The Sundance Kid Died of Old Age in San Diego

First Edition

Published by
Journeys Press
200 K St.
Chula Vista CA 91910

Author photo by Jeanie Kirk of Selma, Alabama

ISBN: 0988264390
ISBN-13: 9780988264397

Library of Congress Control Number: 2013939908
Journeys Press

The Sundance Kid Died of Old Age in San Diego

The Diary of Etta Place

Syd Love

Journeys Press
2013

This story is dedicated to Maya, who cherishes a good adventure and who dearly loved her Great-Aunt Maggie.

ACKNOWLEDGMENTS

Countless thanks to superstar readers Óscar Cruz, Catherine Fritz, Audrea Liszt, and Dave Ward and to the other friends who read this tale or listened to it, offering valuable suggestions, and to Lola S. Kohen, who understood the latest publication methods.

"You've seen her shoot. Now watch her ride."
Sundance to Kid Curry following a jail break

1

I was never a prostitute. Every time I read that libel about me I could spit porcupine quills. Still, the printed word is so convincing, and our nature such that we tend to believe it, I suppose. But what especially annoys me is how one writer will repeat another's misstatement and maybe not even identify that first one as the source. And soon a third writer will echo what that second one had borrowed and will set it down as gospel, and so on.

It's got to where you can't pick up a book or an article about my late husband without seeing some mention of how we met in a bordello where I "worked." The town might be different every time, but it's always some brothel in Texas, except when it's in Colorado or Utah, Wyoming or Louisiana.

Sometimes they say I merely played the piano there. But I never worked in any of those places in any capacity. If I had, however, I might have been the best-paid attraction, because my husband called me the beauty of my time. He was biased but I enjoyed hearing him say it.

Obliterating that vicious rumor about a bawdyhouse is one reason I'm writing this, so you nieces and nephews will know the truth once and for all. I kept a diary off and on, and one of my sisters returned the letters I mailed to my parents. And I have the ones I sent to my husband's mother. So I'll be able to refer to all those for certain dates, places, and names. Other times, I have to rely on my memory, which is not infallible. After all, if I live until the twenty-seventh of November I'll be ninety-three years old.

Another reason for my setting all this down is that those same people who have written incorrectly about my past have also misstated much of my husband's life, what little that's been made public. I will present his story accurately.

Also, I want to tell about some of the folks we met and the exciting things we did and saw. Our biggest times occurred in the last few years of the 1800s and the first four decades of the 1900s, many of them in South America and Mexico. So I'll write mainly about those days.

Now, my husband and I raised Cain now and then. I can't deny it. And I'll include all that, for I'm guessing you nieces and nephews and maybe a few other descendants might enjoy reading about us and our world, for those were different times.

Perhaps it's my experience as a schoolteacher that urges me to write this. If I don't set it down, all will be lost like my husband's grave would be because of the wind-fired desert sand that skids across it, obliterated if not for the marble headstone I ordered put there, just as the details of our lives would disappear when I'm gone, erased by time.

I'll seal this when I finish and put it alongside my will and certain valuables with an annotation that it's not to be opened until I'm planted beside my husband. I suppose the statute of limitations has expired on most of our deeds. But I don't want to take any chances, even though all I ever did was hold the horses.

Yes, my husband sometimes rode on the far side of the law. But remember, the going often became difficult, economically and physically. You never knew if some stranger might yank a six-shooter or a knife and take your valuables, maybe your life. When Harry broke the law, he had to because of his nature and the times.

He had something inside him he had to nurture and that compelled him to do what he did. I call him a thrill-seeker. And if he were a young man today he would be a deep-sea diver or a stunt flier or maybe one of those astronauts I'm watching in the background on the television while they try to reach the moon and land, something that has never been done. I hope those boys make it.

And let me make one thing perfectly clear, as our president would say: My husband robbed only banks, stagecoaches, railroads, an occasional store, or payroll train. So no individual ever got hurt in the pocketbook. Oh, he had a temper. I'll grant you that. And he could use his fists, always stood ready to light into any jasper causing trouble for him or me or one of his friends. I've seen him lay out many a bozo, and they all deserved it.

And he gambled but never cheated. He could gather stray cattle and horses quite effectively, ride like a Comanche, and shoot like Wild Bill Hickok. But Harry's reputation, the part that some folks feared in him, rested more on what he could do to people than what he actually did. Friends and anyone else who treated him the way a gentleman deserves found him gentle, compassionate.

I partnered with him as sweetheart and wife for fifty-five years, and I can testify that Harry wasn't the unmitigated terror so many people have painted him to be.

When I met him I didn't know anything about him. But I noted his courtliness and devastating handsomeness. I found out pretty soon about his activities, plus his daring and his courage, along with the way other men and women admired him and liked him, fearing him only if they had cause.

Folks generally called me Etta or Maggie in our first years together. Then the Mexicans we got to know called me Margarita. Most people knew my husband as Harry Place, sometimes Parker. His real name was Harry Longbaugh. The Old West knew him—history knows him still—as The Sundance Kid.

2

In mid-March of 1895 we had a warm spell. The men needed to do an early planting, so I got time off from my teaching job in Colorado, and I'll explain how I got there. But first you need to know how I met Harry. I enjoy recalling that episode.

It happened in Denver at Annie Dort's Boarding House, where I got a smidgen off my bill by playing the piano for the boarders a couple of hours each night after supper, which folks today in California call dinner. On this particular night I had played *Sam Bass*, *I Rode With Ol' Jeb Stuart*, and *Oh, Polly, I'm a Rebel Soldier*, and had just started on *Dixie* when I heard some laughing and jostling off to one side of the lobby. I glanced to my left and saw them, two young men in business suits settling into overstuffed chairs.

When I finished *Dixie* everyone applauded, although some shouted for Yankee music. And the two newcomers walked up to me, removed their headpieces, and introduced themselves as Harry Jones and Leroy Smith. Harry had hair as black as mine, Leroy a sort of auburn. He tried to sit on my bench but Harry pulled him up.

"Sure like your music," Harry said.

I couldn't think of what to reply, he becharmed me so. I settled for "Thank you, sir," and plunked a few keys.

"How's the food here?" Harry asked.

"Oh, it's fine. Just fine." I plunked a few more keys, could hardly talk, being so stunned by Harry's good looks and trying to watch him without staring. When some of the guests shouted again for Yankee music, Leroy turned and glared at them. But Harry excused himself and Leroy and led his friend to their seats.

I recommenced playing but wasn't worth reins on a mad hog the rest of the evening. *The Battle Hymn of the Republic* became a war between me and the piano, and so I quit early, stood, grabbed my purse off the top of the piano and, trying not to be obvious, glanced toward Harry.

Mrs. Dort came right at me. She had that way about her. "Your time's not up."

"I'll make it up tomorrow night."

"See 'at you do," she said real mean.

Heading for the stairs to my room, I hoped Mr. Jones would talk to me again.

When I walked close he stood and said, "We liked your recital very much."

That's all he said. But I think I would have run away with him then and there if he'd asked me. My legs felt like clabber and my tongue seemed nailed to my teeth, like he'd offered me a cattle ranch with barbecue every afternoon and fandangos in the evenings. Anyone as courteous and handsome as this tall dark-haired man, who had such a pleasant voice, had to be the kind to treat a woman right. And I guessed by his fancy business rig, expensive boots, and gold watch chain across his vest that he had money, even though he didn't seem much older than me.

His hands looked smooth, not rough like a cowpuncher's, although I sensed their strength. His eyes, deep dazzling blue, captured me right off. Instead of a batwing sombrero or Stetson, he carried a city man's felt headpiece. He wore a medium-size mustache.

I stood flabbergasted at the foot of the stairs. Here, I guessed, might be some of the excitement I'd sought when I came West. But due to my wobbly legs and uncooperative tongue, I could only smile and nod and hold on to the banister.

"Leroy and I have taken rooms here for a few nights."

I nodded.

"The snow's light and the wind has died down. Maybe we could take a walk."

I gripped the banister tighter.

"Maybe you'd like to get your coat and scarf and galoshes?"

I'm sure I looked dumb or naïve. He smiled, hadn't given up on me. I suppose I retained my poise well enough. I nodded again, finally found my voice. "What about your friend?" I glanced toward Leroy, slumped asleep in a big leather chair.

Harry looked that way, then back to me and smiled. "Oh, Leroy'll be all right. He's just tuckered out from a long train ride and thinking about the important business we have to conduct in a few days."

I climbed the stairs as serenely as I could, put on my galoshes and heavy black woolen coat, and wrapped my head in my best scarf, red wool with tassels. I managed, by sliding one hand firmly along the banister, to gracefully descend the stairs.

After we had walked a short piece I regained enough composure to talk, even relaxed and laughed when he told me a couple of funny stories about his friend Leroy.

"I'm having trouble placing where you're from, Mr. Jones."

"Call me Harry. Wyoming. Crook County."

"I'm Etta. Etta Margaret Place. You're joshing. Oh, maybe from the city."

"No. Farm country. Ranching."

"You plain don't sound like it."

"I worked hard to speak proper . . . properly."

"That's good. For some special reason?"

"I thought it would help in the cities. For business."

"Does it?"

"So far."

"How'd you do it?" The educator in me jumped out.

"Listening to city men in banks and hotel lobbies."

We turned a corner. Snow had become slush. Harry took my arm as if he thought I might slip. I said, "I bet you have trouble guessing where I'm from."

"Down South, for sure. Georgia?"

"Alabama. Dallas County."

"And Ireland."

"My grandparents on both sides came over during the Potato Famines. Momma and Pappy were born here and met in Alabama. They talked Gaelic before English."

"You're a long ways from home."

"Yes, and I'm just getting started. There's so much I want to see, that I've read about. With school closed for a while at Leadville, the Harmsworths, the folks I board with, figured a few days in Denver would be all right since they know Mrs. Dort. She runs the place where I'm playing. You saw her when I quit tonight."

"You're so pretty, you should lodge at the Brown Palace."

That flustered me. "Not on my pay. But you could afford it, I reckon."

"Sometimes we like to avoid crowds. Besides, I wouldn't have met you."

I disliked flattery. But from him I loved it. "Oh."

"And you play well enough to earn your living."

I laughed. "Oh no, Mr. Jones, Harry." I wished I could talk. I wanted to say the same kind of thing to him, but I couldn't be that forward, even though I felt ready to become his Sunday girl then and there.

He and Leroy Smith, Harry told me, toiled in the world of finance. "We deal mostly with banks, railroads, and stage lines. We have several associates and operate throughout much of the West, primarily Wyoming, Montana, Utah, South Dakota, Colorado. But we plan to expand as the West develops. You go where the money is."

"Naturally." I felt I tried to sound like a tycoon even though my business acumen didn't match that of Jacob's mule. "I imagine you meet and work with a lot of important people. Wealthy men and their womenfolk."

"All kinds, Etta."

He didn't say much else. As we strolled I thought of what I'd read about San Francisco, Chicago, New Orleans, and I wanted to go anywhere, everywhere. I thought of fancy food and symphonies and champagne. And I found myself wanting to enjoy all that with Harry.

Then I found myself at the front door of Mrs. Dort's Boarding House. *Should I turn and run inside or face the humiliation of a formal good-bye and his not asking to see me again? But no. I'm nineteen, educated, have taught school, and been on my own.*

I offered my hand and a bright smile. "Pleased to make your acquaintance, I'm sure." I turned and strode through the doorway.

Leroy still slept in the chair.

Harry reached my side before I gained the foot of the stairs. "Could we take a buggy ride tomorrow after breakfast? If the weather's right?"

I began nodding before my words came out. "That would be quite pleasurable."

I tried to not bounce up the stairs like an antelope. In my room I examined myself in the mirror for a few minutes before dressing for bed. I couldn't get to sleep for an hour or even read, I felt so excited.

With the weather cooperating, Harry and I drove around town or into the countryside on each of the next few days. I felt a thrill every minute, it seemed, like the first time I got a good look at the Brown Palace Hotel, which I'd heard had opened only a couple of years earlier. I took my time and counted all ten floors.

"Denver's a good-sized city," I said.

Harry nodded.

When we passed the Tabor Opera House and the Broadway Theater, I promised myself I'd get to see performances there someday.

At the intersection with Market Street, Harry kept the horse moving, though at a glance I thought the area looked interesting and popular.

"It's full of vice," Harry said. "Maybe you've read about Storyville in New Orleans or the Barbary Coast in San Francisco."

"Can't say as I have."

"Someday if you do you'll you understand Market Street."

I let the matter drop, though a glimpse had whetted my curiosity. "Did you see Denver or work here during the silver boom?"

Harry flicked the reins. "Sort of on the outskirts. Not regular mining."

We crossed Cherry Creek and rolled into the flats, enjoying the scenery and each other's presence. Sometimes we took lunches so we could stay longer. And I learned he didn't talk much, not about his personal life nor business either. Just plain reticent, quiet.

"Talking about myself would bore both of us," he said. "A little farming. Some cowpunching. Then Leroy and I became pards."

So when a silence became awkward, I filled in. I'd already told Harry I'd been born in 1876 on a farm near Selma. Now I elaborated, sounding like a school marm. "That's the year Custer and lots of his troops got massacred. And Bill Hickok got murdered. Mr. Bell patented his telephone. Grant occupied the White House."

"A big year, sure enough, with you arriving, and all." He smiled at me and flicked the reins on the black Tennessee walker pulling us. "Brothers and sisters?"

"Four brothers and then me and two younger sisters. The boys spoiled us. But we all worked the farm, cotton and sugarcane, corn and string beans, right alongside the colored people who'd stayed with us sharecropping after the war. Pappy had been in the fighting but didn't get hurt bad. Lucky. Just nineteen when he rode back on a young mule that became the family transportation and plow animal."

"Farming's tough."

"Things haven't got better, either, from what I've heard and seen, and I wanted a different life. Got what schooling I could, and Momma made sure we got books and magazines by mail. We had *National Geographic* almost from the day it started. Also *McClure's*. The reading must have influenced my urge to get away. I wish Pappy had been able to read too. But he just can't. That's about it."

"No it isn't." He smiled at me again.

"I thought you might need a break. All right. I taught a spell in Birmingham and came West for a job through Pappy's cousin Risteard only to learn that Risteard had just died. But the Harmsworths took me in, and I got the job in Leadville. Whew. You'd better talk awhile."

Harry steered us to a copse of pines and we stopped to picnic on a bed of pine needles. "How'd you learn to play piano so well?"

"Pappy bought it used for Momma when they got married, and she taught me."

The day soon came when Harry and Leroy had to move on. "We have a big business powwow in Wyoming," Harry told me.

Breakfast had just ended, and everyone except Harry and me had left the table. I didn't know quite what to say, so I kept shut. Harry walked me to the stairs.

"We'll be back in the area before too long, Etta. I'd like to pass through Leadville to see you, if that would be all right."

I reached into my purse for my calling card. "That would be just fine." We sat on chairs near the stairs. On the back I wrote the Harmsworths' names and rural postal route, and handed him my card. With my best smile I said, "It's down the road a short piece east of Leadville near a branch of the Blue River."

Harry frowned at the card. He jiggled it, turned it over, and frowned some more. I saw exasperation and embarrassment. And I realized that the well-dressed, nicely spoken, exceptionally handsome businessman Mr. Harry Jones could not read a lick.

"I'll draw you a map." I found a piece of paper in my purse and began a map when Leroy joined us. I hadn't seen much of Harry's sidekick since the first night, and I liked him well enough. But sometimes he acted bossy.

"We got business, Pard," he told Harry.

"Hold your horses, Leroy." Harry nodded toward me.

Even in his suit, Leroy looked like a cowboy. He seemed to want to scratch, to be looking for a steer to throw, or a bronc to ride. Harry, on the other hand, sitting calmly beside me, well-groomed, slim in his elegant dark suit, appeared at home in the city.

Leroy frowned at us and walked off brooding, his boot heels heavy on the parlor's thin carpet, Leroy pouting, it seemed, even as I observed him from behind.

I handed Harry my map, and he studied it before folding it carefully and stuffing it and my card into his vest pocket near his gold watch chain. When I stood, he did too, and, the most natural thing, he leaned toward me and I moved forward.

We shared a brief kiss, nothing passionate, but far-reaching, exciting, and memorable—for the hope and friendship and the promise it evoked and that I wanted.

3

The first time I ran away from home my thirteenth birthday had just passed. I loved my family. But I had to get going. I toted a few extra items to school with me, and when class ended I climbed up on a mule behind two of the Lee boys—they claimed kinship to General Lee but admitted they couldn't prove it—and they carried me into town. From there I got a ride in a farmer's wagon heading for Prattville. But we hadn't gone more than three miles out of Selma before Pappy on First Manassas caught up with us.

"Jump on up here," Pappy said.

While I rode behind him, Pappy never said a word. But when we got home I experienced my worst switching ever, ate supper standing up, and went to bed pouting that no one loved me nor understood me nor gave a hoot.

I was fourteen the next time and chose a summer day. I didn't know how to just light out for Chicago or San Francisco, but I trusted in Providence. In one paper bag I put the chicken, biscuits, and dill pickles left from the Sunday church picnic the day before. In another I stuffed sweater and comb, toothbrush and ribbons, things like that. Wearing my best bonnet and Sunday dress, I set out long before the roosters started squawking.

For two days I caught rides along country roads with corn or sugarcane, beans or cotton growing on both sides, and I accepted snacks and one good meal while creating answers to fend off questions. Late one day resting under a Chinese elm opposite the Pickens County Courthouse at Carrollton, I waited for someone to come along so I could ask the way to Tuscaloosa.

"You ain't from around here."

He called himself Billy Turnipseed. He had walked up behind me without my knowing it, my being so pooped and hot on a typical sultry day in that part of Alabama.

"No," I told him.

"What's your name?"

"Maggie."

"What else? Who's your kin?"

"Just Maggie."

"Where you from?"

"Over yonder." I pointed where I'd been heading instead of where I came from. The day had got so hot the flies quit buzzing. I yearned for a persimmon or a glass of water.

"Your eyes are darker than inside a gopher burrow. I can't make them out."

"They're black is why." I judged Billy to be about my age, a little taller, as bowlegged as an old cowboy, as muscular as a grown man, which he tried to act like, chewing tobacco and spitting. Billy wore a thousand freckles, homespun shirt and overalls, clean except for the pants cuffs, which showed splatters of tobacco juice. So he needed practice with his spitting. When he stepped into the shade and removed his straw hat I saw he had short black hair parted in the middle. This boy owned feet like a Clydesdale's with gnarled, tough-looking toes. Tobacco juice speckled his toes too. But he smiled, seemed friendly.

"You here to look at the face?" Billy said.

"On my way to Tuscaloosa. What face?"

"In the courthouse window. Hell, you been looking right at the damn thing."

So he practiced his swearing too. "Didn't notice. Too busy thinking."

"Well, look." He spat on and around his toes again. "Hell." Billy pointed to the top window, just under the courthouse roof, in the third story, or attic.

I looked and, sure enough, I could make out the face of a wild-eyed Negro peering out of the lower-right pane. He looked scared to death.

"Name's Henry Wells. He been arrested for burning down the courthouse in 1876. During the night a sombitchin storm hit. The men started drinking homemade corn to keep warm and get their courage up. Then someone brought a rope."

"So they lynched him?"

"He pressed his face agin the window and yelled out he didn't do it."

"But they lynched him?"

"Pap says they did. But Ma says lightning killed the pore sumbitch with his face up agin the glass, ten, eleven years ago."

"You'd think the face would have gone away."

"He said he'd haunt 'em. I reckon he is."

"Good Lord." That scared me, Billy Turnipseed too. I stood. "Which way to Tuscaloosa?"

"Up yonder," he said. "I'm headed there myself."

"I thought you came from here."

"Got an uncle there with a job for me. Probably help you find a place to stay, unless you got kin there."

I didn't want to answer that. "Why aren't you toting a bag of some sort?"

"Ain't necessary."

I studied him. "Maybe I'll see you there."

"I know where to borrow a horse and buggy. We'll be there tomorra sure."

That sounded good to me, so we set out together even though I didn't know whether I liked the boy, showing me that face in the window.

At dusk we started looking for a place to sleep, found a creaky old barn occupied by owls and mice and probably many other critters, and climbed into a loft full of hay. I went right to sleep. After full dark I woke up to find Billy trying to pull my drawers off.

No fourteen-year-old girl raised in the country, especially with older brothers, could help knowing what that skunk had planned. I felt frightened like never before, but I didn't want him to know and I doubted I could beat him at Indian wrestling. "Is that how you Pickens County boys do it?"

He continued tugging my drawers. I shoved his hand aside and pulled them up.

Billy said, "What you talking about?"

"Haven't you ever done it with your clothes off?"

"Well, I—"

"It's more exciting. More comfortable too."

"Well, I—Hell yes."

"Then get off me and let's do it right."

He rolled away and began removing his shirt.

"Put your clothes over there." I pointed. "And I'll put mine over this way so we won't get them mixed if we have to dress and leave in a hurry."

Billy took a few steps in one direction, I in the other, and I could hear him shedding his pants as though he had fire ants in them. I felt around the straw against the wall near me. My hand touched a two-by-four about three feet long. I picked it up.

I hope I didn't kill him. But for all I know his bones still lie there with the cats chasing the mice through them. It's a chance I had to take, his misfortune if I hit too hard. I took off running, and I fretted for quite a spell over what I'd done.

The next day at the edge of a country road I stood hungry and exhausted in the shade of a white gum and yearned for a drink of cool water. I had been listening to a mockingbird and watching a squirrel climb a nearby elm when a familiar-looking horse ridden by a stern man I quickly recognized stopped in front of me.

"Jump on up here," Pappy said.

4

But the whipping I dreaded all the way home never material-
ized. Instead, we held a family parley and made a deal: In
another year, when I would be fifteen going on sixteen, I could go
to Birmingham and live with an older cousin and attend school
year-round.

"That'll satisfy you," Pappy said.

I only had to behave until then and handle my usual chores.

Pappy, tall and thin, serious, didn't laugh much. And I had
never known him to string so many words together.

I behaved.

And I did my chores.

I kept up my reading too.

When the day came I felt just as sad as happy because I
especially hated to leave Momma, but my sisters and brothers too.
Pappy, I figured, would be so busy working that he wouldn't miss
me. Then he surprised me by giving me his Philadelphia derringer, a .41-caliber single-shot percussion muzzle-loader with a
wrought-iron barrel. He took it off a captured Yankee officer who
had already lost the other one of the pair.

"This is one of the early ones," Pappy said. "Not one of
those imitations."

It was a Deringer derringer, after Henry Deringer Jr., who
wrote his name with one *r*, regardless of what happened to the
spelling later. The gift thrilled me, my knowing what it meant to
my father. "Are you sure, Pappy?"

"It's a city gun. You're going to the city."

In those days, everybody toted a derringer, usually a pair.
Pappy gave me six extra cartridges he'd made, plus molds and

powder so I could make more if I could find the lead as soon as I had shot at least a half dozen people, I suppose.

On a hot Saturday afternoon my brothers Flann and Dunleavy prepared to drive me in the wagon to Selma, from where I could take the stage to Montgomery and then go by train to Birmingham. I felt ambivalent. I would miss my people and the piano, and I knew Momma would cry. Me too. But I had to do it.

Momma fixed me the grandest box lunch I'd ever seen: fried chicken, baked ham, biscuits, persimmons, apples, apple pie, and chocolate cake. She also sneaked me ten dollars in money over and above what Pappy had provided for my transportation, and she gave me her best heavy coat.

"I don't need to look good in winter slopping hogs," Momma said. And then instead of crying and rushing back into the house, my mother, chunky and jolly, gray hair in a bun, gave me a big kiss and hug. "Go, Etta Margaret. Go see all the exciting things happening in the world. Then come back and tell us all about them."

With the chickens and ducks and dogs around her feet, she stood in the yard waving and smiling, Pappy's arm around her, while we drove off. Maybe she cried later. I did.

I found Birmingham to be a blessing, the soul of world culture, learning, and excitement, as far as I could see. It had mule-drawn trolley cars, some electrical street lighting, plus a few telephones, and a daily newspaper. And lots of the people talked different from us in Dallas County.

"Yankees," older cousin Molly told me. "They turn up all over a big city like this, pesty as bedbugs."

I went to the school library every afternoon to get books for class, to keep up with *McClure's* and *National Geographic*, plus, for the first time, saw *The Saturday Evening Post*. That's how I finally enjoyed the thrill of reading in detail about such people as the James boys, Buffalo Bill, Belle Starr, Wyatt Earp, John Wesley Hardin, and others. Most got killed or otherwise retired before my time, but their stories fascinated me, not the killings, but the adventures. When I was little, Jesse and Frank James spent a lot of time in Selma in the saloons along the river, and we were sort of proud of that. Pappy had seen them.

The only comparable activity we had in my time occurred when they brought in Rube Burroughs's corpse and displayed it in Selma on a Saturday afternoon. I was twelve, and we all got a look. A shopkeeper standing on the street in Linden, over in Marengo County, shot him after Burroughs broke out of jail. Good thing too, for Burroughs had been a cold-blooded killer who deserved every slug he took.

"I'd say you were born twenty years too late, Etta," Cousin Molly told me one day. I had been running on excitedly about reading up on the Northfield Bank Robbery, where the James Boys and the Youngers had so much trouble years earlier.

"I know, Molly. But I can't help it, the West attracts me so. I want to go there."

"Well, hold on. I read that Buffalo Bill's bringing his Wild West show to town. That ought to satisfy you."

"We'll see," said I.

Through the newspaper I learned about what the article called the last of the outlaw gangs active in the West. The paper called it Butch Cassidy and The Wild Bunch, never listing anyone else in the outfit, although identifying one other rider by nickname, The Sundance Kid. The names stuck with me. The article described Cassidy as a jovial, free-spending beloved Robin Hood, while depicting The Sundance Kid as a hard-drinking, hot-tempered killer feared throughout several territories and states. It said even the rest of the gang gave him a wide berth.

I sure didn't want to meet up with that hombre, but Cassidy sounded like good company. I told older cousin Molly about them.

"Riffraff," she said. "Let's hope they stay away from our part of the country."

"I hope there's going to more articles about them." I felt melancholy, thinking they could get shot before any more stories appeared.

Before my seventeenth birthday I earned my credential and became a schoolmarm at a rural school in the Birmingham outskirts, good work, for a while. Once again, my reading helped to pacify my anxious soul, or itching feet, whichever I suffered, while also agitating them. I'd have to move on before long. My credential would carry me hereafter.

5

Mr. Armstrong and the boys look like they need quite a bit more time to reach the moon, so I'll continue my history on this July day in the Year of Our Lord 1969.

One of the many fine things about large families: You could go live with an aunt or uncle or cousin if you got into trouble or merely had the itch.

Several of our kin had gone to Texas, even before the war ruined Alabama and a lot of other places, and had ended up fighting with local outfits and later raising families in Texas. Others had gone there after the war, never to be heard from again, either by accident or choice, and I hesitate to speculate on motives. It's the old American story.

About the time I felt ready to see the world beyond Birmingham, I spent a few summer weeks at home helping around the house and in the fields, riding Traveller or First Manassas, hunting and fishing. On Sundays before the sermon and picnic at Ivy Creek Baptist Church I'd take rifle practice with my family. I outshot all of them.

One day at supper Pappy and Momma discussed a letter they had received from an older cousin in Colorado. It contained the usual topics, like crops and kinfolk and snows of the previous winter. But I listened carefully: *Colorado. Denver. The West.*

"I'd sure like to go visit," I told them.

I looked at Momma. She waited.

Pappy said, "Too far."

Three days later at breakfast I asked again.

"What for?" Pappy said.

"It sounds exciting."

"So's Birmingham," he said.

"You could write to them. I mean, Momma could. Maybe there's work for me. I mean, teaching."

Pappy grunted and poured honey on his grits.

The following summer after another year teaching in Birmingham I tried again.

"You've got a good job," Pappy said.

I felt a three-day sulk coming on.

The next morning as I helped Momma with the breakfast dishes I asked where Pappy had gone so early on Traveller.

"To town."

I kept drying a big pan.

"Aren't you going to ask why?"

"I suppose it's to the bank or to pay a bill."

Momma said, "He's sending a telegram."

"Who to? How come?"

"He's asking Cousin Risteard if there might be a teaching job up that way for a restless girl with two years' experience already."

"Oh, Momma!" I hugged her.

"Wrote it out for him myself."

"I never thought—"

"He studied on the idea all winter."

The feed-store owner's son brought the answer two days later. Cousin Risteard had contacted the school board. They had a job for me.

"Pappy, Momma." I hugged and kissed them both. "Just think. Denver!"

"You'll see Denver on your way to Leadville, where the school is."

"That's all right. We'll go to Denver on Saturdays, like we go to Selma here."

"They say it's a far piece," Pappy said. "But they go once in a while."

"Their home is in the country about a mile from the school," Momma said. "You'll live with them. They say the land's beautiful there. Winter's a little cold."

"I'll love it. And after a while I'll have enough experience to teach in Denver."

"Yes. Go, Etta Margaret," Momma said, "so you can come back and tell us about the wonderful things out yonder."

I arrived just in time for Cousin Risteard's funeral. He had been seventy-eight and not well, and though I didn't know it they were saying over his grave at the little cemetery on the edge of Leadville as the stage bringing me from Denver rolled past. At the Wells Fargo office I learned about his death when I asked directions to the Risteard place. I left my suitcase at Wells Fargo and walked down the street to the graveyard, where I introduced myself to Cousin Lillian. "My sincere condolences, ma'am."

She took my hand. "Poor thing. I just . . ."

I assumed she meant Cousin Risteard. I nodded.

"I just . . . You see, I . . . You poor thing, and so slim and pretty. I sold the farm this morning. And I'm going to Texas to live with our oldest son."

"Oh."

"He's on his way now to fetch me."

I fidgeted, lost, muddleheaded, doomed.

"But don't you worry none. The neighbors contacted Mr. Harmsworth. He's the school board president. You'll be welcome to live with the Harmsworths on their place east of the Blue River. They have five younguns. Three of them are big fine boys about your age. That lovely black hair of yours will make them boys fall all over themselves."

The Harmsworths raised corn and wheat, although they had a few calves and hogs for meat, two milk cows, two mules, a fenced garden patch near the house, two hounds, with chickens and ducks running everywhere. The boys were sixteen, eighteen, and nineteen, all tall and skinny like their pappy, their daughters fourteen and eleven. Another boy had been killed at age six by lightning. Their first born, a girl, had run off two years earlier in a screaming hand-flinging rage, crying about the wicked winter weather, the hard work, and how everything kept passing her by. She had written them some, a different city each time. I was sorry I missed that girl.

I shared a room with the remaining daughters, and we womenfolk had our own outhouse, same as at home. I had to walk only a mile to the school, and in bad weather, they told me, we would take the wagon, both girls and the youngest boy and me. I taught the older boys what I could at home in the evenings with the others usually participating, pestering some but encouraging too.

At home I presented the same subjects I taught at the school: US and world history, geography, Latin, arithmetic, algebra, grammar, spelling, penmanship, and shorthand, with some literature, including a dab of Greek plays in English—naturally not all this to the same students or on the same day. It depended on their ages. Since they had to work, none of the older boys from any of the families attended school from spring to fall. They told me none of us went to the schoolhouse during heavy snows, especially not in a blizzard. On Saturdays I worked with Mrs. Harmsworth, Dorcas, a short portly woman whose fat cheeks made her seem to be puffing. She tied her hair, gray and straight, in a bun atop her head. I also collected the eggs and fed the chickens and ducks.

On Sundays we made a picnic basket and rode in the wagon to the Baptist Church in Leadville and stayed all day, eating and talking after the service. The young people played baseball and flirted.

Mr. Harmsworth, Ezekiel, reminded me of my father, his big jaws, smiling eyes, reticence, the man firm but fair.

"You getting on all right?" Mr. Harmsworth asked after the first week.

"Took a few days before the altitude quit nagging me."

"We're a lot higher than Denver. But a young person gets used to it easy."

"I hear it snows here a lot."

"You get used to that too."

I circled one hand in the air. "These mountains sure are pretty."

"Yep. We're heaven-kissed."

The boys tried sparking me but gave up graciously when I discouraged them.

And I knew after the first week that I'd have a chore fulfilling my one-year contract, that living on the outskirts of Leadville and teaching in a rural school would plainly not satisfy me for long, when even Birmingham hadn't been able to hold me. Denver beckoned.

One weekend in the late fall the weather let up and I rode the dawn stage into Denver with Mrs. Harmsworth and the girls. We had just a few hours to shop and walk around, spent the night together in the same room at Annie Dort's Boarding House, went the next morning to the Baptist Church service, and caught the afternoon stage back to Leadville. The oldest boy, Homer, met us with the wagon long after dark.

"Wasn't that wonderful, Etta? Girls?" Mrs. Harmsworth smiled at us.

"Yes, ma'am," I said.

"So many fine things we could do if we had the time and money."

I sure agreed with that. Still, it had been a nice respite, anodyne too, and the memories helped me through the next weeks. I got to make a return visit in a few months. The Harmsworths didn't think I should go alone. But they didn't expect more big snows so the menfolks had to do an early planting. And I had saved a few dollars.

"Probably going to stay this way for a spell," Mr. Harmsworth said. "Go ahead."

"But don't get snowed in," Mrs. Harmsworth said. She laughed.

I smiled and started packing.

So that's how I happened to be in Denver playing the piano when Harry and his pard showed up. Getting to know Harry helped me through the following months, the memory of him and the desire that someday he would stop by the farm to see me.

The day came sooner than I had dared hope.

6

With spring well along and my contract nearly fulfilled, I had no intention to renew it, though the board wanted me to. I didn't have any idea how to find Harry, although of course I would be on the qui vive. I just couldn't wait any longer, had to do something different, stimulating, and soon. I would go to Denver. If I couldn't find work there I'd cross my fingers and move on. I plainly didn't thrive, not in my brain, my heart, nor my soul. Like Aristides, I had to run.

I didn't recognize Harry until he got close. I stood out front drawing water from the well when he rode up on a beautiful sorrel mare with a blaze and white front feet. And so I just about forgot returning to the kitchen to help with Saturday dinner, so glad to see him I wanted to hug him and kiss him right there in the daylight.

"I never knew where to write you," I said.

"Couldn't have read it anyhow."

"Leroy or somebody could have."

"I wouldn't want that," Harry said.

"No, I suppose not."

"We moved around a lot too, Texas mainly, down around Fort Worth, San Anton, where the winter isn't so mighty."

"You and Leroy?"

"Him and other associates because we had some complicated transactions."

"I suspect so." I sounded like a financial wizard again.

I couldn't move my eyes away from his, the prettiest blue I'd ever seen. He had the same mustache, the long lean hands I'd admired, looked a bit thinner than earlier, and sun-browned more. He wore different rigging, not the fancy well-cut business suit this time with the gold watch fob and city hat, but a big Stetson suitable for fighting off the sun, a nice brown corduroy jacket, red bandanna around his neck, good denim shirt and pants, spurs on the same boots, though the shine he'd recently put to them, probably in Leadville, couldn't revive them. I suspect the wear came from riding, not walking.

And this time I could see his six-gun on his right hip and tied to his thigh, no doubt routine protection against snakes and other varmints along the trail. The stock of the rifle in the saddle boot under his right stirrup looked like it belonged to a Spencer carbine, a dandy repeater like my brothers owned and which I had practiced with so often. When we entered the house, and Harry removed his jacket, I saw an inside gun holstered near his left biceps. Of course a businessman had to watch out for himself in those times. You never knew what you'd come up against out West, highwaymen and all.

And didn't Mrs. Harmsworth and the girls carry on when I introduced them to Harry! By the time Mr. Harmsworth and the boys came in for dinner, the women treated Harry like family, and I had been busting my buttons, I felt so proud, Harry so tall and tan, and probably the best-looking man any of them had ever seen.

Mr. Harmsworth took to him right away too, called him "Son," and brought out his jug of corn liquor, something he commonly didn't do until just before supper. "You can hang your hardware on that peg over there." He motioned toward the kitchen door.

The boys acted polite to Harry, but only Ulysses said anything other than howdy.

"You ain't no farmer," Ulysses said. "Hands too soft."

"I quit all that some time back," Harry told him.

"Gambler?" Ulysses continued watching Harry's hands.

"In a way. Banking, mainly."

"Mind your own business, boy," Mr. Harmsworth said.

I said, "Mr. Jones is a financier."

"What's that?" Ulysses asked.

Mr. Harmsworth told him, "He works with money. Let's have another drink."

After their second drink, he and Harry seemed like old fishing buddies.

During the meal, the boys hardly spoke, seemed sullen, maybe jealous. After we ate the roast beef and the chicken, with all the buttered rolls and fresh-cooked vegetables, everything washed down with ice tea, Mrs. Harmsworth set out an apple pie.

"That pie's for church tomorrow," Ulysses said.

"Better to enjoy it with our company." Mrs. Harmsworth brought out a blueberry pie and set it beside the other. "Try a piece of each, Mr. Jones."

Ulysses frowned at Harry's hands.

Mrs. Harmsworth fluttered. So did the girls. Harry ate a piece of each pie.

Afterwards, the men sat on the front porch, rolled cigarettes and smoked, spat past their feet and talked.

The boys disappeared somewhere while the girls and I helped clean up from dinner and do the pots and pans. Then I brushed my teeth, washed up, combed my hair, and put on my Sunday dress, pink and white, sleeveless, and with a modestly low neckline. I stepped onto the porch. A meadowlark sang from somewhere out of sight.

Harry stood. Coatless, he had strapped on his inside gun. "Let's take a walk."

You bet. How about Denver? "There's a nice path along the branch. Shade from the pines." We went hatless.

"That would be fine. It is a little warm for this early."

We walked a short piece along the branch, watching the water and listening to it gurgle, until I spotted a stump. "I wouldn't mind sitting." I didn't feel tired, just nervous.

Harry spread his bandanna on the stump for me and stood off a few steps.

"Oh, we need another stump." I stood.

"It's all right. I prefer this." He faced me, both of us in the shade of an elm, the creek behind Harry. A kingfisher skimmed the water, missed its prey.

I sat again, glad I did, for he didn't give me any warning.

"Etta, I want you to come with me."

I started to stand.

"Please sit. I've been studying on this. I mean go with me during my travels."

"To Denver?" I asked.

"Everywhere. Etta, I'm asking you to be my woman."

I couldn't speak for a minute. I tingled. "Are you sure that's what you want?"

"More than anything."

Naturally, at nineteen going on twenty, I didn't want to be an old maid. But I realized I didn't know Harry well, hardly at all. I didn't want to get bound up into a situation I would have trouble getting away from if necessary. I took a good look at him standing there tall and strong and handsome. And I could see the love in his eyes, the same as I felt in my heart. My momma had raised me right, but not everything she tried to teach me took. No doubt in my mind, I wanted to be his woman.

"If I go with you, do you think someday we'll marry? Maybe in five years?" I don't to this day know where I came up with "five years."

"How about one year? I'm in between major transactions and under a certain amount of pressure from my . . . opposition. But in about a year . . ."

I stood, and we had that hug and kiss I had wanted in the front yard. And if I thought kissing him in Denver had been special, let me make it perfectly clear that the Denver kiss related to the one beside the creek near Leadville like collard greens to homemade ice cream. Then I sat again and Harry told me the rest, still standing, formal, serious, the first time he'd talked so much or that I had seen him jumpy, not so smooth or confident. It seemed almost as though he might lead a prayer meeting.

"My name isn't Harry Jones. It's Harry Longbaugh. And while it's true I'm in the financial world, it's not like I led you to believe. And I don't want to deceive you any longer, on account of how I feel about you. And if you go with me you'll have to tolerate things you might not like, including some people, men mostly, that will disgust you once in a while. Some of my associates are pretty low-down no-good varmints. Fortunately, we go our separate ways much of the time and just meet for business."

He shifted his weight, one foot to the other and back, didn't seem to know what to do with his hands.

"Etta, my profession is robbing certain types of businesses. Every county sheriff and US marshal in several states and territories is after me and the boys, as is the Pinkerton Detective Agency, especially a pigheaded operative name of Charlie Siringo, with his persistent sidekick, Frank Dimaio." He paused.

Did he want me to comment? I didn't what to say, couldn't work my mouth anyway, I felt so stupefied.

"We have to be cautious how we act and what we say when we're not active."

I swallowed hard.

"We never acquire cash or valuables from individual people, and never harm anybody if we can help it. We're against killing, most of us."

I didn't know what to think or say. I had wanted more adventure. All of a sudden, I stood on its doorstep, offered up as simply as grits for breakfast. I had never been a lawbreaker, not even on a small scale, such as fishing on someone else's land without permission. Now I had the chance to cross the line into outlawry and hook up with an expert. The creek bubbling over the rocks became a torrent to my ears. *What would my folks think?*

Harry noted my hesitation. "Etta, I wouldn't allow you to do any of the actual work. You would not carry a firearm or go with us when there's danger. We have a camp in northern Utah we spend a lot of time in, and you could stay there or in a city hotel when the boys and I had work to do." He watched me, asking but not pleading.

I looked unseeing at the creek. I pondered, wanting, scared.

"I want you to know these things, Etta, because if you go with me I can't have you opposing me. I'm twenty-five years old and I've been outside the law since fifteen. That's a long spell and I'm not going to change. It's what I know and like and prefer. There's all the freedom in the world, better than cowboying before the fences came, except on the occasions when we have to be on the watch for the opposition. That's mainly the Pinkertons. The others aren't dogged or very savvy."

When Harry paused, I looked up from the creek, saw him studying me. And I again saw the love in his handsome face, noted the restrained proud request there, saw the untamed strength, and a wildness. I saw the life and the man I wanted.

He said, "Maybe you need time."

I watched the creek. If I did this, what if my folks found out? What would they do? How could I explain? I looked at Harry again.

He extended a hand.

I took it. "I'll go with you, Harry. I want to." I stood. And we shared another kiss and hug, a transcendental embrace that made me trembly weak one moment and all-powerful the next, unconquerable, unfettered.

On the walk back to the house Harry told me I'd have plenty of money.

"But remember," he said, "much of the time we'll be in the hills, where there's nothing to spend it on."

"But once in a while a fancy city too? Fort Worth? Denver? San Francisco?"

"I'm promising you that."

"I don't have anything to wear." As soon as I said that I felt silly.

Harry laughed. We held hands, excited, jabbering as we approached the house. "Is Leroy still one of your partners?" I hadn't recalled him again until then, being so caught up with Harry. "I know you're good friends. I hope you don't mind my asking."

"Leroy and I have partnered for quite a spell. You see, he's the head of our organization, which, I should add, is sort of famous. And his last name is not Smith. It's Parker, though nowadays he calls himself Cassidy."

I nodded, my thoughts on me and Harry, on Denver and San Francisco. Still, I had asked, and Harry seemed to need to talk.

"I suspect you might know about him from his nickname, same as most folks do."

"What's that?" I only half listened, enjoying my hand in Harry's.

"Butch," Harry said.

"'Butch'?"

"Sugar, Leroy is Butch Cassidy."

That shook me from topknot to toes. Still, the information didn't mean nearly as much as anticipating what lay ahead for me, and caused just a puny emotion compared to what I experienced later when I learned that my outlaw lover, Harry Longbaugh, that handsomest man I'd even seen, and the only man I'd ever love, was The Sundance Kid.

7

The Harmsworths urged Harry to spend the night and go to church with us the next day. But he told them he had paid for his room in Leadville and should get on back. Later I learned he didn't want to spend Sunday morning in any church. Also, I found out, he had to make a business transaction to be able to properly take care of his bride, as I thought of myself, and arrange for my transportation.

"We'll be traveling light," Harry said. "Do you ride side-saddle? Or like a man?"

"Like a man," I told him.

So I finished my teaching contract with my mind on Harry and fancy places and sometimes thinking about jail and my momma and hoping I wouldn't have to shoot anybody and that Harry wouldn't either. I had to wait only a month, but it seemed so much longer. My students must have thought me daft, the way sometimes I'd teeter through an explanation. Just before I expected Harry back to take me on our honeymoon, I broke the news to the Harmsworths.

"We'll go to a preacher first thing in Denver. I'm so excited."

"Me too." Dorcas hugged me.

"We're happy for you," Ezekiel said.

"If I'd a known you wanted to get married . . ." Homer said.

"We need you on the farm," Ezekiel told their oldest boy. "Besides, Mr. Jones spotted Miss Etta first."

Homer grabbed a .22 rifle from near the door, hurried outside, and started shooting at magpies on the barn roof.

Harry arrived midmorning this time, a Saturday again, and once more rode a beautiful horse, a chestnut gelding fifteen hands easy, a Thoroughbred, looked like. For me he led a good-looking young gray, also a gelding, about a hand shorter than his. Harry certainly knew horseflesh if my gray handled the way he looked.

The gray's saddle wasn't new, but I didn't mind. The rifle boot hung empty, though Harry still had that Spencer in his. And he had tied down the holster that held his revolver. When we kissed and hugged I discovered he toted his inside gun.

"Let's go," Harry said. He had taken his time hugging me but sure acted eager to leave. He also seemed nervous, maybe afraid I'd changed my mind. *Do cats bark?*

"You have to stay for dinner," Dorcas told Harry.

"You need some of my missus' cooking before hitting the trail," Ezekiel said.

I also urged him to stay. "Besides, I still have some books to pack for sending to Momma." And I wanted to get accustomed to Harry a little before racing down the road to Leadville and the hotel, which is what I reckoned to be our agenda. So Harry slipped the bits on the horses, gave them oats Ezekiel offered, and loosened the cinches while Mr. Harmsworth got his jug. They sat on the front porch and sipped toddies and rolled cigarettes and smoked and talked and spat.

I packed everything for shipping except what I had on and what I could stuff into the saddlebags. So I retained a Shakespeare in type so small I almost had to squint to read it, a French reader, a Thomas Hardy reader, and *The Adventures of Tom Sawyer.* In Leadville the week before, I had bought man's clothes—shirt, pants, hat, and light jacket—for my first time to dress that way since my days as a rootin' tootin' tomboy.

By dinner, Harry no longer seemed jumpy. Good toddies, I suppose. The girls competed in passing dishes to him.

"An outstanding meal, Mrs. Harmsworth," Harry said. "Much obliged."

She blushed, and I agreed and thanked her. I had enjoyed that meal as though it could be my last special feeding for a while.

It was.

We'd hardly ridden out of sight of the Harmsworth place, and my gray handled like he could read my mind, when Harry, sitting a couple of notches down on his spine and as comfortable and smooth as I had ever seen a man on a horse, turned off the road and onto a trail at the edge of a field of young corn hosting an army of magpies.

"Leadville is over yonder." I nodded toward the right.

"I don't think we should ride too close to Leadville for a year or two."

That gave me my first sensation of belonging to The Wild Bunch.

Before long we had nearly reached the foothills. And though I didn't feel lost, being as I could easily find the sun on its descent behind the Rockies, I could not have told where the next town sat.

And I had my second experience of being in the gang. It came when Harry's horse fell a second before I heard the shot. The horse pinned Harry by his left leg, and as I jumped down to help him another shot gouged up dirt on the trail. I kept one arm looped through the reins with my gray acting up, as could be expected. And for the first time I heard Harry swearing.

"Ride like hell for the stand of trees up ahead."

"What about you? That poor horse is hurt bad. Bleeding from the muzzle."

"Let that go for now. I'll get loose here somehow. And when that bastard rides up I'll be able to shoot him. Make tracks, Sugar."

"Who?" I looked back and toward the northeast and saw a rider half a mile off loping our way, a rifle in his right hand, the butt of the stock on his hip. "Must have a buffalo gun. And an uncommon eye."

"I wouldn't be surprised. Get going." Harry pushed on the saddle with his free leg but didn't make any progress. "I hope it's the rancher I selected our horses from."

"'Selected'? Bought?"

"Not hardly."

"Then we don't want him catching us."

"But if it's not the rancher, it's that damn Charlie Siringo. Do like I say."

Certain family members described me as hard-headed or strong-willed. And while I felt happy to obey and cherish Harry even before we married, I had to think for myself too. Praise the Good Lord that Harry's horse had fallen on its left side. The boot with the rifle showed in front of the saddle. I still had one arm linked through the reins of my gray as I grabbed Harry's Spencer carbine and turned to face the rider. I hoped to hit the horse, much as I hated to, rather than the man, even though I suspected I'd like the horse more.

They continued closing in on us.

Harry lay mostly on his back, but he twisted around to watch. He held his six-gun. "Wait'll he's close enough."

"He's close enough." I sighted, squeezed the trigger, and watched horse and man fall. I estimated the distance at around five hundred yards.

"Jesus!" Harry said.

I slid the Spencer into my saddle boot, took the lariat fastened on the other side, looped one end around Harry's saddle horn, mounted the gray, and wrapped the other end around my saddle horn. And I dragged the poor suffering chestnut enough so Harry could slide free. As soon as he stood he shot his horse in the head. He pulled off his bedroll and saddlebags, limped over to me, placed his bags in front of my saddle, his bedroll on top of mine, and climbed up behind me, bedrolls between us.

"Let's run for cover, Sugar."

We galloped to the trees and through them and kept on hurrying toward the foothills, the gray hardly affected by the double burden, a strong, wonderful swift mount carrying us to safety in the wilds beyond Leadville.

"It's all right to slow up a little, Sugar."

In a smooth walk we continued westward.

"You made an outstanding shot."

"Don't mind saying so myself."

"Such a lucky shot."

Harry sounded so proud of me I didn't contradict him.

"The boys are going to have a hard time believing it when they find out."

I didn't say anything.

"Going to josh hell out of me for having my neck saved by a girl."

I kept shut. But I urged the gray into another gallop.

Harry had one hand on each side of my waist, for comfort more than balance, our ride being in that equable stage, moving swiftly, when there isn't any motion up or down, just forward, level and rapid, susurrous, reposeful. The wind we created riffled my shirtsleeves and blew my hat back until it hung by its thong between my shoulder blades. My eyes watered. My nose ran.

When the trail began to rise, I slowed us down. My eyes still teared and my nose continued to drip, except now my crying caused it. I tried to not let Harry know. But pretty soon he found out, reached around me with both arms, and hugged me. He put his lips close to my ear.

"Don't fret, Sugar. My leg doesn't hurt much."

I didn't let on I bawled for the horses.

Every time we reached a knoll or a ridge we stopped and looked back to see if anyone followed. Along about dusk we traded positions, and one time I suggested we stop and rest.

"I don't see anybody," I said. "Besides, I shot his horse."

"Yes, but the man might have been that damn varmint Charlie Siringo, or his partner, that other varmint, Frank Dimaio, just as determined. They find ways."

So we kept on, the gray alternately walking or loping, until full dark caught us on a moonless night and we stayed at an easy walk while the stars came out. Even then we kept moving until after midnight. And throughout the chase, that flight, I felt a thrill, an exultation. I supposed similar feelings helped to form Harry.

By then we'd ridden well into the foothills, with more boulders and caves and trees than ever, pines, firs. Plenty of cover, Harry called it. We dismounted near a creek.

"Yes, Etta Margaret."

"Yes what?"

"You do ride like a man." He tied the gray to a sapling, removed bridle, saddle, and blanket.

Close by we found a cave to our liking. So we had fresh water, plus the music of its swishing by, and plenty of broken dried limbs and twigs. Harry built a fire in the mouth of the cave. Nights remained plenty cool that time of year, and the cave and fire were a blessing, romantic too. While I fixed supper of bacon, biscuits, and beans from Harry's saddlebag he watered the horse at the creek and retied it, this time near a patch of grass. Then he sat beside me, his leg hurting too much for him to squat on his heels. He cleaned his rifle and six-shooter and talked about his transaction in Leadville.

"General store on the edge of town. Clerk by himself. Didn't give me any trouble, and I acquired enough cash to do us a spell."

For a moment I pondered how I felt about this first evidence that I had run off with an armed robber. Then I nodded at the fire, smiled at Harry, and stirred the beans.

He wanted to know about me, so I filled in some of what I'd left out during our brief courtship in Denver. Then I urged Harry to tell me about his early years.

For the first time since I'd met him, Harry seemed to want to talk.

Turns out he was born July 20, 1870, on a small spread in the northeast corner of Wyoming at the southern slope of the Bear Lodge Mountains.

"We raised enough sheep to get by," Harry said. "Had some hogs, a milk cow, chickens and ducks, a mule, and a saddle horse. And two smart dogs to handle the sheep. High country, close to seven thousand feet. Lots of big game."

When he first told me this I couldn't understand why anyone would want to homestead way up there. Later, I learned to deeply appreciate the particular marvels of such country, despite the hardships of heavy winter snows and subzero cold.

"There were just my parents and me. We had a branch most of the year, with the nearest important water being Inyan Kara Creek and the closest community a tiny town called Sundance. We went there every Saturday to buy essentials and talk to folks.

"My Pa got murdered when I was four. He'd taken the wagon down the trail into a stand of pines to chop firewood. When he didn't come home by supper, my mother and I got on the horse and went looking for him. Found him stabbed to death, probably by a renegade, Indian or white. Whoever did it stole the wagon and mule along with his rifle and ax and lunch sack."

A year later Harry's mother married an older widower from an adjacent ranch. The widower and two sons moved in with Harry and his mother.

"I didn't like him or his kids. A foul-mouthed unwashed snuff-dipping hot-tempered heavy-handed son of a bitch. In a few years I realized that life didn't have to be that way and that I'd have to run off unless my mother or me killed the bastard. I suppose my ma considered him better than nothing."

When Harry was ten, beatings replaced the switchings and slaps. By the time Harry turned fifteen he'd grown big for his age and strong.

"The next time my stepfather slapped my mother I knocked him down. I only got to smack him twice before he hit the floor, but I still drew a heap of satisfaction from it. I tried to get Ma to run off with me, but she said she wasn't up to it. I pulled out anyhow. Far as I know, she's still alone with that snake."

"You haven't been back?"

"Some, last time a year ago. He always left the house."

I dished the food onto tin plates. We used biscuits to scoop up the beans, our fingers to lift the bacon. As I sipped coffee I thought of my own momma, and tears came to my eyes. I resolved to get Harry to let me write to his mother on his behalf, maybe even take me to visit.

"Interesting thing." Harry fed twigs to the fire. "Deadwood is just across the line from my home place. In South Dakota. When I was six, a drummer peddling thread and cloth and other household essentials stopped by. Everyone welcomed itinerant peddlers. They brought gossip, sometimes news."

On this visit the salesman reported that James Butler Hickok, the famous Wild Bill of the Old West—and hadn't I read about that man?—had been shot in the back of the head and killed in a Deadwood saloon by a drunken poltroon named Jack McCall.

"I thought my mother showed uncommon grief over the death of a man I had never heard her mention, and that I'd never seen, though us boys talked about him and pretended in our games sometimes to be Hickok. You could say we felt we knew him well. But my ma, for a long time . . . I just didn't understand how sad she got. I knew she grew up in Deadwood. Still, you wonder." He stood. "I'll spread our bedrolls."

8

I washed our tin plates and cups in the creek and put them into Harry's saddlebags while he laid our bedrolls side by side next to my saddle, his rifle still in its boot. He spread his bandanna near the head of his roll and laid his inside gun there, a beautiful lightweight Iver Johnson .32-caliber five-shot revolver with oak grips. He put his six-shooter there too, an 1871 Colt Frontier model single-action center-fire .44-40 with a seven-and-one-half-inch barrel. He sat to remove his boots, black Justins with beautiful filigree. From above his ankles Harry unstrapped his derringers, .41-caliber single-shot nickel-plated Remingtons, and placed them with the other weapons.

"You tote a regular arsenal," I told him.

"Sugar, sometimes a regular arsenal comes in handy."

I removed my Philadelphia derringer from my saddlebags.

"Etta, that little fellow is awful old. Does it work?"

"Far as I know."

"We'll re-outfit you in Denver."

I felt nervous wondering what to do next, I mean how to go about my "wedding night," as I thought of it, felt like a little kid heading to school for the first time, knowing its importance but with it so mysterious that the apprehension got to me. Growing up around farm animals hadn't prepared me for this. So when Harry, cross-legged on his blankets, started making a cigarette, I felt pleased to postpone the big moment. "I want to know more about you, Harry." I'd swear he seemed relieved too. He crawled to the fire, near the end of the blankets, lit his cigarette with a burning twig, and propped himself on an elbow. He pulled a half pint of bourbon out of a saddlebag and took a sip.

"First thing I did when I ran away," Harry said, "I stole a neighbor's horse. Got caught and sat for eighteen months in the jail at Sundance. Too young to hang, I figure. A week after they let me out I got into a fistfight and spent two more days in the same cell. I won the fight."

Later when I saw Harry "in action," I realized he was a natural-born scrapper, strong and fast and agile, could take a punch, unafraid to get hit. He stayed cool in an emergency, not only as a youth but in all our years together.

"I took whatever work I could get. For a spell I did some wrangling at the Suffolk Ranch on the Cheyenne River, at the mouth of Lodgepole Creek. But the foreman gave me the worst jobs and liked to cuss me out. Reminded me of my stepfather. After the second month I drew my pay and laid him out."

Harry took another sip. "I drifted all over Wyoming herding cattle and breaking horses: Laramie, Sheridan, Cheyenne, Fort Bridger, and around, and got good with cattle and horses both. On Sundays a lot of us practiced shooting, and I got good at that too. Also got tired working from can to can't, usually for only a dollar a day and found."

One day Harry and a young friend selected two dozen steers from the herd they worked and drove them into the next county, selling them no questions asked. He also "selected" the horse he rode.

"I had a big time doing that. I could see my future. I could also see the need to get out of that part of the state. I went one way and the other boy the other. I kept on taking an occasional job punching cattle or breaking broncs, mainly to get the lay of the land or hide out after a robbery. I'd team up with one fellow or another in one state or another. But I like to work alone too, small-town banks, country stores."

Harry wasn't evil, just a good man burdened with an ungovernable quirk that demanded excitement and freedom. Now this is not any litany of Harry's acts outside the law before we met nor afterward. I wouldn't give the Pinkertons that satisfaction. But Harry took part in one especially significant robbery that the Pinkertons know about and which is recorded in histories. I'm referring to the holdup of the Great Northern train at Malta, Montana, nearly into Canada, in December of 1892. A fellow named Bill Malden and another named Harry Bass participated with him. Harry labeled them "good men."

I still had some jitters about my approaching initiation, but Harry's talk helped.

"On a train there's so many folks to look out for," he told me. "Women offering their watches and jewelry, some even smiling a little, men giving up their watches and stickpins. But I didn't take any of that. I just kept everybody under control while the other boys handled the express car. The Pinkertons said we got nine thousand dollars, but we got nineteen, my first train. You don't forget a thrill like that. I loved it.

"We split the money and stashed it separately. Got caught the next day."

Harry carried hidden derringers even then. In the jail he got the drop on the guard, and all three of them escaped out the back, stole the nearest horses, and split up. Malden and Bass soon got caught. Malden drew ten years in prison and Bass fourteen. Harry didn't know what happened to their shares of the robbery.

Harry had traded horses, having selected a good-looking black from a rancher on the edge of town, and after riding far into the night he returned to collect his loot and board the Great Northern at Wolf Point, not far from Malta, riding it into North Dakota as a respectable paying customer. When he left the train Harry acquired a different mount and headed south. He wanted to see his mother, though not his stepfather, so he didn't go to the ranch after all, instead wound up in a saloon at Belle Fourche,

South Dakota, where he met Butch Cassidy, several years older and a head shorter.

"Leroy, wobbly drunk and silly, stood at the bar arguing with a big mean-looking s.o.b. about the advantages of the Dakotas having got statehood. I sipped my beer and listened. Pretty soon I realized that Leroy merely pestered the other fellow in a friendly way. But the other man, more my size than Leroy's, and red angry in the face, looked ready to smash Leroy bloody.

"Leroy had something sympathetic about him I liked. I felt an instant friendship with him. And I didn't want to see a happy drunk get beat up. So I told the guy to lay off. And he started in on me. Of course I knew something he didn't, such as that I didn't plan to stand there arguing and wait for him to swing first. Besides, I hadn't had a fight recently and felt tense from all the hurried traveling since leaving my former associates outside the jail in Malta. I laid him out."

Harry sipped his bourbon. "I finished my beer, and Leroy finished his. We stepped outside and introduced ourselves. 'Heard of you,' I told him. 'Likewise,' Leroy said."

By then Butch had ridden with the Hole-in-the-Wall Gang and the Rock Springs Gang, and more recently established his own outfit, which the newspapers and Pinkertons called The Wild Bunch. And so the incident at Belle Fourche led my late husband to get mixed up with that crowd, most of them not the sort of pals he would seek but that he had drifted into by stopping for a beer and a place to rest. Butch asked Harry to call him Leroy, the way some of his family did.

Harry and Butch conducted a series of business deals that summer and fall, and Butch occasionally contacted other members of the Bunch to participate in a project. It depended on the magnitude and location of the transaction. Also, several of the no-goods in the outfit wouldn't have hardtack and beans and coffee if they didn't get included from time to time.

"When cold weather set in we'd usually head for Robbers' Roost in northern Utah, although we also split time in winter on a ranch near Alma, New Mexico."

When I looked for Alma in my atlas, to include in this memoir, I couldn't find it. Alma must be a ghost town by now.

So that's Harry's life before we met in 1895. Malden and Bass had been locked up for three years, and Harry had been a fugitive all the time since and would never be held for long in any jail. No doubt the statute of limitations expired on many of his episodes. I don't know about such laws in South America. Certainly in Mexico they're not hunting for either of us, being as what we did had been common during those wild times of the Mexican Revolution. They'd have to jail the whole country, just about, including several men who became president. Still, I didn't do anything except hold the horses.

As for Prohibition in and around San Diego, everybody—law-enforcement agencies, politicians, and respected businessmen—ignored the Volstead Act. Remember, those were different times. Anyway, all I did was drive the car.

Finally Harry finished his cigarette, his second. "I haven't talked liked that in years. Must be the whiskey." He lay on his back and stretched and yawned. If he felt nervous with anticipation, it sure didn't show. Before long his hand touched mine. He turned toward me. And I turned toward him, and he kissed me. And we kissed for quite a spell. And pretty soon I lost my nervousness.

The first two or three times Harry did it to me that night I felt terribly excited and awfully pleased to be his woman, not just his Sunday girl. The other times, my enthusiasm had mostly expired, but I became contented to lie there and hold him while he did it. After a while my tailbone quit hurting because of numbness. I never realized people did it so often. But after a few days I enjoyed it, and instead of his doing it to me we did it to each other. Maybe I'll delete this part.

Anyhow, I must have eventually nodded off. Next thing I knew, first light arrived and I heard him whistling *John Brown's Body* while currying the horse. Harry already had a fire going, so I rolled out and worked up a breakfast of coffee, bacon, and hardtack. Still whistling, Harry led the gray to the creek and back, then gave him a handful of oats out of his saddlebag. Harry no longer limped.

"Are you hurting any from your fall, Harry? Stove up?"

"Nope. How'd you sleep?"

"Well, I was awake a lot." I limped toward him with a cup of coffee.

After breakfast we left our idyllic little honeymoon site, saddled and mounted that outstanding gray gelding, and continued our circuitous path toward Denver, where hot baths, good food, and a real bed awaited. Harry sat the saddle. I rode behind. And we looked for another horse to acquire.

The sun hung about thirty minutes high, the birds hunted and chattered, and the air still nipped us when we topped a hummock in the cedars and paused to look back. An antelope sprinted across the path in front of us.

"No sign of the Pinkertons," Harry said.

I faced the direction of the Harmsworth place, though I knew I couldn't see it. Thing is, I realized I had begun a far different life. I wanted this one last look at the old one. The Harmsworths had been wonderful to me, and I decided to write them and my own people when we got to Denver.

And I did. I wrote the Harmsworths every few months, even when Harry and I lived in South America and Mexico, wrote until they died during our San Diego years.

I taught Harry to copy words so he could add "Having a fine time" and "Thinking of you." When he asked how to write "Etta is still beautiful," I smiled and showed him.

I always regretted not stopping back to visit. Seems like one situation after another kept us from it. Of course I never told them everything, just about the sight-seeing in the countries we lived in or visited and a few of the interesting people we crossed trails with.

And I never told them that their dinner guest on those two sparkling Saturday afternoons near Leadville, Colorado, in the spring of 1895—that amiable, handsome man who came to court me and take me away—had been The Sundance Kid.

9

In midmorning we spotted several horses in a pasture.

"I don't see a house anywhere," Harry said.

"Maybe behind those trees?" I pointed.

"Could be." He nudged the gray with his spurs and we followed the barbed wire until reaching a gate.

I noted a black Morgan stallion that looked good, plus a couple of Quarter Horses, along with run-of-the-mill stock.

"They won't think two for one is fair," Harry said, "but it's the best trade we can offer. I wish to hell we had another saddle, though."

"'Two for one'?"

"We leave the gray, so we have to take two."

"But the gray's wonderful."

"He is, Sugar. But he belongs to a man who has had two days to get the word out about his disappearance, not to mention that if that had not been a Pinkerton operative, one of us shot an innocent man's horse out from under him. The gray could cause us to be recognized."

Harry never would say "steal" or "rob." Thus the gray had experienced a disappearance. And Pinkertons weren't innocent for they pursued Harry.

"We've come a long piece, Harry. Folks out here won't have telephones."

"Etta, I have been in this business and its related activities for a long time. I trade horses a lot and never been detained due to one giving me away."

"Anyone looking wants to see a man on a gray, not a woman. Besides, I'll wager he can outrun anything in the state if I'm the only one he's carrying." I watched the back of Harry's head for a reaction.

Harry seemed to study the horses.

"Besides," I said, "I've already named him. He's Cuchulain." I could almost hear Harry's question, so I added, "Ireland's national hero."

I didn't know if he'd ever traveled with a woman, had to compromise with or try to cater to one. I prepared to say "Please" when Harry swung a leg over the saddle horn and slid to the ground.

He faced me and smiled, the handsomest man I had ever seen and the only man I would ever love. He took the lariat off the saddle, opened the gate, and stepped into the pasture. "If someone gets after us," Harry said, "you'll have to ride like a man again." He "selected" the Morgan stallion, rode it bareback with rope twisted around its muzzle.

In Denver we lodged at the Brown Palace and enjoyed a week of fine meals and glamorous shops, and attended the Broadway Theater show, where we saw Lillie Langtry, the famous Jersey Lily. She looked pretty, thrilled us both.

"Hard to believe she's past forty," I said.

"Sure is."

Harry had let his whiskers grow ever since coming back for me. But the night before we left Denver he went somewhere for a couple of hours, and when he returned to our room he tossed some packages onto the bed and started shaving his beard.

"I like your whiskers, Harry."

"They'll grow back. I find it's good to change appearance from time to time."

Uh-oh. "Anyone get hurt?"

"No. The clerk acted pleasant. New clothes for both of us." He pointed to one of the bundles. "And fancy weapons for you." He motioned to the other bundle. "Also cash to pay our hotel bill and finance our travels for a while."

I unwrapped the clothes first: a frilly yellow dress for me, new jeans, a heavy coat and wool scarf, a denim jacket. For himself he brought jeans, shirt, and an antelope jacket. My new arsenal, as I thought of it, comprised an 1894 lever-action .30-30 carbine made by Mr. Oliver F. Winchester; a .32-caliber five-shot Iver Johnson revolver to be my inside gun, just like Harry's except with ivory grips; and a brace of .41-caliber derringers, single-shot rim-fire Colt Number 3s, only four and one-half inches long, nickel-plated with brass frames, spur triggers, and beautiful ivory grips.

When so many people carried Model 94 carbines like mine to the Alaska gold rush in 1898, everyone started calling it the Klondike Model. People today still know it by that name, a dandy weapon using smokeless powder in a twenty-inch nickel-steel barrel, both features innovations in that model, with a magazine of six cartridges.

Here we are today making spaceships like the one taking the boys to the moon, and yet we still produce that fine carbine I carried in my saddle boot during my younger days. When the Winchester people turned out their two-millionth Klondike Model in 1953 they gave it to President Eisenhower. I don't know what Ike did with his, but mine hangs on the wall above the fireplace.

For his shopping spree, as Harry called it, he told me he'd acquired a common-looking horse from the livery in case anyone connected him to the robbery. And he enjoyed a good night's sleep. I, however, did not, having lain awake most of the night waiting, I reckon, for the law to bang on the door.

In the morning, after deciding which older clothes to discard, we rode northeast out of Denver, I on my gray, Harry on a little brown mustang with saddle and bridle.

"Where'd you get that horse?" I asked him.

"Bought him." He smiled at me. "I'll show you the bill of sale."

"The saddle and bridle too?"

"Sure."

"What about the Morgan?"

"I gave the liveryman a good deal. He wrote both bills of sale for me."

Just before we crossed the South Platte, Harry moved his saddle and bridle to a large black mixed-blood gelding with huge chest and long legs, a beauty he spotted in a pasture. We left the mustang, a losing deal some rancher would be confused about and lament, though that little mustang could sure run, all day, I suspect.

We stepped up our pace for a couple of days, rode through the Pawnee Bluffs to Scottsbluff, and on to Central City and Deadwood, finding good cover each night. This beautiful high country thrilled me. I realized how someone would want to endure the winters in exchange for enjoying the other months there.

Nearly twenty years had passed since Bill Hickok's murder in Deadwood, but we still found people there talking about it, quite a few claiming they had been in Saloon No. 10 and saw the whole thing, more people than could have fitted into the place. But Harry acquired a certain amount of information he considered accurate.

"My ma's going to appreciate any news," Harry said. "And I might find out something I've wondered about for a long time."

A few days later we arrived, Harry pleasing me no end by introducing me as his wife. His stepfather, whom I never got a good look at, left the house immediately, so Harry wouldn't have to slug him. We never saw that man again.

The affection between Harry and his mother made me happy, but sad too, they saw each other so seldom. And it made me think about my own momma, how she might have changed in the year I'd been gone. But my momma had a good husband, plus several fine younguns still home to help out. I suppose I'm the only one who misbehaved. I wondered, though, when I would see my ma again.

From time to time I took a walk so Harry and his mother could talk privately.

When Harry and I were alone he told me.

"As I guessed," Harry said. "Hickok had been her beau before she met my father."

"That must have been thrilling."

"She called it 'scary.' Said she feared he'd get killed. Then she met my father. Felt she'd be more secure with him. In love too."

"With Hickok?"

"Both of them."

After two days Harry wanted to move on.

"Let's get your mother to come with us. I mean, let's set her up in Deadwood, wherever she wants."

"I asked her. She won't do it."

"But this life and your stepfather are making her old before her time."

"Momma's a plain and simple woman, Sugar. She won't leave him."

When we packed, and Harry had the horses ready, Mrs. Longbaugh, as I thought of her, stood with us in the yard. She'd have been so pretty if she'd been able to take care of herself.

"We'll come back every once in a while," I told her.

"I hope you can," she said.

"And one of us is going to write you regularly."

She smiled and hugged me. I guess she knew which one that would be.

Harry kissed her on the cheek and hugged her, but never spoke, just nodded.

She faced me. "Go, Etta. Go and see everything, just everything, and someday you can come back and tell me all about it." *Just like my mother talked.* She hugged me again and kissed Harry again, and I cried so much I could hardly find the stirrup.

Harry and I stopped and looked back after a few yards, and she waved, sort of flapping her hand. Momma used to do the same when company left or one of us would be gone for a while. When his mother wiped her eyes, we rode on.

Harry said, "She might be crying—"

"Yes."

"Because she won't be able to read those letters one of us is going to write."

That made me feel awful, embarrassing his mother that way, and I stayed angry at Harry the rest of the morning for telling me.

Harry had promised to meet Leroy in early December at Robbers' Roost, so we started that way, sight-seeing and honeymooning leisurely along the trails. We rode through the southern lip of the Bighorn Mountains, along the Sweetwater a piece, through South Pass, and across the Green River near Fort Bridger.

Harry reined up, rested a leg on his gelding's mane, and got out his cigarette makings. "Sometimes life gets tedious, spending the winter holed up with the Bunch."

"I wouldn't be one bit surprised."

"Gets cold too up there in northern Utah."

"I would think so."

"Might be all right to visit a big city first."

"Sure might be, Harry. Yes, sir."

"But we need to improve our finances."

I sure knew what that meant.

Near the Wind River, Harry acquired a beautiful chestnut Quarter Horse mare, leaving the black gelding in the same pasture—he called it "trading up"—and before long we camped near the stage line.

"I'll need a few days to study the stage schedule," Harry said, "so let's make ourselves at home."

We settled in near a creek with plenty of cover provided by pines and cedars, boulders and brush and hummocks. From one of those little rises Harry could watch the stage pass a quarter of a mile away. Every time we heard anything moving along the road he grabbed his pocket watch, jumped onto the mare bareback, and with a twist of rope for bridle cantered to a high spot for a look.

Harry accompanied me every day while I hunted with my carbine for our meals. After we struggled through the meat of a jackrabbit, I bagged a small buck and we upgraded to venison. We ate well. So did the horses in lush wide-spreading meadows. Antelope and deer grazed in the distance, and once we saw an elk. The creek provided water cool and clean, almost as nourishing as our food, and twice it gave up a trout.

I read to Harry from my Shakespeare, and he liked it. We also played cards and took short walks around what we thought of as our estate. Harry didn't like long walks and wouldn't let me go anywhere alone on account of bears and maybe strangers.

In a few days, Harry knew the stage schedule.

"One goes east every day at four in the afternoon," Harry said, "west in the mornings at nine. Usually carries passengers. The driver's always alone, meaning he probably won't be toting a lot of money. But he should have enough in his strongbox for us to at least visit Salt Lake City in style."

"Which stage do we take?"

He gave me a surprised smile. "Sugar, you can watch from a distance. The four o'clock. Now, what makes this a good idea is the driver has to slow down on the hill. I'll handle him there. That time of day it'll get dark soon and that'll be good cover in case anyone's following us."

On the afternoon of the appointment, as Harry called it, he reviewed his arsenal, cleaned and oiled each piece, and armed himself around three, in case the stage arrived early: Derringers strapped to the outside of each leg inside the boot; six-shooter in the holster tied down on his right thigh; inside gun holstered in front of his left biceps; and his repeating Spencer, that needle gun, in the boot on the right side of his saddle. For his six-shooter and carbine he carried extra ammunition in his jacket pockets and saddlebags. Rather than his business suit and city hat and gold watch fob, Harry wore his cowpuncher outfit. Around his neck he tied his red bandanna so he could pull it up to hide his face.

"I'll let my whiskers grow all the way to Salt Lake," he said.

I tried to smile but felt so scared it didn't come out right. Seeing him prepare made me realize I would be watching Harry negotiate one of his business transactions much more dangerous than what I'd observed previously, which had been stealing a horse he'd let loose later, if it didn't get shot out from under him. I wondered if becoming involved in the demise of the Old West might be more than I could handle. But when I watched him tighten the cinch on the Wind River mare, I knew that anything Harry Longbaugh did was all right by me.

"You ride your gray with me to a little stand of cedars just off the road," Harry said, "and you wait there with the horses. After I get the strongbox and you see the stage leave, bring up my horse. That's it."

"Got it."

"We'll have a good hour of dusk for riding toward Fort Bridger on a road that's traveled so much no one can track us."

"And the stage is going the other way," I said, "so it'll be the next day before any kind of law can get moving after us."

"Sugar, you'll do all right."

I felt the same way. I hitched up my jeans, put on my jacket, grabbed my hat, and mounted the gray. My inside gun hung in front of my left arm, my Winchester in its saddle boot. Apprehension coursed through me but not fright.

And then we waited in the cedars. Harry made a cigarette and prepared to light it when we heard the stage. He stuffed the cigarette into his shirt pocket, dismounted, and started toward the road.

"Be real careful." I emphasized "real."

Harry stopped, faced me, smiling, calm. "Sugar, if I'm real careful, I won't get anything done." He also emphasized "real" and pulled his bandanna over his lower face.

He didn't have to show himself until the last minute. When he did, his Colt in his right fist, the stage stopped in a rattling fog of dust and clattering hooves, with the driver and shotgun rider beside him raising their hands. That guard shouldn't have been there. Now Harry had an extra pair of hands and eyes to watch. I heard him cuss.

Then a door opened and two men in suits climbed down. I heard them try to talk Harry into surrendering. I'd never heard of such fools.

Sitting my horse, watching from the trees, gave me fits.

When the shotgun rider threw down the strongbox and raised his hands again, one of the city preachers, for that's how they acted, walked to the box, stood in front of it, and put his hands out toward Harry, as though protecting the box. He said something I missed. With a swift left jab, Harry knocked him down and out. The other preacher started toward Harry, and the

- 59 -

guard grabbed his shotgun. Harry gave his attention to the driver and the guard, who set down his scattergun and raised his hands again.

I couldn't sit still any longer. My first rifle shot tore up the dirt right where I'd aimed, near the feet of the fool passenger. He scrambled back to the stage and jumped inside as though he'd met a mountain lion on the trail. My second shot splintered the top of the door, right where I'd aimed.

The driver had his hands full trying to control his horses, so when Harry yelled and fired a couple of shots into the air, the driver had no trouble sending his team the rest of their way up the hill. The fool Harry knocked down began to stir, then stopped.

Harry shot the lock off the strong box. When he opened it we saw mostly twenty-dollar gold pieces, but paper money too.

"That's a lot," I said.

"Yep. And heavy. Let's put all we can tote in the saddlebags."

We did that and mounted our horses, the stage long out of sight. We lit out in the other direction.

In my few days with Harry Longbaugh, I had participated in horse stealing, a stagecoach robbery, and some shooting.

I felt like a full-fledged member of The Wild Bunch.

And I enjoyed the feeling.

10

Salt Lake City didn't compare to Denver, not in the fall of 1895. We registered as Mr. and Mrs. Place in a nice hotel and stayed for a couple of weeks. We had our city clothes cleaned and ironed first thing and enjoyed a big time taking advantage of hot baths, a good bed, and decent meals. I saw lots of cattlemen and farmers walking around and in the lobby, so I felt good in my jeans and boots, cleaned and shined. But twice I had occasion to wear my frilly new yellow dress. That pleased Harry. Me too.

Staying in Salt Lake didn't cost much, and the three thousand dollars acquired from the stage would have lasted us several more glorious weeks if we had chosen to stay. I did some shopping, mostly through store windows, being as we couldn't carry much with us. We also saw Buffalo Bill's Wild West, a show that thrilled us, all those Indians and cowboys, exhibitions in horsemanship and shooting, and a mock holdup of a stage.

"What did you think of that holdup, Sugar?"

"I liked ours better."

Harry agreed.

Late at night he often went to a saloon and played cards, usually cooncan or faro, while I stayed in our room reading, waiting up for him. He'd wear his business suit and city hat while packing only his derringers and inside gun. He never needed them on those nights. Harry usually won at cards, so he didn't throw our money away. And as far as I know he didn't have any fights.

But Harry fretted that someone would recognize him if he stayed long in a place, and that the someone would notify the Pinkertons.

"It's mighty concerning sometimes," he said one night as we lay propped up in bed in the dark, "knowing that damn Charlie Siringo is out there somewhere." He sipped tanglefoot from a jug he'd bought.

I held his other hand. "I'm glad they don't have a picture of you."

"Yes. Or of you."

"Nobody saw me. Besides, I just held the horses." I giggled.

"And firing away like a sharpshooter in Buffalo Bill's circus."

I couldn't see Harry's face, but I heard the levity. "I did that extra." I smiled recollecting my participation in the robbery.

"You did right. Things took too long."

I knew he looked at me.

"You liked it, didn't you, Sugar?"

I squeezed his hand. "You bet your boots."

"There's nothing glamorous about Robbers' Roost," Harry said. "It's regular camping out in cold weather, sometimes snow. But we have a wood floor in our tent and a wood stove. Luxuries."

The sun showed low in the east as we rode north out of Salt Lake City, Harry on the Wind River mare, I on my great gray Cuchulain. I'd been pestering Harry to explain to me about that hideout no outsider had ever found. He finally said he would.

"We're in a valley with a couple of natural springs and snow melt for drinking water, for the horses too if the creek is dry. But we skimp on water, just in case, especially for bathing, and nobody minds. When the snow's heavy we're pretty much stuck until it eases up. There's big game, rabbits, and birds too. And we dry meat for lean times. Sometimes one of the boys takes a wagon to a ranch down the slope and returns with essentials like whiskey and coffee, sugar and flour and salt, grain and fodder for livestock. Winter grazing's poor.

"And all around it's hilly and rocky, mostly barren. Give me the Wind Mountains or the Black Hills any day."

The way Harry described Robbers' Roost, it might be called a commune.

"Everybody chips in toward provisioning food and firewood and for care of the horses and other livestock, like a couple of mules, some cows and calves. There's not much need for cash. Even the card games are penny ante. That's why I left so much of our money in that bank at Salt Lake City. It should be safe. Most of the boys will be holed up for the winter."

I had to laugh at that. "I suppose it's rowdy, what with all the robbers and thieves and cutthroats raising Cain all night. I hope we can sleep." I tried to be funny.

But Harry took me seriously. "It might be an interesting study for a schoolteacher like you, Sugar. You see, when you put a lot of desperados together they find camaraderie, seldom friction. Besides, all the boys aren't usually there at the same time. Another thing: They don't have the jealousy like in some outfits. You see, there's a prostitute or two with them. And several of the men bring their own women."

I noted, with relief perhaps dictated by jealousy, that Harry said "they" and "them," not "us" or "we." I kept shut, instead asked him to fill me in about some of the Bunch I'd be meeting. I'll quote Harry on only those I think have been in print so, just in case, none of their families will come after me for exposing them.

"Leroy you already know. He should be there by now. Let's see. Elza Lay. He's Leroy's best pard after me. Elza's one of the few in the Bunch, other than Kid Curry, who's killed anyone, but that took place in a shootout during a messed up robbery, not in the back or in the dark. His woman, Maude Davis, will be with him. America Connolly, he's sort of new to us, a happy little half-breed still in his teens. Can just about outshoot me in pistol practice. America can also throw a knife expertly, same as any full-blooded Mexican or Indian. I hope he's still with Janie Bowen. You'll like her.

"Ben Kilpatrick, who's so tall everyone, even the Pinkertons, calls him The Tall Texan. There's Tom O'Day. He's just a rustler and bank robber. Will Carver, a pleasant fellow I don't know much about. Harry Tracy, an ordinary holdup man. Lonny Logan, a general no-good. And Lonny's brother, Harvey. That's Kid Curry, a braggart I wish would hook up somewhere else."

I'd read about Curry: twelve men killed "of record" but bragging that the number had reached eighteen. I didn't want to meet him. But I did, him and the others too, in addition to several who popped in and out but didn't make much presence, or I have forgotten their names. Most of those the law didn't kill within a few years got imprisoned for long periods. At the Harmsworths', when Harry had explained his profession, he mentioned that the Bunch tried to avoid killing. I wanted to ask if he had killed anyone, but I didn't. I swore to myself I would never ask.

The last part of the trail became especially steep. But we made it easy. When it leveled off and narrowed, Harry looked up high and waved.

"Who you waving to?"

"Signalling. Don't recognize him from here."

"I don't see anybody."

"Up there high in the rocks." Harry pointed.

I kept looking and squinting and finally spotted the upper body of a man in a Stetson and heavy coat. I waved in case it mattered. It made me feel important.

A few minutes later on that cold day in late December 1895, with tall outcroppings of pine-grown hills on all sides like the walls of a bowl, we rode into the meadow that held the camp: tents and outhouses, with desperados and a few women scattered about except for a nearby cluster of folks that included Leroy "Smith," that is, Robert Leroy Parker, Butch Cassidy. Leroy got to Harry first. When Harry dismounted they had a big hug and a laugh. I dismounted and extended my hand to Leroy, who acted pleasant enough, though not enthusiastic like in his greeting of Harry.

One after another the others approached and shook hands with Harry while he introduced me. With respect, sometimes affection, they called him "Kid" and "Sundance," and I wondered about that. Finally I decided "Kid" referred to his youth, "Sundance" to his birthplace in Wyoming.

A few moments later I put the two words together. And for the first time—surprised when I maybe should not have been, stunned because I couldn't help it, and thrilled for I had a right to be—I realized that Harry was The Sundance Kid.

You can imagine my pride and excitement. Harry himself had already become my white knight, my rock. But now, knowing he belonged to such a famous part of the last of the Old West, that fascinating era I thought I had missed out on, I reveled in shivers of happiness.

I drew some attention of my own, and the men and women treated me courteous and respectfully, though I suspected they came from impoverished upbringings and had cultural shortcomings. I felt glad, by the way, that none of the unattached women, apparently the prostitutes, seemed to know Harry.

The breeze changed direction and I smelled barbecue.

"Been cooking all day," Leroy said. "Stop by my tent when you're settled and we'll have some tanglefoot."

Our tent sat off to one side, and I enjoyed seeing that stove he mentioned. Harry put our saddles and saddlebags on the floor, led the horses to the corral downwind, returned with the bridles, and hung them on the center pole. He left the saddle pads, sweaty and dusty, in the shed at the corral.

"Leroy sure seemed glad to see you, Harry."

"He's been a good pard for a long time."

"Why didn't you let me know you were The Sundance Kid?"

"Figured you'd find out sooner or later. Change your mind?"

"What do you mean?"

"Want out of this lash-up with me?"

"Do you want me out?"

We shared a big hug and kiss. That topic never rode our way again.

"Let's get on over to Leroy's tent," Harry said. "By the way, around others he'd probably appreciate it if you'd not use his family name, but call him Butch."

Our breath frosty in the cold, and with me looking around like a tourist, we walked the short distance to Leroy's tent and joined him in front of it, Elza Lay and Maude, America Connolly and Janie, and a few others sitting on crude handmade benches surrounding a fire. America, holding the jug, stood and, proud as could be, handed the whiskey to me. I took a sip to be polite, passed it to Harry, and we sat.

Each gave an account of his or her activities since the last time the Bunch rode together, sort of reporting to Harry, I figured, knowing they'd have had such powwows before our arrival, I'm sure. I didn't hear much exciting, although Butch made himself sound heroic.

Harry didn't like to list his exploits. "Not much," he said. "'Cept one thing." He put his arm around me. "I captured Etta."

I heard applause and cheers, like from a friendly audience at a play, although Butch frowned before slowly joining in.

Elza Lay, still smiling at Harry's comment about me, asked, "Sundance, did you meet up with that damn Charlie Siringo anywheres?"

"Not from up real close," Harry said. "But probably close enough."

I saw a puckish smile indicating he planned to reveal something good in his quiet, pleasant way.

"Etta Margaret here shot his horse out from under him, Siringo or some rancher who had winged mine and knocked us down. Pinned me under him. She made just a spectacular shot."

Harry told how I used his rifle and made the shot from five hundred yards.

"Amazing," Elza said.

"I'd like to have seen that, Miss Etta." America nodded and smiled.

Others nodded and made similar comments, except for Butch, who sipped from the jug, and tough-looking Laura Bullion, whom I'd pegged as one of the prostitutes.

"Yes," Laura said. "Unusual shooting for someone little more than a girl."

I looked at the fire and kept shut.

Harry put his arm around me again. "Etta tied my lariat from her horse to my saddle, pulled my horse off me, and we hit the trail riding double." Then, polite but firm, he told Laura, "Etta not only shoots like a man, she rides like one too."

That shut her up, but I felt embarrassed, being the center of attention. "More like three hundred yards."

"No need to be modest around these folks, Etta. It was a shot few could make, five hundred yards and you know it. We can go back and measure if you want."

I said, "I think we'd better stay away from there." That brought some laughs.

"Kid, let's have a shooting match," America said. "Men against the women."

"No," Butch said. "All together. Pass the word. And I'll be there."

Butch sounded like he had the contest won and no one else need show up. I'd certainly do my part unless Harry didn't want me to. But I knew there'd be plenty of competition in a roundup like this. We wouldn't have to worry about running out of ammunition or empty cans or bottles for targets either.

We talked until the embers began fading. All of us left in our separate directions, and I got a mean look from Laura Bullion. I smiled and kept going, later informing Harry how she'd scowled at me.

"Don't fret, Sugar," he said. "It's probably that she's not pretty and you are."

Thanks to later achievements by the Pinkertons, you can judge for yourself, in one book or another, her pictures side and front view, number across her chest. She probably also felt jealous, for I had Harry. I never minded prostitutes, in fact felt sorry for them. But Laura Bullion had apparently declared herself my enemy. So I declared to myself to leave her be.

As for the rifle match the next day, I won that easily with my new Klondike Model 94. America Connolly took second and Harry third. Butch finished quite a way back although none of the other women beat him. On the following day we held a pistol shoot. Harry using his Colt won that easily, with America Connolly second. I shot with my inside gun and beat all the women and several of the men, including Butch.

A few nights later while we sat around the fire at Butch's tent, just the three of us, he got to talking about himself, things Harry probably knew, so it was for my benefit.

"Just seventeen when I took off," Butch said. "No dirt-poor farm could hold me. I did a little cowpunching but that's no better than farming. I met some good boys I got along well with and we partnered for a few holdups. Then I started my own outfit. And one day I met this rascal sitting beside you, and things got better all at once." He turned to Harry. "We've been all over, haven't we,

Pard?" Butch faced me again. "You may have read about me back yonder where you lived."

I read about him, all right, and he should be ashamed of himself: the oldest child, running off to raise hell when they needed him at home. Imagine their despair when he turned outlaw and served prison time for stealing a horse. But I kept shut.

Leroy's nickname fitted him like the spurs on his boots, with his round pugnacious face and boxed ears and stubby nose. I have to admit I liked him most of the time. But that murderous Kid Curry was also likable most of the time. Even women liked Curry. Leroy didn't seem to especially like women or respect them. I never saw him involved with a nice girl, though Harry told me Leroy visited prostitutes. I believe to this day that he tolerated me in order to avoid any problem with Harry.

On Christmas Eve, the air cold and breezy, Harry cut a little pine tree and surprised me with it. Snow still clung to it, making that tree so beautiful I wouldn't have decorated it even if we'd had doodads to hang on it.

"You're going to make me cry," I said. "It's the prettiest tree I've ever had."

"You deserve the prettiest, Sugar." He reached into his pocket and brought out a diamond ring and put it on my third finger, left hand. My tears rushed out.

"Got it in Salt Lake. Paid for it."

I nodded.

"Hope you like it."

I nodded and hugged him. "I didn't get you anything."

"You got me you. That's enough."

I had to struggle to keep from bawling. When I could speak I said, "I wish your momma could be here. And mine. And the rest of my folks. And the Harmsworths."

"Someday we'll have a big reunion, Sugar."

"Maybe by then we'll have children."

"Would you like that?"

"Oh, yes," I told him. "Someday. Not too soon."

The sun began to set on New Year's Day when Butch stopped outside our tent and looked through the open flaps. "Kid, we need a meeting."

"Come on in."

"I mean the whole Bunch. It'll be spring soon. The boys need to know what we'll be doing."

"How about tomorrow?" Harry said.

"That's what I figured."

"I reckon there's a lot of hangovers around today."

"I was just fixing to say that. What time do you figure?"

"How about midmorning?" Harry reached for his cigarette makings.

"My thought exactly, Sundance. In front of my tent?"

"Wouldn't behind it be better? Every dab of sun helps in this cold."

"Yep. That's what we'll do. Happy New Year, Etta." Butch left.

"Spring to most of our men is mid-February," Harry said. "They can't stand being here much longer, the cold and lack of excitement, even though it's safe."

"I think I saw some riding out already. At least they had bedrolls."

"That's right, Sugar. They left word where they'd be when needed. Good thing is the Bunch has friends and friendly contacts over several states and territories."

At the planning session the next day the women sat in, all of us perched on benches or our heels in the mild sun. But the men did the talking. It's been so long ago I don't recall the details, though I remember mention of Belle Fourche and Casper, Omaha and Dodge City and Tucson, a couple of places in New Mexico.

"We could just work our way south from here," Butch said.

I heard some agreement and some opposition.

Will Carver, one of the boys I liked best, said, "What do you think, Kid?"

Butch looked at Harry.

"From Belle Fourche and Casper, for instance, we could get back here in a hurry to hide out," Harry said, "but that's like adding to our winter. I favor the lowlands of southern Arizona, southern New Mexico."

Butch frowned at the ground. "Such a long ways before we get anything done."

"Easy to scatter after a job, like last year," America Connolly said.

Butch frowned at the young fellow.

Harry had told me Butch resented America, being so new, and also a half-breed.

"The little guy's right," Elza Lay told Butch.

Butch looked at Harry, who nodded.

"South it is," Butch agreed. "Now: Trains are good."

"Hard to case," Kid Curry said.

"Might be full of Army," Ben Kilpatrick commented.

Butch looked at Harry.

"Anything's all right," Harry said, "if it's well planned. But maybe we should consider warming up on something simpler to handle, like a small-town bank."

Butch stood, turned a little circle, and sat. "I'll study on that. Now . . ."

All morning, Butch acted as though the agreed-upon decisions and strategy originated with him. I don't know if the others noticed, but I saw as plain as skimmed milk that the brains of The Wild Bunch was Harry Longbaugh.

11

We enjoyed a pleasant enough winter at Robbers' Roost even with the cold and the snow and despite the Comanche looks I received from Laura Bullion. I became good friends with Janie Bowen, Maude Davis, Annie Rogers, and a couple of the other women. So that made up for Miss Bullion's being on the warpath.

Harry and I took lots of short walks and rode Cuchulain and the Wind River mare regularly so they wouldn't pitch us onto the rocks when we started to leave the hideout.

When that day came, we were ready.

"Time to spend some of that money we have in the bank," Harry said.

We said our good-byes and packed.

As Harry had suggested at the big powwow, several of us rode south to Salt Lake City to retrieve our money and to sightsee, though just briefly, for Salt Lake still experienced winter weather. So Harry, Butch, and the others soon began talking about Phoenix or Tucson, maybe Houston.

"Looks like I'm going to have to get back to work," Harry told me.

"May I hold the horses again?"

I can't recite all the Bunch did, or what Harry did alone, in the way of business transactions as I can't recall it all and don't want to mention certain activities in case the Pinkertons don't know. But one that is significant occurred eighteen months later, following another winter at Robbers' Roost. It has been written up plenty.

Several of us traveled together.

"Deadwood should be a good starter," Butch said. "What do you all think?"

I didn't hear much response for or against.

"Sundance, what about you?"

"I feel like Belle Fourche would be better. Less law."

"Less money too," Butch added.

They wrangled back and forth. Then Butch and some others chose Deadwood, figuring there would be plenty of money around from the gold rush in territorial days.

Harry and I with Tom O'Day, Walter Putney, and Kid Curry headed for Belle Fourche. It gave me fits every time Harry worked with Kid Curry. But, in my time at least, Curry never killed anyone while riding with Harry.

Anyway, they got out of the bank with ten thousand dollars but never got out of Belle Fourche. I learned this almost immediately, being as I waited in a clump of trees ten miles down the road with a change of horses saddled and rested and grained and known to be fast. I had Cuchulain, best of the bunch by far.

So when the boys didn't show up by the appointed time I left the rendezvous and, leading the Wind River mare, rode into Deadwood as agreed "in case," and sent the sheriff an anonymous note about three horses hitched to saplings down the road a piece. I didn't want them going hungry. And I still felt bad about the horse I shot near Leadville.

As much as I needed to see Harry and help him if I could, I didn't want to show up in Belle Fourche too soon after the robbery, just in case. So I had been in the hotel at Deadwood two days when the townspeople became enlivened considerably by the arrival of a wagon toting four trussed-up men said to have recently robbed the bank at Belle Fourche. Several deputies on horseback escorted the prisoners along Main Street.

I stood and watched from in front of the hotel across the dusty street from the Deadwood jail. Such a sorrowful day, seeing

Harry bound hand and foot and hobbling to be locked up. Kid Curry, Tom O'Day, and Walter Putney followed him. I bit back my tears and started studying about what to do.

When the weekly newspaper came out two days later it made a fuss over the captives.

"One of the dangerous new guests in our exclusive Inn of the Iron Bars," the main article said, "is the notorious killer, highwayman, and horse thief, The Sundance Kid. He is a desperate fugitive still wanted for the Great Northern train robbery four and one-half years ago at Malta, Montana, and no doubt many other robberies and murders. He is legally known as Harry Longbaugh or Longabaugh. Another is the infamous cold-blooded killer, Kid Curry, legally known as Harvey Logan. Curry, or Logan, is wanted for murders and depredations in several states and territories.

"Their two companions are still working to improve their glorious reputations although they now will be delayed quite a spell from pursuing their goals. All four, easily apprehended by valiant townspeople before they could flee Belle Fourche with their ill-gotten gains, are believed to ride with that gang of ruffians, killers, and thieves known as The Wild Bunch and directed by the intrepid Butch Cassidy."

Right away I visited Harry. "What in the world went wrong over yonder?"

"Everything, Sugar. Somehow they got wind of us. Met us in overpowering numbers, shotguns leveled, when we stepped out of the bank."

After my first few visits, the guard, a slim young towhead with freckles, didn't ever pay me hardly any heed, smiled, and brought me a chair. Harry and I could talk freely, even hold hands and kiss between the bars. He shared a cell with Kid Curry, but Curry stayed back so we hardly noticed him.

One day I brought Harry news about Butch. "Leroy and the others never got a penny here in Deadwood. I heard it at the hotel."

"What happened?"

"A couple of them got drunk and made too much ruckus. The sheriff ran them out the night they got here. Either didn't recognize Leroy or didn't give a hoot."

Another time when the deputy went out back to use the outhouse, Harry and I talked about the need to escape from the jail. "Depart," Harry explained.

"This is no rabbit hutch like the one in Belle Fourche," Harry said. "That's why they brought us here. We'll need help."

This was a sturdy building of bricks and heavy timber with iron bars well fitted into the windows upstairs and down, most of the cells on the second floor.

"It won't be easy, Sugar. But there's no big hurry as long as we get out before November, when the circuit judge is due."

In the end, Harry departed almost as easily as I checked out of the hotel.

At lunchtime on Halloween of 1897, I took advantage of the deputy's being accustomed to me, and therefore a little careless, to pass my derringers with extra cartridges through the bars to Harry. After supper, in full dark I checked out of the hotel, traveling light, as usual, walked to the livery stable, and had Cuchulain and the Wind River mare saddled. I put my Shakespeare, Thomas Hardy reader, Sunday dresses, and other essentials into the saddlebags and rented the three best horses available.

"They don't show so well," the liveryman said, "'longside that gray of yours."

"Few do. But they'll pass muster for tonight."

"You and some friends going for a Halloween ride?"

I told him, "That's the plan."

"Don't let the goblins get you." He laughed.

So did I, and I ran a line from horse to horse, mounted Cuchulain, and with my remuda started walking north out of town, away from the jail in case anyone watched. I passed a batch of saloons, some bordellos, and rode through Chinatown before looping around and returning, finally reining in behind the hotel.

Late that night at the agreed-upon time, Harry opened the alley door in front of me and stepped out. Curry, O'Day, and Putney followed a few seconds apart. Not a shot had been fired nor a voice raised.

"The deputy's hog-tied and gagged," Harry said. He returned my derringers, had the deputy's six-shooter in his waistband. The others had found revolvers in a desk.

"Much obliged, Etta," Curry said. "Reckon we'll be seeing you around."

"Etta goes with us," Harry said. "You've seen her shoot. Now watch her ride."

We rode like thunder the rest of the night, and just before first light the men traded horses at a ranch south of Deadwood.

"That's a good-looking sorrel watching us from the far corner of the corral," Harry said. "I'll get him for you and you can leave your gray."

"I don't think so," I told him.

"What if the liveryman remembers you?"

"I hope he paid more attention to my face than my horse's."

I knew he didn't like giving in. But he never had a runner like my great gray.

"Boys," Harry said, "let's keep in touch."

Curry, O'Day, and Putney left together.

"A friendly rancher has a spread not far away," Harry said, "still in the Black Hills and in a nice little valley."

"Is that where we're headed?"

"I have some gold pieces there."

"And then San Francisco?"

"Count on it."

Right away I started thinking about having my hair done and acquiring a new dress. But we had to take a roundabout route.

First we stayed a couple of days at the spread Harry mentioned and where the rancher and his wife treated me regally, called Harry "Kid," and hosted him like an old friend deserved.

"Red and I used to ride together," Harry told me during the introductions. That gave me all I needed to know. Red, skinny and freckled, stood near Harry's height.

He returned Harry's cache of gold pieces and outfitted him with a new arsenal. This included an 1894 Winchester carbine like Harry had bought for me in Denver, two derringers, and a good but worn holster with a brand-new single-action .45-caliber Colt Bisley center-fire revolver. It had red oak grips, a blue round barrel seven and one-half inches long, a half-fluted cylinder, and side-rod ejector. This became Harry's all-time favorite six-shooter. He gave the deputy's pistol to Red.

"You all going through Leadville on your way to San Francisco?" Red asked.

"We can," Harry said. "What can we get you?"

"Not that," Red said. "But something you ought to know. Ever hear about the Pinkerton operative who got his horse shot out from under him near there a couple of years ago?" Red showed a crooked smile.

"Sounds familiar."

"Yep. One of their top men, Charlie Siringo. They say a woman got him." Red, still smiling, looked at me. "They say she rode with a fellow who had robbed a store in Leadville a day or so before. Young couple. No names. Got clean away. No good description of the woman." Red looked at Harry. "Man's description fits you, Sundance. Course it could have been 'most anybody."

"That's my guess." Harry squeezed my hand.

"Hell of a shot, though. Imagine, a woman." Red scratched his vermilion hair.

I smiled. But I kept shut.

The next day, heading in the opposite direction from Leadville, we left riding south and into New Mexico, where we stopped on the railroad line at Folsom and stabled the horses. The liveryman would remove saddles and bridles, gaining a surprise windfall.

"We won't be gone long," Harry told him, hugging me. I watched the liveryman lead Cuchulain and Harry's mare to a stall. I knew we wouldn't return. I felt like bawling.

"They say the weather's better in San Francisco now than in the summer."

I nodded.

Toting our saddlebags, we walked toward the train.

Harry took my hand. "I'm sorry, Sugar. But we'd be too tied down otherwise."

"I know."

"He's an awfully fine horse. Outstanding."

I reached for a handkerchief to wipe my eyes.

12

San Francisco was everything I had hoped for. I felt like dancing all the time.

We stayed at the Palace Hotel; bought me a nice dress and coat, shoes and hat; saw the Pacific Ocean for the first time; strolled along the rocky shores; and ate at the Cliff House, where we could watch seals on the big rock a little way out in the water. Such a thrill, seeing the Pacific. Ever since, I've loved walking a beach and watching the waves. We saw the opera, the symphony, the park, and a Lillie Langtry play. Overall, we had just a grand time, including some boat rides on the bay and a close look at Alcatraz Island, where the military had its prison.

But one night in our room Harry said, "Sugar, we're running low on gold pieces."

"Are we going to replenish our supply?"

"One of us is, Etta. But I don't feel comfortable about performing a transaction here. Everything's unfamiliar, and we don't have friends or hideouts around."

"Can we stay through Christmas? I'd like that."

We stayed through New Year's Day, packed our saddlebags, took a train eastward quite a piece, then acquired horses and tack for the last part of the journey to the ranch near Alma, New Mexico, where the Bunch occasionally rendezvoused, especially in late winter. Butch and a few of the other boys with certain of the women got there first.

The plan, which Harry worked out and which Leroy accepted and promoted as his own, concerned the bank in Fort Sumner.

"Sundance and I will handle this one alone but split everything equally with you all." Butch tugged up his gun belt. "You all rest up."

"I want Etta along to hold the horses," Harry said.

Leroy hesitated, but said, "Sure, Kid. I'm thinking the same thing."

"Etta and I'll register at the hotel and wait for you."

"I'll follow in two days," Butch said, "and we'll take it from there."

We rode out on a couple of good horses, Harry on a young buckskin gelding, mostly Quarter Horse, I on a blue roan mare about eight years old with a sweet canter.

We spent four days in Fort Sumner. Harry found a card game every night and I had plenty to read, but we became annoyed with Butch when he didn't show up. Finally a telegram addressed to "Mr. Place" arrived for Harry.

"Read it to me, Sugar."

"'Ulcer attack. Return home. Leroy.' I didn't know he had ulcers."

"More likely alcohol poisoning. It's happened before."

Harry and I mulled the situation over. Fort Sumner was tiny, just a village, maybe a few hundred residents, including those on the far outskirts. The fort had long been closed. But we knew there'd be money with the longhorn trail nearby. And now we had eaten at every place in town, ridden into the desert, and done a fair bit of walking around, considering that Harry was a cowboy by birth. But the need for funds made us feel like hungry bears in winter. Harry said, "Looks like I have a new helper."

As it turned out, Harry probably could have handled this job alone. But you never knew in our business when some fool not realizing whom he dealt with might try to disrupt the transaction, or somebody could arrive unannounced.

So the next day, carbine in hand, derringers strapped outside my lower legs but hidden by my boots, and my inside gun holstered under my jacket in front of my left biceps, I stood guard just inside the bank door. Harry with his Colt Bisley in his right hand walked behind the counter and acquired the cash from men reaching so high you could almost hear their shoulder sockets squeak. No customers arrived.

Harry collected sixteen hundred dollars in paper, saving the vault for another time after the clerks insisted that the only man who knew the combination had taken off sick.

If a posse formed, we never heard about it.

Leroy's "ulcer" problem had cleared up by the time we returned to the ranch, and he apologized for disappointing his pard.

"That's all right, Leroy," Harry said. "I picked up a nerveless cold-eyed helper who worked out just fine."

The others of the Bunch had left but soon reunited with us and Butch to perform several successful fund-raisers during the next few months.

Then Harry and I went to Alabama.

"Do you mean to say, Etta Margaret, that folks drove their buggies right into the hotel? Didn't the horses and mules mess up the rugs something shameful?"

So I had to explain to Momma how the Palace Hotel in San Francisco had a roofed driveway permitting buggies and carriages to roll in and stop at the entry. "Park, they call it, so people can get out without getting rained on and footmen can unload."

"'Footmen'?"

The first day with my folks on the farm near Selma went like that. Poor Momma and my sisters had never been out of the county, and here I rattled on about San Francisco and the Pacific

Ocean, Denver and Salt Lake City and Cheyenne. I had written the folks about most of the places, but their hearing about them was different. That included Leadville and Deadwood, though I omitted certain salient details. I knew they wouldn't understand, even though those were different times.

Harry, of course, was the successful financier, and therefore I didn't have to teach school any longer. I had written them that Harry and I got married in Leadville two years earlier by the circuit judge and that I had become Mrs. Parker. Harry thought it funny to use Leroy's true last name, and he clearly couldn't use his own.

For weeks I'd been feeling as awkward as a baby goat about the idea of sleeping with a man in the house I grew up in, especially as we hadn't married. Now I had to throw in my cards or call.

"Momma," I said just before dark on our first night there, "why don't I sleep with the girls? We've got so much catching up to do."

"Why, that would be fine, Etta Margaret," Momma said, quickly enthusiastic.

"Harry won't mind sleeping on the porch, I'm sure." I smiled sympathetically at Harry. "It's got good netting to keep the mosquitoes and other bugs from getting at you."

I saw the relief wash through Momma's and Pappy's faces. Harry didn't like the arrangement but hid his disappointment well.

Along the way at Montgomery, Harry had bought me a gold wedding band and we checked our saddlebags, rifles, and all at the train station. I persuaded him to check his six-shooter and holster. I left my inside gun and holster, my Model 94, and derringers. But in my purse I still toted the old Philadelphia derringer Pappy gave me. He would appreciate that. Harry bought us a satchel and stowed his inside gun in it.

But after breakfast on the first day, when Pappy and Harry sat on the porch to smoke, I saw Pappy looking hard at one of Harry's boots. Where Harry had a leg crossed, Pappy could see the strap holding a derringer and guessed the reason.

"Habit, Mr. Place," Harry told him, "and a good one. Out where your daughter and I've been, it's best for my type of business. There's desperados, even today."

"Have to be on your guard."

"All the time."

"I hear there's still a few robber gangs."

"They're an occasional threat," Harry said, "like that dreaded Cassidy bunch."

"Well, you take good care of my daughter, young man."

"Mr. Place, around me, Etta's as safe as in her bed."

Harry told me after supper when we walked in from the separate outhouses that he had a tussle understanding the way my folks talked, especially my mother. "It's not so much the Alabama in their speech as it is the Irish."

"Really? I don't hear it."

"You wouldn't, Sugar. You sound about like your pa."

My pappy was born on a farm near Raleigh, North Carolina, in 1846, one year after his pap had taken the family out of Ireland during the Potato Famines. One ancestor had ridden with Hugh O'Neill in the seventeenth century, and another somewhat later had been an outlawed rapparee. When I turned out to be more ambitious, you might say, than most girls, my father feared that the old rebel's wild blood had bubbled up in me, not to fight any tyrannical king this time but the boredom, the confinement. Our more immediate family came from the Dingle Peninsula, at the foot of Macgillicuddy's Reeks, those splendorous mountains that are the highest in Ireland.

I saw that my father liked Harry from the beginning. I confirmed that feeling late one afternoon when I sat with them on the porch and noted that Pappy had entered a rare mood to talk. The liquor jug between them might have helped. I kept quiet.

"My folks brought us down here to Dallas County when I was six," Pappy told Harry. "When the war against the Yankees broke out I was only fifteen, but like so many others I rushed off and joined the Autauga County Guards. Going to put an end to it and get back before fall harvest. Wound up in the Army of the Tennessee. Shiloh, Chickamauga, Atlanta, Bentonville. Lucky. Got the hell scared out of me and nicked by a couple of minié balls, but returned safe, though worn out and ragged and skinny, and mad at getting whipped. Riding a Yankee mule."

He sipped from the jug, passed it to Harry, who obliged.

"Now Flann and Dunleavy want to join up to fight Spain. But I don't cotton to that. Need those boys here. What I did was different, defending my country."

Just a year separated my younger brothers, Flann short and red-haired, Dunleavy tall and dark, and always together, work or free time.

We soon went inside for supper. Flann and Dunleavy had learned that Harry years earlier did some cowboying—Gareth and Tyrone had farms but planned to visit—and asked about those days. Harry told them the truth, about the hard work, some of it hellish, like nights in the rain or snow, all for poor pay, and nothing glamorous about it.

"Do you ever see any Indians?" Dunleavy asked.

"Some," Harry said. "Mostly making a purchase at a store in town."

"You ever shoot any?"

"Hell, boy," my father said, "Old Man Zimmermann shot one stealing from his still just last month, over near Linden."

"Just one of our tame ones, Pappy."

"The Indians out West are tame now too," Harry said, "not like when I was a boy." He paused. "In fact, everything's pretty much quiet out West these days. The olden times are gone forever."

I'm sure I'm the only one who heard the irony in his voice.

"Can you shoot?" Flann asked.

"Some."

"We got rifles," Flann said. "Let's have a match tomorrow after dinner."

Dunleavy said, "Etta's lost her eye by now. I been itching to get even."

The next day they brought out two fine Spencer .52-caliber rimfire seven-shot repeaters like the Yankees had at Gettysburg and elsewhere.

I walloped my brothers, although Harry and my father finished close behind me. Harry took it well, but I knew he felt tempted to give a pistol demonstration, in which case I wouldn't have been able to touch him, nor could any man alive, although I didn't know for sure about John P. Belden nor Buffalo Bill. But then Harry would have to do some explaining, and we didn't want that.

I played the Kimball upright every night after supper, Irish tunes like *Cockles and Mussels*, *The Men of the West*, and *The Girl I Left Behind Me*. I had learned them from Momma while she taught me to play, and I added some ditties I'd picked up out West. Everybody sang and Momma and I played a few duets. She had a lot of musical talent, a good ear. But she liked just playing and singing for the family.

Momma and Pappy had been sweet on each other before he left for the war, and they married as soon as he returned from it. She was Kate Muldoon, a beautiful brunette with roots in County Derry, and her parents had also fled the Famines. She had been born on a farm near Selma, two years younger than my father. I used to hope I'd look as good when I reached her age. I don't know if I made it or not.

We stayed a week. Momma never tired of hearing me talk about the ocean, San Francisco and Denver and Salt Lake, and Pappy never wearied of telling Harry about the war and farming and the faults of the McKinley administration. But one late afternoon when we strolled through the sugarcane, Harry broached the subject of leaving.

"I know you're not ready to ride out, Sugar."

"It's all right," I told him. "I've had a wonderful visit. And we'll be back."

"I'd like that."

"I suspect you're tired of sleeping alone on that porch."

"Well, yes, I kind of formed a habit with you."

"'A habit'?"

"A good habit, Sugar."

We told the family that night. The next morning after breakfast of oatmeal, scrambled eggs, ham, grits, and biscuits with butter and honey, Momma prepared a lunch for us: fried chicken, biscuits, pickled peaches, molasses-pecan pie, chocolate-chip cookies, and apples dried and fresh. Pappy handed Harry a pint of his best corn whiskey.

I had forgotten most of what little Gaelic I learned as a girl. But I thought a minute, then, in that old language, asked Pappy, "What do you think of my man?"

When he smiled and nodded I knew I'd said it correctly. "Daughter, there's a lad who could ride with O'Neill. With Jeb Stuart too."

I understood what high praise that meant.

"You still tote that old derringer I gave you?"

"You bet."

"See that you continue to do so."

Momma hugged and kissed me, then hugged and kissed Harry. I felt so proud to see that. "Go see more wonderful sights, Etta Margaret. Then come back and tell us."

My sisters, dark-haired dolls in their mid-teens being sparked by half the boys in the county, whispered to me at the same time that they considered Harry the handsomest man they'd ever seen.

The girls and my younger brothers would carry us in the wagon into Selma, where we could catch the stage to Montgomery, claim our things, and board the train.

Momma and Pappy stood on the porch and watched us leave.

I turned around just before the wagon rolled onto the road, and I waved. Momma had one arm through Pappy's. She waved the other hand for as long as I could see.

I wondered what my parents would think if they knew their most troublesome child, who left home early and could never be like the rest of the family, had become the woman of The Sundance Kid.

13

I have read where the Pinkerton agency says The Wild Bunch could have been responsible for the train holdup near Folsom, New Mexico, on July 11, 1899. Pinkertons, you may adjust your files to be more positive: As sure as a barnyard rooster crows at dawn, The Wild Bunch did it.

As usual I wrote about it in my diary, but I remember this date anyway, my first train robbery. A girl doesn't forget a thrill like that. Harry never tired of talking about his first one, that time in Montana, and I enjoyed listening. So I had been looking forward to my first, as you can imagine. I suspect I have certain details the Pinkertons don't possess.

Some of the boys rode up the track that morning and felled small trees at the top of a rise where the conductor could see them and stop before having a wreck. He'd already be rolling slow on account of the hill.

We'd packed essentials into our saddlebags so that afterwards we could abandon the ranch we'd gathered at in recent days. We also prepared a change of horses.

"Me and Curry and Elza will take the express car," Butch said. "Kid, you and Connolly handle the passengers. Sound good? Etta waits here at the ranch."

"She better stay with us," Harry said. "Something could go wrong."

"But what could she do?" Butch said.

Harry told him, "Pard, you've seen her shoot."

I dressed as a man and rode a hard-running piebald mustang gelding about six years old with a stubby tail. Harry had acquired a gray Thoroughbred mare that reminded us of my great Cuchulain.

We rode to where they'd felled the trees and we hid in what little cover remained, mainly boulders and smoke trees and willows.

"Looks like the boys cut down too much of what we need for cover," I said.

Harry shook his head and smiled. "Leroy gets too rambunctious sometimes."

We heard the train, saw it steam into view, moving slower each moment. When it stopped, we rode into the open and shot into the air and at the train wheels. Then Harry and nice young America Connolly handed me their reins and entered the passenger car. I could see them through the windows, Harry at one end of the car, America at the other, revolvers in hand, keeping everyone covered.

Harry and America didn't take anything from the passengers. Butch and Kid Curry would have, but they and Elza Lay had entered the express car. In a few minutes I saw them jumping down from the train. Harry and America did the same and ran up to me. I handed them the reins to their horses.

The others joined us, and we hurrahed the train a moment, firing into the air. Some men passengers had begun removing the trees. We started riding off.

And we found ourselves facing a batch of men two hundred yards off riding hell for leather toward us, shouting and shooting. We pulled up.

"I caught a reflection from a badge," I said.

"Posse!" Harry yelled. "How in hell did they find out?" Harry yanked his carbine out of its boot and shot the horse out from under the lead rider.

America threw a couple of pistol shots their way, and another horse fell.

I grabbed my carbine, gritted my teeth, apologized to the poor animal I aimed at, and spilled it and the rider with a shot into the horse's chest.

The remaining riders stopped, then spread out and started up again, not as enthusiastically, I judged. Most posses comprised townspeople not real good at the shooting, anyway, but who afterward in the saloon enjoyed talking about the chase.

I spotted Butch and the others veering off to the right, America not far behind them, when a shot sliced through the willows near us. We turned to see a short man and a tall one aiming pistols at us from outside the passenger car.

"I'll take the tall one." Harry, who could have nailed him in either nostril from that distance, winged the tall fellow in the left leg, and the varmint fell. To the best of my recollection that's the only man Harry ever shot.

"My turn." I plugged the other one in the right boot, proud of my aim. He howled and hobbled off.

Meanwhile I saw Curry and Elza firing their six-shooters at the posse as fast as they could. Butch did the same with his rifle. When we drew close to the others I glanced back and glimpsed three men on the ground. *Had we spilled their horses?*

We spurred our ponies, got a big lead on the posse, and circled around to the ranch, changed horses, and raced off again. I felt like a Pony Express rider.

No doubt about it, I seldom lived a more exciting day. I didn't care about the foot I shot, though I fussed with myself concerning the horses we knocked down.

"They were just old plugs, Sugar. Don't fret."

I don't know how Harry knew that, if he did, but he made me feel better.

Elza Lay got shot in the back of the left shoulder but didn't bleed much and didn't have to slow down.

The Pinkertons claimed two sheriff's deputies got killed that day. I hope not. If it happened, however, Harry didn't do it, nor I, and not Elza nor America, despite his pistol skills. That boy was timid. America never should have joined up. But I reckon he had been misguided and lonesome. No, if any of that posse died, the blame goes to Kid Curry, and you know what I think about him.

That night at camp we counted the money: five thousand dollars, mostly in paper but a lot in coins of gold and silver.

"I saw some new hands at the ranch," Harry said. "I reckon one of them tipped off the sheriff."

"I'd like to get aholt of him."

"I'm with you there, Pard."

The Bunch experienced other excitement during those months. Harry allowed me to participate occasionally.

With winter coming on, Harry and I treated ourselves to three days in Denver before rendezvousing with Butch and America to ride through Cheyenne, Laramie, and Salt Lake City on the way to Robbers' Roost. America had taken a fancy to Harry and me, and we liked him a lot. America now said he was twenty-four, but this two years after he claimed to be nineteen when he couldn't have been more than seventeen.

A year after the Folsom train robbery the Bunch pulled off another one the Pinkertons list as a possibility for us. I thank the Pinkertons for the date, being as I forgot to write about it in my diary, and my recall of my early years is sometimes faulty. In exchange I can confirm for the detectives that we performed the transaction. I refer to the train robbery near Tipton, Wyoming, on August 29, 1900.

Harry had let his whiskers grow, his disguise. You know that sent me to tingling. "I want you in the passenger car with me," Harry said at our camp. "We'll be regular travelers until Leroy and the others stop the train at a blockade. Then you cover everyone from the back. I'll handle the front."

"Do I get to dress up?"

"Yes, and you'll be the prettiest girl in Wyoming."

I dressed like a lady in a white blouse, long gray skirt, large matching bonnet, and a beautiful red jacket that hid my inside gun. I guess I looked pretty good despite nervousness because two nice-looking young men tried to flirt with me when I sat near them at the rear of the car. But their expressions changed when I stood, unholstered my Iver Johnson, and told everyone to face the front, from where Harry had them covered.

In a few minutes Butch gave us the high sign from outside through a window.

We jumped to the ground to mount horses the others had brought us, and the trouble began. I had a boot in the stirrup and swung halfway up when my horse started bucking and crow-hopping. With me bouncing on one foot we must have looked like Pawnees doing the Ghost Dance. I suppose my fancy dress and bonnet spooked him. Anyway, he fell one way and I the other, except he got up running. Harry on his horse also danced around, trying to stop mine and help me at the same time until he had to take off after my horse. Then damned if a passenger didn't jump out and grab me by the arm, a big mean-looking cuss.

"Are you crazy?" I told him. "Let go of me, damn you."

The other boys had ridden off, but Harry caught my horse and came nearly back to me with it while that fool held me by both wrists and tried to force me back onto the train. Of course the fool didn't know Harry.

It was like hell broke out in Georgia.

Then Harry reined up next to us. "Leave her be, Mister."

"Go to hell," the varmint responded. "This girl's my pris-oner." He let go of me with one hand and drew a revolver. If he could have read the look on Harry's face he would have run like a rabbit from an eagle.

Harry shot him.

The blood splattered all over my face, frightening and shocking me almost out of my boots. But I jumped onto my horse and we lit out.

I don't know where Harry's bullet struck the man, or how bad he'd got injured, but he fell, and I never looked back. I hope he survived.

And that became the only man Harry ever shot.

All of us got away all right. Ten miles down the road we switched to our relay horses and kept moving until after dark, then camped. Supper became cold beans and water as we didn't want to risk a fire in case someone had followed us.

"Should we post sentries, Sundance?"

"That's my thinking, Butch."

"Mine too," Butch said.

"It'll surprise me if we're not tailed."

"We do so damn much running." Butch finished his beans.

"Getting harder to make a good living, the way the West is growing and changing. Etta read where there's only five territories left."

"I never knew that," said Butch, who never read, even though he knew how. I disagreed about the changing times, though of course I had been involved for only a few years. But I fully enjoyed the activities of my time with Harry. So I kept shut.

"Kid, you think you killed that man back there?" America Connolly did the asking. Kid Curry stood sentry but wouldn't have cared either way.

"Don't know for sure, 'Merica."

I'd been wondering the same thing while trying to not think about it.

"He shouldn't have grabbed Miss Etta."

"No," Harry said. "His mistake."

Butch replaced Curry on guard duty before long and we turned in.

"Tired, Sugar?"

"Some. Still excited though. There's something special about a train robbery."

"Indeed there is."

"I'll never forget my part in today's. It's like a painting before me right now. It's so fascinating, so illogical, the way men, riding horses that have been around for thousands of years, can stop a powerful, modern contrivance and take control of it, like today and earlier at Folsom, make everyone pay attention, and then ride off, returning to the past."

Harry took my hand. "You're a philosopher, Sugar."

"It's such a thrill. When do you think we'll do that again?"

"We'll have to study the train schedules. How soon are you thinking?" He squeezed my hand, and in the glimmer from the moon I caught a sliver of his smile.

"Such a thrill," I repeated, and I went to sleep with that thought. Of course I wouldn't try it nowadays. Those were different times.

The moonlight conversation, not my excitement about the transactions at Folsom and Tipton, but concerning changing times, soon galloped back to us. We had gone to Cheyenne for a big rodeo, just Harry, Butch, and me, and enjoyed buffalo steaks in the hotel one evening when we overheard two well-dressed men talking at a table close by.

"You'd think this is twenty years ago," a little man with a big beard said.

"Hell, it's not that bad, Horace." This from a tall flint-eyed older man.

"It is when it's your train or bank," Big Beard said. "We have to get the Pinkertons after them."

"They already are, Horace. It's just a matter of time."

"The Tipton job sounds like the Cassidy gang."

"So they say," Flint-Eye commented.

"Yes, and I'm getting tired of hearing that too. 'Sounds like the Cassidy gang . . . Might be the Cassidy gang . . . Could be The Wild Bunch . . .' Some of those worthless brigands have been jailed now and then. There should be photographs. When in the name of decency and justice are pictures going to be distributed so we'll know who in tarnation we're looking for? And recently a woman too."

"Oh, she's one of those sleazy wenches that . . . you know."

When he hesitated, I saw Harry tense. Big Beard had looked at me and looked away. If he had grouped me with that Laura Bullion, I'm not sure I could have kept Harry from knocking him cockeyed. And that was not the place.

"No, my friend," Flint-Eye said. "I've heard she's a black-haired beauty."

"'A black-haired beauty.' That won't help find the road agents. You think there's only one of those in this vast land?"

"Maybe just one who can ride and shoot."

We ate slowly to not miss anything. And my description didn't flatter me, the way Big Beard spat it out. The last comment I recall from those two expressed hope the politicians would soon be clamoring for more and better law enforcement.

After supper when we walked around town in that pleasurable high-country twilight, Harry and Butch stayed mostly quiet. Once, though, Butch said, "Pinkertons keep turning up, it seems."

"Like finding a lizard under every rock you kick over," Harry said.

I asked, "Do you think those two suspected us?"

"Probably not, Sugar. But we'll want to be extra careful."

Butch commented, "Like you said, it's getting harder to make a good living."

We didn't much enjoy the rodeo the next day either. But at the rodeo dance that night, Harry and Butch got lively again and had a big time with a jug of tanglefoot. I enjoyed dancing with Harry once despite his lack of skill, though I refused one dance request after another from the rodeo crowd, even though Harry urged me to accept.

"I'm stepping on you so much, Sugar, you'll be crippled up tomorrow."

I finally accepted a cowboy's invitation. But when the dance ended he grabbed my arm and wouldn't let go.

Harry joined us and laid him out.

That night in my and Harry's room, Butch and Harry planned the robbery of the First National Bank of Winnemucca, Nevada. You may have read about this episode. It is quite famous, for it was an important bank with plenty of cash.

"We'll need at least four of us," Harry said.

"At least," Butch said. "Big banks are dangerous."

"We'll ride in separately but tie up at the same place in front of the bank. One man stays outside with a carbine and the horses. We'll need a change of mounts waiting a few miles off."

"We can get those at the ranch," Butch said.

He meant the spread where the Bunch was protected outside Winnemucca. Harry had told me some of the other boys hung around there this time of year.

The night before we planned to ride into Winnemucca and make ourselves rich again we enjoyed a suckling-pig barbecue and a few drinks at the ranch. America Connolly, carrying a plate of food, joined Harry and me. He was so young and likable, and I felt motherly toward him, as Harry felt fatherly. Butch wanted him to participate in the holdup. None of the other boys showed up at the ranch after all, except Bill Carver, and Bill could be unreliable.

I no longer felt the strangeness of hearing America, a head shorter than Harry and ten or twelve years younger, calling Harry "Kid."

"I'm scared, Kid. There's too many people in town nowadays. And Pinkertons are more plentiful than sow bugs under a damp log."

"Things have sure as hell changed, 'Merica. You should have been with us eight, ten years ago."

"Sure wish I had been, Kid. But I remember when I first joined up how we used to be able to go into town a couple of days afterward and have a big time spending our money. Now it's run like greased lightning for a week, hide the money, maybe not be able to spend it for months."

Harry nodded, sipped his drink.

"I'm going to get me a ranch job in New Mexico, Kid. I got a special girl now. I won't be any good to the Bunch no longer."

"I understand, 'Merica. And we'll miss you. Best tell Butch, though."

"Do it for me, Kid. He'll just fidget and bluster and try to shame me into staying. I don't mind you knowing I'm quitting. But Butch doesn't have good sense sometimes. You know that."

"All right, 'Merica."

"I hope you won't have no trouble replacing me."

"Don't fret that." Harry smiled and squeezed my hand.

14

In one way, the negotiation with the First National Bank of Winnemucca, Nevada, went off without a hitch. In another, if you've ever spent a day with a polecat, you can't call that day pleasant, although memorable in a way.

Harry, Butch, Bill Carver, and I separated soon after we left the ranch so we could ride into Winnemucca singly and from different directions.

"We should all arrive 'bout the same time," Harry told me when Butch and Bill made dust. "The routes I suggested won't leave them enough time to get drunk in some saloon before we get there. And it won't be necessary for you to wait outside with the horses. You come inside the bank with us."

How excited I became when I heard that!

I wore jeans and jacket and floppy hat with a cute blue ribbon holding my hair behind, and rode a medium-sized dun gelding with suspect heritage. But he had a friendly attitude and four sweet gaits. Harry chose a black stallion, a Quarter Horse, if I recollect correctly, with three white feet and a forehead star, a beautiful fellow I would have liked for Harry to keep. But I had learned my lesson about loving a horse. Butch had selected a white Morgan, and tall skinny old Bill Carver rode a paint, both geldings.

"They can all flat out run," Harry had said when we rounded them up at our rendezvous ranch. "So can our relay of horses."

On Sept. 19, 1900, Harry and I followed our separate trails, and I drew a few looks, like any stranger riding into town alone. I pretended to adjust my saddle outside the bank while Harry and Butch stood in front of a feed store across the street and studied the town.

And the smell arrived, faint at first, but unmistakably the insidious spray of a skunk, and drawing closer, riding in on the breeze. Soon the odor became so overpowering that I looked around to see who had gotten sprayed. I had to calm my dun, the poor frightened creature, then turned my attention to Bill Carver, older than most of the Bunch, stepping down from his paint beside me. "Oh, Bill," I gasped.

"I'm sorry as all hell, honey," Bill told me.

Harry and Butch crossed the street toward us.

Bill's horse—snorting, ears laid back, nostrils big and twitching— fidgeted and looked at him wild-eyed.

Butch stepped close, then jumped back. "Jesus, Bill!"

The boys never called one another by name while doing business, but Butch just blurted it out, he got so flustered. I started giggling. Harry tried hard to not laugh.

"I got off to—excuse me, Etta—make water," Bill said, "and didn't see the damn polecat. I got him. Then he got me. We had hell proper there for quite a spell."

Butch finally saw the humor and we all laughed, except poor Bill.

"Maybe," Harry said, "this'll keep folks from chasing us. Come on."

Still laughing and smiling, we entered the bank in a cluster instead of singly and a few seconds apart as you're supposed to do to avoid attention. Harry told me and Bill to watch the door. Harry and Butch stepped to the tellers' windows.

"Bill, please don't stand so close to me."

He gave me an apologetic look and walked to the side.

I drew my inside gun. Right away a customer, revolver obvious under his coat, entered in a business suit, saw the pistol in my hand, and stopped. "Lay your six-shooter on the floor," I told him, "and get over there by that man in the corner." He disarmed himself, and I motioned toward Bill. The customer approached Bill, stopped, stepped away, but stopped again.

Almost everyone glanced at Bill, so easy to pinpoint the origin of the odoriferous catastrophe. As other customers walked in I ordered them toward Bill, but they wouldn't stand close.

Harry grabbed a money bag and collected side arms from employees, and he and Butch cleaned out the cash drawers. I heard Harry say he didn't see any shotguns stashed handily for occasions such as this, and he and Butch escorted the manager to the vault and cleaned that out too. They had the money in two large canvas bags, heavy looking.

All of us, including customers and workers, got just about asphyxiated.

As soon as we stepped outside we distributed our take into saddlebags.

"You ride last," Harry told Bill.

We lit out.

On the run to our change of horses I thought mainly about the thrill of participating in the holdup, and now about the excitement of the escape. After ten miles we reached a sycamore grove where a boy about twelve, a pleasant young fellow named Vic Button that Butch had taken a liking to, held our fresh mounts, saddled and bridled. We changed horses and split up to return to the ranch from different directions. When we got there, Bill burned his clothes and took a good bath, which he had needed for a week or more anyway. He scrubbed the best he could and killed most of the smell.

The next day while I cleaned up the breakfast dishes, the boys sat on the porch, smoking and spitting and keeping an eye out for strangers.

"Somebody coming," I heard Butch say all the way to the back where I worked. I hurried to the porch and stood behind Harry.

"I recognize those horses," Harry said.

"And I recognize the wrangler," Butch told him.

Sure enough, here came young Vic Button with the horses we'd ridden to and from the bank. Harry left the porch and placed a generous number of gold coins into the boy's saddlebags. "Nice work, young man. We needed your help."

"Much obliged, Kid." Vic could barely speak, so excited that Harry acknowledged him.

Then Butch left the porch and put his arm around the boy. "What do you think of that white Morgan, Vic?" Butch nodded at the gelding he'd ridden.

"He's a beauty, Butch."

"I rode him myself for the Winnemucca job."

"I bet he really flies."

"He's yours, Vic."

That was one of the few generous things I ever saw Butch do, and I never saw a happier boy. I don't know whom Butch stole that horse from.

Later, America Connolly got to know Vic well and told us nice things about him. I've seen Vic's picture with the horse and a write-up about how Butch gave it to him, though not why. Robin Hood Cassidy, don't you know.

I have read that our loot, as the newspapers called it, totaled thirteen hundred dollars. I suppose banks don't like for the public to know how much of their customers' money disappears, as that figure is grossly incorrect. It amounted to a dandy sum in those days, more than thirty-two thousand dollars, lots of it in twenty-dollar gold pieces and gold coins of five or ten dollars. Paper money included fifty-dollar bills, Benjamin Franklin on some. Others sported William H. Seward, the Yankee secretary of state during the Civil War.

Butch had been strutting around the kitchen while I counted the money. When I announced the total he stopped and said, "A little over ten thousand apiece. Good."

Harry looked at me. "Does that sound right?"

"What do you mean?" Butch said. "Three into thirty is ten. That's easy."

"There were four us."

"That's right, Butch," Bill Carver said.

Butch waved his hands. "I know that. But Etta didn't do nothing. And she and Sundance, they're together. That's just one share."

"Maybe," Bill said, "you and Sundance should have it all. You two did the collecting. I just stood in a corner, like Etta."

"But," Butch said, "you're . . . you . . ." He looked at Harry, who waited calmly while his friend reddened and stammered. Butch glanced at Bill, who frowned at him. "Well, sure," Butch said. "I didn't mean nothing."

I gave Bill a thankful look and divided the money four ways.

Two days later we said good-bye to Butch and Bill and left the ranch.

"There's a cabin I often use in northeastern New Mexico," Harry said. "We can stash some of our money there and bank some in Salt Lake City."

"I need to shop in Salt Lake," I told him.

"Whatever you want, Sugar. Then on to Wyoming."

"And let's buy a pretty dress for your mother."

The poor woman had aged more than she should have in the time we'd been away, and she looked awfully sad, just sorrowful, and skinny too, like a lamb long-separated from its mother. But she perked up, couldn't do enough for us.

Mrs. Longbaugh told us Harry's stepfather had again taken off on a mule for that neighbor ranch where two of his sons with their wives and children lived on a spread as poor as the Longbaugh place.

After we'd chatted a bit through coffee and cookies Mrs. Longbaugh bounced up. "I'll be right back." She returned with a cigar box encircled by a red ribbon. She undid the ribbon, opened the box, and handed it to me. It contained letters I'd written. "My friend at the store in Sundance read them to me as they arrived," she said. "That is, when I could get to town. Now I'd be much obliged to hear you read them all the way through."

So the three of us sat by the fire the first night, and I read each letter to her in the order I'd sent them. Some of the compliments I paid Harry embarrassed him, but Mrs. Longbaugh, nodding and smiling, dipping snuff and spitting into a small can she held in her lap, accepted my praising Harry as his natural due.

As I read, I made a decision. I explained it to Harry that night. "Let's try again to take your momma with us when we leave. We could set her up in Cheyenne or Salt Lake, anywhere she wanted. Would she leave him?"

"I'd hope so, but she'd be leaving this place too. Her home."

"But she's suffering here, and not just on account of him. In a city the winters wouldn't seem so harsh. And there's shopping and entertainment and new people. That would be almost like luxury for her."

"We'll ask her, Sugar."

Harry raised the subject at breakfast, and I seconded him.

"I'll be fine right here," she said.

We used every argument we could think of to pry her out of there.

She kept thanking us and shaking her head. "I'll do fine right here."

One day while I helped clean up the kitchen, Mrs. Longbaugh mentioned that Harry's father, grandparents on both sides, and some other kin rested in a little private graveyard off the road to Sundance.

"Take me to the cemetery," I told Harry.

"What in the world for?"

"I want to see your father's grave and the others."

"But they've all been gone so long."

"That's why we should go visit. Bring them up to date about you. Introduce me. And see how they're all doing."

Harry gave me a strange look. But I talked him into it.

When we got there and dismounted I counted about fifteen grave markers, most of them in the blessed shade of elms and pines and spruce, a lovely spot considering.

"Where's your father's?"

"Don't recall."

"What kind of marker does he have?"

"Doesn't have one."

"Who's he next to?"

"Not sure."

I followed a little behind Harry as he wandered, some tombstones crooked, others broken and lying down, trails uneven, the whole patch wanting a good weeding. Occasional wildflowers gave much-needed life to the place, and from high in a tree a mockingbird sang an elegy. That helped too.

"Sugar, what's this one here say?"

I stepped close to Harry, who stood at a large horizontal marker. "'Eldridge H. Longabaugh.' They put an *a* in the middle."

"Some of the family spelled it that way. The *H* is for Harry. My grandfather. My father is right here." With his boot he pointed to the adjacent weed patch.

"Talk to him a bit, Honey. Then let's go into Sundance."

"What for?"

"Have a marker made for your father. And spell his name your way."

From his mother we obtained the dates of birth and death for his father. Then we rode into town and ordered a headstone from the barber, who also served as stonecutter.

The next day we left Harry's home place. His momma sent us off with a sack of fried chicken, fresh-made rolls, and blueberry preserves. She hugged me, and she and I cried. Then she hugged Harry, and he slipped a bag of gold coins into her apron pocket.

When we mounted our horses and turned them toward the road, she stood on the porch flapping one hand in a good-bye wave, while using her apron to wipe her tears.

Harry had to balance the food in front of him as he rode, but we lightened it considerably at dinner in the shade of a white pine by a burbling creek. We put the rest into our saddlebags along with our traveling money.

Several of the Bunch had decided to winter in warm climes rather than at Robbers' Roost. We felt the same. After all, there's safety in scattering as well as in numbers, the way times kept changing. So we rode south out of Wyoming and passed right through Butch's home country, the Uinta Valley of eastern Utah.

"Do you think Butch is there at his home place? We could stop if you want."

"Leroy won't be there," Harry said, "and I don't know his folks."

"How do you know he won't?"

"Never has visited, not since I've known him."

"Harry, that's awful thoughtless of him."

"Says he doesn't want to bring them trouble."

I shook my head and studied my horse's ears. "Do you think your mother knows about you? About us? She never said anything."

"She knows. She'd have heard from people in town or from Deadwood."

"I hope my folks never find out. I don't know what I'd do."

Harry didn't comment.

I studied my horse's ears again.

While riding to the ranch near Alma, New Mexico, we conducted one business transaction, traded horses a whole batch, and got there just in time to get a roof over our heads during a light snow. Butch greeted us, as did a couple of others I didn't know well and whose names I've forgotten.

Around the chimney fire that night we made warm-weather plans.

"We haven't been to Arizona recently," Butch said.

"A fact," Harry said.

"So?" Butch moved closer to the fire.

"Remember we told Ben Kilpatrick and Curry we'd meet 'em in San Antonio."

"We could send a telegram," Butch said.

"We already sent our word."

Butch stood, fidgeted, sat again. "Well, hell. I forgot."

I liked Ben, The Tall Texan, but never felt comfortable around Kid Curry, that no-good Harvey Logan. I kept shut, but Harry knew. Butch never noticed.

After a few days we said our good-byes, left the horses, toted our tack, saddlebags, and bedrolls, and one of the boys drove us in a wagon to the train stop.

"We gonna do some work in Texas?" Butch asked.

"Wouldn't be surprised," Harry said. "But let's first see what Ben has in mind. He knows the area best."

"My thinking exactly."

As the wheels tattooed the rails and the train rocked on the bends and the New Mexico desert filled our windows, they discussed the difficulties of our profession.

"I feel like civilization is gaining on us," Butch said.

"Indeed it is." Harry nodded at the passing scenery.

"I suppose we could consider another line of work."

That became the sum of their profundities for a few hundred clackings of the wheels.

Then Harry, with a smile in his eyes and a chuckle in his throat, said, "Maybe instead of changing professions we should change countries."

We laughed, joked briefly about that, and dropped the subject, started discussing what we'd do in Texas. Still, that might be when we began thinking about relocating.

We had a big time in San Antonio, except I longed to see my people again and to visit New Orleans. So Harry and I decided to leave within a week. Bill Carver showed up at Fanny Porter's bordello, a regular meeting place for the Bunch, and Butch brought him by our hotel. Naturally the boys started celebrating to observe our impending departure but also to acknowledge Bill's arrival without a skunk. He got joshed plenty about that, even in the lupanar, where, I'm told, Butch had made certain everyone knew.

Harry surprised me one day bursting in to our hotel room when returning from a whiskey purchase. "Have to spruce up," he said. "Put on my Sunday best. We're going to have our picture taken."

"Oh, Honey, it'll take me hours to get ready."

"No, Sugar. This one's just me and some of the boys." He cleaned up, put on his suit, combed his hair, trimmed his mustache, and brushed the dust from his hat. "See you soon."

The photo came out good, a regular studio portrait with the boys dressed like church deacons and trying to look serious. Harry had traded his fedora for a bowler.

Two days later Harry burst into our room again. "Guess what, Sugar?"

He looked so angry I didn't dare say anything frivolous. "What is it?"

"That loco Leroy sent a copy of that damn picture to the Bank at Winnemucca."

"Uh-oh."

"He included a thank-you note for the swell time we had there."

"Must have been drunk."

"I've never allowed a picture of me. Now the first one goes to a bank." After a while he simmered down and decided he wouldn't say anything to Butch. "Leroy didn't mean any harm. But I'll never let him get his hands on another picture of me."

We knew Butch had been photographed years ago when arrested for horse stealing. "This will make the Pinkertons' job easier, won't it, knowing what some of you besides Leroy look like."

"Count on it."

15

We shipped our horse tack, saddlebags, and bedrolls to Montgomery, bought new traveling clothes, and took the train to Fort Worth, then to New Orleans. How I looked forward to seeing that grand city! Even having Butch and Kid Curry along didn't diminish my enthusiasm. As it turned out, their being with us led to a decision that altered our lives considerably.

I believe the presence of another train passenger, a Spanish Creole, started the boys thinking about South America, not that the Creole knew anything about it, but just hearing him talking to his wife in a Spanish sounding different from what we'd heard in Texas, even though he also knew English, which he spoke to us.

"We'd never been to Fort Worth before," the man said. "Never so far West."

"It's almost east to us," Butch told him. "Next time try Wyoming and around."

I feared Butch would invite those nice folks to Robbers' Roost, and I whispered to Harry to head him off.

"I'll keep an ear cocked," Harry whispered back. "Don't fret."

I suppose I needn't have worried. Harry could keep Butch in the saddle, and the conversation soon became New Orleans, the couple's home. They recommended a hotel on Jackson Square, also some restaurants. I wrote them down.

That night at our hotel on Jackson Square, Harry mentioned the couple from the train, and we began talking about South America. Kid Curry had gone out.

"We don't know nothing about South America," Butch said.

"Good reason to go look," Harry told him.

"And I reckon they're bound to have banks and trains and stagecoaches."

"You mean for getting around, or for business?"

"We gotta make a living, Sundance."

"I still enjoy what we're doing," Harry said. "But with telephone lines spreading like a spiderweb, and the Pinkertons so contrary, maybe we should get jobs."

"I don't know nothing else. Neither of us has any schooling to speak of."

"But sometimes I feel like a buzzard in peacock feathers."

"Know what you mean," Butch said.

Of course, things weren't the same, even in my time with the Bunch. Elza Lay and a couple of others had been imprisoned. Some of the boys were dead. And others, like America Connolly, had drifted away.

New Orleans looked every bit as marvelous as I had heard and read, and then some. We ate like moguls, toured the Mississippi on a paddle wheeler, hired a carriage with driver and rolled all around town under more magnolia trees than I dreamed existed, and slept in the best bed east of Denver. Celestial weather blessed us.

And a certain topic returned continually.

"I pine for the olden days," Harry said.

Butch nodded. "Know what you mean."

"Maybe we could try some legitimate cowpunching," Kid Curry said.

"Rough work," Butch told him.

Harry nodded. "Buy a spread, hire some hands to work it."

"Makes sense," Curry said.

"Live like gentlemen." Butch grinned at his comment.

"Why not?" Harry asked.

"My thinking exactly," Butch said.

"We could disband the Bunch. Free-lance. Me and Etta, you and Curry."

"Yes," Curry said. "Just us four."

And so, although the Pinkertons, the newspapers, and the public in general wouldn't know it for quite a while, Butch Cassidy and The Wild Bunch, torment of the West for fifteen years throughout several states and territories, no longer existed.

After a few days in New Orleans, Butch and Kid Curry decided to move on.

"I heard about a boarding house in New York," Butch said. "Meet there?"

"Good. How about around the first of February?"

"Then what?" Butch asked.

"Sightseeing. Then take a boat to wherever in South America sounds good."

"Be lazy for a while?"

"Might do us some good, Leroy."

I'd believe that when I saw it. Same as Harry punching cattle again.

Naturally I didn't like the idea of going anywhere with Kid Curry. But of course I kept shut. As for Butch, he and I tolerated each other, although he surprised me by not making a fuss about my going along.

"I thought sure Leroy would want you to leave me behind," I told Harry.

"No, Sugar. He says we'll need you to do the cooking and washing."

Before we left New Orleans we bought gifts for my people. Then we caught the train for Mobile and on to Montgomery, where we sold our horse tack and stored some of our guns. We reached the farm near Selma in time for Christmas of 1900.

"South America," Momma said the first day at dinner when we told our plans. "Now there's a land I have longed to see." She nodded twice.

"It'll probably take a year to get a letter from you," Pappy said. "And how you going to make a living down yonder?"

Harry stopped his fork on the way to a bite from his second helping of molasses-pecan pie. "We're fortunate enough to have some savings, Mr. Place. I'll look for a good business investment there. And I'll set aside enough money to bring your daughter right back if things don't work out."

Pappy nodded.

"What kind of crops they got?" Dunleavy asked.

Harry looked at me.

"I remember that from my teaching," I said. "Wheat and alfalfa and corn."

"So probably plenty of cattle to eat it," Flann said.

"Yes, in Argentina, at least. That's the place I've read most about."

Grania asked, "Is there gold? I bet there is."

"I think the Spanish conquistadors got it," I said. "But I'll let you know."

"Just bring it back," Dierdre said.

"Watch out for Indians," Flann told us.

I said, "In Argentina, the Spaniards got all of them too."

They'd had a dry but mostly cold winter and didn't have much work except daily chores of milking the cow and caring for her and the hogs and plow mules, chickens and ducks and dogs and cats, plus two good saddle horses growing old.

Everyone doted on Harry as usual. He and Pappy, Dunleavy, and Flann played cooncan and dominoes, talked about President McKinley's re-election on his promise that we'd all have a full dinner pail, and they sat on the porch and smoked and spat. And every evening just before supper we all enjoyed some of Pappy's corn whiskey. Momma and I took polite sips only.

We cut a young pine tree and brought it in to decorate for Christmas the same way we used to do when I lived at home. That made me feel wonderful but sad too, knowing about the ones I'd missed, and who knows what Christmas would be like in South America.

After dinner of turkey and ham and all the side dishes, Momma stood and tapped me on the shoulder. "Come with me, Etta Margaret." She led me into the kitchen and sat me down with pencil and paper. "I want you to have some of my recipes in case the food down yonder ain't good or is too strange."

Momma dictated recipes for many of the wonderful dishes I'd enjoyed all those years before I left home. Molasses-pecan pie topped the list, and green-tomato pie. Other preparations I wrote down included fried okra, hush-puppies, collard greens, grits, chitlins, squirrel stew, fried possum, pig's feet, and brains.

"You wouldn't stand still long enough to learn cooking when you were a girl," Momma said. "Maybe this session will help." Momma's measurements included a pinch, a smidgen, a dab, or a dash.

"Yes, Momma. Now my man will eat royally, even in a foreign land."

The train rolled northward leisurely, giving us a good gander at Atlanta, Charleston, Philadelphia, Richmond, Baltimore, and Washington. We watched through the windows the whole time, Spanish moss dangling from lots of trees at first in the Deep South, and once in a while a nice stand of pines. Seeing the poverty upset us.

"Look at that old mansion," Harry said. "Ruined."

And a little later: "There's another must have been a fine home one day, Sugar."

Neither of us knew this area, but I had read about it, and I'd seen some of the destruction around Selma. Harry couldn't stop marveling. Everywhere the Yankees had been you could still see how people struggled to get on their feet, and this thirty-five years after the war.

"My mother told me they hardly knew about the fighting," Harry said.

"But here you can see it, sure as warts on a toad."

I felt grateful we had money for such a trip, and I reminded Harry that we owed it to the splendid acquisition in Winnemucca.

"Yes," Harry said. "And to the one in San Anton."

"What 'one in San Anton'?"

"Leroy and I did a little business one night when the poker game slowed down."

Despite that revelation, I knew Harry had lost much of his enthusiasm for his doings in the financial world. For instance, never once on the trip to New York did he suggest conducting a transaction.

Not needing money for quite a while contributed to that attitude, Harry plainly weary of being on the dodge all those years, including the time I had known him. If so, I could accept that, although I knew he might resume his activities after a spell. That would be all right with me too.

16

We reached New York in mid-January and took a carriage to the boarding house Butch recommended, Julia Thompson's place at 325 East Fourteenth St., ten dollars a week. It seemed clean but not what we expected from New York. After two days we left word for "Leroy Smith" and moved to the Hotel Metropole at twice the money. But the Metropole meant New York, classy.

It stood at Broadway and Forty-Second Street, with a palm garden, such a nice touch in the cold, and a basement restaurant, which nowadays is called a rathskeller. It offered first-rate chuck, so we had steak or fish with a fresh green salad every night and fresh fruit with breakfast, Harry the handsomest and most distinguished man in the dining room. If he would have let me teach him to read and write, he could have become a United States Senator or an ambassador at least.

And we got married. The ceremony gave me joy and relief I hadn't expected.

"I hope you didn't think I'd forgot, Sugar." He hugged me.

"I was just fixing to remind you." I felt thrilled, wanted to sing and dance and announce to the world. But I'd already told my home folks, Harry's mother too. For a while I felt sad, not being able to spread the word. But now I knew I wouldn't feel ashamed if I became pregnant. Still, having a baby wouldn't have been timely then.

The move to the Metropole might have jogged Harry into talking about marriage. Our five-year trial had come and gone, being as Harry never remembered dates, and I had decided to not say anything for a while longer, being happy enough as things stood.

"My new suit fits real fine," Harry said one day. He had just finished dressing, stood in front of the mirror. "Collar's high but I'm getting used to it."

It had three pieces, black and formal, among our first purchases after arriving.

"As nice as anything we saw in Denver or San Francisco."

"What's the fancy name for this tie?" He touched his foulard.

I told him. "And don't lose that diamond stick pin."

"No, Sugar." Then he had popped the question, as young people say nowadays. "While I'm all dressed up, let's get married."

"Just like that?"

"What do you mean, 'Just like that'? It's been three, four years."

"Closer to six, Mr. Longbaugh."

"All right. But the courthouse is just around the corner. Come on."

"Quit joshing me. You're not serious."

"Am too." He grabbed me and kissed me. Seriously.

That convinced me. "But someone besides you has to get spruced up. And she doesn't have anything to wear." I leaned close to the mirror.

So we went shopping again. I found a beautiful floor-length belted dress, maroon with ruffles below the elbow and on the cuffs, extra-fluffy white blouse, a high collar, and matching jumper. "Now why don't you walk around town while I have my hair done?"

That would be too much walking for a cowboy. I saw him into a hansom cab and I entered a beauty salon, where they arranged my hair high in a pile, making me taller. Harry returned with two shots of Kentucky courage in his belly and, in his hand, a hundred-and-fifty-dollar gold lapel watch he'd bought me at Tiffany's. We wanted to say the word. And we did.

When we left the courthouse, my arm through Harry's and my hand pampering our marriage certificate, we went to DeYoung's Studio for a formal portrait, standing close together for it, proud of our fancy outfits, and Harry holding a top hat in his right hand. The hat, a studio prop, completed our look, elegant and sophisticated. I pinned on my new watch. We appeared to be classically Grecian even though Harry was bowlegged. Yes. Mr. And Mrs. Sundance Kid had presence. Harry could pass for a statesman.

I had extra prints made for my folks, Harry's mother, and the Harmsworths and mailed them before we sailed. Ours is framed on my living room wall alongside our framed marriage certificate. I still have the watch and Harry's stickpin, although I had to leave the dress in Bolivia a few years later. It's probably being worn by some poor Indian woman in a homburg. It will help keep her warm.

Next we rode the ferry to New Jersey and took a carriage to the Lakewood Hotel, a fancy winter hangout for all the best people. We fitted right in, you can bet your boots on that. The grub tasted good too but no better than at the Metropole, just more expensive.

When we returned late that night we found a commotion outside the theater near our hotel. As we drew close we saw the reason: Miss Lillian Russell, after her show, leaving in her carriage and everyone wanting a good gander or an autograph.

"Would you look at that, Harry? Six white horses pulling her buggy."

"Overfed and spoiled too, the way they're strutting and holding their heads."

"Think they'd make good relay mounts for the Bunch?"

Harry smiled. "If we decide to do any business here we'll acquire them first off."

Our driver guided us around the crowd and stopped in front of the Metropole.

Harry said, "I hear she has a fellow named Diamond Jim."

"So what? I have Diamond Harry."

We enjoyed a big time in New York. Like any cowboy, Harry hated to go anywhere if he had to walk, so we took a street-car or buggy. We loved spending time on the waterfront watching the Statue of Liberty and all the boats, liked eating in Central Park and going to the shows, including Miss Russell's. I have some of the programs beside me and don't need to look in my diary. So I know we saw Molly Barrymore at the Garrick Theatre in *Capt. Jinks of the Horse Marines*, Blanche Bates at the Garden Theatre in *Under Two Flags*, and Edna May at the Herald Square in *The Girl From Up There*.

One night when we returned to the hotel Butch surprised us in the lobby.

While Harry and he hugged each other and pounded one another's arms, I gave an apprehensive glance around for Kid Curry. When Butch turned to me and we shared a brief hand-shake, I asked the whereabouts of the Bunch's most vicious member, supposed to go to South America with us.

"Harvey decided to see California," Butch said. "He don't like foreigners."

"Know what you mean," Harry said. "I always thought Harvey and 'Merica Connolly would get into it."

I felt happy enough to shout. But I kept shut.

We had the most fun the night the three of us went to the Savoy to see The Four Cohans in *The Governor's Son*. Tickets cost $1.50 each to the evening show for the best seats in the house. Those Cohans had a way of reaching out to the audience, and you couldn't miss noting that the son, barely out of his teens, would become a big star. He had written and produced *The Governor's Son* himself and put on quite a show.

Between acts, the son, George M., stepped out from behind the curtain and asked a tough-looking lug in our row and off to the left several seats to stand. The applause started before the big bruiser fully gained his feet. He hadn't been champion for nearly ten years, but what a prizefighter he'd been, all the way back to the bare-knuckle days of my childhood. I still get a tingle when I think about Cohan's introduction. Yet, he merely said the man's name, "John L. Sullivan." But he dragged it out: "John . . . L . . ." After the *L* everyone knew and rose and cheered and whistled and shouted.

Butch stood and yelled like a teenager. After the applause subsided, Sullivan sat, and George M. said, in that dramatic way he had, "And he can lick any man in the house." A cheer went up, but Sullivan smiled and shook his head and made negative motions with his hands.

Butch leaned across me. "You could take him, Kid."

Harry kept a straight face and started to stand. I grabbed his arm next to me with both hands, and he leaned back, grinning like the devil on Saturday night. At least I think he pretended.

I said, "Shut up, Leroy, damn you."

Butch laughed.

After the show Harry bought a pint of Hunter Baltimore rye. He and Butch sipped from it on the ride to the hotel, and I participated to be polite. I went to bed to read the *North American Review*, which I had purchased for fifty cents three days earlier. Then I switched to *Moby Dick*. Harry and Butch stayed in the sitting room of our suite sipping rye and talking. They had a lot of catching up to do and planning.

I could hear them, with Butch getting loud, the same as many folks who can't hold their grog. When they finished the bottle, they said their good nights.

"Hell," Butch added, "they should have introduced me too."

Harry came to bed. "I could have taken him, Sugar."

The next morning in bed Harry gave me highlights of their reunion confab.

"Leroy says there's a flier out. Seems the first National Bank of Winnemucca and the bankers' association have put up a thousand dollars each for information that helps get any of us arrested for the Winnemucca job."

"Each?"

"Yep. He says they don't have your name, Sugar, but they claim Leroy and I were in on it. They also offer a reward of twenty-five percent of any recovered money."

"A thousand dollars. Leroy finally amounts to something."

Harry laughed. "The flier says one robber smelled like a polecat."

By midmorning Harry had revived enough to leave the suite on a day warm and clear, pleasant enough to eat in the palm court at the hotel.

"This must be as grand a day possible for late winter in New York," I said.

"Yes, but I still feel like I was sent for and can't go."

As we sipped coffee I read a few items to Harry from *The New York Times*: Admiral Dewey going to make a speech at Annapolis, Kitchener chasing the Boers in Africa, and the Colombian army fighting rebels down yonder.

"I reckon we could make a side trip to Colombia," Harry said.

I rattled the newspaper. "Do you want to hear anything from the financial page?"

"See how the Bunch is doing."

We had such fine weather I kept the front page, have it before me now.

After lunch I suggested examining merchandise through store windows.

"Sure. I'll get a buggy."

"On foot. It will help your head and stomach feel better."

"I'm better already, Sugar."

"And it won't hurt."

I dragged him along and, bless him, Harry didn't complain. At Wanamaker's we bought clothes for both of us, plus ribbons and a few yards of red silk I probably didn't need, and for seventy-five cents dress gloves for me.

"Look, Sugar. There's an opera cape." Harry stepped close and spread it for a better look. "Must be satin. And you know how I like red."

"I don't need one, Harry."

"I'm considering it for myself. Only twelve dollars."

I realized Harry hadn't fully sobered. I tugged his hand. "Come on, Caruso."

At a bookstore I bought the new Jack London collection, *The Son of the Wolf*; a Washington Irving collection; and Henry James's *Daisy Miller*, *Washington Square*, and *The Portrait of a Lady*. I also purchased a Spanish-English/English-Spanish dictionary, a Spanish grammar book, and an English guidebook to South America.

"When we walk down that gangplank somewhere in South America," I said, "we'll at least be able to eat, drink, and find a hotel." I had enjoyed French and Latin in school, so I hoped I would take to Spanish right away. "One of us has to learn Spanish, and I don't figure it to be you or Leroy." We also bought a steamer trunk and had it delivered to the hotel.

"Let's find a livery," Harry said. "Buy some horses to ship."

I decided I'd better fill him in on some of my readings in *National Geographic* about Argentina. "Let's have some coffee." The poor man seemed more tuckered out from walking than after an all-day getaway run with changes to fresh horses.

Two nights later we attended Josef Casimir Hofmann's piano recital at Carnegie Hall. I wore a new gown, sleeveless and black and silky, with low neckline, and a fancy topcoat with my gold watch pinned outside. I'd put up my hair, as black as my dress, in a splendid roll. Harry wore his dark formal outfit showing off his diamond stickpin. Judging by the glances we drew, I'd say we were the handsomest couple there.

When the Polish maestro's last notes sounded, Harry caught me wiping my eyes.

"Such marvelous music!" I sniffled. "I wonder if I'll ever play again."

"Sugar, I'll buy you a piano in South America. If we don't stay put I'll hire men with a wagon to haul it around after us."

I squeezed his hand and sniffled again.

"You play better than him too."

I knew Harry meant it, but he lacked an appreciation of classical music and was tone deaf. He'd rather hear *Mustang Grey* or *The Dying Cowboy* any day.

The next morning Harry and Butch went to the office of the captain of the port and found out about a liner sailing at the end of the week for Buenos Aires. We studied on that possibility that night while Harry and Butch drank Old Crow rye. I joined them just to be polite. And we agreed to head for Buenos Aires.

"It's not so close to the Equator to be too hot," I said, "but not so far to be cold."

"And too far for the Pinkertons to come after us," Butch said.

"We can't count on that," Harry told him.

So our New York venture neared its end, and it had been grand, at least for me and Harry. Butch had spent most of the time playing cards and drinking in one saloon or bagnio or another.

The morning before we left we happened to stroll past DeYoung's Studio. The display window caught our attention, for square in the middle sat our wedding photo in a fancy frame, the largest picture of the most elegant couple.

I smiled, planning to say what a nice gesture the studio had made. But when I saw the black look on Harry's face and the squint in those blue eyes, I stopped. "What is it?"

"Sugar, we can only hope the wrong people haven't asked about it. Come on." He led me inside, confronted the manager, and insisted that our picture not be displayed. I feared Harry would slug him, but the man didn't argue, removed it immediately.

Harry brooded about the photograph most of the morning but cheered up by lunchtime. "I hope our picture didn't find its way back to that window as soon as we walked away. We'd better check before we sail."

After lunch at the Metropole he wanted to nap, so we went to our room.

"I want to walk some more, Harry. Get one last look at this great place."

So I enjoyed taking in the sights and the clean cool air, try-ing to record it all and keep it forever, when, following my custom I entered a bookstore. I thought the steamer trunk could carry one or two more volumes. And one title on a corner shelf caught me up so that I almost cried out. I instantly bought it as a surprise for Harry and walked out eager to start reading it to him.

"What's it about, Sugar?" he asked when I reached our room. "What's it called?"

"It's called *A Texas Cowboy.*"

"By that favorite writer of yours? What's his name? London?"

"Not this time. This book is by that varmint, Charlie Siringo."

17

On March 6, 1901, on the passenger liner SS *Soldier Prince*, we sailed from New York into the Ocean Sea, as Columbus called it. Our ship did some princely soldiering too when we chugged right through a walloping storm on the third day and didn't sink, just rolled and pitched and yawed for several hours. The three of us, and a lot of other folks, didn't feel so princely then.

Harry stayed in our cabin and Butch in his, but I watched from the rail until a crewman told me the sea acted up too much and that I'd better go inside. Lots of passengers, including Harry and Butch, got sick. Some became scared. Some prayed.

But that became the only unpleasantness of the trip. By the time we could see some of the buildings of Buenos Aires on March 25, we had our sea legs, and "Mr. Place" and "Mr. Jones" had yapped so much with the purser that they'd about worn the poor man out. And I had learned enough Spanish to keep us fed and off the streets.

Along the way I'd read *A Texas Cowboy* to Harry as we sat on deck in wooden chairs or in a saloon—that's what they called them—in those big soft morris chairs we'd learned about in New York. The book had been published in 1885, the year Harry punched out his stepfather and left home at fifteen. Siringo had to be about thirty and already calling himself "an old stove-up cowboy."

"Nice, Sugar."

I had just finished the last page, and Harry had enjoyed the whole book.

"But," he said, "we didn't learn anything about his investigating techniques."

"No. He didn't join the Pinkertons until later. But we found out the man had a sense of humor, could laugh at himself, and ride well, shoot well enough."

"Yes, if he's not a natural liar. Sugar, it seems like Siringo ought to be getting too old to run all over one continent after another looking for two simple cowhands gone astray."

"We'll find out, won't we?"

"Besides, I still lean toward trying our hand at livestock raising."

"Of course, Honey."

Butch could read some, but I doubt he could have handled a whole book. However, he had another reason for not borrowing my copy.

"I know all I want to about that son of a bitch—excuse me, Etta," he said.

By the time a tug put a local pilot on board to direct the *Soldier Prince* to a pier, we could see the city's vastness and guess at its importance.

"I've never seen so many big boats with all the different flags," Harry said, "except in New York."

"And the buildings look modern. I think we're going to like the place."

Harry agreed.

Butch didn't comment.

The ship quit moving without a bump or any unusual sound I could detect, and we began saying good-bye to friends we'd acquired. Two Argentines who spoke English and an American who had been there, told us to be sure to visit Iguazú Falls, which they called "one of nature's most-magnificent creations."

We decided on the hotel one of the Argentines recommended, the Europa, a short walk from the dock, through the Plaza Colón and the Plaza de Mayo to Florida Street. But Harry and Butch felt the same distaste of walking. And we had the steamer trunk and some smaller bags. We needed a carriage.

Good thing too. That "short walk" became quite a piece.

Pedestrians crowded the streets, especially Florida, packed with shops and small restaurants.

"I smell grilled beef," Harry said.

I told him, "And I smell fresh bread."

Harry registered us as "Mr. and Mrs. Place." Butch signed in as "Jim Lowe," the way they knew him in some parts of New Mexico and Utah.

When we walked away from the desk I said, "Is that wise, Leroy?"

"Is what wise?"

"Using a name you're known by in the States. Maybe the Pinkertons know it."

"I doubt it. And it makes me feel comfortable in a new place."

You could never tell Butch anything different once he said something out loud.

Harry and I took a suite: sitting room, large bedroom, balcony, bathroom, and plenty of closet space. Butch got a room nearby. I began hanging up things from the trunk, and Harry had removed his money belt and started unstrapping his derringers when Butch called out and knocked. Harry let him in. "Get settled, Pard?"

"Yep," Butch said. "You?"

"Just about. Let's go find a bank."

"Jesus, Kid, we don't have the lay of the land yet."

I decided that their plan to be ranchers hadn't lasted long.

But Harry said, "Not that. I want to open an account, stow most of my cash, and maybe ask about a spread for sale."

I knew how to ask in Spanish for a bank, *un banco*, simple enough, and the hotel clerk directed us back to Plaza de Mayo nearby. Right away we entered a place where we hoped they'd speak English. After all, I couldn't talk land deals in Spanish yet. We had chosen the Banco de la Nación, with customers crowding the lobby and tellers' lines. This time while we crossed the lobby we didn't case the place but looked for an official.

"Did you hear all those foreign languages, Harry?"

"I guessed that's what I heard."

"I detected German, Italian, English from England, and American."

"I think I heard the American."

Harry opened a joint account for us under my maiden name. Butch opened his as Jim Lowe. Those were different times, don't you know. Passports and drivers' licenses didn't exist, much less credit cards, and plenty of folks lacked a birth certificate. A bank accepted you on your word, especially when you showed a formally written letter of credit from a New York bank, as we did, and toted a money belt bursting with hundred-dollar gold pieces. We also rented safe-deposit boxes and purchased Argentine pesos.

From a real estate specialist, Harry and Butch got an idea of prices and the best areas to live and work, and we walked out onto Plaza de Mayo and into the warmth and clarity of what south of the Equator in late March was a beautiful fall day.

"We'd need the whole Bunch to take that place," Butch said.

Harry laughed. "And a full belly. Let's eat."

Several small restaurants rimmed the plaza. We selected one where we could sit outdoors at the edge of the sidewalk, enjoy the day, and study the activity around that historic square commemorating Argentina's independence from Spain. And I prepared for my most important test yet of my nineteen days' study of the Spanish language. I pretty much failed. You see, I had looked up a lot of words in my dictionary and memorized them, specifically several connected with eating. But when I examined the menu

I couldn't find any of them except the Spanish for bread, salad, milk, beer, and wine. Our stomachs would get bored or drunk.

"Boys, I feel dumber than Jacob's mule."

"What is it, Sugar?"

"The menu's so foreign to me."

Butch laughed.

"I mean, I thought I'd do better by now. But *fiambres, puchero, churrasco, humitas, chorizo*. The closest I come to recognizing a meal is one called *bife a caballo*."

"What do you suppose it is?" Butch asked.

"I think it's horse meat."

"Count me out."

Harry said, "As long as it's not an old hammerhead mustang."

"I need a beer." Butch pushed his hat back and looked for a waiter. We hadn't unpacked the store-bought cigarettes, so Harry and Butch got out their makings.

We had a round of a good local beer while I studied the menu. But I didn't become any more fluent. I waved for the waiter. Much to my surprise and pleasure I recognized a few of the words in his explanations. The food turned out to be not so different after all.

I told Harry and Butch about it the best I could.

"I vote for *churrasco*," Harry said.

Butch and I followed suit. And we got the biggest, thickest, juiciest, tastiest steaks any of us had ever tackled. They looked and smelled wonderful, sounded good too, still sizzling.

"Get us some red wine, Sugar."

I misspoke: The waiter brought us a fifth each.

So we ate and drank and talked and overall had a grand afternoon right there at the edge of the Plaza de Mayo in downtown Buenos Aires, Argentina, on just a splendid afternoon with winter rushing toward us in the Year One.

By the way, as my Spanish improved I learned that *bife a caballo* meant "steak with a fried egg riding on top."

Back at the Hotel Europa we took siestas, just like I'd read you were supposed to. Well, we did something else first. Just let me say that a good meal and some loving when you arrive at a strange place go a long way toward making you feel right at home.

When I woke up I shook Harry's shoulder. "Let's walk around before supper."

"On foot?"

"Honey, that's the best way to walk."

We showered and dressed. I said, "What about Leroy?"

Harry walked along the hall and quickly returned. "No answer."

We exited the Europa and strolled Florida Street.

"Not even San Francisco or New York had this," Harry said.

I agreed. The street seemed extra-crowded with people gawking, shopping, sitting at the sidewalk cafes, or just ambling, in motion but loafing.

"This is actually entertaining," Harry said.

I squeezed his arm. "To promenade. That's the idea. Or watch the promenade."

I got Harry to walk all the way to 9 de Julio, an avenue named for an important date in the war for independence. "My guidebook says it's the widest street in the world."

"I'm convinced," Harry said.

Carriages and pedestrians roamed all over, and shrubs and trees prettied it up. We walked back to Plaza de Mayo, saw the City Hall, the government building they call the Casa Rosada, and the cathedral where San Martín is buried. Harry showed interest in hearing what I had read about San Martín. But he'd finished walking for that day. And I felt proud of his accomplishment, mine too: getting him to do it.

Harry and I seemed about ready to find a ranch on the plains, which they called the pampas, but first we wanted to visit that local phenomenon our shipmates mentioned, Iguazú Falls. Meantime, Butch could investigate ranching possibilities.

Except the falls weren't local. The trip took us three days each way by boat on the Paraná River through the wildest country, mostly jungle, I've seen to this day, way north of Buenos Aires to where Argentina, Brazil, and Paraguay meet on the Iguazú River. We heard the falls roar for a long time before seeing them, and we walked as close as we dared without getting soaked. Still, we got sprayed lightly, cool and refreshing after all the heat and humidity on the boat. Also, the spraying water, like a curtain of damp gauze, kept the mosquitoes away.

We stood marveling at the thundering and crashing water, wide and spectacular and marvelous, when a young Indian approached to identify himself in quivering English as a guide who could explain about the falls and wouldn't charge anything.

I didn't believe the part about no fee, but the young fellow seemed likable. Harry and I exchanged nods and let him begin. I've checked the facts, and they seem to be pretty much as the guide told us: that Iguazú Falls dropped two hundred feet and stretched a mile and a half wide, making them wider than Niagara Falls or Victoria Falls.

"I've never seen so many orchids and begonias and ferns just growing wild," I told Harry. "I recognize them from *National Geographic*." We saw lots of multicolored birds, including a toucan, easily identifiable by its huge yellow beak. We heard chatter from the jungle, monkeys, I supposed. And we walked past bamboo and palms, scattering more gorgeous butterflies than I thought could exist in one place.

Harry inhaled deeply. "Seeing this area is worth the trip to South America."

I agreed.

We stayed two days at a small primitive inn. When we prepared to start back, Harry tipped our guide so generously I thought he'd follow us to Buenos Aires, but we finally convinced him we'd be all right, that the boat would take us almost to our hotel.

In our absence, Butch had a big time too, having discovered the underbelly of Buenos Aires, La Boca, on the waterfront, the raucous heart of cantinas and brothels.

"Sundance, you should have been with me."

I glared at him while Harry shifted from one foot to the other.

"Sorry, Etta," Butch said. "I just mean it's exciting around here."

We sat in our suite at the Europa, sipping rye before heading for a restaurant.

From outside we heard the fuss of vendors, carriages, foot traffic.

Butch hadn't been anywhere near Avenida 9 de Julio, had not learned any Spanish, and didn't have any idea who San Martín had been, although he seemed to know several bartenders, sailors, and women from the demimonde. Harry might have been the same way if he hadn't found me.

Butch had two black eyes and a fat lip.

You see, "Butch Cassidy" might have won him a wide berth at certain saloons, bordellos, and banks in various towns of several states and territories back home, but "Jim Lowe" didn't give goose pimples to anyone in South America.

"Who slugged you, Pard?"

"Big bastard," Butch said, "off a German freighter. 'Kraut,' everyone calls him."

"I've heard of German efficiency," I said.

"He'd been asking for it all night," Butch said, "boasting about being a tough hombre. I decided to let him have it."

Harry said, "You mean he's worse off than you?"

"No. I misjudged by a right smart."

However, mixed in with his capers along the water-front, Butch had done some serious investigating of ranching possibilities.

"You still hankering to nurse cattle and break broncs for a while, Kid?"

"For a while. Can't do any harm. Sugar?"

"I'm with you, Honey. But I won't believe you two are ranching until I see you dusty and sweaty and throwing calves for branding."

Harry kissed me on the cheek. "How about building fence?"

"That too."

This would be nothing like the old days. But I got left out some in those times anyway, or told to stay with the horses. And I reckoned they wouldn't last long at cowboying. So I kept shut. Still, anything would be all right by me.

Harry and Butch checked around some more. They didn't need an interpreter, so many foreigners around that lots of public officials spoke English, and some even sounded as though they came from England. At the government land office we obtained four square leagues at a tiny inland community named Cholila in the area called Patagonia. That put us in Chubut Province sixteen hundred miles away, about as far south from Buenos Aires as you can go without freezing in winter.

"Think it'll be warm enough down there?" I asked.

"We might have to bundle up once in a while," Harry said. "But if we stay around here the Pinkertons might show up."

Butch said, "If we live in the jungle, we could hide out easy, but there wouldn't be any stores or banks, and I'm talking about for legitimate transactions."

"I recall folks on the boat saying Patagonia is wide open spaces, Sugar, desert, much like where we've spent so much time in the States. And they say it's primitive."

"We know all about rough times," I said. "Let's go."

First we had to make several purchases, and every time I asked someone what we'd need, the usual answer came back "everything except firewood and livestock." So I gave my guide-book and dictionary a good going over. We spent several days buying what we needed or wanted and packing it into boxes or big canvas bags for shipment by sea: cooking utensils, dishes and silverware, matches, bedding, tents, a camp stove, axes, saws, picks, shovels, nails and hammers, ropes, knives, and what all.

"We'll need a branding iron," Harry said.

Butch looked up from fastening a bag. "My thinking exactly."

We designed a cliff with a narrow notch at the top, like a hole in a wall if you knew what to look for. Butch said it reminded him of the outfit he used to ride with. A smithy made it.

A whiskey bottle would have done as well. But I kept shut.

We purchased plenty of shells for our various guns, which we'd brought all the way. Each of us selected a good saddle and bridle and new boots and hats and other clothing, including some for cold weather.

Butch saw a big knife, its blade half as long as on a Mexican machete, and had to have it as soon as I translated the engraving on it: "Death Before Dishonor" on one side, "Unequaled Lover" on the other.

We also bought several cartons of Argentine cigarettes, two cases of Cutty Sark, and two of Old Bushmills, examples of the advantage of being in a cosmopolitan city.

"But," Butch wanted to know, "what'll we do for liquor when that runs out?"

Harry told him, "Man at the land office said the Indians or gauchos there would have some locally made wine or liquor, maybe both."

"But will it be any good?"

"He said it would taste fine if that's all there is."

When we were ready to sail south, the steamer wasn't, so we had to wait a few days. Harry and Butch passed much of that time playing two-handed card games or dominoes, sipping beer or whiskey at an alfresco café, usually La Argentina, on Florida Street a few doors from the hotel. Right away they had learned how to ask for their drinks and the check.

I walked around and gawked at shop windows, saw the Colonial buildings in San Telmo, studied up on Spanish, and joined them for dinner and supper if Harry didn't already accompany me.

But they showed signs of restlessness and that bothered me. You never know what a cowboy will do if he's penned up for long. And that is all Harry and Butch were, cowboys, even though they had wandered from that toil, the same as many men who found their lives so altered by the Civil War and the barbed-wire fencing of the range.

The night before we sailed from Buenos Aires we ate in the Europa's dining room, a *churrasco* and a small bottle of red wine apiece, low lighting, clean linen tablecloths, guitar players, and an auburn-haired beauty singing love ballads.

"What's she saying, Sugar?"

"I'm missing most of it. Songs are too tough for me."

"I need to know too," Butch said. "She's singing straight to me."

"I believe that's to help a vocalist concentrate, Leroy, and create emotions."

"She's doing that. I want to meet her."

"Her emotions," I said, "not yours."

We finished eating, the boys smoked a cigarette apiece, and Butch twisted his neck looking for the singer, who had taken an intermission.

"Sugar, Leroy and I are going to ride a buggy around town, have a few drinks."

I had been thinking about our big soft bed upstairs. I gave Harry a look, but the way he smiled I couldn't be angry, not at the handsomest man I'd ever known, and the only man I'd ever love. "Sure, Honey. I won't wait up. You boys have your inside guns?"

Of course they did. Harry continued smiling.

I knew better than to tell him to be careful, especially when he headed out with his best friend. I gave him a grin and a kiss. "See you at breakfast."

But I hadn't been reading an hour when I heard them in the hall outside our room, then heard Butch laughing as they walked into the bedroom where I read propped up on pillows. Butch fell to giggling. Harry removed his coat and hat and kissed me, my husband laughing lightly, the devil in him.

"Well, Leroy," I said, "what is so god-awful funny?"

Finally he got hold of himself enough to talk. "The big German sailor? Kraut?"

"Yes," I teased. "Your best friend from La Boca."

"Sundance knocked him cockeyed."

18

The swimming season at the long white beaches south of Buenos Aires is December through March, and if you so much as swish a toe in the ocean before December or after March you are perpetrating a social faux pas, never mind how warm the water or ideal the day.

So we missed that. And now May had arrived with the theater season beginning just as we prepared to leave for our spread. May to October, that's when the shows run. I wouldn't have understood much anyway. Maybe my Spanish would be ready for the next season. Harry would want a few days in the city by then.

We rode the steamer down the coast four hundred miles to a port called Bahía Blanca. There we had the good fortune to learn about the imminent sailing of a smaller boat on one of its sporadic trips to our next destination, Rawson.

"Why Rawson?" Butch asked.

"It's the closest port to where we're heading," I said, "and capital of Chubut Province, like a county seat, like Selma or Autaugaville." I felt like the navigator.

At Rawson we disembarked at a pier in clean little Bahía Engaño where cliffs came down to the water north and south. We had our possessions unloaded onto the beach, paying an unoccupied Indian fish peddler a few pesos to guard them with the promise of that much more when we returned. After I asked him a few questions, we walked around town and spotted a bank first off, a general store, a saloon, a livery stable, some little wooden houses plopped down here and there, and a telegraph office.

"Not many folks live here," Harry said.

"No," I said, "but the fish peddler told me it fills up some on Saturdays. Lots of sheep ranchers and herders come in from the outback. And there's a community of Welshmen nearby in a town called Trelew."

"No phone lines," Butch said. "Just the telegraph wire leading out of town."

We enjoyed a fine dinner at a wooden shack on the beach away from the dock, one of the best meals we'd had in Argentina: a freshwater salmon apiece skewered on a small green cutting from a tree and broiled on a wood fire right in front of us, served with lemon and salt and a roll. Our restaurant sat in a little cove with small rhythmic waves and fresh salty air. I loved it, just to sit there and nibble my fish and look out to sea.

"This beer's not cold," Butch said.

"I'm drinking mine." I sipped.

"Me too," Harry said.

With Harry speaking English and me 5 percent Spanish, we bought three saddle horses and put our new rigs on them, purchased two pack mules, and hired a string of Indians, men and women accompanied by their children and dogs. We rented horses for the Indians. The horses looked about the same as in the States, but the liveryman called them criollos. He said they could run forever, live off the pampas, didn't need much water. Harry selected duns for me and him, Butch a buckskin.

"The clerk in the store reminded me we have three hundred miles to go," I said. "And it's midafternoon. We start now or wait until first light tomorrow?"

"It's pleasant here. What do you think, Sugar?"

In my mind I continued enjoying our respite on the beach. "I wouldn't mind staying over. We could curl up on the beach. Get going when the sun peeks at us."

"There might be fleas or crabs," Butch said.

We hashed it out for a spell. But Butch couldn't understand the beauty and originality of the adventure, so Harry and I gave in. That's a situation you sometimes have to put up with when your man's best friend is around. Swallow or spit.

We made some final purchases at the store: bandannas to cover our noses and mouths in case the trail got dusty, dried beef, shipped-in canned beans and fruit, and a water pump for a well the clerk said we'd probably have to dig.

"Wind comes up," the clerk told us. "Dust storms once in a while. Mostly desert. Not much rain. Mild weather most of the time."

"Much obliged," I said. I'd relay the clerk's comments outside.

"Watch out for highwaymen," he added.

I interpreted that remark right away for the boys.

Harry smiled ever so slightly. "Thank you. We'll sure keep an eye peeled."

So we rounded up our people and mules and started out.

Chubut Province—Butch pronounced it "SHOEboot," but it's "chuBOOT"— stretches north, south, touches the Atlantic on the east, and toward the west reaches the eastern slope of the Andes, where we'd bought, around Cholila, almost to Chile. For the rest of that day and all the next we followed the Chubut River, which flowed to the edge of Rawson. But it soon bent northwest, and we needed to keep on due west.

Within a couple of days we missed being near the river, and noted few streams. I chatted with the Indians about the situation and reported to Harry and Butch.

"They say there's big grassy valleys in this part of Patagonia as we climb toward the foothills. Rains enough. Livestock thrives. Mostly sheep, especially in ravines and canyons. Some beeves. Lots of ravines to cross."

"Mountain lions?" Butch asked. "Bear?"

"No enemies until real high up. Where we're going, just wild dogs and red fox."

"Good," Harry said, "and there'll be water and grass."

"Exactly."

Butch frowned at his horse's ears. Probably disliked the idea of the sheep.

I had read up on Argentina, and while I rode I studied the Indians we hired. They looked pretty much like our Indians back home, but had suffered a worse fate.

"Few are left," I told Harry at one of our first campsites. "They're scattered across the plains, like ours, and into the Andes, plus some in the jungles up north."

"I never saw a one in Buenos Aires," Harry said, "and not any in New York except the Ojibway dancers."

"At least we saved a few for reservations and Wild West shows. But in Argentina the government gave huge land grants to soldiers for killing Indians." I felt a pang in my heart just saying that.

A couple of the boys we hired spoke adequate Spanish, so I got in some work on the language. Fortunately I had packed my dictionary and grammar where I could reach them easily and wound up carrying both by hand for much of the trip. I must have looked like a circuit rider toting his Bible. But I enhanced my vocabulary with terms essential to ranching, such as "pasture," "fence," "A storm is coming," "when the rain quits," "about to foal," "Get to work," "branding time," and "Draw your wages and hit the trail, you varmint."

My guidebook also received regular use. For instance, sometimes at a rest stop our helpers built a little fire, heated water, and soon began passing around a small gourd like a bowl. They took turns sipping from it with narrow metal tubes, each "straw" privately owned, as near as I could determine.

"What is it?" I asked.

For answer I received more words than I could swallow, Spanish or Indian. And one showed me the gourd. I saw leaves and twigs in the liquid and, with encouragement, sipped some through a borrowed straw. I liked it, made me think of green tea. I dug into my guidebook before losing track of two words they had repeated, *yerba mate*, and paraphrased for Harry and Butch what I found.

"Yerba mate is a holly that grows into a tall tree, and they dry its leaves and twigs and soak them in hot water. The drink and the gourd are called mate. The 'straw' is a *bombilla*. Drinking mate is an afternoon social custom dating to Indian days."

"Might be a nice pick-me-up for us too," Harry said.

"I'll keep an eye out for a store," I commented.

Butch gave each of us a funny look.

The Patagonian desert is one plateau after another, stony here and there and windy from time to time. It's sort of a murky brown with splashes of color in the flowers and in berries yellow, white, and red among the shrubs. Some areas are grassy. And the Indians identified several animals new to us.

"That one's a guanaco," I told Harry one day, and pointed to it.

"Looks about like a llama," Harry said.

I'd shown him a llama earlier. "A little different. And they say a guanaco is awfully fast."

When a small animal like a deer skittered across the road in front of us, the Indians hollered almost at the same time, "*Mara. Es una mara.*" Later I found out the English-speaking residents called it a Patagonia hare. We also saw armadillos, which we recognized from our time in Texas, and rheas, which we thought were ostriches until I read in my guidebook they were rheas and that ostriches lived in Africa.

"The rhea's smaller," I told the boys, "but also plenty fast."

The next rhea we saw raced across the pampas right in front of us. A cowboy riding a smallish brown horse, the man in a floppy hat with his poncho flying behind him, sped after the rhea while twirling a rope with three fist-size balls tied to it. Then he flung the thing and tripped up that huge long-legged bird in a pile of dust and feathers.

"I'll be damned," Harry said.

Butch shook his head. "I've never seen that before."

We rode to the scene of the capture and introduced ourselves.

"*Tirosolo*," the cowboy said. "*Gaucho*." He pointed to his chest.

I'd been trying to recall that word for two days when we started seeing similar riders on the pampas, for I'd read some about gauchos. I asked Tirosolo, "What are you going to do with the bird?"

He smiled a little, maybe at my use of *pájaro* for such a large creature, being as I hadn't guessed that *rea* meant rhea. "*Las comen si no son viejas y duras*," Tirosolo said, "*y mandamos las plumas a la capital para adornar los sombreros de las elegantes damas.*"

"He says they eat the meat if it's not old and tough," I told Harry and Butch, "and send the feathers to Buenos Aires for women's hats."

Tirosolo, medium tall, dark and weathered, slim and muscular, smiled with good teeth and happy eyes, boasted a big mustache proving he wasn't Indian.

"I'd say he's a match for our cowboys," Harry said. "You reckon he'd let me examine that flying weapon of his?"

I struggled to interpret that but figured I said it right when Tirosolo smiled again, bent down, and bound the rhea's big ugly feet with a piggin' string. He undid his weapon and held it up for Harry to take.

We examined it: three long cords tied together at one end with, on each loose end, a heavy leather-covered wooden ball.

"*Boleadoras*," Tirosolo said nodding, twirling a hand over his head. He told me the Indians invented the weapon long ago, that gauchos use it to capture any man or beast, and that they also have friendly competitions with it. I believe Tirosolo encouraged us to try the thing, but we refused, graciously, I hope, and started off.

That night in camp I reviewed in my guide the part about gauchos and summed it up for Harry and Butch.

"It says the gaucho can mount or dismount a galloping horse, same as you boys, and can throw a lariat and a knife in addition to the *boleadoras*. He helped drive out the Indians, who are gone as a force, and now peons are replacing him. This is good: 'The era of the gaucho is just about over. For many years when he hadn't been soldiering, this magnificent horseman and cowboy had been a wild nomadic buffer between civilization and the Indians. The few gauchos remaining are proud people still admired in many quarters, especially by country folk, for their independence and skills. The gaucho is the last Argentine.'"

"Out of date," Harry said. "Like us."

"We should have thrown that thing when we had the chance," Butch said.

I guessed Tirosolo might be an unusual name, so I went to my dictionary. "Best I can figure, it's a nickname meaning 'single shot.'"

"He's good, all right," Harry said.

"If he'd been with us at Winnemucca, we wouldn't have needed Etta."

I'd read that Patagonia had plenty of forests farther south, but for trees we saw only the *ombú*. They were widely scattered but you could see one from miles away, the plateaus being so vast. It's medium-size, a welcome shade tree, but that's all.

"They say it's worthless as firewood," I told the boys, paraphrasing from my guide. "Lives five hundred years. No fruit, and a cyclone couldn't uproot it."

"They said there'd be some trees where we're bound," Harry said.

"Yes. Relief from all this flat land."

"What's that tall peak we keep seeing yonder?"

"My book calls it Aconcagua, highest point in the Andes."

"Doesn't stand out much above the others," Butch said.

"It's that the whole Andes range is so high."

After several more days of riding toward Aconcagua, passing an occasional ombú or rhea or llama, and ascending slightly we reached a dusty crossroads with only one structure, a small wooden store with a false front.

"You reckon this is Cholila?" Harry said.

"Couldn't be," Butch told him. "No saloon. No bank. Nothing."

Harry and I dismounted and entered the store. I talked with the proprietor and his wife for quite a spell. Finally Butch joined us.

"This is it," I said.

"Gawdamighty." Butch looked around the little store.

Harry told him, "They say Sunday's lively, Indians sitting on the stoop."

"Me llamo Juan," the owner said, and nodded toward his wife. *"Ana. Somos argentinos puros."*

"Pure Argentines" they might have been, but they looked like pure Indians too. Didn't matter: short and dark, wiry and smiling, sincere. I liked them. They made us feel welcome. They had a general store: horse tack and feed, work clothes, canned food, coffee, salt and flour, farm tools. I'm sure it also served as the local center for gossip and news.

"Juan says we have several neighbors," I told the boys. "Some are no more than eight kilometers away, maybe five miles or so. One's an American or Englishman, Juan's not sure. A dentist. And anything we want, Juan will get for us, though it might take a while, on account of there isn't any telegraph."

We bought a small sack of dried mate leaves and twigs, two gourds, and two *bombillas.*

"Harry and I can share," I told Butch. "You get the other gourd and straw."

Butch gave me the same funny look he had on the trail when I explained about mate.

After obtaining directions, we thanked Juan and Ana and stepped outside.

"Etta could take this place by herself," Butch said.

We rode south a bit and up the slope quite a piece into those eastern foothills of the Andes. Just before nightfall we found a level spot for camping in pines near a stream.

"We're so high," Harry said, "we can just about see the Atlantic Ocean."

"Yes," I said, "and look at all the valleys, green and beautiful, cutting through the plain in all directions. High grass. Llamas and vicuña grazing. Just wonderful."

Harry agreed, turned to look up the slope. "Plenty of timber up higher. And we'll need it to build with. What do you think, Leroy?"

"They don't understand a damn thing I'm saying." Butch had been instructing our Indians, he thought, about where to camp and where to tether the animals.

I took over for him.

The next day we scouted around some, but one place seemed as good as another within what we estimated to be our property. So we decided to build where we camped that first night out of Cholila. We hired two Indians and their women without kids or dogs, paid off the others, and sent them back with the rented horses they'd ridden. I hoped they'd turn in those ponies. The two mules would be good for plowing in case we wanted a big garden and for dragging timber from the slope when we started to build. And we admired the criollo horses we'd purchased.

Once in a while rains muddied the place. The winter got awfully cold at times, but mostly stayed mild, so we accomplished a lot: corrals, a barn, a small log house we added to in the summer, and our Indians dug a well in case the stream went dry. Harry installed the pump. From neighbors we bought unbroken horses, beef cattle, sheep, a dairy cow, chickens, ducks, and sheep dogs, which quickly became excellent cattle dogs too.

Harry and I adopted the custom of the afternoon break for mate, but the idea never caught on with Butch. Sometimes Harry substituted whiskey.

One of those neighbors we bought from turned out to be the dentist, John Newton, an American who had a practice in Buenos Aires during the rainy season. We would run into him in one grassy valley or another of that vast unfenced land. We liked him.

Harry and Butch started right in breaking horses and soon built a nice string to sell in Rawson. One of the Indians, a reliable older man as honest as the clouds, took the horses there and handled the sales.

Our Indians had been farmers and laborers, but could ride a little. So Harry taught them to make a lariat from cowhide and to throw a loop. He also showed them how to make rawhide bridles and to mount and ride bareback. They took to the horse business with enthusiasm, but didn't mind the other work. With supreme effort and insistence, I taught Butch a few words of Spanish, and with those and body language he became good at directing them in the chores. We found them trustworthy and hard working.

I helped part time in the outside work, planted a garden, got in some reading, and showed the women my way of cooking, while they showed me theirs. And every day I learned a little more Spanish, though I suspected it included a lot of Indian. Harry and Butch didn't pick up much of either language as they spent so much time talking to one another. And if they couldn't get one of the Indians to understand by showing him or by talking slower and louder, they called on me.

19

In the Argentine they measure three miles to a league. So I did some math and figured out that our spread comprised 7,680 acres. From the start, we felt rich.

No one's land had fencing except for sheep pastures, so our cattle shared several of the little valleys with our neighbors' stock. And due to the brands, our dogs, and an attitude of camaraderie that had pretty much been lost in Wyoming and Utah and around, we never had any trouble.

I frequently wrote home and to Harry's mother and the Harmsworths.

Early in 1902 we had our first cattle drive into Rawson along with a small string of newly broke saddle ponies and shipped everything on consignment to Buenos Aires.

By May of 1903 we had twelve hundred sheep, seven hundred head of cattle, and thirty-five horses, mostly broodmares giving us a foal apiece every year. Business thrived. We enjoyed the life. We hired more hands.

And Harry said what I'd been thinking. "Let's make a visit to Buenos Aires."

"Good," I said. "It's the rainy season, so it's also the theater season."

"Let's bring back some good whiskey," Butch said. "The local tanglefoot don't set well with me."

I thought, *Except at time for your nightly toddy.*

We told the hands we'd return in a couple of months and set out on horseback for Rawson and the boat to Bahía Blanca, where we'd catch the steamer to Buenos Aires.

On the first day out of Bahía Blanca, I picked up a Buenos Aires newspaper, *La Prensa*, about two weeks old, and read an article that stunned me. "Boys, a story out of Washington refers to Teddy Roosevelt as president."

"What's the matter with that?" Butch asked. "He's the hero of Cuba."

"But he's McKinley's vice president, and McKinley's second term isn't over."

Harry said, "Something must have happened to McKinley."

"That's what I'm afraid of," I said.

At the Hotel Europa the clerk told me about McKinley's assassination at Buffalo in September of 1901. I explained to Harry and Butch. I had been only five when President Garfield got shot, but I remembered the excitement and consternation at home when we heard. Now I had those same feelings.

We saw the sights of Buenos Aires right away, did justice to several first-class steaks, and caught a couple of plays. Out of fairness to Harry, I dragged him to only two. Besides, I couldn't understand as much of the plays as I thought I would.

And one day we saw the announcement in our bank.

"Look, Kid," Butch said. "They spelled your name wrong."

"I'll have Etta speak to Mr. Siringo about that."

"Looks like the pictures of me and Sundance are from the one we mailed to the bank at Winnemucca."

"You mailed it," Harry said, "not me."

"I only thanked the bank for its cooperation."

"You did that and a lot more, Leroy." I became angry all over again, the way they had taken my photo off our wedding portrait in New York and printed "Wanted" under it.

Years later I read that in the Pinkerton's New York office, an agent who knew about Winnemucca and the photograph going to the bank had noticed our picture in the studio's front window, where it had sat until Harry and I spotted it just before we sailed.

So the law had been close behind us.

Butch admired his photograph. "How do they know to look for us here?"

"Once they learned we'd visited New York and maybe wondered why," Harry said, "they might have gone to the steamship lines, also the courthouse. I thought we'd gone far enough East we could get married under our real names."

"I'm glad we did, Honey."

"I just wanted to make us legal."

I squeezed Harry's hand.

The poster described me as Harry's "female consort." I suppose the authorities included me only to help them find Harry and Butch, as they didn't taint me with a single violation of law. Besides, I dressed like a man whenever they let me go along. "Maybe we'd better start calling me Margaret or Maggie."

"Yes," Harry said, "around any more people we meet."

They identified Harry as highwayman, bank burglar, horse thief, rustler, and murderer, Butch the same except "bank robber" instead of "bank burglar."

"What's the difference?" Butch asked.

"You're the leader," Harry told him.

The American Banking Association put out the notice, offering a thousand-dollar reward for each of us. It told anyone with information on our whereabouts to contact local authorities, who would notify the Pinkerton National Detective Agency. It said the loot included a fifty-dollar bill, and that one of the robbers smelled like a polecat.

I saw Butch frown at the poster. "What's wrong, Leroy?"

"I ought to be worth more space than that."

"Don't fret," Harry said. "You did the best you could."

We had remained near the door, blocking anyone who entered from seeing our faces and the poster simultaneously.

"While we're here," Harry said, "we might as well conduct a transaction."

I'd swear I saw Butch's knees buckle. "Hell, Kid, we don't have no horses, no plan, no hideout. Jesus!"

Harry grinned, satan in his smile and eyes.

"Let's have a drink," I said.

No one opposed that idea.

We'd begun sipping beer at a sidewalk table on Florida Street when our American neighbor, the dentist our hands called *El Doctor Juan*, saw us and stopped to chat. He stood tall and lean, a sun-browned, mild-looking man, probably in his fifties.

"Sit with us," Harry said.

"Can't. I have a patient due. I got here just a week ago and I'm already swamped. Been drilling teeth high and low. Yanked some too. How about you folks?"

Butch sipped his beer.

"Vacationing," I said. "We've taken in a couple of plays."

"Etta's our interpreter." Harry nodded toward me.

"Not very good though," I said.

After a few more pleasantries, Dr. Newton tipped his hat and stepped into the crowd rushing along Florida Street.

"What do you think, Sugar?"

"Seemed like he eyed us mighty close."

"My thought exactly," Harry said.

"What are you talking about?" Butch asked.

"Dr. Newton," Harry said. "Studying us. Maybe he'd seen the poster."

"Could be just surprised," Butch said. "He'd never seen me and you in our city clothes. And Etta's nice to look at."

Talk about surprise! Butch usually joshed me or argued. I felt like thanking him, gave him a tiny smile.

"We haven't broken any Argentine laws," Harry said.

"Got our spread fair and square, treat our Injuns white, and pay fair wages, and we've been working hard. We shouldn't have anything to fret about unless Charlie Siringo himself comes to town."

"Or his sidekick," Harry said, "Frank Dimaio."

"You know we could take 'em, Kid."

"Yes, though it's best to avoid them. And we're so far away, maybe they won't even look personally."

"The banks must have got up a pile of dough to pay the Pinkertons to be after us way down here," Butch said.

"I'm sure they did." Harry lifted his bottle, put it down.

"This is such a big country." I took Harry's arm. "Chances are slim any local folks will memorize our looks and start searching for us."

"Let's finish our vacation," Harry said, "then head back to the ranch. Even if they learn where we live, probably no one will want to guide 'em way out there."

Harry didn't sound convinced, but we agreed that was our best idea short of pulling up stakes.

An hour later, Butch set out for La Boca. Harry and I stayed at the table awhile before returning to our room. The next day while the girls in the shop beside our hotel tackled my hair and nails, and I thought Harry rested in our room, he all of a sudden showed up and surprised me with a kiss then and there. I'd swear I heard the girls flutter when they saw him.

"What's going on, Honey?" I wished I could hide my hair full of rag curlers.

"I have a job."

I knew he joshed me but I played along. "I hope the pay's good."

"Should be. It's detective work. See you in a bit."

The girls had just finished with me when Harry returned. "How'd work go?"

"Profitable, Sugar. I'll explain in our room."

He shut the door behind us and leaned his back against it. "I investigated the lobbies of several banks, the Post Office, City Hall, and the government house, where the president issues orders after Gen. Julio Argentino Roca tells him what to say."

I couldn't read his expression.

Harry stepped forward and took my hands. "Sugar, we are all over town."

We sat and he explained how everywhere he looked he found copies of that same wanted poster we'd seen at the Banco de la Nación.

"My wedding portrait."

"I'm sure sorry, Sugar."

Profitable work, all right. Now we knew to be more concerned.

After capturing Butch between his escapades to La Boca we took the next steamer south, arriving at the ranch without getting rained on, though one dust storm caught us.

The winter turned out unremarkable, not too cold, just hard work complicated by an occasional shower. And knowing the Pinkertons had got word to Buenos Aires, I continually expected Harry and Butch to return to the old ways. If ever a land lent itself to our previous kinds of activities, Argentina did, so huge, virtually unpopulated for mile after mile of cattle ranches, grain farms, sheep ranches, yerba mate plantations, and vineyards, plus all that jungle in the north. But the boys never raised the subject. As for me, I kept shut, although I wouldn't have minded some excitement of the former kind.

We played cards, and Harry and Butch taught our Indians cooncan and cassino. One day Butch blustered into the kitchen where one of the women showed me how to make a stew, *puchero*, and I'd begun demonstrating how to create molasses-pecan pie. He gulped from the first jug he saw, even though he'd grabbed Indian liquor, and started out again, knocking over a chair and bumping the table.

"What's wrong?" I had seldom seen him angrier.

"Damn Injun beat me at cassino."

I continued working to improve my Spanish. Seems like the more I learned, the more I discovered I didn't know. And once in a while I tried to teach Harry to read English. But it didn't take. Meanwhile, Butch had to be forgetting what little reading he knew. I guess the schoolmarm kept showing up in me, but those boys exasperated me.

And I wrote to home and Harry's mother and the Harmsworths even though a week or two usually passed before Harry or Butch or one of our hands took the letters to the store at Cholila. And from there the letters wouldn't go to the port at Rawson anytime soon, depending on travelers going that way, and the memory of old Juan the storekeeper. Juan and Ana never missed a chance to mention that they were "pure Argentines," not any ignorant scruffy Indians.

20

Around the middle of November, Harry and I took a recon-naissance ride to the lip of a small green valley where we grazed some of our cattle. I sat the biggest blackest prettiest geld-ing I had ever owned. Obviously, some American blood had mixed with the criollo. Now, don't believe that racetrack superstition about not putting your money on a horse with three stockings. This boy had them and could flat out run. I called him Ventarrón, which means "big wind" or "hurricane." Harry had broken him and given him to me. Harry had his favorite of the moment, a beautiful chestnut stallion not as big as my horse but faster over short distances, a six-year-old with a chest like Hercules and an obtuse streak like Butch's. But, same as with Butch, Harry could handle him.

"There's one of our neighbors." Harry pointed across the valley, where I saw the dentist, Dr. Newton. He waved. Harry waved back, and we cantered toward him, scattering a few lazy beeves and calves, flushing two chinchillas and a red fox.

"I wonder how he'll look at us this time."

"Like a lucky couple in love," Harry said.

El Doctor sat a sturdy skewbald mare of the type back home we'd call an Indian pony, some sort of Argentine mustang. He seemed glad to see us. "First time I've seen you folks since Florida Street."

I took a few deep breaths.

"We've been in one of the other valleys and around home mostly," Harry said.

"I've seen some of your hands out and about. They keep busy."

"They're a good bunch. And Etta herds their women and kids around."

I suppose Dr. Newton would naturally look at me for a moment after Harry said that. But I'd swear he scrutinized us both. I wished Harry had called me "Maggie," but Dr. Newton already knew me as "Etta." I smiled and inhaled deeply.

He faced us. "I have such a big spread and so many hands I don't have much to do except ride around and supervise. And pay the bills."

"You have your dental practice."

"Yes. Once a year at least I can keep up on what's going on in the world."

I gasped, pretended to cough, looked at Harry. He smiled, looked calm. No wonder he made such a good highwayman. He toted his full arsenal, I my inside gun.

Harry's stallion bobbed his head and snorted. Dr. Newton's mare executed the fastest 180-degree turn I'd ever seen and pumped her hind legs straight at Harry's horse. She'd have sent Harry and his mount a considerable piece if she'd connected.

Dr. Newton kept his seat, despite the surprise, and spun her back facing us. He and Harry laughed.

"So your mare's not in heat," Harry said.

"No. Maybe I could let you know when she is. That's a fine stallion of yours."

"You bet. I'll bring him over. They'll make good babies."

"I suppose you know," Dr. Newton said, "there's been a lot of crossbreeding with the original Spanish stock, mostly with Thoroughbreds and draft horses."

"We figured they had some of that," Harry said.

"If anything, their endurance and intelligence are greater. Let me know when you want to buy more stock."

"Count on it. You've helped us a lot."

We jabbered a bit more, mainly about livestock and the weather and how General Roca had run the country for more than twenty years no matter who held the presidency.

I kept expecting Dr. Newton to ask our partner's whereabouts, maybe throw in a few casual-sounding questions about what we used to do in the States.

But in a few minutes, with a touch to his hat brim, a smile, and a wave, he rode off on the little brown-and-white mare that broke the heart of Harry's stallion.

"What do you think?" I said.

"I think he knows but doesn't give a hang."

We worked all through the 1903-04 summer, enjoying a bright warm Christmas and New Year's like those we seem to have nowadays in San Diego. In late March while we played cassino one night and talked about one thing and another, Butch offered an idea we liked immediately.

"Let's take a break from all this ranching and visit the States," Butch said.

"We could see our folks and old friends." I used a seven from my hand to pick up a three and a four.

Harry took a king with a king. "And find out the law's official attitude toward the Bunch."

"Maybe they've decided there isn't any Bunch," I said.

We made our fall sales, hired a foreman Dr. Newton recommended, packed our essentials for camping and traveling, loaded everything onto mules, and started for Rawson with two of our hands who would return with the mules, saddle horses, and camping gear.

On the second day out we had to hunker down in a ravine during a sandstorm, gritty and powerful and even a little scary. Fortunately it lasted only an hour or so.

The next day on the plateaus we had passed our second ombú and a Patagonian hare with her brood when we encountered a sorrowful sight. I mention it to counteract the malignant lies some people have said or published about my husband, embellishing their Sundance Kid stories about Harry being a vicious killer, hot-tempered, and other such calumnies.

So we encountered a young Indian couple with five little ones, the oldest, a boy not more than ten. They sat on the side of the main route where a trail intersected it.

"Be careful," Butch said. "They're probably robbers." He yanked his carbine out of its saddle boot.

"Ease off." I thought he might shoot.

"They're harmless, Leroy." Harry pushed the barrel of Butch's carbine down.

When we drew closer I could see the children better and how the man and woman seemed frightened, and that some of the youngsters sat crying their eyes out while hugging a dead mule lying on its side. Their parents looked every bit as upset.

"Looks like their life's possessions piled up there," Harry said.

I wiped my eyes. "I've never seen a sorrier sight."

The woman squeezed one of the man's arms in both hands. They looked too timid and scared to even spit.

"Watch his free hand," Butch said. He pointed his carbine at the man. Harry motioned for Butch to lower the rifle. Slowly, frowning, Butch did so. We reined up.

"Ask them what happened, Sugar."

The man stood and removed his sombrero, holding it in front of him with both hands, a little fellow about my size, spoke fair Spanish and understood mine. His woman stood beside him.

I soon had their story. "They had to pull up stakes in a hurry where they worked," I told Harry and Butch, "way out where Christ lost his jacket. That's the Spanish equivalent for 'way over yonder.' Turns out the overseer, a white man, and the

Spanish version of 'a mean s.o.b.,' threatened to dismiss them and confiscate their mule if the wife wouldn't come to his bed. On command."

"I'd have shot that son of a bitch," Butch said.

"You would, Leroy," Harry told him, "but this poor farmer wouldn't. Around here Indians don't shoot white men. The whole countryside would've been after him."

The man had a dribble of a mustache, his sombrero not fit for his dead mule. No, they had to run. The poor woman, so skinny and plain. But it doesn't take much in the looks department when a man has lived in Patagonia all winter without a woman, or in plenty of other places, for that matter. As an example, Butch had a romance going for a while with an Indian girl down the trail from us. He got red and huffy when Harry and I found out and kidded him, so we never mentioned it again.

"The farmer tried to draw his pay," I told Harry and Butch, "but found out he owed it all to the owner's store. So they stole some food and lit out, not having any idea of their fate. They couldn't work just anywhere. And fearing their former boss would have the law after them, they had to get far away where nobody knew them."

"I know that feeling," Harry said.

And the mule dropped dead on them.

"That mule had been their transportation, a big wage earner, and almost a pet, already old when they got him before the oldest child arrived. And here they are."

Butch fidgeted. "We'd better get a move on."

"Leroy . . ." Harry faced me. "Sugar, have our boys distribute our youngest mule's load to our other pack animals and turn that one over to these Indians." Harry undid his shirt, removed a few twenty-dollar gold pieces and a passel of Argentine pesos from his money belt, and dismounted. He handed the money to that poor farmer. I never saw such grateful expressions as those on the faces of that unfortunate couple. I hoped they wouldn't have trouble, wouldn't draw suspicion, spending the gold coins.

One of our hands led the young mule to the children, whose faces immediately beamed like sunbursts, shined like the gold in their father's hand.

And before any of them could speak, Harry had remounted and spurred his horse toward Rawson. There is your Mr. Terrible Sundance Kid for you.

At our last camp before Rawson we packed most of our weapons. The next morning I put on a pretty red dress, braided a red ribbon into my hair, and placed both derringers into my purse. Harry wore his inside gun and, strapped above his ankles, covered by his boots, his derringers.

Butch, toting his inside gun, took off ahead of us to get to the cantina.

On the boat trip from Rawson we were the only English-speaking passengers. But when we changed in Bahía Blanca to the Buenos Aires steamer we had company Harry and Butch could talk to, an older man with silvery sprigs of hair squirting out under the crown of his brown city hat, a medium paunch, and a mountain of words to unload.

"I'm from New York," he said. "Going home. How about you men?"

"Florida," Harry said, right on top of Butch's "California."

I sat nearby listening. The talk, all from this fellow, smelled of braggadocio and dullness, even lies, until about thirty minutes up the coast.

"Just before heading this way," he said, "I read in the *Herald* that we have entered the age of flight. Yessiree. You folks probably missed it." His look included me.

Harry and Butch nodded. I waited.

"They say a couple of bicycle-makers from Ohio, brothers named Wright, claimed to have built an engine for one of their gliders, lay down on the bottom wing, and drove it through the sky." His chest puffed out as though he'd done this craziness himself and proud of it. "The first time, you see. In North Carolina. *The Times* wouldn't print it. Didn't believe it."

Another lie. Obviously, this man's bubble moved off plumb. If we had any doubts about his being anything but a big bag of wind, that convinced us.

21

We passed through Buenos Aires and New York without lingering except to buy gifts for everyone. Butch took the train west directly from New York, planning to leave word at Robbers' Roost or the ranch in New Mexico.

"I'm praying Leroy won't return with Kid Curry," I told Harry.

My husband patted my hand. I didn't know how he meant it.

So late May of 1904 had arrived when we checked most of our belongings at the Montgomery train station and boarded the stage for Selma.

We enjoyed a splendid homecoming, as everyone called it, even though my home was on the road with Harry. In our absence, Dierdre and Grania had married Dallas County boys. Dunleavy and Flann still helped on the home place but had leased a section nearby and would be marrying soon, like my older brothers.

"So now you speak five languages, plus the English."

"How's that, Momma?"

"The Spanish you've learned since leaving. And you already knew Gaelic, Latin, Greek, and French. I'm mighty proud of you, Etta Margaret."

I tried to explain that I knew only enough Latin to explain the grammar, some French phrases from my introductory teaching and reading, that the Greek I taught had been the Greek plays in English, and that I had forgotten most of the Gaelic. She wouldn't hear it.

"You're doing what I would have done if I'd had the opportunity," Momma said. "I wish all my younguns could be like you, instead of follow a mule or churn butter."

My folks seemed mighty pleased with their gifts, which, being from New York, had added pleasure and value. At Abercrombie and Fitch, Harry had purchased three new .44-caliber lever-action Henry repeating rifles and a box of cartridges each for Pappy, Dunleavy, and Flann.

"That's that damn Yankee rifle like Sherman's troops had," Pappy said. "You load it on Sunday and it fires all week." He loved it.

For Pappy, Harry added a silver half-pint flask, a fifth of Glenfiddich, and a pith helmet. "Pappy won't wear that jungle hat," I had told Harry. He smiled, looked away.

At Wanamaker's, I'd bought Sunday dresses for Momma and my sisters, Sunday hats for each, and, at Tiffany's, a diamond lapel watch for Momma.

"I hope you didn't go and buy me real diamonds, Etta Margaret."

"They are real, Momma, and you'd better wear that watch."

We sat on the porch that first night, a lovely evening, and caught up on the news while explaining to Pappy and Momma about our life in Argentina. Dierdre and Grania would visit another time with their husbands, but my youngest brothers joined us for supper. We referred to Butch as "Leroy."

I said, "Leroy is Harry's good friend and investing pard from banking days."

We sipped from jars of Pappy's best corn, although he and Harry drank most of it. I noted, however, that Dunleavy and Flann had advanced considerably in that department.

"James J. Jeffries is still heavyweight champion," Pappy said. "But he couldn't have whipped Sullivan in John L's prime." He spat off the porch and nodded.

Pappy looked thrilled to learn we had sat near Sullivan during the Four Cohans' performance. And Momma tittered to hear about our spotting Lillian Russell. Teddy Roosevelt seemed like a good president, Pappy said, despite being a Republican and only forty-two years old with just six months as vice president before succeeding the murdered McKinley.

"You know you're getting old, Etta Margaret," Pappy said, "when the president is younger than you are. I thought the war would put an end to assassinations. Still, there's no such connection to this one, I don't reckon."

McKinley had been dead for only a week when the folks heard.

"Dunleavy learned about it in Selma when he took the wagon for coffee, salt, and sugar," Momma said.

I mentioned what the braggart on the boat told us about the Wright brothers.

My people hadn't heard that report.

"No man has ever been able to invent a flying machine," Pappy said.

"It's not natural," Momma said.

The rest of us agreed. Dunleavy and Flann spat off the porch and laughed.

Full dark came on slowly and bright with stars, reminding me of similar nights in Patagonia. "Down there we have constellations, like the Southern Cross, that can't be seen from Alabama. Lots of things. But not the Big Dipper."

"Just an astoundment," Momma said.

Pappy nodded. "During the war we followed the Big Dipper all the way north."

They loved hearing about Buenos Aires and New York.

"We want to know more about Lillian Russell," Momma said.

"Yes." Flann leaned forward. "Is she real pretty? How old is she?"

Dunleavy asked, "Did she have Diamond Jim with her? What'd he look like?"

I told them what I could and urged Momma, "You've just got to take off one day soon and go somewhere."

"But there's so much to do here."

"It'll wait till you get back."

"Pappy and me have talked about visiting his kin in Montgomery."

"That's a start, Momma, but not what I mean." She had never been to Montgomery, fifty miles away. Momma wouldn't have seen electric lights if she hadn't gone to Selma some on Saturdays. The next day I told her about Montgomery.

We stayed a week. Harry and I had a bedroom together now that my sisters had married, though in such a creaky old wooden house we felt embarrassed to do anything. But Harry remained patient and understanding. My sisters when they visited got flustered around him, same as usual, as did the wives of my older brothers, Gareth and Tyrone, though they tried hard to not show it.

One day when all the boys visited, Dunleavy and Flann suggested having a shooting match. "You too, Harry," Dunleavy said.

Harry glanced at me.

I hesitated, but nodded. "Sure. Me too."

"No you don't, Sis," Dunleavy said. "You showed us last time you can still shoot. Now let Harry represent you."

Flann backed him. "No women this time."

Pappy, Dunleavy, and Flann used their new Henrys, while Tyrone and Gareth, who had missed the last match, shot the Spencer.

"You're at a disadvantage, Mr. Parker," Pappy said, "not having a rifle of your own. Not fair."

"It's all right, Mr. Place. I'll do the best I can."

Harry borrowed a Henry and won easily.

I played the piano every day. I missed a few notes but nobody complained.

And one night Harry said, "Sugar, I'm going to buy you that piano I promised."

"I don't see how we can take one so far south, and to the foothills of the Andes."

"We'll buy it in Buenos Aires, build a special wagon for it."

"I know you mean it, Honey." I'm sure my tone told him I didn't expect it.

Momma prepared another of her wonderful lunch baskets for us to take along. I sat in the kitchen with her and could see by her expression and starting sentences and stopping in the middle that she hesitated about saying something, or asking it. We had plenty of money, with more where that came from, and I knew Harry wouldn't mind, if that's what she asked.

Momma finished tightening the lid on a jar of peach preserves and faced me. "You still don't have no younguns."

"No, Momma."

"Gareth and Tyrone and their wives made us grandparents sometime ago."

"I know, Momma. You wrote me."

She picked up the preserves and fiddled with the lid. "It's that, you being our oldest girl, but Dierdre and Grania are going to make us grandparents before you do, looks like, and you've been married lots longer."

"I know, Momma." I felt too embarrassed to say we were "trying," the way couples announce to everyone nowadays. "We'd like babies, but they haven't happened."

"You're twenty-seven going on twenty-eight."

"I know, Momma."

"You and Harry. Why, your children would be so beautiful." She smiled. "Is it all right I mentioned this?"

"Of course, Momma."

My parents walked us to the front porch, where Pappy gave Harry a quart jar of his good corn whiskey. Pappy reentered the house while Flann brought the wagon and team around to carry us to the stage stop in Selma.

We stepped off the porch and into the yard.

And Pappy returned, strutting toward us and wearing his pith helmet.

Later Momma wrote me that, for the remainder of his life, he wore it every time he went into town, took his flask too.

22

After a few days of hard dusty traveling by stage and train we reached Cheyenne, where we purchased a nice-stepping mostly white Appaloosa mare for me, a big blue-black Morgan gelding with one white front foot for Harry. We called them Sullivan and Jeffries, and we directed them north.

When we rode close to Harry's home place I couldn't see any laundry hanging on the line or on the bushes in back. Any dogs could have been under the house, but they should have been bouncing out and barking. I didn't see any chickens or ducks, and the chimney didn't smoke. The corral gate hung open. The barn door sat askew. I got a bad feeling.

Before we rode into the front yard we could see boards on the windows. Weeds, high and scraggly, that Mrs. Longbaugh had battled so successfully, dominated the place. My apprehension grew. Harry frowned as he took in the scene. A small hook, just high enough to keep little children out, I suppose, held the door closed.

"He killed my momma," Harry said.

"We can't be sure."

"No, Sugar. He killed her if he never laid another hand on her. He killed her with his yelling and spitefulness and niggardliness. He worked her to death and then probably turned his back and walked out without a second thought."

We dismounted and hitched the reins to the porch railing. Inside, nothing seemed changed, just dusty, unlived in. There hadn't been much worth stealing unless you were poorer than

Harry's mother and stepfather. And I couldn't find our wedding portrait.

Harry opened the bedroom closet. I saw a few of her clothes, though not her best dress, which we brought her from Denver three years earlier. That convinced me.

"She would have wanted to be buried in that dress," Harry said.

"I'm so sorry, Honey." I put my arm around him.

We looked some more. On a flimsy bedside table I spotted a small stack of opened envelopes, letters inside. I picked them up and showed Harry: letters I had written to her for both of us. The cigar box that had held the letters sat empty beside them.

"Judging by the date of the last one," I said, "and the time it takes them to get here, I'd guess she's been gone quite a spell. But there should be more letters."

I never saw Harry's expression blacker nor wilder. If his stepfather had been there, Harry might have beaten him to death with something akin to pleasure.

I put my arms around him. "Let's ride into Sundance and talk to the woman at the general store. Your mother's friend. She handles the mail."

"Yes, but first I want to swing by the place where the son of a bitch lived before Ma married him."

"What if he—What if you—Never mind."

When we reined up amid barking hounds at his stepfather's original place nearby, a skinny blond boy about sixteen sat on the porch whittling. He seemed friendly enough, left his chair, and walked up to us.

"You one of the grandsons?" Harry asked.

The boy nodded.

"Where's everybody else?"

"It's just me and my ma and pa and brothers. They're in the trees over yonder gathering a store of firewood. I'm getting over a sick spell so they let me stay home."

"Your grandpappy with them?"

I studied the boy's face. I hoped he wouldn't lie, and I don't think he did.

"He lit out right after your ma died. Texas, he told us."

Harry studied him. I watched my husband like a shotgun rider eyes a highwayman. I didn't see any trouble, felt relieved when Harry spoke.

"Much obliged." He nodded, started to turn his Morgan away.

"Miss Etta," the boy said. "Kid. I'm proud to meet you. I've only seen you from a distance. But we hear a lot about you and The Wild Bunch."

"We've been split up and out of the country for three years," Harry told him.

"That's what your ma said. But you hear talk in town like the whole Bunch is still going. I'm awfully sorry about your momma, Kid. She was mighty good to all of us."

Dusk came on as we reached Sundance. Mrs. Bohanan stood with a key in her hand near the door, about to close the store. She'd known Harry since he'd been a tyke, of course, and right away she started hugging him and carrying on, glad to see him but upset all over again about his mother's death. They'd been best friends, and Harry had told me Mrs. Bohanan probably had read my letters to his mother for her.

"Your momma died of pneumonia, Harry. About a year ago now." She thought a moment and gave us the date. "Miss Etta, your letters kept coming. I saved them." She walked to the counter, reached under it, and handed me six unopened letters I'd mailed from Argentina and a card from Alabama. "Been expecting you since I read the card. The postmaster in Deadwood didn't know how many stamps to put on, or I'd've wrote you about her passing."

"How did she look in that Denver dress?" Harry said.

"Oh, how she used to brag about that! I guarantee you, she looked beautiful. I sent word to the mortician at Deadwood and he come over and did just a wonderful job. She looked so like being alive. And so many folks went to her funeral. The preacher—"

"What name is she buried under?"

"Why, his. They were married a long time."

"She never loved him. And he treated her mean."

"I know, Harry. No. She loved only your father. And before him . . . Well, I reckon you might as well know now."

"Mr. Hickok. Ma told me last time we were here."

"She and Wild Bill made a splendid couple, Harry. But she felt Bill didn't seem ready for settling in. Then your father come along and nothing else mattered."

"I should have been here. I wouldn't have allowed her to be put to rest under that man's name."

"Your momma told me time after time how you had tried to get her to Denver or someplace where you could take care of her. And the money you gave her. And she felt so proud that you learned to write."

"Just a few words Etta taught me."

"And you, Miss Etta, all the letters. Fort Worth. New Orleans. New York. South America. They thrilled her so, I had to read them to her over and over, including a batch when she got bad sick. She tried to do the right thing, Harry, staying here, what she was cut out to do. And she felt mighty proud of both of you."

"I'm reimbursing you for the undertaker and burial."

"No, son. She was my good friend. Let me do that for her."

Harry paused, then: "What about the headstone?"

"Her death certificate carries his name, of course. But he wouldn't pay for a marker. He come to town to let me know she passed away. Then lit out. Texas, they say."

Harry said, "Much obliged, Miz Bohanan."

"Wait." She walked behind the counter and brought out our wedding picture, pin holes in the corners. "She had me take this off the wall. Gave it to me just before—"

"Keep it if you want," Harry said.

Mrs. Bohanan nodded. "I'd be mighty proud to."

Full dark had come by the time we left Mrs. Bohanan and walked the horses along the main street to the livery stable, paid for their keep, and walked to the boarding house to spend the night. There at supper and at breakfast the next morning a dozen men, including old-timers, recognized Harry, using his first name, except the younger ones, who called him "Kid" or "Sundance." Each shook his hand, stopped to chat, tipped their hats to me, and said "Howdy, Missus." I saw as plain as snow in the Rockies, some knew Harry but that others had wanted to meet him, heard he'd come to town, sought him out.

Harry had one question for all of them: "Any Pinkertons been around?"

We found the grave of Harry's father right away. But his mother's lacked a marker so we couldn't be certain of it. We returned to town and talked again to the barber, that sometime stonecutter, who confirmed that she rested next to Harry's father. We arranged for him to make a new gravestone in fine marble and place it at Mrs. Longbaugh's resting place. Harry ordered carving of his mother's dates of birth and death, her place of birth, and "Beloved Wife And Mother." Her name said "Longbaugh" too. Bet your boots on that.

23

America Connolly had been mending a barbed-wire fence when I noticed him look up at our approach. A little boy, barefoot and hatless, in jeans and plaid shirt, played around his feet. America's horse, the same steel-gray Quarter Horse he rode the last time we saw him, watched us from the corral nearby. Two hounds ran up barking, but America quieted them. He still gripped the pliers in one hand when he hurried toward us, boots kicking up dust, America grinning, almost laughing, taking off his Stetson with the other hand and pitching it into the air and giving out a little yelp.

And when Harry dismounted and they met, he and America gave each other one of those big hugs, an *abrazo*, the way Mexicans do their men friends, like men do in Argentina.

"My God, Kid," he said, and "Jesús, María, and José" and "Miss Etta, you're prettier than ever," plus "I'd been hoping you'd show up ever since Butch rode through a while back," and, picking up the little fellow, who had followed him, "This *pequeñito* is Little America." He stepped toward his house. "Come on."

America seemed to have made an easy transition from best knife-throwing member of The Wild Bunch, a good shot too, to farmer and rancher, husband and father.

We dismounted and tied our horses to the front-porch railing.

"How'd you all find me?"

"We asked around in Alma," Harry said. "We'd heard you liked the area. They told us where you had a little spread here in the middle of the desert."

"I got it cheap right after I left the Bunch and married Catalina. We built this little two-room house of bricks we made from adobe dug at the edge of the creek. Got wood for the roof in Alma. I break and sell horses, raise a few beeves. We got a milk cow, some goats, chickens, cats and dogs, and a little vegetable garden. Catalina planted the roses and geraniums. The cactus was already here."

America pointed northwest. "The Sangre de Cristo Mountains, part of the Rockies. Our creek starts up there and has water most of the year. I have a windmill and a well in the back." He pointed due west. "Those mountains are the Manzanos."

A young woman stepped onto the porch near us. "This is Catalina." She carried a tot about half as big as Little America, now on the ground and hugging his father's leg while watching us with wide-open eyes blacker than the devil's heart.

Catalina, lovely, hair as dark as mine, eyes as black as her hair, had skin the color of the handmade adobe bricks of their bread oven in the yard near us. When she smiled, her teeth showed as white as the spectacular high clouds in the sky that day. Catalina owned a fine figure, and just nineteen, we learned, with a third youngun on the way.

America got out the tanglefoot, and he and Harry sat on the porch and sipped quite a bit of it while I helped Catalina prepare supper. She spoke good English so I didn't try to show off my Argentine Spanish, just washed and chopped vegetables and enjoyed watching the little boys play on the kitchen floor while she told me about the sunsets and star-filled nights and how hard America worked to make a life for them.

"Sometimes it's difficult, Miss Etta, but we love it out here in this high desert."

She had a soft voice, her accent slight, charming.

"And you love each other. I can see that."

"You're wondering, aren't you, Miss Etta?"

"About what?"

"If I know about you and your husband, about America and The Wild Bunch."

"All right. I suppose so."

"My husband told me everything after Butch Cassidy visited. But America says he personally never shot nobody, and I believe him."

"What I've seen, the Bunch was mainly robbers."

"That's what America says. But he wouldn't say nothing about his conversations with Mr. Cassidy. Said he thought it better not to. I felt they talked some kind of code. Never gave me details. Changing subjects or falling silent if I walked close. It's good Mr. Cassidy didn't stay long. We didn't feel much friendship."

"Butch takes some getting used to." Butch never liked the young fellow, so it surprised me to hear he'd visited America. Perhaps Butch needed something.

"Miss Etta, I've heard so many nice things about you and your husband. America admires you both." Her "things" came out "theengs."

Catalina said she was sixteen when America quit the Bunch and married her. "My father went from spread to spread shoeing horses and mules. I was the oldest girl, didn't have any brothers, and he often took me along. America and I met on a ranch where he'd hired on as a hand on the other side of Alma and I showed up with my father. I'm educated through seventh grade. That's two years more than America. But he had learned English from his father and helped me with mine."

I didn't admit that America had two more years' learning than Harry. "You're the prettiest Spanish girl I've seen, even in South America. And your English is good."

"Mexican. Thank you, Miss Etta, but I have mistakes."

"I thought everyone in New Mexico was Spanish."

Catalina laughed, her teeth again humbling the clouds in whiteness and beauty. "So many say they're Spanish instead of Mexican. I don't know why."

In those days, sometimes you hesitated to ask a person's race. Harry and I had wondered about "Connolly" and felt just by looking that America had to be a half-breed. But we never asked him about it.

Now Catalina seemed to want us to know about them, same as they knew about us. "America's mother was an Apache from the White Mountain Reservation in Arizona, his father a whiskey trader, an Irishman. They traveled around selling. When America was twelve his parents died in a blizzard in Colorado. He worked four years as a ranch hand for next to nothing. Then one day Butch Cassidy and Elza Lay stopped at that very ranch for something. When they left, America lit out with them."

"So America was only sixteen when he joined the Bunch?"

"And now he's twenty-two." Catalina smiled. "My husband retired at nineteen."

That's one way of viewing it. But I had seen enough of their digs, just on that afternoon, to know they worked from can to can't but remained as poor as Jacob's turkey. They plainly didn't have much. And the eastern New Mexico desert, although beautiful, is harsh on a man if he's trying to scrape an existence out of it.

After a while, just to be polite, I helped Harry and America with the tanglefoot.

Next we had a meal of tasty beef enchiladas and beans. When Catalina put the boys to bed we took chairs into the yard and sat under the stars, listened to the coyotes, and talked. America brought us up to date about some of the Bunch.

"Elza Lay is still in prison," America said. "Too bad. So decent, nice to me."

"And he has a family," I said.

America nodded. "Harry Tracy broke out of prison in 1902, killed several people, and got cornered over by Davenport, up in Washington. Didn't want to visit no prison again or hang either. Shot himself."

I estimated that as good riddance. But I kept shut.

America saved the good news until last.

"Kid Curry dynamited the Denver and Río Grande railroad train at Parachute, Colo., just last June. On the run when he got wounded and trapped in a gully two days later. Shot himself in the head."

Kid Curry, that worthless no good Harvey Logan, done in. My husband looked at me, his expression difficult to read. But he lifted his jar and tilted it toward me, ever so slightly. I took a big swallow from mine. As books and articles have come out mentioning those times, I've read in detail about the deaths of Tracy and Curry.

"Butch didn't mention any others," America said. "Claimed his horse moved too slow and had a mean streak, so I traded for one of mine. His is fine since getting rested and fed right. Little America rides him bareback with a rope for a bridle 'round his nose. He's mighty good with the kids." He hesitated, then added, "We call him Sundance."

Back inside, America built us a fire in the living room chimney, and we pitched our bedrolls in front of it, feet toward the flames. We felt good.

"What do you think, Sugar?"

"Wonderful evening. A fine young couple, sincere, hard working. Cute boys."

"They sure have it rough though."

"And winter's closer every minute in this high country."

"Sugar, what would you think about staying here a spell and giving them a hand?"

I leaned over and hugged Harry. "As Butch might say, my thought exactly." I also felt that their ability to procreate might rub off on us.

At breakfast Harry said, "'Merica. Missus. Etta and I'd like to help out a few days. We could pitch our tent. Wouldn't get in the way. Earn our keep."

The expressions on America's and Catalina's faces warmed every bone in me.

"The west side of the house don't get much wind," America said.

Catalina squeezed his hand. "And the afternoon sun will heat it up some for you."

And so we stayed on. I milked the cow, helped care for the vegetable patch, and pumped water from their well to the troughs for the livestock. All of us cleared brush so America could plow the land and plant a feed crop for next spring. I helped Catalina with the boys and the cooking. And Harry broke horses with America, expanded the corral, and took a wagon into Alma for a load of hay.

For my birthday Catalina fixed a delicious meal of beans, tortillas, chiles, and *albóndiga* soup with the best meatballs I ever tasted. For regular meat we had roast beef, a cottontail rabbit Harry bagged with America's 20-gauge shotgun, and a chicken, whose neck I wrung myself.

"This is a feast," Harry said.

"The best we've had in a long time," I added.

America said, "I can't help bragging. This meal is worth photographing."

That echoed a Spanish saying I'd heard in Buenos Aires. I agreed.

"Save room for dessert." Catalina had made a chocolate cake. I'd concocted a molasses-pecan pie that would have made Momma proud.

By then we'd had a few drinks and went into the yard to a paloverde tree and strung up a piñata Catalina made out of paper and sticks to resemble a donkey. But only three-year-old Little America could hit the thing when blindfolded. When the boy broke it and just a few individually wrapped popcorn balls tumbled out, I started sniffling. He couldn't know what that toy donkey might have carried if his mother and father had been better off. But we had a big time. Besides, we celebrated my birthday, not his. Of course, the boy didn't know that either.

The first snow just dusted the cactus. But we knew what lay in store.

"Sugar, this is going to remind us of winter at Robbers' Roost."

"I know, but shouldn't we stay through February, until Catalina's baby is born and she gets back on her feet?"

"Of course. I'll help lay in more firewood."

"You think our tent will hold up?"

"If the snow's not too heavy."

We didn't look forward to the weather of the next few months.

Two days later America told us, "Catalina's first babies came in spring and summer. Her mother stayed with us to help. We're scared about this one, the cold and the isolation, and all. I need to take her and the boys in the wagon to Fort Sumner to be with her parents until after the baby's born. We just follow the Pecos. We hope you understand. You all can stay on here in the house."

"Thing is, 'Merica, I promised Etta we'd spend the winter in a city. Let's hire you a hand or two to take care of this place while you're gone."

America agreed. Harry insisted on giving him money to cover a helper's wages, and we started for Denver, where we had funds in a bank.

Denver in those days didn't match Buenos Aires, but at least it had plays and musicals in English. We enjoyed them a lot more, especially Harry. And we lodged at the Brown Palace. In March we rode to the ranch at Alma, New Mexico, found a few friends holed up there, and sat around and jawed for a couple of days. Anytime someone brought out a jug I participated to feel included.

"Butch came through a few months ago asking about you, Kid," one of the ranch hands said.

Harry asked, "Any news about Charlie Siringo?"

"It's a girl." Catalina stood on the porch and held the little scamp up for us to see. Catalina looked as beautiful as ever, and I'd swear the baby smiled at us.

America said, "We hoped you would get here about now." Their sons hugged his legs.

I couldn't imagine a better reception. We dismounted. They stepped off the porch, and we had hugs all around.

"The little heiress is going to be a beauty," I said.

"She can't miss." Catalina smiled. "We named her after my mother and you: Etta María Guadalupe."

Again, we set up our tent and pitched in on the chores, the work plentiful and hugely satisfying, for we knew how much we helped out. But before long I began to notice that Harry seemed restless, and I thought America looked preoccupied.

That didn't surprise me concerning my husband. Nearly four years had passed since we'd conducted any financial trans-actions in the former way. I suspected he had the itch. But did America have it too? He hadn't lived such a long time in the old style, the way Harry had, and now he had stakes in the ground, with Catalina and three little ones, and a small spread that at least gave them a hardscrabble independence.

I noticed Harry and America stopped work frequently to talk beyond hearing from the house, Harry leaning on his ax or a shovel, or the two of them sitting on a corral fence, or squatting in the shade of the barn. Sometimes they'd not even look at each other, just smoke, lean against a fence, watch the Sangre de Cristo Mountains.

One night while Harry and I lay in our tent I tried to ease into my concerns. I might as well have blurted it out through a megaphone.

Harry politely interrupted me. "'Merica needs capital. The winter killed some of what little livestock they had." Harry told me the plan. "We won't take our best horses."

"I understand, but what's my part?"

"Sugar," Harry told me to my profound disappointment, "'Merica wants Catalina to think we're in Texas buying horses." He hesitated.

I knew it hurt him to say the rest.

"You'll have to stay home."

24

America Connolly, quite an animated little fellow anyway—probably the Irish in him more than the Apache—was more excited than I'd ever seen him, funny too. He waved his arms and danced around and made faces to illustrate the various situations. The humor didn't rest so much in what he said but the way he presented it and the entertainment I received from it. But I got annoyed again over not getting to go along.

"So after a couple of days in Amarillo," America said, "we knew the stage schedule and the lay of the land, and we planned our move for just before dusk."

Catalina, in the kitchen bathing Etta María Guadalupe, called Lupita, couldn't hear us. Harry and America had returned just that day, and now in late afternoon the three of us sat on the porch while watching the Manzanos and Sangre de Cristos. America should have gone on the stage. Make a better living than throwing knives or ranching.

"We didn't get a thing, not a trinket or a tiepin or a Mexican peso. I know Sundance wouldn't take anything from individuals anyway, although I might have if any passengers had been on the stage. Kid, I thought you'd shoot their horses, you were so disappointed, our planning and all. Miss Etta, we hid out a couple of days and tried again."

Harry smiled, sipped his drink from a small jar while smoking a store-bought cigarette from some packs he'd purchased in Amarillo. But I imagined his wrath in the scene America described.

On their second attempt at returning to financial transactions of the old sort, Mr. Longbaugh and Mr. Connolly enjoyed more success.

"We got a thousand dollars in gold coins," America said. "The stagecoach driver told us the money belonged to a wealthy Easterner with a ranch on the Canadian River. Said the man would order up a posse and chase us down. We laughed at that."

That rancher must be a greenhorn or had made a mighty small sale, no more than that for his shipment. America and Catalina's half didn't stretch near enough to help the way they needed. Harry, smiling and sipping and smoking, seemed contented to let America present the whole story.

"So we rode south into the Llano Estacado and hung around Lubbock in one cantina or another, talking horses and cattle and weather and horse thieves. Nobody recognized Sundance or me either. One man after another told us The Wild Bunch had been split up and run off by the Pinkertons and progress. That had some truth in it but we didn't like hearing 'run off.'" America laughed. "Kid, I thought you were gonna slug the second man who told us that.

"Around Lubbock we had to ride through one dust blow after another. Awful country. And the rattlesnakes! Spooked our mounts a couple of times, but nobody fell off. At Lubbock just before dark we got around two hundred dollars from the railway station. Had to tie up and gag the only man still working. On the way out of town we broke in to the bank by the rear door, dynamited the safe open, and made a nice collection. Then we skedaddled out of town into the night."

America had become dramatic. That term "nice collection" was one of Harry's.

From Lubbock, America said, they continued south through the Llano Estacado to the Mustang Draw, turned west and followed it into New Mexico. "We'd reached the other side of Roswell when an eastbound stage surprised us. We made a collection from it, laid low overnight, and rode into Roswell the next day after looping around to come in from opposite the stage holdup.

"The bank and assaying office sat side by side. We found out the sheriff and a posse had gone looking for us to the east. We did all right in Roswell, didn't we, Kid? But I thought the clerk in the mining office wouldn't never cooperate."

Uh-oh. "What happened?"

"Sundance knocked him off his feet and through the back door."

Big trouble finally caught up with my two happy marauders while they rode in the twilight just beyond Roswell. Someone possessing a fair aim, but fortunately not an excellent one, thank the Good Lord, fired a high-powered rifle bullet through the rump of America's horse and apparently right into the poor animal's heart.

"My horse dropped like he'd been clubbed. It must have been a buffalo gun like a Sharp's .50. I fell clear and stepped close to get my rifle and saddlebags. Miss Etta, Sundance had thirty yards on me by then. He sure knows horseflesh. But I felt like a goner, due to be a jailhouse guest.

"While I jumped around figuring what to do, Sundance raced back for me, fired one round at full gallop from his Colt Bisley, and knocked the pins out from under the shooter, maybe an old-time buffalo hunter at least a hundred yards away. A marvelous shot, Miss Etta, especially in that light and off a galloping horse.

"Then Sundance came alongside me. With saddlebags and rifle I jumped up behind him. We lit out flying. Pretty soon it was full dark. I think Sundance hit the retired buffalo hunter in the leg. He could've killed him if he'd wanted. We all know that."

I felt relieved knowing Harry hadn't killed the hunter, probably the only man Harry ever shot.

"We found another good horse for me during the night, saddled and bridled, and lit out north for Fort Sumner. Bought that string of mustangs we herded when we arrived in time for dinner today. I figured it up, Miss Etta. We rode seven hundred miles in sixteen days, traded horses seven, eight times, and acquired more than four thousand dollars, gold and paper. And Sundance saved my life, Miss Etta. I'll never forget that."

Not sixteen days, but seventeen. And I fretted every minute.

Over the next few weeks Harry helped America break the mustangs, found some good ones for selling. And they cleared land, which they planted to corn, more for the livestock than for America and Catalina. She and I conditioned their vegetable patch for another season and planted it in early April of 1905, when Harry and I decided to leave. I must have been every bit as restless as Harry to get moving. At least he'd had that long diversion to Texas with America.

"We sure wish you all would stay on," America told us.

"You'll want to see my next baby," Catalina said. She patted her belly. "It'll get here long before winter, so I won't be going to Fort Sumner."

"We'd best see after our investment in Argentina," Harry said. "But if things don't work out here, you good folks come on down to Patagonia. We've got land to spare and mountains that would make you feel right at home."

"We're grateful, Kid. Maybe someday. But we'll be fine, thanks to our trip."

That reminded the boys of their days with the Bunch, I suppose, for all of a sudden America proposed a pistol shoot, and Harry agreed.

"Count me out," I said. "My weapon's the rifle."

Catalina giggled. "Me too. Mine's a measuring cup."

We walked a few yards to the east, close to a stand of prickly pear cactus, which Catalina called nopal, with its apples still green and small. She called apples tunas. They selected a plant with twelve small apples hanging on one fat thorny leaf, a *penca*.

"Six shots a piece, Kid?"

Harry looked at me. I realized he didn't know that two into twelve made six. Quickly, I said, "Sounds good to us."

With Harry firing his Colt Bisley and America his Frontier Model that seemed almost too big for him, they took turns knocking off the little green tunas one at a time from thirty yards.

"You haven't lost your eye, 'Merica."

"You neither, Kid. But I'll admit I practiced some at Fort Sumner."

"Do we go another round?"

America smiled big, happy. "I reckon not."

Of course not. America couldn't keep that up. Harry would start pulling away.

They holstered their revolvers and gave each other an *abrazo*.

"I didn't know my husband could shoot so well," Catalina said.

I smiled. Let her wonder.

I helped Catalina prepare a royal breakfast on our last day: biscuits, tortillas, eggs, bacon, steak, frijoles, milk, coffee, apple pie, and molasses-pecan pie. She put the leftovers into a saddlebag for us along with dried apples and a pint jar of whiskey.

Catalina and I cleaned up the kitchen while Harry and America saw to the horses.

I put down a plate I'd just dried, faced her, and put my hands on her shoulders.

"Catalina, you're too pretty to live way out here. Nobody can see you."

She laughed. "My husband can. That's enough."

"Sure and that's the main idea. But you belong in Denver, San Francisco."

"America's promised to take me to visit when we get a little bit ahead."

"That's good, honey. Make him keep that promise."

"He will. Maybe we'll have enough when we sell the mustangs they brought back from their trip." Catalina looked down, then square into my eyes. "I've hankered to tell you, Miss Etta: Nobody's as pretty as you. You make me feel like a horned toad."

I laughed and hugged her, and we joined the men.

Harry and America finished tightening the cinches on our mounts. They had rolled our tent tightly and tied it behind John L. Sullivan's saddle. The bedrolls lay snug behind James J. Jeffries's saddle.

"That ought to do 'er," America said.

Harry wiggled Sullivan's saddle horn. "Yep."

For a moment we stood in the warm splendid sun, looking at each other and at the mountains, the little boys hugging America's legs, Catalina holding tiny Lupita. A few clouds hovered over the Sangre de Cristo ridge.

As though someone gave the high sign, we exchanged hugs all around. The men also shook hands. Catalina and I wiped our eyes.

America picked up their sons, held them together against his belly with one arm, and placed the other arm around Catalina. "Everyone take a look at your daddy's best friend. He is the greatest man I ever met. Make it a real good look. Because we know The Sundance Kid."

We ate cold biscuits and the steak at midday on the trail. That night, Harry set up our tent, and in a ring of stones built a fire from mesquite and sagebrush.

"We haven't had any luck yet." I set a pan of beans and bacon to warm.

"What do you mean?"

"All that time around that fine young couple and nothing rubbed off."

"Sugar, I don't know what you're talking about."

I sat and began filling our plates. "I'm still not pregnant."

"Oh." Harry knelt beside me and put an arm around me. "It can still happen."

"Honestly?" I wanted to believe it could, but I needed Harry's support.

"Of course, Sugar."

"Maybe it's not in the cards."

"Let's don't think that way."

I had my doubts, but I nodded at my plate and took a bite of biscuit, as good cold as hot. "Do you think America will tell Catalina he jumped the traces on that financial-improvement trip you boys took?"

"Not any time soon."

"Maybe never?"

"Maybe never. She felt happy and secure when he quit the old ways and they married. He may never break out again. Best to not say anything."

In those days, plenty of men did like America, straying across the line of the law just to acquire a stake and eventually settling in another territory and becoming honest ranchers or businessmen, even politicians and lawmen, and obscuring their pasts.

When we lay snug in our bedrolls, our feet toward the dying fire just beyond the tent opening, I got a yearning for a few days in a city. "Do you think we could go on to San Francisco, Honey?"

"Have a big time at the Palace Hotel and the Cliff House and around?"

"That's the idea. Use our half of what you and America just acquired."

"We can go to San Francisco and do those things. But we'll have to conduct a little business along the way, maybe stop by one of our stashes."

I turned onto my side and looked at him.

"You see, Sugar, I gave our half to 'Merica."

25

A long the way to San Francisco we conducted several business transactions, mainly involving stagecoaches and two small-town general stores. At one, I winged a clerk in the back of the leg when he tried to jump Harry. And Harry plugged one fool who grabbed me as a hostage, got him right through the ribs when I kicked and jerked away. I hope he survived. But that fool should never have angered Harry by grabbing me.

I don't believe my husband ever shot anybody else.

Financially we did all right. Naturally, we had to trade horses a few times, though I sorely hated to give up John L. Sullivan, as good a little mare as you could wish for.

We did San Francisco like cowboys after a long and dusty trail drive. Through friends on the way, we had learned Butch's whereabouts, and I wired him that we'd be in New York at the Hotel Metropole by late January or early February. We took our time, determined to avoid any snow. Why be uncomfortable? We had money.

That's how we got to see San Diego for the first time, arriving by train from San Francisco. We registered at the Horton House across from a nice little plaza of grass and palm trees with a fountain on the main street, rented a buggy the next day, and drove all over downtown and the waterfront, along the big harbor, a beach, and through other fine scenery, saw several poker palaces and saloons, a Chinatown, and, I suspect, a few bordellos. This was a small quiet town except for sailors just off the boat.

"The bartender in the hotel told me last night Wyatt Earp has a card room close by." Harry motioned to the street on the east. "This is Fourth Avenue, isn't it?"

"It is but Mr. Earp isn't there."

"How do you know? Let's go see for sure." Harry took my hand. "He's probably not marshaling anymore. I just want to say hello."

"Absolutely not." I grabbed my husband's arm. We stood on the plaza near the Western Union office, across from the Horton House. "The hotel clerk told me last night. Said everyone asks, so he right away volunteers. Earp moved to Los Angeles several years ago."

"Damn."

I saw disappointment in my husband's face. "Harry, he might have friends in the Pinkertons. Be glad you missed him. Come on. Let's walk." I felt mighty glad Mr. Earp lived in someone else's town.

We considered staying a spell in San Diego, the fall weather being so pleasant. But we voted against it and, after having to double back to Los Angeles by train, rode the stage and train to Yuma, El Paso, and on, spending two days in New Orleans and taking in the sights. We reached my home place near Selma in time for Christmas, had another good visit through New Year's Day of 1906, and went to New York.

Nowhere did we see any posters with our pictures.

We enjoyed a late breakfast at the Metropole Hotel our first morning in New York, and I purchased *The Times* to catch up on the goings-on.

"Land o' Beulah," I told Harry and Butch. "Listen to this." I summed up an article from *The Times*. "A motorcar struck a trolley broadside on Twenty-Eighth Street and knocked it six feet onto its side."

Harry lowered his coffee. "What happened to the horses pulling the streetcar?"

"They're all right. Here's the rest. The motorcar had four men in it. It bounced backward twenty-five feet. Then it drove off in a hurry. Before they got hit, the driver of the trolley, Mr. Miller, shouted, 'Look out. We'll all be killed.' And the driver of the motorcar yelled back, 'Get out of the way quick.'"

"So they saw it coming," Harry said.

"Looks like it." Butch had been in the city a week, had seen several motorcars.

"Let me finish. Only one passenger rode the trolley. She jumped out before they got hit. Then the conductor and Mr. Miller jumped clear."

"Lucky," Harry commented. "How long ago did it happen?"

"Last night, it says."

"This automobile business. I reckon it's here to stay, for folks with the money and interest. But they should use different streets from the horses."

Butch said, "Let's go see where it happened."

"Good idea," Harry said.

I agreed. The waiter kept pouring coffee, and there is nothing better than coffee and the local newspaper your first morning after reaching a town.

"Here's another good one." I summed up a story about how a provocative photograph of a society lady named Mrs. Harry K. Thaw had got displayed the night before at the opening of the Second American Photograph Salon in Pittsburgh. Wearing a flowery Japanese kimono, she lay in a sensual pose on a polar bear rug. The prissy Thaw family didn't like that one whit.

I reported that a painting by John Singer Sargent, *An Ideal Head*, brought the top price in a sale at the Fifth Avenue Art Galleries, seventeen hundred dollars.

And I read to them where Col. and Mrs. John Jacob Astor visited Chinatown and The Bowery the night before with another couple. Stops included The Chatham Club and Nigger Mike's.

"First, however, the distinguished party attended the Thalia Theatre to see *The Curse of Drink*."

Harry said, "I have seen the curse of drink many times."

That night I wrote to my parents. *We are having a more enjoyable visit in New York than the first time, maybe from being a little familiar with the place. Harry and his pard, Leroy, take carriages all over, but Harry will walk some when it's just me and him.*

I wrote that the Auto Show impressed us the most. They set it up at Madison Square Garden and the brand new 69th Regiment Armory. I told the folks the automobiles didn't excite us much but what they called air-locomotion vehicles did. Yes, sir: airplanes. They spelled it "aeroplanes." My family would be thrilled to hear about them. I picked up a program at the entrance.

The main attraction for the three of us was Captain Baldwin's big fat air bag, a dirigible, they called it, *The California Arrow*.

"We heard about it in California," Harry told Butch.

"What's it do?"

"We didn't see it, but we talked to plenty of folks who had. Flew right over the bay from Oakland to San Francisco."

I nodded toward a young man talking to visitors by the machine. "That skinny fellow looks like the pictures we saw of Roy Knabenshue, the famous parachutist. He did some of the driving, Leroy."

"Sugar, let's hire Mr. Knabenshue and the dirigible for returning south."

"But is it cheaper than the steamer?" Butch said. "And where would we sit? And what if some bird hits the air bag and puts a hole in it? Does it sink in the ocean?" He shook his head. "Big ugly thing like that's probably damn slow too."

"I suppose you're right, Leroy," Harry told him.

As long as those two had been pards, Butch still didn't know when Harry joked.

We also saw Professor Langley's airplane that had flown off a boat and straight into the Potomac two years earlier. Dr. Bell showed up with his man-carrying kite. And we saw the Frenchman, Santos Dumont, with his tiny machine, the *Demoiselle*.

"Good that he's a little fellow or he couldn't get into that thing," Harry said.

"He flew it in Paris." I tapped my program.

But none of the machines did anything during our stay except squat on the floor.

"Where are the Wright brothers?" Harry looked around.

"Not listed in the program."

"I'm saying they never flew no machine into the air," Butch said.

And, yes, the Auto Show displayed automobiles, foreign ones too, so many I can hardly recall any of their names. Since our return we'd seen several being driven in New Orleans and San Francisco, though not San Diego. One brand I recollect, however, is Studebaker, which had long been famous for manufacturing covered wagons.

Harry and I took in several theatrical productions. As before, I kept the programs. So I know we saw Molly Barrymore at the Criterion in James M. Barrie's *Alice, Sit by the Fire*, not one of his better plays. But the next night at the Empire we saw Maude Adams in his more popular *Peter Pan*. We saw Eddie Foy at the Casino in *The Earl and the Girl*, Robert Loraine at the Hudson in Shaw's *Man and Superman*, and George M. Cohan, so vibrant, at the Grand and without his family this time, in *Little Johnny Jones*.

"Remember I said the Cohan boy would become a big star?"

"And you were right, Etta Margaret, as sure as cactus blooms in the spring."

Only a concert by John Philip Sousa at the Hippodrome could get Butch to accompany us to a show.

"Leroy gets excited," Harry said, "with that loud brassy music and the drums."

Mainly, Butch studied The Bowery. And he didn't look for any Col. and Mrs. John Jacob Astor.

Before we sailed, Harry and I went to Carnegie Hall, where we heard the New York Symphony play Berlioz, Schumann, and Weber. Harry didn't enjoy the concert as much as I did, but he sat still, stayed awake, and pretended to listen.

"Sugar," he said afterwards, "I'm getting you a piano in Buenos Aires."

I had one big day by myself. While Harry and Butch went to find out about sailing schedules and accommodations, I selected some dresses and riding clothes to be sent to our hotel. Then I had my hair done. The hairdresser told me I had the finest head of black hair she had ever seen and that I looked pretty too.

I bought books for the trip but also for our time at our ranch house, so isolated. These included a new edition of the complete works of Thomas Hardy; the plays of Oscar Wilde in two volumes, just $2.50; *The House of Mirth,* just out, by Edith Wharton, for $1.50; and Jack London's newest novels, *The Call of the Wild, The Sea-Wolf,* and *The Game.* I had to buy another steamer trunk.

I picked up a new *Collier's* and a *McClure's,* three decks of playing cards, a set of dominoes, two bottles of Cutty Sark, and two of Old Bushmills. I took a cabriolet to the hotel and would be ready to sail as soon as I wrote my folks once more.

And we still hadn't seen a reward poster displaying our pictures. I commented on that fact to my husband.

"This city hides us," Harry said, "like quails in the brush."

"I suppose our recent work in the West will make the Pinkertons think about us."

"They might know where we've been, but not where we are."

Later I realized that, for us, that time in California in the fall of 1905—just a few months earlier when Harry and I on a dusty trail halted a stagecoach toting a strong box stuffed with bags of paper money, gold dust, and gold coins—marked when the Old West expired, as dead as Andrew Jackson's horse. The revelation saddened me.

We couldn't know that we'd be bringing the olden days, you might say, to South America. And, unlike in the States, that I'd participate regularly.

26

I never became jaded with traveling, what some people think of as acquiring sophistication. But our third ocean voyage resulted so unremarkable that I can't remember much about it. I read a lot and reviewed my Spanish grammar so I wouldn't sound funny after so much time away. I read to Harry some, and we talked and played cassino, but he spent plenty of time with Butch too, in the bar usually, drinking or not, but usually playing cards or dominoes, working up games of poker or faro or cooncan with others.

We just didn't meet any interesting passengers. We didn't sail into any storms, and the ship didn't break down or hit a reef. Butch remembered to be "Jim Lowe," and Harry didn't have to clobber anyone.

No, our "sophistication" didn't cause the trip to be routine. It was common, is all, as plain as the paint on the side of the ship, even if we did leave winter in New York and find summer in Buenos Aires nineteen days later.

We requested that our possessions be sent to the same hotel on Florida Street, and in our best duds descended the gangplank in Buenos Aires harbor. So they wouldn't look too much like their photos in case those damn Pinkerton posters continued to complain about us, Harry and Butch planned ahead and had grown beards.

We hired a buggy for the ride to the Hotel Europa.

While we rolled along we craned our necks, looking high and low and all around for familiar sights, probably for Pinkertons too, whether we realized it or not.

"Everything seems the same to me," Butch said after a few blocks. "Kid?"

"I'm not sure. Etta?"

"It's different, boys. I can feel it."

At the Europa a bellboy unloaded our things, Harry paid the cabriolet driver and sent him away, and "Mr. and Mrs. Place" and "Jim Lowe" registered.

"Let's head for the bank before going to our rooms," Harry said.

"We gonna walk from here?" Butch frowned.

"It's only two blocks," I reminded him.

Harry took my hand and we entered the bank to exchange some cash for pesos and deposit the rest. Butch grumbled all the way there.

The posters remained up. We paused in the middle of the lobby.

"Damn," Butch said softly.

"Well, Leroy," Harry said, "you made The Wild Bunch permanently famous in two hemispheres."

"Hell," Butch said, sounding modest, "but there ain't any Bunch no more. Just me and you."

"And me," I told him.

Butch looked at me, his big round face, jaws even fatter with his whiskers, and he smiled, just a little. He seemed to tolerate me, but I knew he liked me some and respected me a lot. However, Butch never accepted the fact that I could ride as well as him and shoot better.

On Florida Street, ebullient customers jammed our favorite café, La Argentina, where we found a table on the sidewalk in the shade at the edge of the passing crowd. I sipped a tall Scotch and water, Harry beside me with a beer. But he seemed preoccupied.

"What is it, Honey?" I touched his hand near his drink.

"Nothing."

"Just thinking?"

"Some."

I didn't press him. I studied the passersby and the other idlers, and I walked to a nearby kiosk and bought a magazine, *Esta Semana.* When I sat and began thumbing through it, Harry and Butch started discussing purchases we needed for the ranch.

"We gotta take more whiskey," Butch said first thing.

I continued turning pages. After a bit, the photographs of handsome men and women in the social and political limelight gave way to an article about an Argentine man with one of those non-Latin names as common in that land as good steaks and wine, what with all Argentina's immigrants from Italy and France, Spain and England. What he had done arrested my attention like a rattler on the trail. I read through it twice, missing several technical words, and my dictionary remained packed. But I understood most of it.

"Boys, listen to this. An Argentine named Juan Vucetich has perfected a way to take a man's fingerprint, preserve it, and match it up, if he has anything to match it with, like images from a door facing or a drinking glass. Says Mr. Vucetich elaborated on a method developed a few years ago by an Englishman named Sir Francis Galton. It says here they can find out who's who from the loops and circles on our fingertips, the designs being exclusive to each individual."

"I've never heard of anything like that," Harry said.

Butch shook his head. "Don't believe it. Too many people in the world."

"There's more. The article says this could be a dandy parlor game but also could match crimes with the people suspected of committing them. First, of course, you'd have to experience the misfortune of being behind bars and having your fingerprints taken."

"Or," Harry said, "we touch something during a transaction, and the law thinks it's us, our fingerprints might show up one day alongside our photographs."

"I'm afraid so," I said.

"It just don't make sense." Butch examined his fingertips.

"But it just might, Leroy. And the article says fingerprinting, in one form or another, has been known since ancient times."

Harry asked, "Does it mention whether the Pinkertons are doing it?"

"No, but it's the kind of thing they'd pick up, I suppose."

"Hell," Butch said. "So what does that mean for us?"

"Wear gloves," I said.

Harry told him, "Don't touch anything."

"Sugar, remember that excursion I took with 'Merica into Texas and around?"

"Seventeen days and you wouldn't let me go with you."

Harry knew I kidded. "It started me studying on how things used to be. We had a mighty big time, 'Merica and me. Same as me and you other times. Remember? Like on the way to California and after we got there?"

We had just gone to bed in the Hotel Europa after leaving the café, unpacking, having supper, and watching the night activities from our balcony. Sure, I remembered, though not so much what we did but the glorious way I felt while we transacted business, and how the thrill remained with me for days. I felt the way Lily Langtry must have when a packed house stood to cheer her.

"It had been just like our first years together," I told him, "the happiest, most-fulfilling times of my life."

We talked so long we grew wide-awake. So we poured some Scotch, added water, and kept talking, sitting in bed propped up against the pillows and the headboard, reminiscing: the Bunch, Robbers' Roost, Denver, Tipton, Cheyenne, Santa Fe, Salt Lake City, Winnemucca, the great horses we'd had, the hard rides and the campfires, and, yes, that varmint in the background, Charlie Siringo.

"I liked Siringo's book," Harry said. "Glad you read it to me. I wonder if he's got one out now about his detective days."

"Maybe he won't write that until he's through detecting." I felt my drink.

Harry took a sip, fell silent for a moment. "And he won't be through until he's finished with us." He took another sip. "Lots of wide open country here."

"South America's such a big primitive land, except for Buenos Aires and a few other cities."

"No automobiles. No aeroplanes, whether they can fly or not."

"No running water except in the cities."

Harry laughed. "Just like back home."

"I bet I know what you're thinking."

He took my hand. "Think so?"

"Of course." Sure: the talk about the old days, the Pinkertons, the posters. "I know you'll want to discuss it with Butch."

"He's my pard, Sugar. But what about you?"

I gave him an extra-large kiss.

We took the next boat south.

"I'd swear the captain of the port at Bahía Blanca acted strange toward us."

"Yes, Sugar. I didn't see any reward posters, however."

And the captain of the port at Rawson acted unfriendly, not like before. He didn't say anything disturbing. But I could feel it. So could Harry. Butch, who'd had a big last night at La Boca after we made our purchases for the trip, didn't notice the change.

We bought saddle horses with tack, two mules to carry our possibles, and hired two men with their own mounts to help out. And we quickly left Rawson.

By the time we reached the crossroads store at Cholila, I had put aside the feeling that people suspected us.

The storekeeper, Juan the true Argentine, revived it for me.

"Did you think Juan seemed extra friendly and accommodating?" I asked Harry.

"Probably wondering which of us is going to shoot him."

27

The place had gone to hell.

For a few minutes I wondered which of the boys would shoot the help.

A lot of the corral fence needed fixing. Goats and chickens walked in and out the house, and the barn doors hung crookedly. My garden patch had become weeds and sand.

Two of the Indian women came out of their huts, greeted us nicely, and explained, a little apologetically, the reasons for the mess. I relayed the news to Harry and Butch.

"The weather has been foul. The foreman got drunk and ran off with one of the younger women. Our other men are camping close to our livestock in one of the valleys. The women say there's a lot of resentment on account of our staying away longer than we promised, and white folks like us had killed off most of their ancestors."

"Oh, hell," Butch said.

Harry and Butch took stock of the damage while the women and I chased the goats and chickens out of the house, shoveled out the droppings, and swept. I sent them to the well for water, which we splashed all over, then swept again. And I started them cleaning dishes and utensils and seeing what could be rustled up for grub.

My cowboys returned before long.

Harry surveyed the results of my industry. "It's like new, Sugar."

Butch opened a bottle of Old Bushmills. I started to suggest we'd never get the outside in shape if he started drinking, but Harry took a sip right after Butch, and they sat at the kitchen table. I kept shut, pretending to sweep for a moment. Then I got jars for all of us and joined them.

"A couple of men are gone but they didn't steal much," Harry said. "We spotted most of the cattle, horses, and sheep, so they might not have taken much livestock."

"What about my great horse, Ventarrón?"

"He's there."

"Good, or I'd be on the warpath after some polecat."

The women fixed a fine meal of *bife a caballo* and *puchero*. We felt better after we'd eaten. We could start putting the rest of the place back together in the morning.

Reorganizing took longer and more work than we'd estimated. Besides, Harry and Butch had started reminiscing heartily about the big times they'd had before we came to South America the first time in 1901. Sometimes they'd stop for a spell, lean on their shovels or the fence, or squat in the shade and smoke and spit.

One day when I approached to ask what they wanted for dinner, I caught them talking about how pleasant and exciting it had been to spend the winter in that god-awful cold and isolated Robbers' Roost.

The fourth day back, Harry and I had been counting our cattle in one of the valleys north of our house, and racing the horses to chase the devil stored up in them, when we spotted that timid man and his poor raggedy family Harry had given money and a mule to on the trail sometime earlier.

They appeared solidly at home on the edge of a small stand of scrubby pines, with two tattered tents and a crooked outhouse, stone fireplace, bread oven of handmade bricks, and a well. Two tethered mules raised their heads and pointed their ears at us.

"Looks like they've been there awhile," Harry said.

"Let's go see how they're doing."

When we got close they recognized us. Smiling, happy, hats off, kids jumping up and down around them, they trotted over to greet us.

We dismounted. Timid hugs and handshakes followed all around.

The couple jabbered away, she in an Indian dialect, the father in his fair Spanish. I jabbered back in my fair Spanish, and explained to Harry.

"After finding work one place and another while on the run, they showed up here six months ago, and Dr. Newton put them on a retainer to watch his stock as well as any of ours in the area. With the money you gave them, they had bought another fine mule and badly needed clothing. Still have most of their money, been buying staples at Cholila and trapping a little."

"I'm happy for them," Harry said. "And Dr. Newton. A good neighbor."

"Indeed he is. As for this little family, the father's name is Juan. His wife is María. The baby she holds is four months old, the toddler fifteen months. The oldest boy is about twelve now. He's also Juan."

"Plus we have Juan the true Argentine and *El Doctor* Juan Newton."

"Don't forget Fingerprint Juan."

Juan the father made sure we noted the two little ones. That sent me to musing about the children Harry and I wanted, and I found myself gazing at that tall eternal peak, Aconcagua. I had to shake my head to redirect my thoughts to business.

We gibbered back and forth a little more before excusing ourselves.

On the ride to thank Dr. Newton we decided, having met two other Juans first, that the man we just talked to would be Little Juan, his twelve-year-old son Juan Jr.

A half mile from his ranch house we found Dr. Newton mingling with cattle and horses while he rode a fine-looking strawberry roan he said had "almost pure criollo blood." He and Harry shook hands, and Harry accepted a store-bought cigarette.

"Good of you to have that Indian family watch out for our stock," Harry said.

"They seem honest and hard-working," Dr. Newton said, "and out here it's good to be on the lookout for predators and bandidos."

His facial expression didn't say more than his words had.

"Maybe we could add a little to what you're paying," Harry said, "and the father and older boy could expand their territory and help us out some at the house too."

"Yes, María and the little ones can keep an eye on livestock and have dinner ready when father and son return home every day."

They agreed on wages and duties for Little Juan and Juan Jr. We talked weather and politics, and we briefly described our stays in New York and San Francisco. He invited us to visit his home anytime, and we made a reciprocal offer.

On the way back at the little family's digs I explained the request for help and the augmented wages. Little Juan happily accepted the proposal.

"What do you think?" Harry asked when we turned our horses toward home.

"Good arrangement."

"I mean about Dr. Newton."

"I know," I said. "Well, he seemed as friendly as ever."

"What else?"

"He didn't say anything to make us think he's suspicious."

"No. But I could feel something. I'll wager you did too."

I didn't comment again until we reached the corral and pulled up.

Harry turned in the saddle and waited.

"I sensed an awareness," I said, "maybe even a tad of fear in him. Like you mentioned, not anything he said. But he seemed like that day in Buenos Aires when he stopped to chat at the café shortly after we'd discovered the Pinkerton posters."

"My thought exactly."

"I think he knows."

Harry nodded.

The next day Little Juan and Juan Jr. rode over double on the mule Harry's generosity had provided for them. They arrived just after sunup, so you know they started early. Right away Harry cut out a couple of good horses for them, and you should have seen their gratitude.

"You giving them Injuns them horses, Kid?" Butch frowned and spat.

"We can afford it, Leroy. They're a big family with transportation needs." He turned to Little Juan and Juan Jr. "Looks like you'll have to ride bareback."

They smiled as though understanding, but that saddles didn't matter. They'd ridden mules. Each grabbed a hemp rope from the corral fence, twisted lines around the muzzles, and jumped on. They needed plenty of savvy, those horses not having been ridden for a long time. But they hung on, laughing and shouting. We had fun watching.

"We should have had Leroy ride 'em first," Harry whispered to me.

Little Juan turned out to be a top hand, with Juan Jr. hardly eating leftovers.

"We made a good acquisition in those two," I told Harry.

"Yes. I'd like for this fine loyal family to be with us for . . . the rest of our time here."

I heard Harry's hesitation, wondered about it, but kept shut.

With help from the Juans we whipped the place into shape, and a couple of weeks passed before we saw Dr. Newton again. Harry and I had ridden out to where our land met his, enjoying the beautiful day, but searching ravines for mavericks and sick animals while looking for busted fences. Sometimes I wondered why ranchers put up any fencing at all in Patagonia, the range being so plentiful and productive, and the neighbors scarce and cooperative. But ranchers needed some fencing to isolate the sheep, which crop the grass so close.

El Doctor rode with one of his hands hazing a cantankerous steer toward the herd. When he saw us he waved and casually rode over.

The conversation began in a usual-enough way, about the weather and livestock and General Roca. Then he said it. This must have been difficult for him, not knowing how we'd react.

"Ma'am. Mr. Place. You folks are fine neighbors. Just first rate. And Mr. Lowe. I certainly—I've given this a lot of thought and I think you should know."

He revealed that every rancher in Chubut Province, probably the rest of the country too, and maybe all the way to Chile and Bolivia and Peru, knew our identities. They had either seen the reward notices or talked to someone who had.

"Not long after you left to visit the States," he said, "a couple of Pinkertons showed up again in Buenos Aires, asking about you." He gave us their names.

They were the varmints Charlie Siringo and Frank Dimaio.

"One day a friend told me the detectives had found out at the land agency where you had settled. Before long they stopped by my office. I had seen the posters and, knowing they'd already learned about your spread adjacent to mine, I didn't deny seeing you out on the range. By the time they interviewed everyone in Buenos Aires who might have done business with you, banks and so on, the rains had started. They couldn't find anyone to guide them out here, and I for one didn't inform them rain wouldn't be a problem in this area. And it's a long trip. They never came here."

I figure they also might not have relished wandering into a grizzly's cave. For all they knew, we had another gang and an easy-to-protect hideout like Robbers' Roost. This country is even more primitive than the Western United States. And they were strangers, didn't know the language.

"I don't like to meddle," Dr. Newton said. "And I'll reiterate that you're good neighbors. That's why I thought I should tell you. Two of my friends in Buenos Aires had been in the States when The Wild Bunch was active. So they're more aware than most are concerning you folks. But we know you're not wanted for violating any laws in Argentina."

"You're sure the detectives returned to the States?" Harry asked.

"The police superintendent himself told me."

He gave us a few more details. In a few moments we thanked him for his consideration and excused ourselves. I felt distressed and confused.

"He seemed relieved, didn't he?" Harry said.

"Yes, either because Siringo and Dimaio went home or he doesn't have to pretend anymore that he doesn't know about us."

"Maybe both. Makes sense."

"What about you?" I asked.

"What about me, Sugar?"

"Are you relieved?"

"I reckon. Happy too."

"About what?"

"That he likes and trusts us enough to know I wouldn't shoot him."

By the time we reached the corral and turned our mounts over to Little Juan and Juan Jr., my distress and confusion had been replaced by an ocean of calm and a mountain of tranquility. Harry's expression and the way he sat his horse told me he probably felt the same.

"That's twice they've come as far as Buenos Aires," Harry told Butch.

"So they might be back," Butch said.

"I hate being hurrahed by that damn pair."

Harry and Butch fell silent. Harry got the jars and Scotch and sloshed us each a good amount. This time I joined them for more than courtesy.

Butch said, "Not much law in these parts."

"No," my husband said. "Not much."

"I don't cotton no more to this being retired."

"Well, Leroy," Harry said, "why don't we just unretire?"

I said, "I'll hold the horses."

28

We wanted to make our first excursion significant, so we gave it plenty of thought. Harry did most of the thinking.

"Let's knock off the store in Cholila," Butch said.

"Too close to home," Harry told him.

"That's why. A short ride. And there's just that little guy and his wife."

"That little guy," I said, "is Juan the pure Argentine. He's a friend."

"Oh hell."

"I've been studying Etta's map," Harry said. "Etta showed me how to do distances. Five hundred miles inland from Buenos Aires there's a city called Mercedes. It's in big type on the map, but not as big as for Buenos Aires. So there's bound to be plenty of possibilities for us."

"Probably take us a week to get there," Butch said.

"More like two."

"Aw, I don't know."

"Give it some thought, Leroy. You decide."

Butch scratched his chin and nodded. "Mercedes it is."

Shortly before making our last camp until riding into Mercedes to get the lay of the land, we picked up a helper. Harry saw him first, cantering toward us, and waited calmly to see what the stranger wanted. But Butch spotted him, grabbed a rifle, and shouted for him to pull up.

"Let's see what he wants, Leroy," Harry said, "before we shoot him."

The stranger reined up. "Name's Dey. Can we parley a minute?"

"We got nothing to say to you," Butch told him.

"It won't take long. You might be interested."

"Keep those hands where I can see them." Butch leveled his rifle at the rider.

The stranger was a dark-skinned young man, slight of build, early twenties, I'd say. Looked to me like his darkness came from the relentless sun of the pampas.

"Wouldn't hurt to hear what he has to say," Harry said. "What do you think?"

"My sentiments exactly. Climb down, buster, and walk over here."

Dey joined us under the shade of an ombú. "I've been in the next town seeing my girl. Didn't expect to run in to you all."

"What's that got to do with us?" Butch asked. "Where you from?"

"Texas. But I live in Mercedes. And I'm ready to pull out."

"How come you live there?"

"Arrived with my folks when I was little. Pappy's a mining engineer. I shoe horses, help out in a general store. No future. Taking my girl and leaving."

"All right. Get going."

"My girl's still packing. I headed home when I spotted you all."

"We're just tourists, boy."

"Sure. And I'm John Wesley Hardin. I want to throw in with you."

Butch turned to Harry. "I heard Hardin got killed."

"He's joshing you," Harry said.

Dey removed his hat, used his bandanna to wipe his forehead. "I know Mercedes right well. I can save you a passel of time, maybe some missteps."

"We ain't going to Mercedes." Butch waggled his rifle.

"You must be the leader," Dey said. "Butch Cassidy."

I'd swear Butch puffed up with the recognition.

"Just speculating." Dey nodded to me. "Miss Etta." Then Dey looked at Harry. I saw the awe. "Heard about you folks when I was little, before leaving Texas. Notices about you all been up in Mercedes quite a spell. English and Spanish."

"Damn," Butch said. "But we ain't going there. Now make tracks."

"Let's talk about it a minute," Harry said.

"But—" Butch spat. "I been thinking the same thing."

"Young fellow," Harry said, "undo your gun belt real slow and hand it to me."

Dey unbuckled his belt. With an admiring look at Harry's Colt and the hand that had given him his reputation, the derogatory parts unfair, he handed it to Harry.

"Take your horse and get on the other side of the tree," Harry said. When Dey did as told, my husband and Butch talked softly.

"Let's shoot him," Butch said. "He wants the reward."

"Maybe so. But he says he knows the town. Let him explain. That way, we can go in late in the day or at night, know right where we're heading."

"All right, but as soon as that jasper gives us the layout, let's shoot him."

"Leroy, we can keep an eye on him to make sure he's not lying. Then take him with us for a spell when we light out so he can't tell the law 'til we're safe."

"All right, and then shoot him."

"Leroy, he's a young fellow maybe just trying to get a stake and marry his girl."

Butch fidgeted.

"If it doesn't work out, I'll take responsibility."

Butch frowned. "All right. But don't give him nothing."

"I'm thinking ten percent."

"That's what I meant."

Dey was a happy young man when we told him he could join us. On the ground in the shade of the ombú he drew a rough map of central Mercedes. As soon as he situated the Banco de la Nación and told us about all the ranchers and miners who traded there, it became our target.

"There's not much law," he said.

Harry and I rode into town, double-checked Dey's rudimentary map, and bought dynamite. Back at our camp, we ate lightly off the grub in our saddlebags, broke camp, reached town again under a three-quarters moon a couple of hours after dark, and got to work. Dey watched the horses. I watched Dey and the back door.

And Harry and Butch ran out with the money in the wake of the dynamite blast.

We split up and rendezvoused at the west edge of town as agreed earlier. First at a gallop, then cantering, we rode for the foothills. After an hour, with nobody tailing us, we pulled up, and I counted the money: around twenty thousand dollars in gold coins, dust, and paper.

"You worked out fine," Harry told Dey. "We'll let you do more next time."

"Much obliged for counting me in," Dey said, "but I don't feel cut out for this."

Butch shifted in his saddle. "It takes a certain type of man."

"Yes," Dey said, looking at me. "I wanted to find out and I did."

So we shook hands all around, and I counted out two thousand dollars in coins and paper, which Harry gave Dey along with the young man's gun belt and revolver.

"Where to now?" Harry asked.

"Get my girl in a few days, get married, go to Buenos Aires to look for work. This place is drier than the Texas Panhandle.

Dustier too." He tipped his hat to me, nodded to Butch, took a last admiring look at Harry, nodded again, and rode off.

"How much did you give him?" Butch asked.

I told him.

"Hell." Butch shook his head and spat.

We never learned Dey's first name and never saw him again. But I suspect that for the rest of his life he talked about robbing a bank in South America during the summer of 1906 while riding with the last of The Wild Bunch.

We rode like fugitives all that night and for the next fifteen days. When we reached the ranch, Ventarrón and Harry's horse had held up well, the famous endurance of the criollo, I suppose. But Butch's would never be worth much again: It had strained a stifle just before we reached home. As soon as it could walk normally Butch sold it cheap to the man who toured the ranches peddling vegetables and wine from his cart and needed a new horse to pull him, about all that poor old bandit pony could do.

"From now on we'd better have relays of mounts like before," Harry said.

"Yes," I said, "but I want Ventarrón to always be on the home end."

I won't list each of our activities during the next years. Some weren't special, and others I didn't make notes about, we kept on the move so much. And we had to make deposits from time to time so highway robbers couldn't clean us out. We used branches of the River Plate Bank and the Banco de la Nación.

Normally we went after trains and pack trains carrying gold, seldom taking anything in our home province, Chubut, which Butch still called SHOEboot. Of course stagecoaches and banks got in our way occasionally. And for a while we usually returned to the ranch to regroup and let things simmer down. We also spent time as tourists, sometimes renting a buggy, other times riding the train, studying stage schedules, departure routes from various towns, where to acquire fresh horses, and locations of banks, general stores, and assay offices.

Of course we didn't obtain twenty thousand dollars every time we went out. Maybe as that had been our take the first time, the law regularly reported it that way for simplicity. But big winnings became as rare as trees on the Patagonian pampas.

Local gangs operated out there too, and we often got blamed for their activities.

I mailed an occasional letter to my folks, and I heard back sporadically.

In between periods of rain, so intense in the north, we conducted business all over Argentina, usually returning to the ranch for long periods. We didn't get into many shoot-outs, though I had to plug a couple of horses in a posse chasing us when we made off with eighteen thousand dollars from the Banco de la Nación at Bahía Blanca.

Throughout, Harry and Butch seemed as though rejuvenated. I felt quite fine myself.

By the way, I can't say we took from the rich and gave to the poor, the way Butch told people years later. But I guarantee you we never took from the poor.

If our work needed any talking, like instructions, I handled it. And everyone took us for three men until I opened my yap, being as I wore men's clothes, put my hair high on my head under a sombrero, and covered my lower face with a bandanna.

Sometimes I didn't need to talk. If we handled a train I'd jump into the express car with my rifle or six-gun leveled, and the same if my job were in the passenger car. A revolver or carbine held steady at the proper angle talks loud and clear.

For handguns I carried my .32-caliber Iver Johnson under my jacket on my left side, my derringers in my jacket pockets or strapped onto the outsides of my legs below my boot tops, the rifle my Winchester Model 94 carbine. I never strapped on a big six-shooter. They're heavy and buck like a rodeo bronc so that you can't shoot accurately unless you have the strength of a man. No. Toting a large six-gun, you can't retain your femininity robbing a train or stagecoach.

"Leroy," Harry said one night in front of the fireplace after supper at the ranch, "we're doing an awful lot of traveling back and forth."

"What are you leading up to?"

"We're not here enough to enjoy the place or get much work done."

"The Injun and his boy do a good job," Butch said.

"Their names," I said, "are Little Juan and Juan Jr."

"I knew that," Butch said. "Why're you picking on me?"

"Leroy," Harry said, "maybe we should lighten our load by selling this place."

"Where would we live?"

"One town or another. Camp out once in a while. See more of this big land."

"Keep moving?"

"Might be worth a try for a while. Sugar?"

That excited me. "Whatever you boys say. Leroy?"

"I been thinking along the same lines."

We got to work right away on pulling out for keeps. I hated to give up my books, but I let most of them go. At least they wound up with Dr. Newton and his friends, folks who could read and pleasure in them. It took me awhile to decide on just a few clothes, but I did it. I filled the steamer trunks, mostly with my belongings, to leave behind.

"We might as well let Little Juan know he can bring his whole family here and use the house until the place sells." Harry started that sentence looking at Butch, but finished it facing me.

"Good idea," I said.

"Let that bunch of Injuns take over the house?" Butch looked toward the door as though expecting them to come trotting up.

"We're not going to be here, Leroy. And they could use it."

"Don't you recollect how the place went to hell when we went to the States?"

"That won't happen. If it does, the new owner will have to fix it."

"I guess we'll find out."

"Sugar, will you give Little Juan the news?"

Butch fussed and fumed some more but finally quit arguing.

Harry and I rode over to Dr. Newton's the next day and asked him to pass the word about our wanting to sell.

"I guess I'm not surprised," Dr. Newton said. "I realize you haven't spent a lot of time there lately." He grinned. I know he grinned. He said, "I could place an ad in the Buenos Aires newspapers next time I go."

"Much obliged. Etta will wire you an address once in a while."

"My pleasure, Mr. Place, Mrs. Place. And give my best to Mr. Lowe."

"We'll be in touch," Harry said.

We shook hands. As we rode away I glanced back twice. Both times Dr. Newton watched from his porch.

"We've been lucky in neighbors," Harry said.

"I guess everyone knows about us except Little Juan and his family."

The next day I told Little Juan we'd be back to complete the sale someday. I never saw such a happy family when they started bringing their belongings over. They must have thanked us four or five times.

We saddled up, tied bedrolls and tents behind the saddles, and rode off. At Cholila I left letters for mailing to my folks and the Harmsworths.

29

We conducted business in San Luis and Mendoza provinces west of Buenos Aires, crossed the Andes into Chile for a few transactions, and traveled north through Córdoba and Chaco provinces and up into Bolivia, around Sucre and Cochabamba, and the big silver lodes at Potosí.

Talk about altitude! But as high as we climbed, Andean peaks towered above us. I looked up some of the heights later, so I know we reached more than ten thousand feet at Sucre and more than thirteen thousand at Potosí. The altitudes didn't bother us, though they might have if we'd had to run foot races or been a lot older.

Whenever possible we traveled by train, with the horses riding in a livestock car or waiting for us at a livery until we could return. Harry and Butch used a lot of different horses, but Harry let me keep Ventarrón, who held up well. I had dreaded Harry might want me to trade him in, same as I had to give up my swift iron-hearted gray.

"That big-wind horse of yours, Sugar, is worth any other five. You don't need to get rid of him, especially with communication so poor between towns and with law scarce. And his color's common."

When Harry said that, my spirit soared like a condor in the Andes.

Once in a while Harry and Butch worked in the more usual sense of the word. In southern Bolivia, for instance, at Tupita, Harry surprised me one day.

"Leroy and I have a job, Sugar."

"Fine. What's my assignment?"

"Stay in the hotel. We're going to ride shotgun for a transportation company hauling supplies all over the area."

"That's it? You mean regular work?"

"We're not going down into the mines. But we can learn the countryside and find out where they keep money and how payrolls are handled and when they go out."

Another time, mainly in 1908 and 1909, they guarded for the Concordia tin mines under the supervision of a nice young American named Mary Seifert, a slight fellow, short, friendly from the first, only in his mid-twenties, but bossing a railroad commission study of transportation around there. And he bought supplies for the Concordia mines. Spoke slick Spanish too.

"Call me Mary," he said. "Let's have a drink."

So you know he hit if off with Harry and Butch. To be polite I joined them.

Maybe he was really Meredith or Meriwether or something similar, but he never said. Mary Seifert is mentioned in a book or two about The Wild Bunch, and he did us a mighty good turn so I include our time around him. We didn't know about the favor for many years, however.

We never conducted business against Mary or any other employer.

I'm not saying we were proud of our hell-raising elsewhere, just happy we could do it, pioneers of a sort in a wild and strange land. Not just anyone could have accomplished what we did. The local elements trying to copy us did not measure up.

While we lived at Concordia we exchanged telegrams with Dr. Newton and learned that he wanted to buy our ranch. There hadn't been much interest, way out there where we had settled, and his offer sounded fair. We rode back to square up.

"Few folks thrive so far from cities," *El Doctor* told us.
"Ideal for us, however."

After Harry's remark I caught that grin again from Dr. Newton.

He knew a good man when he saw one, so he had hired Little Juan to stay on and run things for him. Harry and I liked that. Butch didn't comment.

Nearing our house, Harry said, "We'll camp tonight and be on our way tomorrow."

"We been camping out." Butch spat. "Let's sleep inside."

"Inside is taken," Harry said.

"The Injuns?"

"It's their home now, Leroy."

"We can boot 'em out, just one night."

Harry looked neutrally at Butch, and I kept shut.

"What the hell," Butch said. But he let it go.

In the morning, Harry had me call Little Juan over to explain his new role and our sale to *El Doctor*. Knowing I'd eventually have to leave my great horse Ventarrón for keeps, I gave him to the new foreman, who thanked me twice. "Call it your present from the Three Kings," I told Little Juan. Though Christmas approached, I said it his way instead of *"Feliz Navidad."*

We had our choice of saddle horses from the herd, part of our deal with Dr. Newton. Harry selected a big fine gelding for me, a chestnut with three white feet, a long pretty blaze, huge girth, and deep chest, part Thoroughbred. I didn't bother to name him, though, and planned to not love him too much. Harry chose a dun mare for himself and a black gelding for Butch, criollos mixed with Quarter Horses, as near as we could figure.

The next day after Harry went to Butch's tent and rustled him out we enjoyed a fine breakfast María prepared of eggs, steak, and mate. The kids behaved well and had become strong. I felt they would live there happily the rest of their lives.

And we prepared to head out.

To my surprise, Little Juan made a speech, and a grand one, considering his humility and that he was Indian. He wished us good luck, promised to pray for us, and thanked us for our friendship and kindness all the way back to when Harry loaded him up with gold coins on the trail that time their mule died. To keep from crying, I told him we'd return to visit someday. Then I paraphrased Little Juan's speech for Harry and Butch. And I wondered what that family would think if they realized their benefactors had been professional robbers famous on two continents.

We exchanged handshakes and hugs all around, except for Butch, who shook with Little Juan only, and without enthusiasm. Then we rode out, though Harry and I stopped after a hundred yards, looked back, and lifted our hats. The whole family stood in front of the house and waved to us. I had to get out my hanky.

"Nice speech," Harry said.

I sniffled. "Good folks."

"Little Juan said something else just as I mounted."

"Yes."

"You didn't interpret that part."

"I didn't want to upset Leroy or make him jealous."

"Well?"

"Little Juan said, 'Be careful, Mr. Sundance.'"

Right after Christmas of 1910 we experienced a memorable episode at the company store of a small Argentine mining community named Arroyo Pescado, and I wrote extra about it in my diary. Like several towns we got to know, it's not in my atlas now.

Harry stepped toward the safe while Butch got some of the workers to load bread and jelly and dried beef into our saddlebags to hold us until we could reach a city to hide in. Assisted by my carbine, I kept an eye on the other employees and the customers.

Things got touchy, so many people around, folks we hadn't figured on, and I reckon that caused me to become jumpy, Butch's normal state, being as he did in tension what Harry did in tranquility.

And Arroyo Pescado turned difficult. The manager couldn't be found. When Harry had trouble shooting the lock off the safe, the customers looked as though they planned to jump us. In the commotion and confusion I had to plug a couple of men who rushed me, just in the legs to knock them down. I couldn't bring myself to raise the barrel any higher. And Harry turned in surprise and shot a stubborn clerk in the chest when that unfortunate man came after my husband with a hatchet. I stifled a cry. I hope the clerk didn't die.

We cleaned out the safe and high-tailed it.

That clerk might be the only man Harry ever shot.

A few days later on a mountain trail, we said good-bye to 1910 and to Argentina, which never saw us again. We also said good-bye to Butch, temporarily.

"I reckon I'd like to go it alone for a spell," Butch said.

"Well, sure, Pard," Harry told him.

"We know each other's hangouts. I just don't want no more hard riding no time soon. And we have plenty of money. Think I'll try being a tourist."

"We'll keep an eye out for you, Leroy. See you somewhere, someday."

They dismounted and gave each other a bear hug.

Butch looked up at me, proffered his hand, and smiled. "Take care of my pard, Etta. Sundance is the best friend I've ever had."

"Mine too, Leroy. Count on it." I dismounted and hugged him.

Butch rode north toward the railroad. He never glanced back.

Harry rode in silence for a long time.

Except for a few transactions too good to pass up on the way to Lima, our South American adventure ended. We'd had a big time, just a marvelous, soul-fulfilling adventure. I have since read that we conducted "the greatest and most successful and intrepid series of holdups ever in South America." That is a direct quote from a book about the Pinkertons. And I believe it. Of course, I only held the horses.

For a while Harry and I became regular bug-eyed tourists and took our time to let the land rest. First we rode up to Sucre, then into La Paz, which we learned is the highest capital in the world, 12,400 feet. We rented a room at the Hotel Copacabana, cleaned up, sold the horses, rested for a few days, and sipped a little *pisco* before taking the train to Lake Titicaca and then the Scottish steamer across the lake to Peru. I remembered from my teaching days it's the world's highest lake. The ruins of an Inca city, Tiahuanaco, stand nearby, but we couldn't see them from the train or boat.

That whole area is high plains inhabited mostly by Indians raising potatoes and various grains, and we saw them peddling robes and blankets and coats of the furs they take off vicuñas, chinchillas, and red fox. Llamas roamed all over, their beasts of burden.

Again, the high altitudes never bothered us.

A scraggly Indian at the station in Cuzco pestered us so much when we stepped into the sunlight after visiting the cathedral I feared that Harry might slug him.

"Big ruins," he said in English barely understandable. "Very important."

I decided we'd talk Spanish in order to get along. "We want to go to Lima."

"Big ruins near here," he said, still in English. "Go today. Return today."

"We're not interested," I said. The conversation went back and forth over the same ground, with him repeating a term I couldn't figure out in English or Spanish. But we were obviously foreigners and, in his mind, rich, so he wouldn't give up. I didn't much blame him, but he aggravated me so much talking his poor English that I considered whacking him myself.

Finally we escaped to the train station so we could go to Lima.

"I understood some," Harry said. "How about that big word he kept repeating?"

"Yes. Sort of like 'machoopeachoo.'" The word stuck with me. Since then I've read about it many times, Machu-Picchu, and how it had been the "lost city" of the Incas and how an American professor "discovered" it in 1911 soon after we stopped nearby at Cuzco.

"An American teacher in Lima," I told Harry years later when my reading recalled the incident to me, "told the professor of an Indian who led him up to the ruins."

"So it hadn't been lost after all?"

"Nope. Now it's famous. So's the professor. That teacher never gets any credit."

"Hell, Sugar. We could have discovered it ourselves. Then we'd be famous too."

"We did all right, Honey. And we don't need another poster saying so."

The train ride to Lima, downhill all the way, followed a contorted route with beautiful hills and vegetation until flattening out near Lima.

In view of our activities in South America during the last five years, we'd decided that Mexico would be a smarter place for us. We wanted to keep moving. So after spending the night at the Hotel Crillón on gray old Plaza San Martín we asked around and learned we had to take the train to the port to find out about steamer sailings.

"I counted on getting my hair done," I told Harry.

"We don't want to miss the next boat by a day if they sail only once a month."

"If I have to look like this, I'm going to get my own cabin and hide in it."

Turns out that Lima had a big port, El Callao, with plenty of sailings. Inside the train station's main building we reserved passage on a Japanese freighter leaving in a week.

My husband continually looked around, not to admire the architecture either.

"See any Pinkerton posters, Honey?"

"Thought it might be a good idea to check."

On the street, Harry looked around again. "This place has a lot of saloons."

"And I'm thirsty enough to gulp seawater." But it was a rough part of town.

"This isn't for you, Sugar, and doesn't interest me. It reminds me of La Boca, and that reminds me of Leroy. He would love it here."

"And you miss your pard."

"Yep."

I squeezed his hand. We reentered the train station and sipped *pisco* in the bar until time to return to Lima, where I found a beauty shop first thing near the hotel.

Of course a busy port isn't the city. At the hotel I picked up a brochure about Lima's highlights, and in the lobby a guide picked us up. This time we hired him. The guide, a pleasant young man in black pants, black dress shoes, and white short-sleeve shirt, like so many of the locals, spoke adequate English. That would make the day pleasanter for Harry and simpler for me.

"My name is Juan," he said.

Harry grabbed my hand as though needing support. I caught his grin. Outside, we hired a carriage and let Juan take charge.

Lima had so many beautiful Spanish Colonial buildings I couldn't count them, and some of Lima's artistically carved wooden balconies looked special enough to be in museums. One of those grand balconies hung on a two-story building where the Palace of La Perricholi had stood.

"La Perricholi," Juan told us, "was an actress a hundred and fifty years back and mistress of the Viceroy Amat. He built the mansion for her. She is said to have been a famous beauty. They called her Micaela Villegas."

Later I read about her in Thornton Wilder's novel, *The Bridge of San Luis Rey*. Made me feel like an insider. I suspect his bridge was the nearby Puente de Piedra, Roman style, from 1610, according to the brochure in front of me as I write.

Juan pointed out Santo Domingo Church. "St. Rose of Lima's ashes sit there."

"Are we going to stop?" I asked Juan.

"Is too dark inside to see anything."

Those old churches are often as poorly lighted as inside a mule's stomach and sometimes stuffy with stale air. We kept rolling. Juan directed our driver to the Plaza de Armas to see all the government buildings and the cathedral.

"Pizarro's coffin is in the church," Juan said. "The coffin has a glass side and you can see the body." Before Harry asked me to explain Pizarro, I opened the brochure and paraphrased its comments about the blood-thirsty old conquistador.

"Let's go look," Harry said.

Pizarro disappointed us.

"Awful skinny and shriveled," Harry said. "And we can't see his face good."

"Probably mean as a cornered bobcat's, though."

We enjoyed rolling around Lima on that day and a couple of others. And we drank a little *pisco*. It's such a smooth clean powerful brandy made from grapes and best taken straight, although you can ask for a *pisco* sour, like a whiskey sour in the States. This being late January, summer down yonder, on a hot afternoon at a sidewalk cafe we often enjoyed *chicha*, a foamy brew made from a local grain.

They had another dandy drink, one made from cherries, *chilcano de guinda*, and sometimes we drank that. They also had Scotch, but we enjoyed the local libations so much we didn't indulge in imports until after we'd been on the boat heading north for a while and our supply of local creations expired.

30

Acapulco Bay has been a seaport since the era of the Manila galleon bringing ivory and silk and other treasures from Asia while trying to avoid pirates. Back then, cargo and passengers had to be loaded into small boats and rowed between the beach and the big galleon. In 1911 our freighter tied up to a wooden pier. But anyone seeing Acapulco nowadays would have a tough time imaging even how it looked to us.

I couldn't find many palms or other trees in close, though the hills nearby looked lush with trees and shrubs so thick a fly couldn't maneuver. And we saw beautiful beaches, most appearing untracked by man, maybe by just an occasional burro or stray horse at night, or a hungry jaguar looking for that burro or horse.

So at Acapulco, on a hot sultry morning at the edge of the huge blue bay in the Mexican state of Guerrero, we stepped off the steamer onto the pier. Armed only with our inside guns and derringers, we walked into a bucolic village and smack-dab into a war.

"Not much here, is there, Honey?"

"I see a saloon over yonder."

We noticed a few low buildings, stucco and brick, plus some huts made from the spines of palm fronds and roofed with palm branches, the immediate street paved with cobblestones, others as dusty as God made them. One of those huts had a little sign, *Restaurante*, and sent out an attractive aroma.

"You think that nice smell is seafood, Sugar?"

"I'm counting on it."

"Let's give it a try."

We found a cook grilling red snapper over a wood fire. We ordered one each and sat where we could watch that magnificent bay and the few ships, steamers and sail. The thump of a generator told me they had cold beer, and so I ordered two bottles of it without any concern for the brand, which I wouldn't have heard of anyway.

"Would you like to try tequila also?" the waiter asked.

His Spanish sounded different from what I'd been hearing, but I understood him. I imagine mine sounded strange to him too, and I suppose he guessed we'd just arrived. He filled two tall skinny jiggers, set them by our beer. "Tequila is very healthful."

"Oh?" said I. We'd heard of tequila in Texas, knew they fermented it from the bole of a maguey cactus, but hadn't tried it. We'd heard nothing about its being healthful.

Harry took a sip. "My tongue is drunk."

To be polite, I followed suit. "Mine's numb."

"Now some beer," the bartender said.

Tequila captured our imaginations instantly, even without beer, and from that moment it became our preferred aperitif, after-dinner drink too.

Following lunch the waiter directed us to the stage depot nearby, where we'd had our possibles sent. Harry agreed to walk there, and we booked passage on the stagecoach leaving on the next day toward Mexico City. For the night we lodged in a one-story six-room inn facing the bay washing the shore in small somnolent waves. For most of the night, dogs played and scrapped up and down the airy see-through hallway.

"Shooting all over like crazy" is how a well-dressed Mexican man riding with us on the stage described the fighting. "Panic. Everyone scared and suspicious. Fellow named Zapata with a bunch of Indians is camped at the edge of the capital."

I relayed this news to Harry.

"Sugar, tell him we've been around a little gunfire ourselves."

The Mexican said Zapata had the Indians stirred up throughout Guerrero and all over the adjacent states of Morelos and Puebla.

I told Harry, "He says you can't figure whose side the Indians are on."

"Probably they're for the Indian, like in the States."

I chose not to send that comment along to our informant. Besides, we didn't know whose side we'd take.

This must be one of the aggravatingest stage rides this side of hell, winding uphill most of the way, not to mention the interminable jolts and our own dust. But we enjoyed the scenery. We had layovers at Chilpancingo and Taxco, then gratefully rolled onto a cobblestone street late one afternoon around the first of March and stopped at the town square in Cuernavaca.

In an old Mexico City newspaper on the freighter I had read about Cuernavaca, which sounded pleasant and quaint, with good weather. I told Harry about the place.

"Let's try it," he said. "You say it's near Mexico City. We can run up there when we want to watch the shooting."

Butch would have taken my husband seriously and responded with some sort of argument, for or against. I didn't comment but told the driver we'd stay.

"This is like spring in Selma," I said when we planted our feet.

"I hear a mockingbird," Harry said.

The driver knew some English. "We say *cenzontle*." He and his shotgun rider lowered our belongings to the sidewalk.

The bird that had greeted us with his song flew out of the top of an Indian laurel where he'd been perched, a mockingbird, no doubt about it. *Cenzontle* became one of the toughest words I ever had to learn to pronounce. "And listen to the sparrows."

"*Gorriones*," our ornithologist-stage driver announced.

A squadron of them changed laurels at that moment. Sparrows, sure enough.

"I don't see any parrots," I said.

"In the hills," he told us.

"What's that big building over yonder in ruins?" Harry motioned to the south.

"The Palacio de Cortés. The conquistador built it for his wife."

"I hope she got out before it fell in on her. Can you recommend a hotel?"

A regiment of mostly shirtless boys ranging in age from, I'd say, three years to fifteen, had clustered around us.

The driver nodded at the building we'd stopped across the street from, the Hotel Delicias, a two-story structure like others around the square, with white stucco façade, red tile roof, a tall, wide entry, its mammoth wooden double doors standing open. Those doors looked as though they could have sealed a church. Or a fort.

"What do you think, Sugar?"

I turned a circle, taking in the rest of the plaza, one side of it dominated by a new-looking hotel much larger than the Delicias. Its sign identified it as the Bella Vista.

"The Delicias is quaint," I said. "And I like all the red roses in front and the window boxes full of red geraniums."

"All right, troops." Harry gestured to our gear. It didn't matter whether they understood his English. They moved quickly. The two biggest boys grabbed most of it and started across the cobblestones. Others picked up the rest, while the littlest tykes trotted alongside, touching our satchels as though helping.

We walked through the entry a few steps, where our bell-boys deposited our possessions, and Harry tipped them, including the little ones who had been shut out of the cargo train. The hotel seemed to have about five rooms. Its patio shouted with geraniums, also bougainvillea, roses, hibiscus, which Mexicans call *tulipán,* and that tall pretty treelike bird of paradise they call *plátano falso,* or "false banana." A well centered the patio, which numerous chickens and, at other times, we learned, the owner's burro, also occupied. We found out he kept his milk cow and horses behind in the corral. The outhouses sat back there too.

A slim light-skinned man, elderly but agile, stepped out of a downstairs room and touched his fingertips to his forehead. "Francisco Alcaide Rambla, at your orders."

They say that as a courtesy, and some mean it. He added, "Would you like a drink?" They don't all say that.

So you can see we hit it off with this man immediately. He spoke good English too, which Harry appreciated.

"Call me Paco," he said.

"Harry and Etta." He and Paco shook hands. Harry registered us as Mr. and Mrs. Parker, and Paco gave us a large room on the second floor across half the front with a balcony from where we could see the street and the plaza all the way past the Indian laurels and other trees to the Cortés palace. In checking out the room we heard the *cenzontles* and *gorriones.* Those happy little vocalists sold us on the Hotel Delicias.

During the next few days, and armed as though for business, we borrowed horses from Paco to explore Cuernavaca and the immediate countryside. On the way north out of town we passed a big stone house with a tower of battlements like a fort might have, then reached the cathedral. It reminded us of the sixteenth-century churches we saw all over South America. We enjoyed the countryside more.

And we shared late-afternoon aperitifs with Paco: white tequila, brown tequila, beer if the iceman had been around or the hotel's generator worked.

"Many Mexicans will drink warm beer," Paco said, "but that's only the poor, and just because it costs less." He didn't have a bar, so in the patio at a round table under the shade of red bougainvilleas we occupied leather-covered bucket chairs they called *equipales*. A huge birdcage and a small one hung nearby.

"That's the prettiest parrot I've ever seen." I motioned to the large bird, red, yellow, and green, in the big cage.

Paco nodded. "*Papagayo*. I call her Carlota."

Harry said, "What about the colorful little fellow in the other cage?"

"That's my baby, Bebito. A *jilguero*. I'm told the English word is 'finch.'"

One afternoon while we sat there waiting for our host to emerge from his quarters at the front, I mentioned to Harry something I'd long been curious about.

"Have you noticed how sometimes you can feel an instant camaraderie with someone you accidentally meet in your travels? Man or woman, rich or poor, black, brown, white, or yellow?"

Harry nodded. "Like in Bolivia, Mary Seifert."

"Sometimes you feel kinship immediately, strike up a conversation, and suddenly have a friendship you hadn't planned and couldn't have thought up."

"I know, Sugar."

"Like with Paco, no?"

"And with me and you."

"And with you and Butch."

"Exactly. I wonder what Butch is doing. No way a letter could've found us."

"No, Honey, but he doesn't even write his momma."

We had brought the Sauza. Paco joined us with jiggers, sliced limes, and a salt shaker. Carlota squawked in greeting, waddled across her cage, stopping closer to Paco. Little Bebito sang a few lovely bars. And, at our urging, Paco gave us his background. He had already told us he turned eighty earlier in the year, born in Mexico City in 1831.

"People say I don't look my age."

"Under seventy," Harry told him.

Paco had gray hair, stood straight and nearly as tall as Harry, and didn't seem fragile in mind or body. His skin, lighter than Harry's, didn't show a wrinkle.

"Swell living," he told us more than once.

Paco had been a sixteen-year-old recruit fighting Winfield Scott and our boys in 1847, all the way from Resaca to Cerro Gordo to Chapultepec Castle, what we call the Halls of Montezuma.

"I plugged one gringo for sure, excuse me, but mostly I shot at the dust and ran or rode one way or another in confusion, all in terrible fear."

Paco had been a young officer under Ignacio Zaragoza when the Mexicans whipped the French invaders and their Mexican cohorts at the Battle of Puebla in May of 1862.

"Porfirio Díaz led us. Such a great victory. Later the Conservaties and French took it back. Then we won again. I fought in all three battles at Puebla. By 1867 I am colonel, thirty-six years old. I stood near Juárez in Querétaro to witness the executions of Maximiliano, Miramón, and Mejía on the Hill of the Bells. So, as you see, during your Civil War we had ours here, with a French accent. Abraham Lincoln kept you together. Benito Juárez did the same for us."

With no wars imminent after Juárez put down the French intervention, Paco left the army and, like a lot of Mexico City folks, bought a home and other properties in Cuernavaca. Unlike many, however, he chose to live there year-round and married a local girl. They built the Hotel Delicias, raised three sons and two daughters, and saw them all grow up, marry, and move to northern Mexico and the United States. His fine little hotel and other investments helped send them on their way. All became successful.

"One daughter is married to an engineer in San Antonio, the other to an accountant in El Paso. I've spent a lot of time in both cities."

"So that's how you learned English?" Harry said.

"Not in Texas. In San Francisco. The waterfront. Waiter. Carriage driver."

Twenty years before we met him, his wife died. Paco didn't remarry.

"I launched myself into the swell living," he said.

He had such enthusiasm for the swell living—dances, fiestas, bordellos all over Morelos, Guerrero, and Mexico City—that Francisco Alcaide Rambla came to be called, affectionately, the Monster of Morelos. We heard that from several people.

"They say another fight's underway here," Harry said. "Going to get big."

"Yes. My weapons are cleaned, oiled, and loaded. My best horse is ready."

"Now, don't be insulted," I told him, "but isn't your age against you?"

"No. I'm not too old to fight. That's what I know best, fighting. The hours in the saddle could be wearisome. But I ride frequently to keep limber."

Carlota squawked. Bebito sang a few notes.

With pleasure and awe and pride, Paco told us of the rebel leader. "Zapata pretty much rules this state of Morelos, but mainly the small towns, villages, and the countryside. He has spent a lot of time planning with other guerrilla leaders and organizing his people in Morelos."

"Man on the stagecoach," Harry said, "talked strong against Zapata."

"You'll find people like that. They are wrong."

The fight against the government also raged in the north, Paco said. "It could expand here any minute. Zapata has thousands of followers."

"You mean troops?" Harry said.

"The same humble farmer you see working in the cornfield is one of Zapata's soldiers. So is the farmer's wife. Drop the plow and grab the rifle hidden in the fence of stones. Set the bean pot off the fire and buckle on the cartridge belt."

"Sounds like a new kind of army."

"Yes. And they follow him out of respect and loyalty. Many are Indians. Others are mestizos like most of us. Of course many mestizos won't admit to being part Indian. I suppose they never served under Benito Juárez or Porfirio Díaz, Indians from Oaxaca."

"I reckon you know this Zapata personally," Harry said.

"Not yet. I don't even know what he looks like. No one around here does. But I know what he's like, what he stands for: freedom and justice. Zapata is symbol as much as he is man. He could fall, and his followers would carry on. *Zapatismo* would endure."

Federal forces, Paco said, continually pursued Zapata but had been unable to corner him or weaken his following. Zapata won several skirmishes.

"The *federales* have destroyed village after village here in the south. They want to—what is that word?—intimidate the people of the villages and small towns, get them to quit supporting Zapata. Instead, the federals drive them to his side." Paco smiled and nodded, sipped his tequila. "Zapata has the right idea, not the federals, and not General Díaz, who is president too long."

Harry raised his glass. "To Zapata."

Paco and I followed suit.

Díaz had been a great soldier, Paco said, and as president did "many pretty things" at first before losing touch with the people. "He became harsh and corrupt and let foreign interests get too influential in Mexico's economy and daily life. The young man from the north, Madero, is pulling Díaz's ears. The people prefer Madero, as they showed last summer in our election."

"We didn't know, moving around a lot," Harry said.

"Madero won but we had fraud, so General Díaz used his power and won. He had Madero arrested but Madero escaped to Texas. Recently he crossed into northern Mexico, to Chihuahua, where the highwayman, Pancho Villa, has raised troops for him. That's where most of the fighting is. But I'll wait here. The fighting will come to me."

"I reckon that's good," Harry said, "having a highwayman on your side."

"Yes. Villa is dedicated and without fear, like Zapata. Another fearless and dedicated warrior is in the capital, José Guadalupe Posada. With his writings and drawings, Posada explains Díaz for many years to the common people. I hope Posada doesn't get arrested and disappeared." The Monster of Morelos paused, took another sip. "I seem to have made a speech."

Carlota squawked. Bebito sang.

31

Paco's hotel staff comprised a cleaning lady and a gardener-handyman, but nobody cooked. So we took our meals at one little restaurant or another, the same as he did, except when he worked up a snack for himself in his quarters, as he called his room. Most of the time we ate at the Hotel Bella Vista on the other side of the plaza from the Delicias. Its two stories stood around a large courtyard, the dining area, open to the heavens, though it had a smaller inside room in case of rain.

A middle-aged English widow, Rosa E. King, ran the Bella Vista, which she'd built the year before, shortly after arriving. It appeared she did well, knew a lot of important people despite her brief residency. She made us welcome.

"Naturally, Governor Escandón dines at my hotel frequently," Mrs. King told us during our first breakfast at the Bella Vista. "The federal generals who come to town lodge here, as will President Díaz with his entourage, to enjoy a respite as soon as the nasty insurrection in the countryside is put down. I mean, one couldn't expect *gente de razón*, as we call the upper class, to lodge at Don Paco's rickety old place."

I don't know what that said for Harry and me, but we forgave her, for Paco had already provided her background. "She's a nice lady," Paco had said, "genteel. But she's ignorant of the political situation." And we liked Paco and his "rickety old place."

Also, by then we'd taken his side in this rebellion.

During another breakfast at the Bella Vista a couple of weeks after our arrival, Harry suggested a change of scene.

"I feel cooped up. Would 'preciate a better look at the surroundings."

"Me too, although Shakespeare and Jack London are excellent company."

"Yes, Sugar, but I'm not good friends with those boys the way you are."

I read to Harry when he'd sit still and let me, and that included the newspapers from Mexico City, *El País* and *El Imparcial*. But he preferred a poker game when he could find one, and he'd already taught Paco to play cooncan and cassino.

"A picnic in the hills would be revitalizing and educational," I suggested.

When we mentioned our plan to Mrs. King, she said, "I'll send you off with a jolly good lunch: fried chicken, tortillas, goat cheese, oranges. A shepherd pie would be best, or a steak-and-kidney pie, but I've not been able to teach either one to my cook."

"We'll add a bottle of tequila," Harry told me, "to wash things down."

"If you go north into the pines and oaks, you must watch out for mountain lions," Mrs. King said. "Whatever you do, don't ride east. You mustn't fall into the clutches of that heinous bandit Zapata."

"We'll be on guard," I said. "Mrs. King, we've been curious about the big mountains off to the east. One's smoking like a volcano."

"Yes, it's active, our Indian warrior, Popocatépetl, which means 'smoking mountain.' But we're in no danger here. The other is inactive, Popo's sweetheart, Iztaccíhuatl, or 'sleeping woman.' That's the legend."

"Lovers for eternity." My hand met Harry's.

We told Mrs. King we'd return in an hour for the lunch, and we walked outside. "'Kidney pie'?" Harry said

"Why not? Remember, where I come from we eat possum."

My husband grabbed my arm and tugged me next door. "Over here."

"What in tarnation for? I need to change clothes."

"Sombreros. Come on."

I couldn't talk him out of it, so we soon left the little shop with a sombrero apiece, those huge fancy ones you see in parades or sometimes on mariachis, lots of embroidery and sequins. Mine was white with a blue band, red embroidery, and silver conchos, Harry's black with a red band, white embroidery, and even more conchos.

"Mine's awful heavy," I said.

"The horses will take all the weight when we're mounted."

I didn't understand his reasoning, and I don't to this day.

At the Delicias, Paco had his worker saddle a couple of good-looking geldings, a pinto for me and, for Harry, a red roan with a white face and a bite out of one ear. Paco gave us a pint of white Sauza. We toted that, canteens full of water, a blanket to sit on, and, in the rifle boots, our Model 94s. Harry packed his whole arsenal, I my inside gun.

"If you see my General Zapata," Paco said, "please announce that Col. Francisco Alcaide Rambla is at his orders."

Paco reminded us that no outsiders knew Zapata's whereabouts. "Anyway, he's on our side."

We sent the horses out at a walk down a trail dropping south past the ruins of the huge palace Cortés had built for him and his Spanish wife. That route took us out of town toward Yautepec, the big volcanoes escorting us on the east.

"I reckon," I said, "we'll be all right if we stay on or near the main trail."

"Yes. I don't want you captured, even by a friendly bandit. But if we hear any shooting, we can ride over and see if we can help."

As mentioned, Harry had enough of being fettered.

After an hour of up-and-down riding we spotted a clean happy stream beside a sandy clearing about thirty yards off the trail in the midst of willows, a *tule*, and several *ahuehuetes* I had learned to identify from a book. We rode to it.

"I don't see any ants or beetles," Harry said, "no rattlesnakes either."

I spread the blanket, we set out our lunch, and sat.

"The chicken's so big," Harry said, "it looks like a baby turkey." We ate only about a quarter of it while also working on the tortillas and tequila.

"Peaceful here, isn't it, Sugar?"

"Romantic too." I smiled around a bite of orange.

Harry leaned close and kissed me.

Before long we began taking each other's clothes off. I couldn't hold back and didn't want to, such a wondrous and exciting situation and feeling, there in the wilderness with the handsomest man I've ever known and the only man I ever loved. We liked that part of the picnic the best, although bathing in the stream afterwards also thrilled us. A frog watched us from a rock. A *jilguero* serenaded us from a low branch.

As we rode out of our little Arcady and got close to the trail, the white-faced roan, in front with Harry, started wiggling his torn ear. Then he shied so suddenly he nearly stepped out from under Harry. I had to laugh. Snakes, wild turkeys, a rabbit, a piece of paper, lots of things will make a horse do that.

At the same spot my horse acted just like Harry's. But I didn't come as close to being grounded as my husband did. I squawked, however.

Harry looked back, smiling and patient. Then his expression changed. "Hold up." He dismounted, unholstered his Colt Bisley, and stepped into the shrubbery at the side of the trail.

I slipped my Model 94 out of my rifle boot.

In a moment, Harry said, "Be prepared, Sugar. We might have a dead man here." A few seconds later he said, "Bring your canteen. He must have missed the stream."

Sure enough, a man lay in there, mostly hidden and just about done for, looked to me. But he merely slept, although he looked plenty scratched and bedraggled.

"He must have crawled in there to hide after we passed," Harry said. "Either that or he made his own trail through the brush and trees."

"I hope he didn't see us frolicking buck-naked."

"This man needed sleep, Sugar, not entertainment."

He looked Mexican or Indian, seemed to be shorter than Harry, must have heard us talking. He looked up surprised, then concerned. But the man didn't try to grab his rifle, which lay half-way under his leg. He had a pistol holster but no pistol.

"Talk to him, Sugar, friendly like, so he knows we don't mean him harm."

I told him we wanted to help, and Harry offered him my canteen. The poor man took a deep breath and gulped so much water I feared he'd founder. "Speak English?"

He shook his head.

I switched to Spanish. "What can we do to help?"

He shook his head again.

"He seems stubborn but awfully grateful," I said. "Should we leave him now?"

"I suppose, Sugar."

But something held us. "He doesn't look like some farmer who decided to sneak a nap when the foreman got careless."

"No," Harry said. "Too far from any spreads. Doesn't even have a hat."

"And he's so whipped out."

"And his rifle and cartridge belt make one thing clear."

"You think he's one of Zapata's guerrillas, Harry?"

"He is, sure as shootin'."

His clothes fitted what we'd heard about the rebels: white cotton pants and long-sleeve shirt, a type of huarache for sandals. "That's it. He's on the run."

The fellow had quite dark skin, and he seemed younger than me, with hair blacker than mine, and eyes just as black. He hadn't shaved for several days, and it looked like he'd trimmed his mustache with a machete and his hair with a hatchet. But I could see courage in that face, intelligence and determination. I figured it wouldn't help to ask too many questions, the man so laconic, probably the Indian in him.

"He's been through hell," Harry said. "He can ride double with us back to town."

I so informed our captive, as I thought of him.

He shook his head. But he stirred enough to squat on his heels, the same as Harry, the way farmers and ranchers and cowboys powwow.

"Are you lost?"

Again he shook his head.

Harry walked to the roan and returned with our picnic leftovers, including most of the chicken, several tortillas, one orange, and at least half the pint of tequila.

Damned if our Zapatista didn't shake his head again.

I said, "Come on. You need it."

Finally he smiled and reached out.

Harry said, "Ask him if he needs shells for his rifle."

I did so.

"It no longer serves," the man told me. He let us have a better look at it. His rifle looked as though pounded by a boulder, the breech bent, the stock broken and splintered.

Harry, who knew a man in trouble when he saw one, walked to the roan again. This time he returned with his loaded Model 94 carbine he'd carried since new, and he handed it to this fellow. Next he gave him a handful of extra cartridges and his brand new black sombrero with the silvery conchos, red band, and white embroidery.

I guess I had a funny look on my face.

"Like you said, Sugar, that hat's mighty heavy."

We liked Cuernavaca more every day, its people friendly, pleasant, and attractive, the cost of living low, weather springtime and said to be that way all year. No doubt we'd want to bust out one day, but meantime we felt as contented as bees that had arrived home with bellies full of peach nectar.

Other guests, including an occasional couple, usually friendly but keeping to themselves, checked in an out of the Delicias. None stayed long-term like us.

I became friends with Mrs. King and some of the Mexican women. Harry drew contentment playing cards and dominoes with Paco and other loafers in one cantina or another or set up under an Indian laurel on the plaza, friendly games, penny ante.

One day Paco suggested having a marksmanship contest.

"Pistols," Paco said.

Oh-oh, I thought.

Paco said, "I was the best shot in my outfit."

And Harry was the best shot in his.

Paco spread the word among his cronies young and old until every man and boy in town seemed to know about it and planned to compete or watch.

"It's like a rodeo or circus is coming to town," Mrs. King said. "Don Paco has won every contest here for years, I'm told. I saw him shoot once. He's good."

And I've seen Harry shoot a lot. I kept shut.

Paco selected a dry arroyo on the edge of town but close enough so that folks would know and not think the federals and

Zapatistas were having at it. As Harry and I walked to the arroyo with Paco, we picked up a battalion of children and dogs. Paco had strapped on an old .41-caliber six-shooter he must have had since the Mexican War. Harry carried his holstered Colt Bisley Frontier Model .45 and had his inside gun under his light jacket.

They shot at tin cans and bottles over various distances. Paco shot well, all right, and he would have beaten Butch and plenty of others from The Wild Bunch. So I figured he didn't get disgraced by Harry's winning the shoot.

"I must admit I'm surprised." Paco shook Harry's hand when the contest ended. "And I'm disappointed that at my age, after all my glories, I have met my better." He turned to the men and boys gathered around. "Mr. Parker and his lovely wife are lodgers at my hotel. Yes. And they're my friends. Very good friends."

None of the other shooters came close to Harry's and Paco's deeds. But they had more fun, joshing each other, trading pistols, facing away from the targets to shoot blindly over the shoulder, all the while drinking tequila and mescal from bottles and flirting with the women and girls. I felt someone would get shot in the foot, or worse.

When Paco pulled a half pint of tequila out of a pocket to share with Harry, they insisted I join them. I didn't have a choice, so I took a sip.

"Honey," I told Harry after my second sip, "let's have a rifle contest now."

"I don't have my carbine any longer," Harry said.

"I'll go to the hotel and fetch mine."

"Sugar, I think another time would be better."

Harry didn't mind losing to me. But he didn't want me to show up the Mexicans.

Many of the contestants trailed us to the plaza and into the Bella Vista bar, where Harry stood for drinks and everyone shook his hand, and a few gave him one of those big Mexican *abrazos*. Harry could handle the hugging if no one also kissed him on the cheek.

As a courtesy to Harry, Paco participated. But I know he didn't want Mrs. King to see him, seemed relieved she didn't show up.

"*El Imparcial* is misnamed," I told Harry. "There's nothing impartial in anything this newspaper prints about Zapata. Everything's a smear, a black eye." I'd picked up the newspaper at the kiosk in the plaza. Now we sat on our balcony after breakfast.

"Being around Paco," Harry said, "and talking with lots of the folks, and seeing the awful poverty of the average man, we can't help but feel that Zapata is in the right."

"So I guess we're not impartial either."

"Mrs. King and a lot of her *gente de razón*, as she calls them, sure don't like Zapata. Afraid he wants to be president and hang them all."

On this day, *El Imparcial* claimed that federal troops had overrun Zapata's headquarters camp and killed several of the rebels—claimed with a gloat.

"Listen to this: 'Zapata unfortunately managed a miraculous escape but will soon be run to ground and strung up promptly from the nearest oak tree for the good of the nation.' And that's a news story, not any editorial. The paper likes Madero in a cautious way, but avoids criticism of Díaz. Straddling the fence, you see."

"Of course," Harry said. "You don't dare play with your mouse in front of an old hawk unless you're rich with mice."

In early May, about the time the grizzlies would be coming out of hibernation in Harry's home state, a terrible fight took place south of Cuernavaca at Yautepec, where Zapata and his people captured the federal garrison in an hour. They had sent in little boys carrying small cans packed with dynamite and dangling burning fuses. The boys tossed the cans into the garrison headquarters and onto the roof, then ran like scared jackrabbits. Federal heads got blown off to all points of the compass.

In mid-May an even bloodier fight took place at an important nearby city, Cuautla. But now the federals expected the dynamite boys, so they hid on the rooftops and slaughtered several of the youngsters. I cried when I read that. The battle lasted four days and the Zapatistas lost a lot of men and horses. But they took Cuautla.

Some of the federal survivors, dusty and sweaty and ragged, reached Cuernavaca, so we heard firsthand accounts of the terror. I could almost smell the gunpowder. Days later they still seemed frightened. Nowadays they'd qualify for therapy.

"Mr. Zapata," I told Harry, "could ride with that damn Sherman."

32

And Porfirio Díaz resigned.

We heard the word on the street before special editions of the Mexico City newspapers arrived. If some folks cared, they didn't show it. Others jumped in jubilation.

"After all these years," Harry said.

"He's been Mexico's president all my life, seems like."

The next day we heard that Zapata and his troops approached Cuernavaca. We couldn't believe that either, too excited to sit still.

Lots of people left town in a hurry, some for good reason, others out of fear of the unknown or of Zapata's fierceness as reported in the newspapers. Others, including the governor and the few federal troops protecting him, hid in attics or fled to the jungle. Mrs. King draped the Union Jack from the second-floor balcony of the Bella Vista.

"Why would she do that?" Harry said.

"Zapata's not at war with the British Empire."

While that took place, Paco washed his shot glasses, restocked his liquor cabinet, curried and saddled his best horse, and put on the uniform he'd worn half a century earlier when he stood near Benito Juárez on the Hill of the Bells.

"What do you suppose?" I asked Harry.

"I think he's going to join up."

On our balcony we placed chairs and a small table and set out a store of goat cheese, rolls, sliced mountain ham, and tequila. I did my hair up and put on a red short-sleeve blouse with a cute fluffy white collar; a multicolored flowing skirt like I'd seen some of the Mexican women wear on Sundays; a delicate white lace mantilla over my shoulders; big golden earrings; sandals on bare feet; and, on each arm, several thin silver bracelets. I colored my toenails red with Paco's house paint.

"You look wonderful, Sugar, just like a beautiful gypsy."

Harry wore his banker's outfit, right down to the pocket watch and gold chain. He strapped on his inside gun but left his others on the dresser, along with mine. He propped my carbine on the balcony just out of sight on his side. "Just a precaution, Sugar. Paco predicts a friendly takeover."

The Zapatistas began arriving in early afternoon. At first the only sign was the racket of hundreds of horses' hooves striking the cobblestones at the edge of town in one of the most portentous sounds I ever heard, ominous, confusing, louder every second.

"Spooky," Harry said.

"Yes. My skin's tingling."

We heard doors and windows slam shut and bolts being slid. People shouted, and idlers ran in different directions from the plaza. The place got so quiet we couldn't hear anything except the horses' clatter. Even the birds in the trees on the plaza shut up. I could feel the tension, my own and what seemed to permeate the environs.

And the strangest army imaginable rode in.

They passed in front of us. Ten or twelve men led the way on horseback side by side in twos, like an honor guard, with the others riding behind them in uneven clusters. Some of their horses looked ready for retirement or the rendering plant. And we saw a mighty scary bunch of armed riders, stern, unsmiling. All dressed in white cotton pants and long-sleeve shirts, like farmers we'd seen, like that bedraggled fellow who spooked our horses on the day of our picnic. Some in the front wore boots, possibly taken off federal troops they'd killed. Most had huaraches, others different types of sandals, each man a straw sombrero large or small, a rifle, and a belt or two of ammunition. A few toted side arms. Several showed big black mustaches.

"They look like they've been on the trail for weeks," I told Harry.

"Yes, but see how sharp-eyed they are, watching every which way, getting the lay of the place, keeping an eye out for trouble."

"They seem as scared as they are scary."

"Maybe some have never been in a town this size. But they're well disciplined." Harry reached for a piece of cheese.

And we saw Zapata.

I reached for the tequila.

Even though we'd never seen his photograph, we knew. Harry and I exchanged looks. I bet everyone knew, the swarthy man riding with others of his troops a few steps behind that first bunch. He stood out, is all, had a presence. His clothes contributed to the feeling, so different from any other attire that day, tight-fitting black pants and short-waist black jacket, good black boots and big spurs, and a white shirt, revolver high on his right hip. Looked like an old Remington double-action .44. His rifle must have been out of sight in the boot on his other side. Zapata's sombrero had a high crown and wide brim like some of the others', but seemed better made. And no one else had a horse like his.

"Harry, that's some magnificent bay stallion he's riding."

"The man knows horseflesh, all right."

Zapata's horse didn't look especially large, though magnificently proportioned, muscular, and long-legged with a saucy step and a blaze on an arrogant, beautiful head.

Another reason we recognized him: the way the men around him looked so proud and confident, yet protective too.

I think Zapata glanced at us. And maybe not. "They might camp in the plaza or take over the church."

"Wouldn't be surprised."

However, they continued riding west, except for a few who dismounted, walked to the plaza, and boarded up the cantinas.

They left the Bella Vista alone, maybe didn't realize Mrs. King had a bar inside.

"Might have been her British flag," Harry said.

Then Zapata and the first batch rode out of sight to be followed by quite a few more riders and lots of men on foot, and the women, also on foot in huaraches. Most of the women carried rifles, had ammunition belts crossed on their chests, and wore long plain dresses with full skirts, female guerrillas of all ages.

"Think you could outshoot Zapata's women, Sugar?"

"I don't know. But I'll say this: I wouldn't trade places with a one of them."

So Harry and I sat on our balcony, sipping tequila and nibbling our cheese and ham and rolls, and we watched the guerrillas pass. By the time the mules came by pulling a couple of wagons, probably camping essentials and grub, some of the townspeople had showed up on the streets to watch, no longer afraid of "the Attila of the South," as *El Imparcial* recently described Zapata. I didn't note even a hint of trouble.

When I heard a movement below us I leaned over the balcony and saw Paco on his best horse. He must have opened the back gate and ridden right through the hotel patio to the front. I nudged Harry and pointed down.

Harry leaned over. "Where you bound all dressed up?"

Paco, square-shouldered and proud in his 1860s uniform, looked up and saw us, removed his hat. "I'm going to offer my services to my General Zapata. He'll no doubt be bivouacked at the edge of town." Paco had belted on his saber.

"Who'll run your hotel?"

"I'll be back tonight and we'll talk about it."

"But we—"

"I came to attention and saluted my General Zapata. He acknowledged me. I must hurry on." Paco spun his horse and cantered him west in Zapata's tracks.

So maybe Zapata had been glancing at Paco, not us.

Following a nap we washed, dressed, and crossed the street to the plaza, where we sat on a bench under a jacaranda. The birds sang and jabbered mightily again, and the whole place had returned to life. Men occupied most of the shaded benches, their animated chatter filling the air. I eavesdropped and told Harry what I made out.

"There's just one topic," I said, "Emiliano Zapata: how he looked and acted, how long he's going to stay, what's he doing here, what's he going to do next."

"So how long's he staying? What's he doing here?"

"Nobody knows."

"What's he going to do next?"

"Nobody knows that either."

About dusk, when we'd moved to the patio of the Delicias and considered where to eat supper, Paco rode up. Harry opened the back gate for him so he didn't have to dismount to put up his horse. "Be with you in a few minutes," Paco said.

When he joined us, Paco wore his usual white dress shirt, black pants, and black shoes. Still, he looked as though transformed. He brought a bottle of aged tequila, salt, limes, three tall jiggers, and sat with us. "We ride in three days."

I saw the tease in Paco's eyes.

"I presented myself with my full rank," Paco said. "My General Zapata asked my military experience. 'War against the Americans. War of the French Intervention.'

"My general nodded. He almost smiled. 'That gives me your age. Can you shoot? Can you drill?' I admitted to being excellent in both categories. 'In that case, while we are here, you can help with marksmanship and drilling, mounted and on foot. And, Colonel, bring your saber. My people will be impressed.'"

Animated, exuberant, ready to saddle up and ride out, Francisco Alcaide Rambla further described his visit to the camp, told us what the rebel leader looked like up close, and how Zapata related to his followers. Paco also relayed rumors. "Factions are forming. Several men from Cuernavaca have already joined up. Others had attached themselves as the Zapatistas marched this way. Díaz is sailing to exile in France. Governor Escandón is sought for interrogation."

The tequila went down as smoothly as the sun settling behind the Indian laurels.

"This has been my grandest day in a long time," Paco said. "It will be topped only by tomorrow when I begin instructing troops for the Chief of the South."

Zapata won't take over the church or the Toluca Theater or government buildings, Paco said, nor a fine mansion for himself. "That's not his way. Leave the townspeople alone. Do not plunder. Intrude as little as possible. His tent is the very heart of the encampment. They say he joins in the singing and card games and that he can be approached by any man, woman, or child to hear requests or complaints or comments. And he will shoot any of his men who violate women or harm children."

I could see that Paco respected Zapata as much as he had Juárez and, when Díaz was younger, Díaz himself. He told us a lot more, and the three of us had a big time. We even talked him into going to the Bella Vista with us for supper, so you know he felt expansive. Besides, he knew Zapata now, and Mrs. King didn't.

When we stood to walk to the plaza, Paco picked up the bottle. "He wants to see you tomorrow."

"Who?" Harry said.

"You both."

"I mean, who wants?"

"My General Zapata." Paco quickly stepped out of the Delicias patio ahead of us, probably already thinking about his duties of the next day under Zapata's command.

We caught up with him across the street. I said, "What do you think's going on?"

"In my general's tent, some local men approached him. They suggested he recruit the glass-eyed gringo who won the recent shooting contest."

"'Glass-eyed'?"

"*Ojo de vidrio*," Paco said. "It's a way of saying 'blue-eyed.'"

"'Glass-eyed'?" Harry said.

"No one in these parts has ever seen anyone shoot like you," Paco said. "Of course, in my prime, I would have given you more competition. Anyway, my general heard you praised so much he wants to meet you. Perhaps he hopes you are a renowned highway-man from Texas."

"'Texas,' hell," Harry said, trying to sound like a Texan. He spat and smiled.

Paco stopped in the shade of a royal ponciana to swallow from the bottle. "My general asked if a black-haired woman, not ugly, accompanied you."

"'Not ugly'?" I said.

"It's just the way he talks," Paco said.

"'Not ugly'?" I repeated.

Harry laughed.

I punched his arm. "Watch it, Glass-Eye."

33

Naturally, Harry wanted to ride the three hundred yards to Zapata's camp, but I tugged him onto the cobblestones. "We don't want to be too conspicuous."

"Horses aren't conspicuous. Everybody has one."

I had to change course. "Maybe you should leave your six-shooter in the hotel."

"Sugar, I don't pleasure in the idea of walking among a bunch of armed strangers unless I have plenty of protection."

Harry packed his whole arsenal, and I had mine, except my carbine.

"Besides," Harry said half-jesting, "he might want a shooting lesson."

"But I left my carbine behind." I tugged his arm again.

Before long the cobblestones ended, and the road became dirt, easier walking.

Zapata had so many troops that by the time we neared his tent, with people along the way pointing or telling us the direction, we had to walk somewhat farther than I'd promised my husband. Harry would remind me of that for several days.

"They're quite a bunch," Harry said.

"And mostly on the sorry side, so poorly clothed and not well armed. Most of the rifles look like they've been through war quite a spell ago."

"I've spotted a few old muskets." Harry motioned behind us. "And back yonder I saw some Virginia Manufactory flintlocks, .69-caliber smoothbores."

"Good Lord."

"Haven't been produced in a hundred years."

These Zapatistas comprised a hodgepodge of ages. They sat on the ground or strolled about, worked on horse tack or cleaned their weapons, while some women fixed meals and others sewed. I caught the welcoming aroma of meat sizzling on grills set over rocks, beans bubbling in pots, dough being pounded and slapped into tortillas. Beyond a big tent in the center of camp a breeze sent reeds and willows to singing the presence of a stream.

"Excited, Sugar?" Harry squeezed my hand.

"You bet."

A sentry stopped us at the big tent. Starting there, I did the talking. When the guard cleared us and we entered the tent a young man standing behind a small table motioned for us to sit in two chairs opposite him. Rifle-toting guerrillas stood around the edges. Other armed men sat in a corner. Each rebel wore the Zapatista "uniform" of large mustache, long-sleeve white cotton shirt and pants, with sandals or huaraches, all except the man who greeted us. That fellow wore a white dress shirt, brown pants, and brown dress shoes. He had rimless glasses, short curly hair, big ears, and a thin pale face with a mouth like a girl's. Clean-shaven. Couldn't have weighed 140 pounds. Unarmed.

Nowhere could we spot the imposing rider in black who'd led the arriving troops.

"We're Harry and Etta Parker," I said.

"I know," our greeter replied. "I'm Gildardo Magaña, counsel for General Zapata." He started right in questioning us.

Now, I'd never been inside a courtroom, but I recognized a third-degree, and Mr. Magaña started right in putting us through one. I quietly cautioned Harry not to cuss him in case Magaña knew English, always a possibility. And on account of the tension I kept one eye on Harry's expression. Maybe I could head him off if he decided to smack the guy.

But I would no more give this man our true identities nor tell him what we had been doing in recent years than I would Charlie Siringo.

He kept flinging the questions, directing them at Harry and concerning Harry more than me. I suppose he considered me merely as Harry's woman, not an individual. Talking through a woman must have galled him like tasting sour milk.

Magaña seemed convinced that Harry had to be a newspaper reporter or a spy for Madero, and he asked the same things in different ways. I steered him with honest denials where fitting, with misdirection where necessary.

"We're tourists," I said, "just up from South America and around. Visited Mr. Pizarro and Miss La Perricholi, high society like that." I don't know if he caught on.

He also inquired about Harry's skill with a six-shooter.

"Everybody where we come from knows how to shoot," I told him.

Magaña smiled for the first time. I don't know what he believed and what he didn't. But he quit the grilling and walked away, not even saying thanks or go to hell.

"I guess we can go," I told Harry.

We stood.

And one of the men in white who'd been sitting in the back walked up to us. "I am Emiliano Zapata."

Harry understood that part.

We shook hands and Zapata led us outside. "That tent becomes as oppressive as a federal patrol. Later I'll introduce you to my brother, Eufemio. He sat next to me in the back."

So the leaders had sat quiet and let that citified lawyer quiz us.

"I apologize for Mr. Magaña," Zapata said, "that is, not for the questions but for his manner. Eufemio and I think of him as

Torquemada. But he is valuable and loyal, and he knows law and politics." Zapata smiled faintly. "Also, he writes better than I, even though I know my letters and have more schooling than most of my people."

I liked him, felt that presence, saw in his face the wisdom and determination we'd heard about, noticed in his eyes a sorrow and a longing.

Harry said, "Ask him how he liked that chicken."

We spent the whole day at the bivouac, mostly sitting in camp chairs in the shade of a *tule* tree watching Zapata talk with his aides and receive his guerrillas arriving with requests or complaints. Everyone called him by his first name. And he got interrupted aplenty, Zapata domestic arbiter as well as military marshal. And now that we saw him up close, cleaned up, and rested, we pegged him for a few years younger than me. I was thirty-four going on thirty-five.

When we tried to excuse ourselves he wouldn't hear of it.

"One more gun won't do him any good."

"You mean two," I said. And that's what I told Zapata.

"No," Zapata said, "but I am grateful for your help that day you found me. Be my guests for barbecue. We will be eating soon. And I have something for you." He turned to one of his aides and spoke so rapidly and softly I missed it. The man trotted to the headquarters tent, hurried inside, and returned with Harry's Model 94 Winchester carbine, clean and shiny, handing it to Zapata. He handed it to Harry.

"It's yours," Harry said. "Tell him, Sugar."

I told him but it didn't do any good.

Finally Harry said, "Much obliged. *Gracias.*"

"Earlier that day," Zapata said, "federals discovered a few of us on the outskirts of Jojutla. Each faction got a big surprise. But they had more men, horses, and guns. We scattered like a secret lover caught by the husband. Excuse me, Missus. No one got hurt on either side, and we all escaped. So did my horse. And my men disappeared. I started on foot across country avoiding roads, trails, and people. You helped me when I needed help the most. I gave the fancy sombrero to my brother."

When I relayed that information to Harry, he laughed, agreeing with the fate of that burdensome big sombrero. I glanced at a smiling Zapata.

In the early afternoon the rebel general suggested having a marksmanship contest. "It will give us appetites for the barbecue."

"Sugar, let him know we'll enjoy watching, sure enough."

Almost as though Zapata understood, he faced Harry, smiled. "This is between me and you." He called it a *mano a mano*.

"But he's our host," Harry said. "I might beat him. Then what?"

"You won't get any barbecue."

A large gathering of men, women, and children followed us to the south edge of the encampment. Tin cans on the ground at fifty yards became the targets.

Zapata used a Remington 1874 Army revolver, a .44-caliber six-shot single-action with a round barrel, ejector rod on the right, walnut stocks, and a lanyard ring in the butt.

"That's a heavy piece of iron," Harry said. "Near three pounds. But reliable." Harry used his .45-caliber Colt Bisley Frontier model.

"Maybe it's too much for him. He's not a big man, though tall for a Mexican."

Harry grinned. "I'll wager he's big enough."

My husband proved prophetic. Zapata could sure as shootin' handle his revolver. He had such a good eye and steady hand that Harry bore down and gave no quarter. To this day it's one of the best pistol matches I've seen.

Harry seemed quite pleased to outshoot our General Zapata. "I feel like I contributed something to the day after all that sitting and listening and nodding but not understanding, like a retired puppet."

Our host requested another contribution. "Your friend who fought alongside Benito Juárez told me about the earlier contest. Would you oblige?"

I interpreted for Harry and got the grin again. He nodded and told me what he needed. I relayed the request to Zapata: a boy forty yards away throwing tin cans one at a time as high and as fast as he could.

Harry with six cartridges in his Colt's cylinder, fired six times at as many cans, and nailed every one. "Ohs" and "ahs" filled my ears. While he reloaded he had me pass another request to Zapata. "Ask him to send another boy. Have them throw cans at the same time, fast as they can."

Zapata smiled at that request and dispatched another youngster with instructions.

Again, Harry smacked every can, quickly sent them flying. The "ohs" and "ahs" blended with cheers, *olés,* applause, and *"Vivas!"*

Zapata, looking between astounded and pleased, smiled frequently and touched his big black mustache. Still smiling, he pumped Harry's hand several times. So did a bunch of other men, including that fancy talking Gildardo Magaña.

"Let's have a drink," Zapata said.

"What'd he say?" Harry asked.

"You get to stay for the barbecue."

Back under the tule, with the second shot of tequila I became Margarita, Harry something akin to "Arry." and Zapata was Emiliano, except when Harry addressed him he was 'Miliano. Others referred to Harry, venerated for helping Zapata that day in the bushes, and now also because he could shoot like none of them had ever seen, as *El Míster* and *Ojo de Vidrio,* Glass-Eye.

Next we enjoyed one of our best meals since reaching Mexico, with all respect to Rosa King and her Hotel Bella Vista dining room. We had thin strips of marinated and barbecued beef, beans, and corn tortillas, food we queued up to receive, Emiliano right there waiting his turn with us and his people. It tasted so savory I'm getting hungry writing about it. There's something about simple grub like that, out in the countryside with fresh air and good company and the appetizing odors, that can be extraordinary.

We had just finished when a messenger showed up with a telegram for Emiliano. He read it, handed it to Magaña, and turned to Harry and me.

"Mr. Madero has agreed to talk with me about the agrarian problems in this part of Mexico. You could be my guests on the train and in the capital."

I relayed that to Harry.

"Let's do it," Harry said.

"Your friend the Juarista colonel," Zapata added, "might like to participate. Please ask him to confer with me."

At the Delicias we planned what to take.

"Do you think 'Miliano just likes having Americans around?" Harry asked.

"Maybe. Or maybe he merely likes us personally and is just being courteous toward foreign visitors."

"No matter what, it sounds like a fine way to see Mexico City for the first time."

"And we couldn't ask for a better guide than Emiliano Zapata."

34

Except he wasn't.

We found out that Emiliano had seldom been to Mexico City and that he loathed the place. He was a horse wrangler, a country boy same as Harry, and never could adapt, just too shy, perhaps, whereas Harry liked a big city for a while, felt at home like a pigeon in his dovecote. We donned our best duds. Paco dressed in white long-sleeve guayabera, black slacks, and black dress shoes.

Emiliano brought along ten or twelve men, including his brother, Eufemio, and Magaña. Except for Magaña, all wore what I thought of as their "peasant farmer" outfit, which also served as uniform: white cotton shirt and pants, sandals or huaraches, and straw hats, though Emiliano's sombrero, better made than the others, spread out more. Magaña wore a brown business suit with black tie, brown shoes, and tan fedora. Emiliano, Eufemio, and Gildardo carried satchels with changes of clothes.

After maybe two hours on the train, which made several stops, we reached the San Lázaro station. Emiliano led us to the Hotel San Lázaro, right across from the station. Our contingent nearly filled the lobby, which had a high ceiling, two white walls, one blue and one yellow; and a few wooden chairs and small tables around the edges on a dingy, once-white linoleum floor, much scratched and gouged. The guerrillas crowded around their leader. They removed their sombreros and stood expressionless, wordless.

I listened in on Emiliano and Magaña.

"This is a pile of trash," Magaña said. "I know nice hotels near the Zócalo."

"This is convenient if we have to leave in a hurry."

"We will not have to leave in a hurry. And this hotel is for short-term visits."

"Our visit to the capital is short term."

"What I mean is—"

Emiliano raised his hand and nodded toward me. "I know what you mean."

"We could stay near Alameda Park at the Regis. You, Eufemio, and me." He paused, glanced at me and Harry. "And the Americans. The others . . ." He motioned toward the other guerrillas. "Here we probably won't have private bathrooms."

"We stay here, Gildardo. Contact Madero's people about a meeting."

So we checked in. Newspapers had printed Emiliano's photo recently, and the clerk must have recognized him. He dropped the pencil twice trying to hand it to him.

We found our room on the second floor, small but clean. Sheets and blanket also seemed clean, though the bedspread looked thin enough to see through. We had a standup wardrobe, dresser, washbowl, chair, and water pitcher, two blue walls, one red, one yellow, and a view of the train station. Disinfectant irritated my nose. Paco roomed next to us on one side, Emiliano and Eufemio on the other, bathrooms at both ends of the hall.

"We'll do better next time, Sugar."

"We've had worse. What did they mean, 'short-term' rooms?"

"Where bar girls and streetwalkers take their customers for an hour or so."

I checked the sheets more carefully.

Harry, Paco, and I got a bottle and jiggers and set up a card game in the lobby.

"My general is intensely loyal to his troops," Paco said.

Harry nodded. "An admirable attitude."

"That's why he wouldn't go to a nicer hotel. That would have embarrassed them. His Indians wouldn't have been admitted."

The next day when the three of us returned from scrambled eggs, chorizo, beans, tortillas, and coffee at the restaurant next door, Emiliano and Eufemio descended the stairs, approached us, and stopped. They removed their sombreros.

"Enjoy your stay," Emiliano said. "We go now to see Mr. Madero." The brothers wore ties, boots, and tight-fitting pants and jackets. "I'll look for you tonight."

"You could take a tour," Eufemio told us. He nodded at Paco. "The colonel owns the reputation of knowing the city well."

I think I saw a conspiratorial smile. I supposed he referred to Paco's fame as the Monster of Morelos. Eufemio tolerated us but didn't seem friendly, maybe felt invidious. He stood shorter than Emiliano, a bit younger, rustic, tough looking, and didn't have as much mustache, though I could see the kinship in their faces. We'd heard he bullied folks. But he did what his brother said, even when he'd had too much to drink.

We stepped into a warming cloudless day and walked toward a nearby carriage.

"I'll pay," Paco said.

"I'll pay," Harry said. "You're the guide."

Paco directed the driver to Alameda Park, already full of loafers, children playing, women pushing babies in carriages. Right away we passed the Hotel Regis, where Magaña had wanted to lodge us. It looked nice. I supposed each room had a bathroom.

Paco pointed to a narrow street at the west end of the park. "That's where the Church carried out punishments during the Inquisition. There's a plaque."

I felt a shiver. "Let's keep going."

At the other end he showed us the National Theater, still under construction.

"I remember when they started in 1900. I've read work's moving slowly now due to the fighting nearby. There's talk of calling it the Palacio de Bellas Artes."

Paco told the driver, "To the Zócalo." We passed a big department store decorated outside with tiles blue, white, and yellow. And soon we reached the Plaza de la Constitución, which they called the Zócalo, same as central plazas all over Mexico.

Paco pointed out the national pawnshop, and we rolled into the square. The big old stone cathedral squatted off to our left.

"It's lopsided," Harry said.

"Yes. There's a lake under the city. Díaz got it pretty well drained, but I doubt it'll ever be completely dry."

"Strange place to build a city."

"Yes and no. They had the materials at hand, big stones from the Aztec temples the Spaniards ordered knocked down."

We passed the government buildings and turned back toward Alameda Park.

And soon we started rolling along one of the longest, widest, prettiest streets I've ever seen, Paseo de la Reforma, lined with trees and statuary.

"We can find many faults in that Austrian intruder the French sent," Paco said. "But Maximiliano did some fine things too. This highway is one of them."

When we reached the end of that magnificent thoroughfare we entered a huge park, Chapultepec. On a hill in the middle of it I saw what looked like a castle.

"Chapultepec Castle." Paco saw me gawking. "The Halls of Montezuma."

"You did some fighting there," Harry said.

"In the outskirts on the other side. A terrible defeat for my country."

We rolled on. Paco enjoyed his guide duties. Though he hadn't been to Mexico City for a few years he remembered how to find a good restaurant, Café Colón, and guided us there for lunch. The driver had his own sandwiches, stayed with his horse.

Next Paco led us to the neighborhood of his birth. A three-story stone mansion had replaced his family's small home. Paco shook his head. We kept moving.

When I spotted *Helados* on a pharmacy window I asked the driver to stop.

"What are we doing?" Harry asked.

I pointed to the window. "That sign means 'ice cream.'" I had read about ice cream and once mentioned it to Harry. Paco hadn't heard of it.

"What's it like?" Paco asked.

"They say it's good, a little sweet. It's a dessert."

"Like flan?"

"Different. It's mostly milk and flavoring, and it's thick. And cold."

All of us except our driver went inside. I suspect he felt angry, feared he wouldn't get a big tip with Paco doing the guide's work.

We sat at the only table. I ordered a dish of strawberry. Harry and Paco chose vanilla. And like hungry younguns we gobbled up that tasty stuff.

The owners must have gotten a chuckle out of us. They came to our table and introduced themselves, the Sanborn brothers from California.

"We're pharmacists," Frank said. "But when we read about ice cream, from that world's fair, we decided to offer it here. No one else in the capital serves ice cream."

"How's it doing?" Harry said, always interested in the financial world.

"Very well."

Walter said, "We thought people would want it in the summer, but they ask for it year-round."

We returned to the buggy and reached Hotel San Lázaro to find Emiliano sitting at a lobby table with Eufemio and Magaña. They sipped tequila from tall skinny jiggers and played cards, so we figured they finished discussing their big powwow with Madero. Other Zapatistas lounged in chairs or on the floor.

Magaña talked while Eufemio dealt. When Emiliano saw us he motioned for the lawyer to turn it off and for us to join them, but we didn't fit. Emiliano escorted us next door to the little restaurant.

Afterwards in our room I filled in my husband the best I could, and Paco contributed where I faltered.

"Emiliano liked the food," I told Harry, "but not the conversation. Mr. Madero wants everyone to quit fighting before he corrects the problem of the land. Emiliano digs his heels in at that. All his life he's seen the government and *hacendados* cheat and deceive their *peones*, who do all the work but are treated like slaves. Emiliano insists that the big holdings be broken up and distributed to the people."

Paco nodded, motioned for me to continue.

"Emiliano says what's just as bad is Mr. Madero accepting the Díaz puppet, de la Barra, for provisional president until legitimate elections can be held. Madero, Emiliano says, is listening to too many Díaz men.

"He had turned and I thought he might spit on the floor. But he didn't. Mr. Madero agreed to talk again soon in Cuernavaca. When Paco said he'd wire Madero, invite him to be his guest at the Delicias, Emiliano said Madero's people suggested he lodge at the Bella Vista."

Paco told Harry, "I said my hotel is just as convenient and is long established. There would be no charge for him or Madero. My general said, 'Thank you, Colonel. I cannot speak for Mr. Madero, but I bivouac with my people.'"

With satchels packed, we stood on the station platform near Emiliano and his entourage waiting for the train to leave for Cuernavaca. Close by, the buggy driver from our tour waved and smiled. Harry had tipped him aplenty.

"I didn't get to do any shopping," I said.

"And I wanted more ice cream," Harry said.

Paco told us, "Me too. Come back with me soon. We'll do those things. And I might still know some women in this town."

35

Harry and I dawdled at Emiliano's encampment a couple of days later when some guerrillas brought in a fellow Zapatista yelling and struggling to get loose. A girl, maybe fourteen, and what turned out to be her parents, walked behind. The girl sobbed something awful. Her mother cried. The father seemed about to explode in anger.

We stood close enough to hear it all, as presented to Emiliano, judge and jury. The soldier had raped her, she said. He denied it. Emiliano heard them out, the parents too. Emiliano didn't say much, just asked a few questions. But he never took his wise dark eyes off that girl, weeping, so frail, so frightened, except he occasionally looked at the accused, who'd become sniveling, slumping, and plenty frightened himself.

When everyone had testified, Emiliano ordered the offender taken out and shot.

On a sunny midmorning around the middle of June, we stood with Paco and a crush of other spectators on the train platform at Cuernavaca not thirty feet from where Emiliano, Eufemio, and Magaña waited, and we watched Francisco I. Madero, the next president of Mexico, step off the train from Mexico City.

His escorts pretty much hid Madero, short and slight. But he had to pass near us to reach Emiliano, and we got a good look: big inquiring eyes behind rimless glasses, short chin whiskers, and on his head a gray fedora matching his gray suit, his hatband and tie red. I liked that. He looked to be under forty years old.

Emiliano, Eufemio, and Magaña shook hands with Madero and others of his group, all in suits and ties, but I didn't see any of the abrazos Mexican friends exchange. All the main people started for temporary bleachers on the street along the plaza to watch the parade Paco had said would take place.

Harry and I returned to the Delicias. On our balcony we set up chairs and a small table with hors d'oeuvres, and Paco joined us. From there we'd enjoy a front-row view of the street. We all wore our best. I dressed in a yellow sleeveless blouse, long blue skirt, sandals, and, over my shoulders, a red mantilla. My hair, like a twisted rope, hung to the middle of my back. Harry sported his banker's outfit, while Emiliano's instructor in drilling and marksmanship wore his hotel-owner's "uniform" of white long-sleeve shirt, black pants, and black shoes. He brought a bottle of mescal.

The municipal band, seated on the end of the bleachers across from us, sputtered and squeaked for a long time, then played martial music long enough for us to have a drink apiece. Emiliano, Eufemio, Magaña, Madero, his contingent, and important local officials sat directly across from us.

Finally, Emiliano's army started filing by.

"They're not exactly marching, are they, Harry?"

"Not any more than 'Miliano's a common general."

This bunch walked by informally, two and three abreast, on foot and on horseback, everyone somber and proud, perhaps thinking of their cause, their deeds, and their leader. But I saw the humility too, in attire, attitude, and weaponry. Many lacked revolvers. They toted few machine guns, and we saw nary a cannon, their principal weapon being the rifle, mainly that outdated multifarious collection we'd seen before.

"My pappy and his companions," I announced to my companions, "were armed about the same half a century ago in the War of Northern Aggression."

When the women started showing up with that same informal, proud step, with several local youngsters trailing them, Paco said, "This is probably the end of it."

But this parade kept moving along the cobblestones, more and more men on foot and horseback following the women and children.

"My General Zapata is supposed to have two thousand troops in this area," Paco said. "My experience in two wars informs me we've already seen more than that."

"Must have got a lot of recruits recently," Harry said.

We didn't mind sitting there longer, didn't have anything else to do anyway, entertainment so scarce in Cuernavaca. Although we'd consumed the hors d' oeuvres, plenty of mescal remained. However, I announced:

"If we get close to that damn worm in the bottom of the bottle, I'm switching to something healthful, like tequila."

And the Zapatista parade kept filing by.

After a while, Harry said, "I've seen that horse before." He pointed out a piebald pinto with short tail and four white feet and ridden by a hatless young man without cartridge belt, rifle, or footwear. Harry nodded. "That same horse."

"So have I," Paco said. "I traded it a month ago to a farmer from Jojutla in exchange for a milk cow that I traded to Mrs. King for her surplus bedding."

"No," Harry said. "I mean today. Just since we've been sitting here."

So we learned when the piebald and its barefoot young warrior passed us again a little while later that Emiliano sent his bunch around the corner and past Madero time after time.

In early afternoon the parade ended. Zapata, Madero, and the other main participants in this political act of their revolution moved off on foot to the Borda Garden for a banquet. Several civic and social leaders had been invited, as well as politicians from throughout Morelos. Guests included Rosa King and Paco, the leading hoteliers.

"I'll report to you what happens," Paco said.

Harry and I walked to a restaurant and ate chicken enchiladas and beans.

Then we enjoyed the Mexican custom of a siesta, which a lot of people had to give up to enjoy that banquet with the Chief of the South and the chief of the rest of the country.

"Mr. Madero talked my General Zapata into agony. And Magaña did the same to Mr. Madero. My general looked bored and uncomfortable all the time. I'm certain he'd rather have been with his people at the encampment. Eufemio got drunk."

We sat in the late-afternoon shade of our favorite red bougainvillea in Paco's hotel patio. His gestures and smile told us he'd had a swell time. Bebito sang.

"I learned that several of the men accompanying Mr. Madero rode with him on the train from the capital in order to try to influence him to not give in to my general. They succeeded. 'After you abandon your arms,' Madero said, 'we'll settle the problem of the big landowners.' Same as ever. My general sat silently. Later, Madero offered to make him police superintendent of the state of Morelos. 'When?' my chief said. He never heard a direct answer."

"So it's a stalemate," Harry said.

Paco seemed bitter. "Madero doesn't understand our country." Carlota squawked.

"And the fighting will continue?"

"Unless Madero changes. Because my General Zapata will not."

Two days later Governor Escandón who, protecting his hide and hair, had relocated to Mexico City, sent a wire saying he wanted to get Emiliano confirmed as state police chief. So Emiliano went to the federal warehouse in Cuernavaca and asked for five hundred rifles to arm his police. The clerk refused. Emiliano took them anyway.

Then Madero sent an order: Emiliano must disarm.

Word of the president's edict spread quickly. Rumors abounded.

"What do you suppose 'Miliano's going to do?" Harry asked Paco.

"It's hard to know," Paco said. "He's been losing faith in Madero while trying to get along without weakening himself or giving up the gains of his rebellion, and he refers to Madero as a good element. But he will not lay down his arms."

So we felt stunned to our toes when a squad of federals carrying a white flag rode up one day and asked Emiliano on behalf of Madero to disarm, and Emiliano did.

Or so everyone thought at first.

"You should have seen it," Paco said. "The Zapatistas brought outdated and broken rifles to the federal warehouse and collected their five pesos of mustering-out pay. That way they could go home and begin planting their crops and also working for any hacienda owners they hadn't run off.

"Somehow my general had gotten hold of those rifles to give up. I personally saw one Zapatista surrender a rifle three times and receive his mustering-out pay each time. And none of those five hundred rifles my General Zapata recently confiscated from the warehouse got turned in."

Harry and I had just finished our flan after a late supper at the Bella Vista when two of Emiliano's boys, swearing and laughing, stumbled in. They seemed more bent on causing devastation than enjoying good clean honest drunken revelry. Each packed a big revolver and wore crossed cartridge belts, and they sported what we thought of as "Zapata sombreros." They looked like they'd stopped several times along the way.

"Those boys are on a toot," I commented.

With cantinas in the central area boarded up on orders from Emiliano, some of the pulquerías and other lower-class saloons on the outskirts of town had become popular with the guerrillas, as had some of the local women.

But these two were up to no good. They sat near the front, pounded on the table, and called for service. When they didn't get it right away, one of them yanked out his six-shooter and fired at the weather vane just visible on the roof. His bullet struck the top of the building and ricocheted into the night. Plaster chips and dust fell into the courtyard. They got a big laugh from that.

We'd been looking that way, so the shot didn't startle us. But Mrs. King's other patrons dived for cover, and the waitress ran to the kitchen.

The other Zapatista gave a drunken sweep with one coarse hand and propelled the hand-painted ceramic ashtray, toothpick jar, hot sauce bottle, and containers for salt, sugar, and pepper crashing to the floor along with a pretty cut-glass bud vase of three fresh red carnations.

Mrs. King arrived quickly from upstairs and approached their table, such a nice lady and far too delicate to have to put up with rabble. I felt a pang for her.

Harry and I heard them ask her for beer. On the way to the bar, Mrs. King paused at our table. "If they don't leave after one pint," she said, "I'm sending for the bobbies."

Poor naïve lady.

Mrs. King brought the guerrillas a bottle of beer each. They sloshed it down, yelled for more, and fired their revolvers into the sky. They laughed and whooped.

I wondered what would happen next, and what Mrs. King might do—maybe send to Emiliano for help despite her being a Maderista—when my husband stood and walked to their table.

Emiliano's hellhounds stopped their racket and looked up at Harry, perhaps wondering what the big glass-eyed gringo wanted.

Harry leaned in and, socking one in the jaw with his left fist, the other in a corresponding spot with his right, knocked them cockeyed onto the floor.

Mrs. King reached Harry's side in moments, observed the laid-out rebels.

"Sorry about the ruckus, Mrs. King," Harry said. "One of my rules is to avoid hitting drunks."

She said, "I'm so glad you don't mind breaking a rule occasionally, Mr. Parker."

Two days later, happily astride excellent horses we'd purchased at a nearby rancho, a gray mare for me and a buckskin gelding for Harry, and accompanied by that ancient, irrepressible warrior who more than six decades earlier had plugged at least one gringo, Harry and I rode out of Cuernavaca with the Chief of the South.

36

So we officially became Zapatistas.

We never went into battle with them, never fired our weapons except in contests or when federals surprised our camp and we felt obliged to shoot to save our hides. We didn't even spend all our time near Emiliano, not with the excitement of Mexico City and the tranquility and beauty of Cuernavaca and other small towns nearby.

But day in and day out, until Emiliano got murdered, and ever since in a different way, philosophically, you could say, Harry and I remained with that doomed, charismatic, dedicated man. I am probably one of the few remaining Zapatistas.

"I reckon 'Miliano wants us along to have you to show off," Harry said.

"Or he wants you handy to give pistol lessons."

"That might be it, Sugar."

"Of course he hasn't seen me shoot my carbine yet."

We packed for the campaign trail, and I had to decide what to leave, items Paco said we could store at his hotel. I toted only those few clothes I could stuff into my saddlebags or tie behind the saddle with my bedroll, plus my Shakespeare, Jack Londons, and grooming needs. Harry made it up to me by buying me as fine a guitar as a girl could want. An artisan in Paracho made it, so you know what I mean. Paco's housekeeper sewed me a carrying bag of heavy cloth for it with a leather shoulder strap. I paid her well and threw in my heavyweight sombrero.

"So we're on the move again," I said.

"On the move, but not on the run."

A good point, but either situation would help give Harry excitement he needed, and I suspect he didn't care which. "You're happy, aren't you, Honey?"

"I'll never change, Sugar. But I'm not figuring the Pinkertons will be poking around 'Miliano's bunch. We should be right comfortable."

"You don't have the itch to do something else?"

"For now, Sugar, I like the idea of siding with 'Miliano. I like his cause and his determination. I feel comfortable following him around. And somehow needed. You?"

"Yes. I'm feeling some of his love for this wild land and its common folk. I'm happy doing what we're doing, as long as you are."

Paco found a brother of his departed wife to operate the Delicias. "He promised to feed my birds and animals and to keep honest accounts for me. We'll see."

"But, Paco, are you sure you want to do this?" Harry asked.

"You mean at my age?"

"There could be a lot of hard riding."

Paco nodded with a smile speaking more than words could.

When we met to saddle up, Paco told us, "I just thank God I lived long enough to ride with a man like our General Zapata." Paco wore his Juarista uniform.

Villa de Ayala, a drab place and so small its folks got water from the plaza fountain, sat square in the heart of Zapatista country near Emiliano's hometown, Anenecuilco. So Emiliano selected it for his new headquarters, for a while anyway. We set up our tent and spread our bedrolls near where Paco established himself on the edge of the bivouac. We had a creek and lots of trees: cypress, madrone, *amate*.

"One of my general's wives lives here," Paco told us.

"One of them?" Harry said.

"She's the one he married, Josefa. He has children, but none with Josefa."

He and Josefa lived in an adobe home in central Villa de Ayala. I empathized with Josefa, so much younger than me, and I had about given up any idea of having children. I felt so grateful Harry didn't have other women or natural children. And we realized that Emiliano lived within the mores of his people and times.

Most of Emiliano's men and women returned to their own homes in the nearby communities to finish planting their corn patch or to take over some of the recently acquired haciendas they hadn't burned.

The troops bivouacking at Villa de Ayala threw together a corral for some of the horses, fettered others and turned them loose on adjacent grazing land. My gray and Harry's buckskin had large deep chests, well-directed legs, lots of haunch, and plenty of spirit. I named mine Cuchulain II and called him Dos, Spanish for "two." The buckskin had a certain swagger, a big barrel, and a fat muzzle, so Harry named him Butch.

Emiliano's brother lived in the camp, and for a while we saw more of him than of Emiliano, who stayed with Josefa. I've mentioned Eufemio's hard drinking and bullying. But he also had admirable traits.

"They say Eufemio is a good leader and fierce fighter," Paco said.

We didn't have any trouble with Eufemio. I know he admired the way Harry handled a six-gun. And everyone had heard about the Bella Vista incident.

"The two men Harry stiffened," Paco told us, "were no-good *cabrones*, excuse me, Margarita. Mrs. King passed the word about how fast and efficient Harry had been, and everyone enjoyed hearing he had laid them out. My General Zapata himself went to the Bella Vista, apologized, and gave Mrs. King money to repair the wall near the weather vane, one of the few times my general set foot inside a building in our town. And he jailed those two for the remainder of his time in Cuernavaca. I wish the incident had occurred in my hotel. I would not patch the bullet hole and could put up a plaque."

The remainder of the summer passed pleasantly, no gunfire there in southern Mexico, good weather, occasional afternoon rains, so many lush valleys and streams, endearing country. The area also had several bubbly hot springs, some isolated in the natural state, so Harry and I could ride out to one, get in the natural state ourselves, and sit down in the water and have quite a big time. You don't have trouble getting your man to bathe when you go in there with him.

We spent a lot of time playing dominoes or cards, monte and faro mostly, a little poker and cassino and cooncan, Harry and Eufemio and Paco, mainly, one or two other men sometimes. I sat in occasionally, but not if Eufemio was on a bender.

Mostly I talked with the women. And I played my Paracho guitar. An expert made it of rosewood and birch and some other woods I knew only the Mexican names for and have forgotten. I learned several Mexican songs to sing and play, and sometimes I'd sing in English, a tune Irish or American. Harry, who couldn't carry a tune, and Paco, who could, would join in. Paco loved showing off his English. It didn't win him any favors from Magaña, but Paco's age and spirit caused everyone else to forgive him.

However, Harry had counted on a different life when we left Cuernavaca.

"Sugar," Harry said one day after breakfast, "I'm getting restless."

"I know you are, Honey."

"It's nice out here, being beyond the reaches of those varmints Charlie Siringo and Frank Dimaio. But . . ."

"On the other hand, we're thoroughly getting the lay of the land."

"I had that very thought, Sugar."

Emiliano farmed a little and horse-traded, kept an eye on his movement's progress, watched the goings-on in Mexico City and elsewhere, while figuring ways to obtain more arms and money for when he had to hit the warpath again.

They finally had another presidential election in Mexico, with Madero defeating the Díaz man, de la Barra. And the revolution saw some successes. Pancho Villa captured Ciudad Juárez about the time troops loyal to a controversial leader named Ricardo Flores Magón, already holding several cities in the interior, took Tijuana. Not long afterwards, however, the federals recaptured Tijuana.

Madero began urging Emiliano again to disarm. Emiliano agreed to do so if Madero would guarantee the property rights the Zapatistas sought. We heard that if Madero wouldn't do that, Emiliano might send his troops through the charade of disarming, like at Cuernavaca, this time nearby in Cuautla. Madero wouldn't budge, and we rode to Cuautla to watch.

"He's doing it again," Harry said when the rebels showed up at the plaza.

"He sure is." Paco laughed lightly. "Good for him."

They must have collected every decrepit or antique busted rifle and shotgun in southern Mexico, the way they kept showing up and turning them in for their five pesos.

"Maybe," Harry said, "they're stealing them back from the federals to turn in."

"Unfortunately," Paco said, "they've had to fight with many of the same kinds."

Meanwhile, *El Imparcial* and *El País,* following the government line, continued to butcher Emiliano in their news columns as well as in editorials. The insiders remained "in," and the newspapers pressed Madero to maintain the status quo.

"Mr. Madero is highly educated," Paco said, "in California and Europe, and is known to be frank and honest. But he's weak. He's trying to please everyone, attempting to compromise when he doesn't have to. That is not going to work."

Only the one-page fliers José Guadalupe Posada continually created and distributed gave the people's viewpoint.

One afternoon following siesta, Harry sat in a camp chair reviewing his arsenal, a routine caution and wise habit for a man in his profession, and I had just started a game of solitaire on a blanket in front of our tent, when Paco approached. On his arm he sported a young Mexican woman who could have passed for a gypsy queen, her beauty, the multicolored skirt, white peasant blouse, her huge loop earrings, and wrist bangles. Sparkling black hair hung in a twist to her waist.

"This is Inmaculada," Paco said. "My new fiancée."

She said, "I've heard so many nice things about you, Miss Etta."

That won me over right off the bat but I still saw her as a man-stealer.

So when Paco introduced her to Harry, I prepared to watch her in action and give her what-for. Harry stood and she smiled at him, then at Paco. She edged closer to Paco, pleasing me no end, for I'd half-expected her to swoon, or pretend to, the way women often did around Harry. That told me her looks had deceived me and that Paco probably deserved his reputation as the Monster of Morelos. The angle of her eyebrows made her eyes seem a little slanted. She smiled a lot. I liked her.

"This lady is a doctor," Paco said. "We say *curandera*. Her herbs can heal a bullet wound, cure fever, kill stomach worms, eliminate a rash, or purify your kidneys."

"Powerful," Harry said. "I don't think we need anything right now."

"So nice to know you." I put down my cards, stood, and we shook hands.

"Inmaculada knows witchcraft too," Paco said. "She's my *bruja*, my witch."

We chatted briefly and they went on their way, arm in arm.

"I bet Paco's showing her off to the whole camp," I said.

We found out Inmaculada came from Villa de Ayala, at least recently, and that her skills also included calming your nerves or waking up your appetite, sexual or gastrointestinal. She certainly made a new man out of Paco, although the old version hadn't been lacking. Inmaculada spoke passable English. Paco called her Bruja.

Late in the year Emiliano prepared to move his headquarters again.

"We're going west," he told us, "to the outskirts of Chilpancingo. It's next door in the state of Guerrero. Merely to wave my sombrero I can raise an army there as easily as anywhere in the south. I invite you to accompany me."

I explained the invitation to Harry.

"You bet, 'Miliano. Sugar?"

"I'll get my things."

"The hunting for wild turkeys is much better there," Emiliano said. "And Chilpancingo is closer to Acapulco, where a boat could land necessities for us."

We knew what that meant. Emiliano had also tired of sitting around. And he had finished with waiting for Madero to redistribute the land.

As Emiliano's drill instructor, on foot or horseback, Paco also would move.

We got settled at the camp near Chilpancingo shortly before Christmas and decided to go to Cuernavaca for the holidays. Paco and Bruja went with us. We all stayed at the Hotel Delicias and had a big time even though Cuernavaca had become a nest for federal troops and officials. It was, after all, the capital of Morelos and only forty-seven miles south of Mexico City and at less altitude. Had better weather too.

Around others we kept shut about our Zapata connections and leanings, and I don't think the Mexico City bunch there ever figured us out. Mrs. King, who knew, apparently didn't gossip about us, stayed as friendly as ever, appreciative of Harry's deed, and looked delighted when we managed to bring Paco and Bruja with us for dinner.

But Harry became itchy again. So after New Year's Day of 1912, the four of us headed back downhill to Chilpancingo.

When we reached the turnoff to Taxco, Harry stopped in midtrail and addressed Paco and Bruja. "You all ride on ahead. We'll join you at headquarters in a day or two." When they reined up to wave their hats, we raised ours in return.

"I heard a lot of talk, Sugar. Let's ride toward Taxco."

"A business transaction like in the old days?"

"Exactly. It's a silver-mining area. A payroll is on the way from Mexico City. We'll get on the other side of Taxco and greet the payroll. Are you game?"

"I'm already tingling."

We pointed our horses along the Taxco road and circled the town.

It's hilly country but we kept moving. After another night on the trail, Harry reined up when we climbed a summit. "Here's an ideal place for the reception."

Harry possessed good timing. Shortly before sunset a pack train of two mules and four guards on horseback approached from the northeast. They didn't make hardly any dust. Two hawks high up had started evening reconnaissance.

We wore bandannas over our lower faces, and I had dressed like a man.

"They'll think we're Zapatistas," Harry said.

"Aren't we?"

The money train turned the bend. Harry spurred his chestnut into the middle of the trail and threw down on the party. Two guards spun their horses around and lit off back the way they'd come, galloping like scared antelopes.

"Let 'em go," Harry said.

The other two guards stood their ground and grabbed their rifles. I tried to plug the horse of one guard, but the fool yanked the reins and spun his mount the instant before I cut loose with my carbine. The slug busted into his left leg just above the knee. He howled something fierce and hit the ground thrashing and yelling at about the time Harry shot the other man in the side, knocking him off his horse.

"Let's hurry," Harry said. "Those other two might ride back with federals."

One mule carried tents and bedding. On the other the payroll turned out to be in gold coins. We loaded several small sacks of them into our saddlebags and galloped toward Chilpancingo until after full dark.

When Harry felt it safe we halted in a stand of pines. "Sugar, I reckon we left more money behind than we acquired."

"But we did all right, looks like."

"Yep. We can give most of it to 'Miliano and still have plenty for us."

I felt bad about the man Harry shot, but that guard had been misguided trying to resist when we had him covered. We never learned if he lived or died, for though *El Imparcial* and *El*

País gave the robbery a lot of play they changed the event no end. They claimed that a frightening horde of Zapatista cutthroats led by the Attila of the South slew the guards and shot the mules, then fled like cowards with all the gold meant for the poor mining families of Taxco.

By the way, I'm fairly certain Harry never shot anyone else.

A few days later some of Mr. Posada's fliers showed up in Chilpancingo and made their way to our bivouac. The fliers, featuring his hallmark skeletal characters, gave a more accurate idea of what happened, except he drew the guards as Zapatistas too and had them cheerfully handing over the money sacks.

37

Emiliano happily thanked us for the gold we contributed to his cause, felt so pleased he threw a jamboree we never forgot. You've never seen so many bloodied and butchered chickens from the cockfights or such loco, hell-for-leather riding of wild steers and broncs. Emiliano got right in the middle of it, the best rider of the lot. That man could have been a champion rodeo cowboy in the States.

We had barbecued beef with beans, tortillas, and corn on the cob, tequila, mescal, and beer. I enjoyed several aromas, lush, irresistible. They had plenty of guitar players, but they coaxed me to join in. Harry, after tippling, tried again to sing. Paco and Bruja danced most of the time, kicking up more dust than anyone. Now that I'm older than Paco had been then, and moving like an old lady, I wish to hell I knew which herbs Bruja fed him.

Two fistfights took place, none involving my husband.

At one point Emiliano broke from his dancing and chatted with Harry and me. Without asking for details he thanked us again for the money. "I think you have done such things before." He gave us a shy friendly smile that we liked so much.

"Let's just say," Harry had me reply, "that we've always been in finance."

We stayed at the camp for several weeks, with wanderings into Chilpancingo for what little city life it provided. We had only two major interruptions. On one occasion Emiliano asked us to scout around Acapulco to see if he could get arms shipments there.

"Maybe I could obtain weapons besides those we win from the federals," he said.

We returned with a positive report about all the isolated and quiet coves and inlets around that regal bay.

The other interruption occurred when Harry and I took on another mule train with payroll money, paper as well as coins. Again, we gave most of our take to Emiliano.

"Yes," Emiliano said, "you understand financing."

And we longed for a soft bed, a hot bath, and ice in our drinks. We told Emiliano we'd be back in a few weeks and rode off to Cuernavaca, where we could catch the train to Mexico City. He sent two boys with us to bring our horses back to camp. I took my guitar.

Paco had recommended several hotels, so we checked them out and wound up near the westerly end of Alameda Park at the nicest one, the Regis, four stories, pale yellow exterior, big dining room, mahogany bar. After that, we stayed there every time we visited Mexico City. On the other end of the park, work continued on the National Theater.

Over the next few days we deposited our gold gradually into banks nearby on Avenida Juárez, such a grand relief to not have to watch out all the time nor wear overloaded money belts. Of course, if any Zapatista had stolen from us, or from anyone else, Emiliano would have had him taken out and shot.

Harry and I became busy visitors for the first few days. We traveled all over Mexico City by trolley or rented a buggy, taking in concerts and stage shows and dining at one good restaurant after another, Cambrinus, for instance, or the San Ángel Inn, Silvain's, the Chapultepec, the American Club. Sometimes we hired a driver with buggy and ventured out to one of the beautiful rural areas. Once when we didn't hire a driver, however, being as directions had been simple, we just about wound up regretting it.

"Harry, I don't think this is the way we came."

"Looks the same to me."

We'd rolled back toward town after a happy drive and long, pleasant dinner in Coyoacán, and had traveled for quite a spell with dark coming on and surroundings looking unfamiliar, though I had to wrangle with my husband for several minutes before convincing him. He stopped the horse, held the reins loosely, looked around.

"Sugar, I reckon I enjoyed that meal a little too much."

"Me too. Let's ask for directions."

We couldn't spot any other people, saw lots of trees but no buildings and nary a street lamp, the sky darkening by the second.

"We'll keep rolling until we find some lights and people," Harry said.

When he flapped the reins on the horse's back to set him moving, two shadows ran out from the trees. One grabbed the horse's halter. The other showed a long-bladed knife. Bandannas covered their lower faces.

"Climb down," the one with the knife said. Both stood on Harry's side.

"What'd he say?" Harry asked.

I told him.

Now we could see they were at most in their late teens.

"They're just boys," I said.

"I know."

"Hurry it up." The knife-holder waggled the weapon.

"Sugar, say we'll be glad to oblige but that I need to show my credentials first."

I did that.

The youthful assailant again told us to hurry.

Harry swiftly had his inside gun in the face of the nearest boy.

With a curse and a shout, they ran for the trees.

Harry clucked the horse into action. "We were lucky."

I slipped my arm through his. "So were they, Honey."

We also frequented the Thoroughbred races at Hipódromo de la Condesa, a dandy track where Harry taught me to bet with a bookie he found first off and who knew his numbers in English. I caught on right away and after that I could bet in English or Spanish with any bookie in the stands or on the concourse.

On the first day, when I cashed my tickets after the last race, Harry took my hand. "How'd you do, Sugar, on the day?"

"Won a hundred pesos, fifty dollars in money."

"Good for you."

I waited for him to announce his winnings. When he didn't, I said, "You?"

Harry hesitated before saying, "I reckon I lost about that much."

"So we broke even."

He laughed and bought us a splendid dinner.

Despite the glamorous outings, something else pleased us just as much without being fancy at all or expensive: stopping by the Sanborn brothers' pharmacy nearly every day and eating a dish of ice cream, just plain vanilla or strawberry. We relished that after all our time at the rustic camps in Morelos and Guerrero. No doubt we ate more ice cream than we would have otherwise.

Frank and Walter always made time for us. This gave Harry an opportunity to talk with someone besides me. Walter, a shy one, held back, so we mostly conversed with Frank, who knew everything going on in the capital, sometimes beyond.

"I read all the newspapers," Frank told us one day, "though their politics haven't changed much even with Díaz in exile. With Zapata staying in the hills to the south and Madero settling in to his presidency, Mexico City is calm. Madero is still trying to figure things out, and most people are pulling for him."

"Will he break up the haciendas," I asked, "the way Zapata wants?"

"It's impossible to guess, with all the Díaz people and landowners influencing him. But he should, or the revolution will start up again. You may have heard that Pancho Villa got angry with Madero at the victory banquet in Ciudad Juárez."

"I read a little about it," I said. Villa wanted justice for all, the same as Zapata.

We didn't let Frank know we had spent so much time with Emiliano, only that we had been in Cuernavaca and Chilpancingo and around and run into him some.

"We're Zapatistas," Harry said.

"Me too," Frank said.

Walter contributed from behind the counter, "Me too."

Frank knew Rosa King from her time in Mexico City before she invested in Cuernavaca and moved there. So we brought him up to date on her and the Hotel Bella Vista, and we told the brothers about Paco and the Delicias.

"Oh, yes," Frank said, "the Monster of Morelos."

"He came with us," Harry said, "our first time here."

Frank smiled. "I didn't recognize him or I'd have given him a free scoop."

They knew the ambassador by sight, Henry Lane Wilson.

"I don't like him," Frank said. "Neither do the Mexicans. But he sends one of his servant girls regularly for ice cream, same as Porfirio Díaz used to do. So we tolerate Mr. Wilson the same as we tolerated Díaz." He laughed. "We liked our own tyrant better."

A boy stopped by with the newest flier by José Guadalupe Posada, and Frank gave him a coin.

A sketch filled the top one-third of the little sheet. This one showed President Madero, tiny and frail and innocent looking, seated at his desk. Several fat men, arrogant and self-assured, stood behind him. Each resembled Díaz. In front of Madero, a shabbily dressed Mexican farmer followed a skinny mule. Man and mule had Posada's trademark skulls. On the mule's flank hung a sign, "Thank God, The Revolution Has Triumphed."

One item told of a man choking his mistress to death for dancing with a stranger. Another said a woman fatally stabbed her husband "from the bottom up," although it omitted the details. Drawings did not accompany either item. The flier contained other short articles, plus lyrics and music for two songs.

"Mr. Posada," Frank said, "is a soldier without a gun and as brave as a good fighting bull. He speaks for the common people, who seek only justice and equality. You would enjoy meeting him."

"We wouldn't want to bother him," Harry said.

"You won't. He's humble and would be pleased to chat with foreigners and show you his shop. Besides, he doesn't get out of town much. You can offer firsthand reports: Zapata, the encampment near Chilpancingo, the mood of the people at Cuernavaca."

Posada's print shop sat near the important art school, Academia de San Carlos. Two days later, mainly at my insistence, we rented a horse and buggy and drove there.

"We're showing a lot of gall, Sugar, busting in on the man this way."

"You want to, don't you?"

"Yes, but—"

"Then let's go in."

"But he's famous all over Mexico."

"Honey, you're famous all over the United States and South America. Let's go."

Harry shook his head and smiled. "I suppose he'd like to meet a pretty woman."

I felt the audacity too, but we'd come this far. Besides, Harry had the presence of an ambassador. I guessed Mr. Posada wouldn't speak English, so I told Harry I'd interpret and we'd keep the visit short. We found out I was right.

This unlikely rabble-rouser, sixty years old, a feisty man, short and stout, a vibrant soul, had his fingertips on the pulse of the people, just as Paco and now Frank Sanborn told us. His mustache would look juvenile alongside Emiliano's.

Mr. Posada smiled when we introduced ourselves, showed us his engraving tools and printing press, then offered chairs and coffee. I smelled ink and metal. He sat with us.

I didn't say anything about the size of Emiliano's army, his types of weaponry, nor his thinking about having arms shipped to Acapulco. But with Harry's prompting I told him what we knew about Emiliano's personality and, without saying why, about the big fiesta he threw. Posada became excited as we talked, for we knew the Chief of the South, something few Mexico City folk could claim.

"Like many older Mexicans," he said, "I started out Porfirista. Then I became Maderista. Now I am Zapatista. I'm going to let my mustache grow large."

Harry laughed when I relayed that comment.

I told about Eufemio's temper and the lawyer Gildardo Magaña.

"Magaña grates on a fellow," I said. "Still, Emiliano says he needs him."

"Indeed he does." Posada rubbed his mustache.

While we talked, customers and friends stopped by. Lupe, most called him, or Lupito, those who seemed to know him well. When he attended to visitors, Harry and I looked through fliers stacked on tables and shelves. His etchings and articles told the social, political, and military history of Mexico for a century and more, even though he said he had been in Mexico City since only 1888.

Posada drew and wrote of politicians, highwaymen, and farmers, bullfighters and dancers, singers and composers. He often printed lyrics, old songs and new, and handled small commercial printing jobs.

"Most Mexicans can't read," he said when he rejoined us. "Or they can't afford a daily newspaper. So the newspapers don't have much circulation. But my fliers cost only one centavo, and every village has someone with at least rudimentary reading skills. The people gather around and listen."

I believed my interpretation of that for my husband struck home hard because of his own inability to read.

When we thanked Posada for his courtesies and prepared to leave, he said, "Next time you're in Cuernavaca, please give my regards to the Monster of Morelos."

Outside his shop, just when we neared our buggy, two men in suits, ties, and hats intercepted us. "*Gobernación,*" the taller one said. They showed us badges.

"Federals," I told Harry. "Some kind of cops."

The taller one, so skinny his friends probably called him Flaco, moved easily into English. "I didn't know you were Americans. Credentials, please." I didn't like his tone, thought of Harry showing his "credentials" on the Coyoacán trail. I stifled a laugh.

"What are you talking about?" Harry said.

"Identification papers. Who are you? Why talk to Posada? Now: Your names."

"The lady is my wife, Belle Starr. I'm Charlie Siringo. Why'd you stop us?"

"We often question Mr. Posada's visitors. He's a well-known enemy of the government. Maybe you are too."

"We're not. We're tourists. Heard about him. Curious, is all."

"I don't believe you. We think you are plotters against the government."

"You're dead wrong."

My husband didn't like his tone either. I wished Harry hadn't said "dead."

"You're coming with us to the office, where we can finish this discussion."

"We're busy," Harry said. "And we haven't done anything wrong."

I saw a big problem approaching, maybe jail, if we had to go with them.

The short man stepped close. "Perhaps we can work something out."

I'm sure Harry knew they wanted a bribe, but he said, "Like what?"

"If you don't want to work something out, let's go." He grabbed Harry's arm.

Harry jerked loose, quickly slugged Flaco, then the other one, hit so hard they fell into the middle of the street. He crouched over them and snatched pistols from their shoulder holsters. "Put these in your purse, Sugar."

I grabbed the guns and climbed into the buggy.

Harry jumped up beside me and got us moving. "'Miliano will 'specially want that boxy-looking one. I heard about it some. Colt came out with it about the time we got to Mexico. A .45-caliber semiautomatic."

"This little one doesn't have a hammer."

"It's inside. A hammerless .38 by Hamilton and Richardson. Different models been around for fifty years."

When I turned to look while the buggy rolled away, the intruders hadn't stirred off their backs. "You think they were really federal officers?"

"Hard to know. I saw them nearby watching when we went into the print shop." Harry clucked the horse into a faster gait. "Doesn't matter anyway."

We never missed purchasing a flier every time one came out. I would translate for Harry, though the intent of many drawings came across so clear they didn't need explanations from me or Mr. Posada. We'd leave them in the lobby of the Regis so others could read them, another of our contributions to the Revolution.

In addition to the Mexican dailies, I bought the English-language newspaper, the *Herald*. It also railed against Emiliano. I suppose the *Herald* didn't want to lose access to the government-controlled newsprint.

We stayed at the Regis for quite a spell, read all about Woodrow Wilson whipping Taft and Teddy Roosevelt in the 1912 presidential election. Then we rejoined Emiliano at the Chilpancingo encampment. For the holidays we went to Cuernavaca.

Paco and Inmaculada awaited us.

"This war is too slow for me," Paco said.

Besides, the vibrant young woman he called his "witch" had begun directing a renovation of the Delicias. Paco had all the war he wanted.

Cuernavaca, Paco said, had become semineutral territory. "But almost everyone considers it federal. You'll see. They say Felipe Ángeles arrives soon."

Sure enough, that important federal general brought his wife to the Hotel Bella Vista, and they were guests of honor at the big Christmas ball in the Toluca Theater.

Harry and I also attended the dance.

"I think I'll run down and tell 'Miliano who's here."

"Don't you dare."

"I wouldn't go without you, Sugar. Need you to do the talking."

I held Harry tighter, felt him laughing.

My husband didn't dance any better than in Wyoming. He wore his banker's outfit, left his derringers and Colt at the hotel, carried his inside gun only. I wore a long red dress, sleeveless with low neckline, held my hair back with a wide green ribbon, and showed off shiny new slippers. Harry bought me a large corsage of white carnations, and I'd pinned on my gold watch from Tiffany. I went unarmed.

When Mrs. King introduced us to General Ángeles and his wife, a plump little lady, I saw jealousy instantly burst into the wife's face. I think Harry noticed it too. He quickly excused us and waltzed me away, stepping on my toes.

Early in 1913 we stayed at the encampment a spell before returning to Mexico City. Harry, in his early forties and not so restless anymore, still couldn't stay put for long. His card playing helped, as did a few drinks from time to time. And he liked being in contact with Emiliano, even though we didn't talk with him every day. Harry could see the fight in Emiliano, knew the cause, felt the imminent explosion.

"We'll be around when 'Miliano needs us," Harry told Paco.

38

A gain, we lodged at the Regis. We enjoyed ice cream with Frank Sanborn and talked politics with him and José Guadalupe Posada. We attended a cockfight, the horse races, and two concerts, watched construction workers at the National Theater, and dined at the American Club, Silvain's, and the San Ángel Inn. The cockfight was bloody.

After we'd been in Mexico City three weeks, bedlam let loose.

The trouble began in early February when several army officers, including Félix Díaz, nephew of the former president, revolted against Madero. They holed up at the main *cuartel* in the capital and began firing cannons toward the Palacio Nacional.

Madero's top general, Victoriano Huerta, set up in the Zócalo to defend the president, or so everyone thought, and fired his weapons toward Félix Díaz.

Extensive rifle fire and terrible shelling from artillery continued in both directions for ten days. Mexicans now call it their *Decena Trágica*, ten tragic days, appropriately named. The streets weren't safe. The shelling killed a lot of residents having nothing to do with the fighting and wounded many others. Lots of folks had to abandon their homes until it ended. The noise at times became hellish, even at night, when it frequently woke us up. Food and water grew scarce in some areas.

Our hotel sat beyond the line of fire, though we could hear plenty of shooting, and stray rifle bullets chipped stucco off the façade a couple of times. We seldom stepped outside, but I kept us abreast of things through newspapers and gossip, which seemed about the same. I read to Harry from the *Herald*.

"Listen to this, Honey. 'People in the poorest parts of the city are eating dogs and cats, even rats. Of course, certain clever, heartless entrepreneurs are earning money catching those dogs and cats and rats and selling them.'"

In case such news reached my family, I wrote them we felt safe and sound. I never mentioned how scared I got at times.

One constant rumor said the Huerta faction and the Díaz bunch didn't shoot at each other nor at military targets but aimed at distant buildings or into the air.

"Sugar, isn't Huerta supposed to be protecting the president?"

"Yep."

"So he and this younger Díaz might be in cahoots."

"Looks that way."

Huerta finally double-crossed Madero openly by entering into a truce with Félix Díaz and arresting Madero and his vice president, José Pino Suárez.

A few days later, the newspapers screamed the worst part of the tragic ten days.

"Lordy, Harry! Madero and Pino Suárez have been murdered. It says here Huerta's soldiers started to move them from the National Palace to the city jail. Someone tried to rescue them. Madero and Pino Suárez somehow got shot and killed. It happened in a dark alley."

"They catch anybody?"

"Not yet. Their guards, if that's who they were, never got a scratch and never had a good look at the attackers, who got clean away."

I felt so bad I wrote my folks about that too.

Huerta declared himself president. And the whole world knew he must have ordered the assassinations. He began burning Zapatista fields and villages.

The rural south flocked to Emiliano's side. Fighting between his guerrillas and federals became fierce all over the south. Casualties mounted.

In the north, Pancho Villa, who had retired after his victory at Ciudad Juárez and opened a butcher shop in the city of Chihuahua, took up arms again, joining forces with Obregón. They made some quick gains against federals.

"That makes the rebels a lot stronger," Harry said.

"Yes. They say Obregón's troops include a lot of Yaquis from Sonora in the north, his home area. Savage Indians. And Villa's a real savvy general too."

"All that should take some pressure off 'Miliano."

Between rumors printed and spoken, and plenty of news stories, we followed the goings on. That's how we learned that Emiliano moved his headquarters to northern Guerrero and that federals occupied Chilpancingo.

"Let's go find him," Harry said.

"The newspapers say everyone needs a pass to travel in territory Emiliano holds."

"There must be a way."

"Harry, we don't have any business being in the thick of this fight."

"Sugar, somehow we've got to help that man."

Mr. Posada immediately started writing and cartooning against Huerta. The general had the reputation of a consummate drinker, and when Posada wrote that Huerta's principal advisors were "Mr. Hennessey and Mr. Martell," we thought sure Huerta would close him down, or worse. But Huerta in his way looked as out of touch with the people as Madero had been in his. No harm came to Mr. Posada.

A little later, however, he died of natural causes. So one of the important voices of the Mexican Revolution fell silent anyway.

Harry and I felt proud to have known him. With Frank and Walter Sanborn, we joined a big turnout for his funeral.

We continued to live at the Regis, same as anyone with money or glamour or ambition would. We never became friends with any of the important Mexicans passing in or out, but occasionally from pictures that had been in the newspaper we'd recognize one of them or a famous foreigner. And a clerk or waiter sometimes pointed someone out to us, our being long-time guests, insiders. I snickered from time to time when the big shot who got pointed out to us looked like an American, making me think how interesting it would be if an employee could identify us for our fellow countryman.

However, no one in Mexico ever knew our true identities except one portly, blondish, middle-aged fat-jawed gringo sitting at the Regis bar late one afternoon.

"Land o' Goshen," Harry said in a friendly way of mocking me.

"I'll be hornswoggled," I responded in the manner of Sundance, Wyoming.

In a big Mexican sombrero and colorful serape, there sat Butch Cassidy.

The reunion took place on a grand scale, though nothing fancy, not between two cowboys. I couldn't keep up with them, so I begged off in the early evening.

Besides, their friendship went back further than mine and Harry's, and they had a mountain of things to jaw about, going over the old days in Wyoming and Utah, Colorado and Texas and around, while rehashing our South America time too.

I couldn't tell if Butch toted any weapons, but I figured he hid at least one derringer inside a boot, probably a knife on a thong around his neck inside his shirt too, something he picked up from America Connolly.

Butch had become handy at drinking tequila, so now he and Harry also had that skill in common. I don't know where they went after they left the Regis, and Harry didn't much recollect in the morning when he returned to our room. But he knew their tour included several pulquerías, those low-class saloons that don't serve anything except a malty *pulque*, sort of like foamy beer. Harry remembered only one name, Pulquería Los Hombres Grandes. When I told him it meant The Important Men, or The Old Men, Harry, sitting on the edge of the bed and removing his boots, smiled as he talked.

"Those guys sleeping with their heads on the bar, or lying in the sawdust on the floor, certainly weren't important men. But we are, Sugar. That's me and Leroy."

My husband vomited into his boots.

Butch had a room one floor below ours. The next day at breakfast, around two in the afternoon for Harry and Butch, I heard a version of no doubt what Butch had already told Harry and which Harry had forgotten.

"First I rode to Bahía Blanca," Butch said, "and caught a steamer for Buenos Aires. Waited at La Boca for another boat heading north but finally got going, you know, the well-to-do American rancher seeing the continent. A week here, a week there, maybe longer. Stayed quite a spell in Río. Hit Caracas, Cartagena. All over. Central America and up to Veracruz, hot and sultry. Sundance, you've never seen so many good-looking women." Butch made sure I heard that before continuing. "Stayed in Veracruz a spell, then came to Mexico City a week ago."

Harry said, "Run in to any Pinkertons along the way?"

Butch poked Harry's shoulder and laughed. "I heard the Regis had good food and cheap drinks, so here we are. Now I'm thinking about Europe. All this traveling helps replace the excitement of the old days."

He neared his fifties, so that might have had something to do with his changed attitudes. I wondered if my husband, a few years younger, would be affected the same way at Butch's age. I doubted it.

Butch claimed to have fattened his South America savings by a few transactions during all that sightseeing. But I doubted that too. After all, Harry hadn't been along to do the planning and to second him, or lead him. Butch had plenty of money anyway, what with our activities down there, including the sale of our ranch. And we all had cash in the States at banks and in tin cans in the ground. However, we weren't fixed for life.

The next celebration never became as transcendental as our first, what might be called "opening night." But we went fancy for dinner at the Jockey Club, then rode around in a rented carriage into that vast square slab of paving stones called the Zócalo and past the national pawnshop, the big stone government buildings, and the huge, tilting Cathedral.

Butch hadn't seen any of those sights. "That big old church sits crooked."

"There's a lake underneath this area," Harry told him.

"The hell you say."

We rolled along the Avenida Juárez business district, showed Butch the House of Tiles, then Alameda Park, green with lawn, packed with trees, busy with people, some relaxing, others walking as though with purpose, all places Butch hadn't seen.

Late one afternoon Harry and I sat in the Regis lobby sipping white tequila, Herradura, I believe, out of tall slim jiggers. We expected Butch to join us any minute when a big commotion sort of exploded just outside the front doors.

39

When the racket reached the lobby we saw it wasn't a holdup or a fight, just people yelling and calling out and cheering, like seeing a popular singer or dancer. We twisted in our seats to see better. In a few moments several men carrying suitcases and looking like hired hands, and a couple of others toting a trunk, walked through the lobby to the registration desk.

"What do you suppose?" Harry said.

"Got me. Maybe some European monarch."

Hotel help clustered around the arrivals, while other workers hurried toward the street. Another herd of men, smoking cigars and wearing dark suits, trouped in like potentates, yakking importantly to one another, all of them swallowing syllables like a hungry child using a tortilla to stuff frijoles into his mouth.

"What are they saying, Sugar?"

"From this distance I can't catch the drift. But their Spanish is more like what I heard in Buenos Aires than here."

"Looks like they had reservations and just arrived."

"They seem to defer to that man with a pigtail like a Chinaman's hanging over his coat collar."

All the men tried to stand close to him, and a bunch of Mexicans with notebooks, newspaper reporters, I figured, pushed and squeezed in, shouting questions and trying to get closer. Other men took pictures.

For certain, everyone focused on the man with the pigtail, a little fellow smaller than most of the others and probably younger than any of them. I never got a good look, just a glance revealing a square face with a huge nose, a bulging jaw he could knock you sideways with, a crooked smile, and dark hair cut medium length, except for the pigtail.

"Isn't that our waiter getting his autograph on a menu?"

"Sure enough," I said. "Now we'll have some answers."

Harry finally got Wenceslao's attention and signaled for another round. Wenceslao spoke English from living several years in Chicago.

"He is the greatest bullfighter Spain ever produced." Wenceslao, talking while drawing close, placed two more well-filled jiggers on the low table in front of us. "He's revolutionary. And so good the stands shake constantly with the cheers. Juan Belmonte, so powerful the bulls act as though trained. Except sometimes they break training and toss him and gore him here and there. We should all go see him fight before he's killed."

All Spain adored and idolized the young man with the pigtail and mighty jaw, Wenceslao told us, an attraction better known than King Alfonso XIII and more popular, already wealthy, just twenty-one years old.

"On Sunday he fights a *mano a mano* with our grand Indian, Gaona, the greatest Mexican matador ever, better than any Spaniard too, even Belmonte."

A few minutes later Butch joined us. "What the hell's going on?" He sat and smiled. "I thought Sundance might have been making a withdrawal from the cash register, so I waited outside to help with the getaway."

We explained about Belmonte and Gaona competing in the bullfight on Sunday.

"We don't want to miss it," Harry said.

"Sure," Butch said. "I'll go. I want to cheer for the bull."

"I've never seen anything like that," Harry commented frequently, even though he'd never been to a bullfight. "Look how they just stand there and the bull runs past." He nudged me. "I think Leroy ought to get in there and try that."

"Hell no," Butch said. "You see how big and sharp those horns are?"

Harry grinned at me and I poked his arm.

We sat close, heard the matadors call to the bulls, noticed the men sweating in those heavy, brocaded outfits, sequined and tight-fitting. We smelled the dust and the dung. By the time the second bull ran into the arena, and Harry had started on his second beer, he said softly, "I sort of see why Mr. Gaona and Mr. Belmonte enjoy doing what they're doing. Hold my beer, Sugar." He stood.

I grabbed his arm and pulled him down. "I know you're kidding. Aren't you?"

Harry concentrated on the big black bulls of Piedras Negras.

I kept my arm run through his the rest of the afternoon.

We didn't know what to look for nor exactly what we saw, except that the sight impressed us: thrilling, violent, artistic, primitive, courageous, bloody, and, when the bulls died, sad, those magnificent animals looking their scary best when they sort of exploded into the arena searching for something to attack.

The band played rousing music that got our feet to tapping and my soul to singing, except when a bull died, or a horse got knocked down, or a bull caught Gaona or Belmonte or one of their assistants and tossed him around and sometimes trampled him, with the spectators screaming in fright.

I loved the men's attire, so many spangles, while the flags fluttering all around the upper rim of El Toreo de Mexico added more color. I never heard so much cheering and so many shouts of approval, the *olés*. Gaona had a pigtail just like Belmonte's.

Harry summed up my feelings. "We are watching two brave young men in a rare spectacle."

Butch cheered for the bull until several Mexican men nearby told him to pipe down. One of them directly behind us kept ranting at Butch instead of making no more than a polite, brief reprimand of an everyday rude ignorant tourist.

He didn't call Butch any names, but I explained what the man said.

Butch got a silly look. Then his face grew flushed, and I think he gritted his teeth. Butch started to stand, but Harry pulled him down.

"We've retired," Harry said.

After the bullfight we had reached the street and stood in line for a buggy to take us to the hotel when a man and woman crowded in ahead of us. That's common practice in Mexico. But you don't elbow and cuss people the way this man did, the same hombre, by the way, who got rude when Butch had been acting smart. I suppose he didn't know I understood his comments.

This time the Mexican said even uglier things, personal, plus some others I didn't understand, some of them low under his breath to impress his woman, I reckon. His tone told everything. A show-off like that nettles me no end. So I planned to give him what-for or relay the personal insults to Harry and Butch when I saw it wouldn't be necessary.

Wild-eyed and looking belligerent, Butch reached for his inside gun and learned he didn't carry it. Then he stooped and pulled one pants leg above his boot top, where he could get to a derringer.

Harry twisted the Mexican around to face us and knocked him onto his back into the street and all over a fresh pile of horse droppings.

40

We encouraged Butch to visit Cuernavaca with us for Christmas and New Year's, but he said he wanted to see London and Paris and around, and then head for the States. Butch never had been one much for the holidays, maybe felt guilty running off to be a horse thief and without ever returning, though his momma and pap and little brothers and sisters needed him at home.

He and Harry had another night on the town that my husband could hardly recall. Then we put Butch on the train to Veracruz, where he could catch a steamer to Europe.

We went to Cuernavaca the next day.

"Soon we take Chilpancingo," Paco told us.

Paco and Bruja had recently arrived at the Delicias from Emiliano's encampment, still in northern Guerrero, so we anticipated a big time.

"The federal military remains in control here," Paco said, "but the town is Zapatista and life goes on the same for us. However, if my General Zapata ever wants Cuernavaca, we will rise up." Gen. Felipe Ángeles and his wife, Paco said, lodged again at Mrs. King's. "I stay out of his way and he stays out of mine."

Emiliano had given Paco and Bruja passes to come and go, so Paco sent a trusted friend to the encampment to acquire passes for us. We soon received them.

"We need to figure out a way to help 'Miliano," Harry said.

After enjoying the festivities of the Day of the Kings we went to Guerrero.

Emiliano was proud to see us again, joking around in his diffident way and asking about the atmosphere in Cuernavaca and Mexico City. Of course he had reports from other sources, especially from Gildardo Magaña, in and out of the capital and anywhere else Emiliano needed him. But he liked different viewpoints. And that made us feel useful and important.

"I regretted hearing that Mr. Posada has gone before us," Emiliano said in that polite way Mexicans say a person died. "Someone will need courage to take up his pen."

This encampment looked much larger than the one near Chilpancingo. Harry asked me to mention this.

"Yes," Emiliano said. "Huerta's conscripts desert regularly to us. Some are mounted. We also acquire other horses here and there."

I saw a shy grin. His saying "acquire" echoed Harry's way of talking.

Everyone, it seemed, felt dissatisfied with the usurper Huerta and wanted him out. That included President Wilson, who had sent a special envoy, John Lind, to Mexico City to replace ambassador Henry Lane Wilson.

"John Lind is not as pushy," Emiliano said, "but he doesn't like Mexicans."

We discussed that exchange. Emiliano doubted it would make any difference in relations with the United States. And he had other concerns.

"I need more weapons and ammunition," he said, "mainly machine guns and modern rifles."

When I sent that comment along to Harry, my husband said, "'Miliano, I've been aiming to talk to you about that."

I interpreted Harry's remark.

Emiliano smiled, touched Harry's arm.

In no time flat we volunteered to go to the States to try to obtain the weapons and ammunition the Zapatistas needed. To Emiliano, I actually said "acquire."

This time, however, Emiliano didn't. "This can be a purchase," he said. "I can obtain the money if you can find the sellers. Shipping the materiel out of your country will take planning, skill, luck, and courage."

"Harry's specialties," I told him.

Emiliano called for a bottle.

We sat on camp chairs under a royal ponciana and toasted our agreement.

Discussing the plan and making arrangements to leave kept us in camp for a few days. When Emiliano suggested target practice with rifles, Harry startled me.

"Sugar, tell 'Miliano I'd like for you to take part."

That set my heart to jumping. I hurried up to Emiliano and asked permission.

He looked surprised, but smiled. "Of course, Margarita, if you are sure."

I was sure, and I smacked more cans and bottles than anyone. That seemed to stun Emiliano. Still smiling, he sat with us at dinner. He and Harry had not participated.

Harry killed time playing cards with Emiliano and Eufemio, and I strummed my guitar. One day after Harry and Emiliano returned from hunting turkeys, Emiliano showed us his new horse, a big white stallion he called *As de Oro*, Ace of Gold.

"My other horse is prettier," Emiliano said. "Good for parades. This one is a war horse, good for fighting."

I've seen photographs many times of a painting of Emiliano with that horse.

When the Zapatistas prepared to retake Chilpancingo, we hurried to Cuernavaca.

"After we take Mexico City," Paco said, "Bruja and I meet you at the Regis."

The four of us—Bruja busied herself redecorating the Delicias again—sat under the shade of the red bougainvillea in Paco's hotel patio, where Harry told them about our assignment from Emiliano.

"When we learn how much the weapons and ammunition will cost," Harry said, "we're to wire Magaña in Mexico City. He'll wire the money to us in El Paso. We'll handle things from then, all the way to Acapulco. 'Miliano's got someone he can trust to meet us in Acapulco. Paco, you'll be our contact here. We might not need you, but . . ."

"I'll be ready," Paco said. Carlota squawked. Bebito sang.

By late March we checked in at the Regis, and I helped Harry send telegrams with double meanings to certain friends in Texas. Then we met with Magaña and created Spanish code words. For machine guns we said "music boxes." Rifles became "toothpicks." For pistols we agreed upon "gloves," while using "tortillas" for ammunition, one hundred cartridges per tortilla. When we shook on the deal, Magaña smiled as though he liked us.

About the time Emiliano took Chilpancingo, Pancho Villa in the north captured the important crossroads of Gómez Palacios and rode into Torreón without any opposition. I paraphrased some of that account for Harry.

"The newspaper says the poor folks got so bad off in Torreón they picked grain out of horse manure to grind for tortillas."

Harry looked disgusted, shook his head. I fought off a sob.

On another day, I read where Emiliano had asked special envoy John Lind for financial help against Huerta. I told Harry, "Lind suggested Emiliano try the Red Cross."

We took the train next day to Veracruz so we could sail to the States and make the purchases for Emiliano. We lodged near the waterfront at the Hotel Diligencias on the colorful central plaza: bandstand, lawns and benches, jacarandas lush in purple blooms.

Early on our first morning, gunfire and screaming and shouting woke us. We had run plumb into the US Marines, landing that very day, April 21, 1914. We didn't see the fighting, didn't know the significance, but I've since read we lost about twenty boys, the Mexicans several hundred. Harry and I walked to the waterfront. Our Marines guarding it made me proud but also ambivalent, knowing the Mexicans must have been bitter. The harbor thrived with ships, theirs and ours.

"Here's an editorial in the newspaper," I told Harry the next day. "Seems to explain what happened. President Wilson, you see, thought Huerta ought to kiss his fanny in apology over a minor incident in Tampico involving some of our sailors. Says Huerta wouldn't do it. Says that's the only popular thing Huerta has done as president. The other will be when he resigns, which is what Wilson had in mind when he sent in the Marines. But Wilson actually plans to seize the Customs House, a large source of income for Huerta, and capture the *Ypiranga*. This is the boat that took Porfirio Díaz to exile in France, and it's in the port here with arms and ammunition for Huerta."

The attack by the Marines helped the revolutionaries' cause, even though the Mexicans felt as angry as new-branded calves about the invasion. But like Pancho Villa told somebody later, "'It's Huerta's bull that's being gored.'"

President Wilson mobilized the Army and a lot of National Guard boys, and I read about talk in Mexico and in the States that our Marines would fight their way to Mexico City. They never moved past the Veracruz waterfront, but we sensed the tension.

"You and I ought to grab the *Ypiranga*," Harry said. "Get those supplies for 'Miliano."

Meanwhile, the US Atlantic Fleet blockaded the harbor, so no one sailed off.

"Sugar, we might as well relax in the shade under the arches in front of our hotel and watch the folks in the plaza. Get out of this heat and humidity."

"Yes. We can listen to the rumors. I hope there's not so much anti-American sentiment, like I've read has popped up in Mexico City."

"We're dark from the sun, and your Spanish is good. We'll pass if I don't talk."

"I suppose. But in Mexico City they set the American Club on fire three times."

"Never liked that restaurant. You and I should have burned it long ago."

I laughed. "Fortunately, with our Marines enforcing martial law here, there isn't much danger for Americans."

I'm not sure John Lind agreed with that assessment. President Wilson sent him to Veracruz to see the situation first-hand, and his office got stoned several times after dark with Lind in it.

One day I read where Emiliano learned that three mid-level aides had passed along inside information to Huerta about Zapatista personnel, weaponry, and activities. They insisted upon their innocence. Emiliano had them taken out and shot.

The famous reporter Richard Harding Davis reached Veracruz first thing, according to what we heard at our hotel.

"I'll bet he arrived in a private cabin," I told Harry, "dined at the captain's table, and probably packed his collapsible bathtub, like in Cuba."

We spotted him a couple of times from a distance.

Another American, however, interested us more.

41

Every day we took a table under the blessed shady arches of one of the many restaurants around the central plaza where we could watch the passersby and the picturesque little square, with its trees and shrubs, kids romping in the old bandstand.

So while we sat out of the sultry heat and sipped Carta Blanca, a muscular young man, short, blond, walked up in a sailor's gait, removed his watch cap, and sat at the adjacent table. I recognized him right away from the times I'd seen his photograph, which I'd often pointed out to Harry. I felt I knew him well, having enjoyed so many of his novels and stories, including several I read to my husband.

I whispered to Harry, "Look who's sitting at the next table."

"Spotted him, Sugar." Harry turned toward him the way a foreigner will often do when he sits near another out-of-place stranger. "Join us for a beer?"

As the world knows, you didn't have to ask Jack London twice to have a drink. Quicker than you could say "call of the wild" he sat with us. My husband introduced us as Maggie and Harry Parker, and I understood the reason when he patted my knee under the table. Out of habit, I glanced around but didn't see any suspicious-looking observers, any posters with our pictures. The waiter rushed up. Harry ordered three more beers.

We were thrilled, and London seemed enthusiastic about sitting with us. After all, Harry was a man's man and I still had my looks. London, a fine-looking man whose eyes, bluer than the skies over Veracruz that day never left our faces as we talked, seemed about my age. I'd be thirty-eight that year.

We let London know right away we loved his stories. Despite his fame, he welcomed the comment. After some chatter about the heat, the humidity, and the US Marines' occupying the place, he asked how long we'd been in town.

"Since the night before the shooting started," Harry said. "We figured to catch a boat to New Orleans after selling our ranch in Argentina. But it looks like we'll be here a spell on account of the blockade."

"Me too," he said, "but it doesn't matter. I'm looking for things to write about. Have you seen much of the trouble?"

"Mostly here. But Zapata's movements in Cuernavaca and around affected us."

"The newspapers and the White House say Zapata's little more than a bandit."

Harry and I started at the same time to disabuse London of that maliciousness. I ceded the floor to my husband, who outlined the entire situation, from Morelos to Chihuahua, from Díaz to Huerta, as well as a history professor could have. How I wish I could have got Harry when he was younger! When he finished, London nodded.

"I see what you mean," our new convert said.

He had sailed in with the Atlantic Fleet, the same as Richard Harding Davis.

"I'm writing for newspapers in New York and San Francisco. I've already been to Tampico. We were as wrong there as a Tahitian in a tuxedo. And I want to meet Madero, then try to find Pancho Villa in the north."

"What about Zapata?" Harry said.

"You sure he wouldn't shoot me?" London smiled around his beer glass.

"Maggie can write down how to find an old-timer in Cuernavaca. He can lead you to 'Miliano."

We sipped beer and talked. Before long a breeze came up. The marimba players, wearing huaraches and white cotton pants and shirts, set up nearby on the sidewalk, and the afternoon got better and better. When the marimba moved on, the harp player arrived with his guitarist and violinist. They dressed like the others with the addition of funny little pointed straw hats. Lots of us loafers hired them for a song or two, so the music, soft and dreamy, instead of fast and raucous like from the marimba band, continued without interruption. We liked both groups equally and had a grand time.

After a while we ordered dinner and ate at the same table, all of us wanting broiled red snapper doused with garlic-and-tomato sauce, with fresh oysters and broiled shrimp on the side, one of the best meals ever. Harry and London felt the same.

We pushed our plates away, and the men lit up cigarettes. When their smokes burned down, London looked from Harry to me and back to Harry.

"We could visit some more places," London said.

In those days Harry's right leg grew weak if he drank too much. And I felt certain London's "places" meant cantinas. "You two go. I'm reading a good novel."

London grinned. "Any writer we know?"

I said, "Wait for me a minute." I hurried to our room and returned with my Jack London novels for him to autograph.

He not only signed them, he wrote a short personal dedication on each one.

I watched the men on their way, knowing Harry wouldn't be able to match him drink for drink, not from what I'd read. But I knew he'd try. I set a slop jar by the bed.

Harry returned to our room in time for breakfast but went straight to bed. Around noon he joined me at a sidewalk table under the arches in front of the Diligencias and sipped a Pacífico while I ate shrimp salad. His drinking leg buckled as he sat.

"Did you have a nice evening?"

"Sugar, I mightily 'preciate your understanding."

Harry had introduced Jack London to the custom of the pulquería. "We didn't stay long. He considered it quaint and something to know about if you're curious but not to hang your hat in. We returned to the plaza and experienced the cantinas there."

"Naturally."

"There are several, Sugar. It took time. And Jack switched to tequila."

"Uh-oh."

"I had to follow suit."

"Of course."

"I mean, a fool alone is still a fool, but it's more fun if he has company."

"Did you run in to any anti-Americanism?"

Harry gazed around the plaza. "I'm not sure which place. Yes, we had one little moment. Neither of us could understand a damn word. But he ranted loud and clear, a big bastard, ugly as an armadillo. Etta, we took it for a long time, just tried awful hard to ignore him."

Uh-oh. "What happened when you couldn't ignore him anymore?"

"Jack knocked him clean through the swinging doors and into the street."

We saw a lot of London during the next week before deciding that the Marines and the Atlantic Fleet had settled in for the duration.

"Jack needs to stay, Sugar. He's getting information to write about. But I'm concerned that pretty soon 'Miliano will want to hear from us."

"London's right good company. But, yes, let's find another way to head north."

London went with us to the train station, brought red roses for me and a liter of Sauza for Harry, plus a flask of Jamaican rum to share while the engine built up steam. We'd become such comrades he'd started calling me Margarita in addition to Maggie.

When we had to board, we exchanged hugs, and I kissed London's cheek.

From our seats we watched him through the window while the train eased away. He waved. We waved back and I held up my roses so he could see them. We watched until we couldn't make him out any longer.

"I wonder if we'll ever see him again," I said.

"Would be nice. Fine man."

I read about him over the next two years. Then, as the world knows, he died. We felt proud to have known Jack London. And we knew he enjoyed our company.

I have often wondered how London would have felt, and what he might have written about it, had he known that his cantina-hopping pard in quaint old Veracruz on those warm and sultry spring nights of 1914 had been The Sundance Kid.

42

In Mexico City we left that train and quickly caught another to Cuernavaca, where we visited briefly with Paco and Bruja, then rode the stage down that worst of trails to Acapulco. There we boarded a coastwise Mexican steamer sailing north. When it docked in San Francisco we got off and rented a buggy and driver to take us to the Palace Hotel, rebuilt since the awful earthquake and fire of 1906. We liked it well enough. But it lacked the warm feeling of the original.

The next day we saw a few other sights and dined on fresh oysters and sea bass at the Cliff House. A day later we began making our way by train, stagecoach, and horseback to America Connolly's little spread in eastern New Mexico.

"Kid! Miss Etta! By damn! I mean, Jesús, María, and José!"

I surmised that America hadn't been speaking much English lately and couldn't easily pull up a lot of his vocabulary. Turned out to be more than that.

"We thought you been killed. Holy Jesus! Catalina, bring a bottle."

We hadn't even dismounted, paused at the hitching rail near the front porch. Their dogs had run out barking from under the house. Chickens scattered in several directions. America, who'd been using a hammer to repair a table, looked like he'd seen ghosts, and I reckon he thought he had.

When Catalina stepped onto the porch I thought she about fainted at the sight of us. But she soon let out a happy cry and bounced up and down in surprise and joy.

Seated on the porch then with America and Catalina, their younguns playing in front of us with the dogs and tossing a ball, us sipping corn whiskey with branch water and ever so happy to be with that fine couple, we watched the sun set behind the Sangre de Cristo range. And we learned that the Pinkertons had reported Harry and Butch killed in South America.

"Supposed to have happened five, six years ago," America said. "Argentina or Bolivia. Maybe robbing a bank or a big store, something like that."

"Loco," Harry said. "Me and Butch both?"

"Both of you."

"Anything about Etta?"

"Not a word."

"Did one of us get to plug Charlie Siringo? Frank Dimaio?"

America laughed. "They weren't there, Kid. We heard the army did it, maybe local police. We didn't hear any more details. But we got it from three people. Damn, I'm glad there's nothing to it."

"Know what you mean," Harry told him.

As the sun sneaked into hiding and twilight joined us, we told about our activities in Argentina and around and how we ran into Butch in Mexico City. I had never written to Catalina and America, and now I felt guilty I hadn't or they would have known we were all right. But we soon got over our surprise of Harry and Butch being reported killed. America and Catalina recuperated from the sight of seeing us ride up strong and healthy, and we had a big time on the porch talking while watching that wonderful New Mexico desert fade into several shades of dark. We listened to the coyotes and other night creatures start up, then went in for supper.

They'd added two more little ones for a total of five, but Catalina still looked slim and pretty. I helped, and she fixed the best meal we'd had since the Cliff House. Catalina and I and little

Etta María Guadalupe cleaned up and joined Harry and America on the porch, where we talked softly in the tranquil wonder of a night resplendent with stars.

Harry had just finished explaining about the Mexican Revolution from our perspective, including our promise to acquire arms and ammunition for Zapata.

"I think I know someone," America said.

"Pard, let's go."

Harry never called anyone else "Pard" except Butch. They rode for Texas the next morning. I stayed with Catalina and the children.

Two weeks later they rode back.

"'Merica knows every revolutionary in El Paso, looked like," Harry told me. "They drove all the latest motorcars."

With America's contacts and speaking Spanish, plus Harry's planning and knowing the shopping list, they had a highly successful trip.

"'Miliano's going to be right proud," Harry said. Over Harry's name they had wired Magaña about materiel available and the money needed. The funds, including a healthy commission Harry could split with America, showed up by wire the next day at an El Paso bank, and Harry paid the suppliers. Before he and America started back, the "music boxes, toothpicks, gloves, and tortillas" had crossed the Río Grande near El Paso on the way to the Chief of the South.

"'Merica's suppliers looked more suitable than those you and I contacted from Mexico City," Sugar. "We paid half down to them and to some escorts. The stuff is going through the deserts of Chihuahua and Sonora to Guaymas. From there it moves by boat to Acapulco. They'll contact Magaña for the rest of their pay."

"Hot country," I said. "And dangerous, Geronimo and other Apaches."

"'Merica says Geronimo gave up long ago. The others went tame. But our boys are fire-tested and armed to their hat brims. And they can trade some guns if need be."

"So with that varmint Charlie Siringo, and that other varmint, Frank Dimaio, thinking you and Butch have cashed in, we can be tourists in our own country."

"Remember, Sugar, they might still be looking for you."

"I'll wear a wild red wig."

We hated to leave America and Catalina, but I promised to write from time to time. "That way you'll know the opposition hasn't whipped us."

"We'll see you again soon," Harry said.

I know Harry didn't want to leave their younguns either. He would have made the most wonderful father. But he didn't blame me the way lots of men faulted their wives in those days. Harry realized he might be the cause of our lack of children.

"Thanks for all your help, Kid."

"Couldn't have done it without you, 'Merica. You earned every penny. If you come visit, I suspect 'Miliano will commission you as one of his officers."

I poked Harry good and hard.

Catalina stepped closer to America and slipped her arm through his.

"Lord o' mercy, Harry honey. Everybody thought you got killed."

"Yes, I got a batch of queer looks as we rode through town."

Mrs. Bohanan, the Sundance storekeeper who had been such a good friend to Harry's mother and read my letters to her, showed about the same expression of disbelief on her face as America and Catalina. But she quickly got her feet under her.

"You and Cassidy both. Argentina or Bolivia, maybe Peru. A bank holdup or a shootout with police or the army."

"It's just as well folks think that," Harry said, "except personal friends. I suppose we'll be scaring certain people one at a time for a while."

We took Mrs. Bohanan for supper at the hotel, where Harry drew additional curious looks, and a few astonished men came up to happily shake his hand. Mrs. Bohanan and Harry had a long talk and in general a big time of its sort.

We spent the night at the hotel and rode out to the cemetery the next day, paying our respects to Harry's mother and father. We felt proud seeing their headstones.

"I wonder," Harry said as we rode away, "if that son of a bitch is back at his old place by now."

Oh-oh. I knew exactly whom he meant.

To my relief, we didn't ride near his stepfather's land or Harry's home place.

"Might be burned down," Harry said, "or wild animals living in it."

We traveled south, horse and stagecoach and train again, through Texas and New Orleans and into Alabama, straight into a heart-warming reunion with my family, who didn't welcome my husband as the ghost of The Sundance Kid but as the finally returning Harry Parker, flesh and blood financial tycoon, son-in-law, and brother-in-law.

Momma and I had corresponded, so my family knew we'd show up that summer, and I knew I had several more nieces and nephews. My sisters, despite all their younguns, still fluttered around Harry. My brothers thought that by now they could out-shoot me and Harry both, and foolishly challenged us. They lost.

Momma didn't say anything about our not having children.

In the years since our last visit Momma and Pappy had aged a lot. I should have expected it, but the realization saddened me. I resolved to never again stay away so long.

Meanwhile, everything felt and looked like old times: the love palpable, meals delicious and hearty, the soil red, the weather hot and sultry. Insects thrived.

"Is the piano in tune?"

"Should be, Etta Margaret. No one's played it much."

Some of the notes could have used adjusting, but my bunch didn't complain, and after supper the first night everyone gathered in the parlor to sing while I played. My playing needed adjusting too but I finally got on track.

Night after night, with at least a few of my sisters, brothers, their spouses, and their little ones visiting, we filled the parlor with singing and my playing. I gave them *The Kerry Cow* and *Darby Kelly* and *Come Sit Down Beside Me*. We all got excited with *Garryowen* and *A Nation Once Again* and a slew more, including *The Bugle Sang True, Her Bright Smile Haunts Me Still*, and *Dixie*. We did *Dixie* twice every night.

On the Fourth of July we enjoyed a spectacular family get-together: barbecued pig, peas, mashed potatoes, corn on the cob, square dancing, a one-turkey shooting contest that I quickly ended, and a certain amount of Pappy's good corn whiskey. I drank some as a courtesy.

Despite all the happiness and closeness enfolding us, I knew I could never return to farming. Just too harsh. I loved and admired my family but felt so glad to have my different life.

The next day we said our good-byes, never easy, and set out to find a ship sailing south to Veracruz. As Harry helped me onto the wagon for the ride to the stage station in Selma, he said softly, "When we get settled I'm buying you the best piano I can find."

43

In Mobile we learned that the Atlantic Fleet continued blockading Veracruz.

"Sugar, we might's well head for San Francisco or San Diego and get on to Acapulco, join up with the shipment to 'Miliano instead of crossing Mexico."

We started west, stopping at New Orleans, where I picked up a daily paper and read that Huerta had resigned.

"Maybe that'll open up Veracruz," Harry said.

"Hope so. Could we stay here a few days and find out?"

"And give you a chance to do some shopping?"

"That too."

I loaded up on essentials, and so did Harry: cigarettes, two new decks of cards, a quart of bourbon, and a few Cuban cigars for special occasions.

But the blockade continued.

With my help, Harry wired Paco to inform Emiliano that the shipment would beat us there, that Emiliano should send someone else to meet it.

"That will be a good assignment for the oldest Zapatista," Harry said.

"I wonder if Bruja's finished redecorating the Delicias."

By train and stagecoach we crossed the country to Los Angeles and rode the train south to San Diego, stopping at a Moorish-looking Santa Fe Depot under construction to replace the old wooden one. We descended, took in the harbor, then faced the other direction where, about a mile away, we saw a hotel we'd been told would be the US Grant, built since our first visit and replacing the Horton House.

"They say the Grant's the best in town," I said.

"And you're the prettiest girl. Let's go."

We wired Paco to update him on our whereabouts. We knew the shipment would be in good hands, and we liked San Diego, decided to stay a spell.

"I spotted at least three daily newspapers," I told Harry. "We'll be able to keep up on the doings in Mexico."

In that summer of 1914 the city leaders in San Diego kept busy preparing an exposition to commemorate opening the Panama Canal later in the year. The San Diego folks figured that the canal would make their town more important as the first stop in the States for northbound shipping. The little place worked at full steam.

"Welcome to our fine hotel and wonderful city," the clerk at the hotel reception desk said. "My name is Pierre. How long will you be with us?"

"Just a few days," Harry said.

"But if you leave too soon, you'll miss so much. We're constructing a bridge into our big park and several Spanish-style buildings for the exposition. President Wilson will be here. Also Thomas Edison. We'll have exhibitions by bird men in their flying machines. So many attractions. Perhaps you can return. It will last a year."

"We'll see how our financial transactions go," Harry said.

"The weather's beautiful year-round here in the Jewel of the West," Pierre said.

In our room Harry said, "Sugar, I thought you were the Jewel of the West."

While keeping in touch with the shipping schedule at the harbormaster's office, we rode a buggy around San Diego, hired a motorcar with a driver a couple of times, took the ferry across the bay to Coronado to see the big hotel and the beach there, and walked barefoot in shallow water, in general having a big time. We felt like honeymooners and acted the same way.

The European War broke out while we visited San Diego, but it was so far away. Our thoughts stayed with Mexico.

One day Harry received a wire from Paco: The shipment arrived in good shape. *"The chief is pleased."*

A few days later an article in *The Sun* more or less confirmed Paco's wire.

"Listen to this, Honey. Zapatistas are threatening Mexico City. The place is in an uproar of rage and fear. The federals made a deal with Obregón. They'll try to keep Emiliano out of Mexico City until the last minute so Obregón can get there first. Then they would surrender to Obregón and he would acquire the Mexican army."

"Don't you know," Harry said grinning, "that Obregón and President Wilson and every rich and fancy Mexican in town are throwing conniption fits knowing 'Miliano's poor ragged Indians are about to rest in the shade at Alameda Park."

Huerta saved his treacherous hide by fleeing—to Texas, some reports said.

On another day I read to Harry how, after a siege, Emiliano took Cuernavaca. That gave him control of the entire state of Morelos.

"Wish we'd been there, Sugar. We know Paco and Bruja enjoyed that."

Another article said Pancho Villa sent emissaries to Emiliano, asking him to meet with Villa and other rebel leaders at Aguascalientes.

"Looks like everybody's getting together," Harry said.

"Yep. Maybe Mexico will be at peace soon."

We stayed a few months in San Diego before sailing south, finally docking at Acapulco on a German freighter in mid-November to learn that Obregón had declared war on Pancho Villa. The following week, the Atlantic Fleet left Veracruz, and Obregón started marching his Yaqui Indians and other boys toward Mexico City. Emiliano beat him to it. We got there right behind him and checked in at the Regis.

But Emiliano didn't seem to want the place. His soldiers—bedraggled and poor and hungry—begged door to door instead of taking food at gunpoint the way any other conquering army would have. Just pitiful.

We had to go to that third-class Hotel San Lázaro near the train station to find Emiliano. He sat at a table in the lobby playing cards and smoking with his brother and Gildardo Magaña, who looked up and stopped talking. Emiliano and Eufemio stood. Emiliano, shy as usual, started to hug me, instead extended his hand, as did Eufemio, both of them smiling. Magaña nodded at us but didn't stand.

Emiliano, so proud to see us, said he was mighty grateful for the shipment.

"'Miliano's got one of the Spencer carbines." Harry saw it lying on a chair beside him.

Emiliano understood that much. He smiled bigger than I'd ever seen him.

"Ask if the fighting's over now he's got Mexico City."

I presented Harry's question.

"No," Emiliano said. "Carranza wants to be president, but he's as bad as the others. And it looks like we'll have to fight Obregón, who supports Carranza."

Harry said, "Tell him we'll arrange another shipment."

When I did so, Emiliano thanked us but said:

"I believe I'll be able to obtain weapons now through Pancho Villa. He gets them in the north from his contacts in the United States."

"If that doesn't work out," I said, "we're ready to help."

He nodded, the gratitude still in his face. "I'm meeting Villa soon in Xochimilco, at the southern edge of the capital. Come with me."

A few days later we went to the most picturesque place I'd ever seen, and during their meeting we had plenty of time to explore. We found a typical village, its attraction the canals in the lake and the way the locals used them. We hired a small flat-bottomed boat, red, green, and white, and a man to pole it.

"My name is Juan," the guide said in English. His spiel contained lots of English and Spanish, so between Juan and me, Harry and I understood.

"The little islands," Juan said, "are earth and grass, *chinampas*. They float, but don't escape *el lago*. Flowers grow on them since before the *gachupines* come here."

Nearby, a boat like ours had an arched roof decorated by flowers. It carried a Mexican couple and a guitar player in addition to the pole master.

Juan caught me watching them, young people in love in an idyllic setting.

"Would want *música?*" Juan said. "Or get married?"

"We're already married," Harry said. "Sugar, you want music?"

"My heart's filled with it, all this beauty and the peacefulness."

In midafternoon while we ate outdoors at the Restaurante Chinampa—it sat on the plaza beside the Cantina Chinampa and near the Hotel Chinampa—Emiliano and Villa with their retinues walked by. All the children in town seemed to be following the rebels. Shopkeepers stood in their doorways happily greeting them.

"What'd they say, Sugar?"

"Couldn't catch a word."

In this our first look at Pancho Villa we saw he stood some taller than Emiliano and weighed maybe forty pounds more, pudgy, with a big mustache in a florid face like a blond. Smiling and apparently joking, he wore a loose brown sweater, khaki trousers with leggings, heavy high-top shoes, and a pith helmet.

Emiliano, somber, attentive, had dressed in his usual rig for special occasions: tight black trousers and short black jacket, white shirt with pleats and ruffles, red tie, good black boots, and big finely woven sombrero with embroidery and conchos.

Everybody toted weapons.

"'Miliano's mustache is bigger and blacker than Villa's," Harry said, "and his skin's so much darker."

"It's the Indian in him. Makes Emiliano look like a small blackbird, what I've heard called a *chanate*. He looks his usual shy and taciturn."

"Yes. But Villa could pass for a politician hunting for babies to kiss."

On the train returning to Mexico City, Emiliano seemed pleased enough with the meeting, although not confident that the revolution would end the way it should.

"Villa is dedicated," Emiliano told us. "But Obregón is also a smart general. And he has many more troops."

Harry asked me to find out if Emiliano thought all factions could work together. I presented the question.

"One would think so," Emiliano said. "But the fact that I control the south is a cactus under Obregón's saddle. If he and Carranza would recognize what we've accomplished, and our needs . . . but they don't."

The Mexico City newspapers, echoing government policy, still called Emiliano a bandit, Villa too, just couldn't see their side. Or wouldn't.

In early December the Zapatistas and Villistas staged a review of their troops in Mexico City along the main streets and into the Zócalo. Too bad Obregón missed it. But we didn't. Then Emiliano and Villa entered the Palacio Nacional to sit for photos. Villa occupied the president's hand-carved chair, what they call the Eagle Chair, with Emiliano seated on his left. We didn't get to see that. But I read in *El Imparcial* the next day, alongside the photo, that Emiliano had insisted on Villa's taking the seat of honor. The boy looking over Emiliano's left shoulder is his only son, Nicolás, about nine years old.

It's a famous picture now, by Mr. Casasola. I've seen it reproduced many times, same as the one in the House of Tiles, the Zapatistas being served at the counter, an impoverished savage-looking bunch. They had a lot to fight for but not much to do it with, mainly their courage and determination, plus their admiration of Emiliano.

"Those poor Indian farmers love their chief, don't they, Sugar?"

"Yes. To a man."

Years later, when numerous historical versions of this conflictive time had been written, I learned that Emiliano became so popular with the poorer Mexicans, and that meant most of them and the ones doing the fighting, that he could have been elected president. "Beloved" is the best word for how the common folks felt toward him. They repeated stories about his prowess in battle and skills as a planner.

They shared his anger, realized it was justified. But they also knew his kindliness, his concern for the weak, and his selflessness. Everyone realized Emiliano didn't seek personal gain but fought so the laws would be the same for poor as well as rich. He didn't want to be president. And since he didn't show much interest in Mexico outside the south, some historians have tarnished him.

44

By early 1915, Emiliano operated out of Tlaltizapán, a small, idyllic town in southern Morelos cooled by Indian laurels and plane trees and several streams, where he lived tranquilly with Josefa and Nicolás.

Some of his guerrilla chiefs and troops continued fighting off and on, in Puebla, for instance, but at that time Emiliano didn't want to get involved that far away. He farmed and horse-traded and saw that his gains in Morelos and Guerrero were maintained and respected. And he talked of retirement.

Harry and I alternated between Mexico City and Cuernavaca while occasionally spending a few days at Tlaltizapán. We had just finished breakfast there one day when Emiliano walked up.

"Come with me." His smile told us a treat lay ahead. "Bring your tent."

So we packed and mounted. I still rode Cuchulain II, and Harry had Butch when we didn't stable them with Paco's horses. We headed north with Emiliano, Eufemio, and quite a few others, going to Yautepec, nearly to Cuernavaca. Since Emiliano didn't take Josefa and the boy, I guessed he had a woman at Yautepec.

"I've called for a meeting of all my chiefs," Emiliano told us. "We need to talk things over and renew friendships. It will be like a fiesta."

Paco and Bruja had learned about the gathering and arrived shortly before us.

"This will be one grand party," Paco said. "All the chiefs and mariachis are here. The women have started cooking. Steers and hogs are butchered. Harry, I told everyone you'd give a shooting exhibition. Margarita, did you bring your guitar?"

When a slim young man wearing jeans, tight cotton shirt, a black beret, and toting a satchel and red cape showed up he caused quite a stir. Paco recognized him right away.

"I heard he'd be here," Paco said. "He's just a novice, eighteen or twenty, but everyone says he'll be a great bullfighter. From Guanajuato. Juan Silveti. Wait until you see him. We call him *Juan Sin Miedo*, Juan Without Fear."

But before the bullfight, we had the Dance of the Drunken Turkeys. I don't know if many folks have seen inebriated turkeys but, believe me, it's a spectacle.

"The poor creatures are going to get their heads chopped off anyhow," Paco said, "so what's the harm? They enjoy a good party on their way out."

We watched as some Mexicans poured tequila into bowls and set them on the ground in front of the three turkeys destined for the barbecue spit.

"Tequila makes the meat soft," Paco said.

That makes sense when you realize how a person feels in the meat and bones after too much to drink. These turkeys became pleasantly inebriated, wobbling around as far as the ropes on their legs would allow, gobbling at one another, trying to fly, and hustling back to the dishes for more tequila, Sauza, I believe.

While the turkeys got tenderized live on the hoof, we played cards, listened to the musicians, and occasionally glanced toward the big ahuehuete tree where Emiliano and his chieftains had begun their powwow.

After the turkeys had drunk their last and been slaughtered and dressed and placed on spits, two of the women used turkey wings to fan the fire. I felt insulted for the birds.

But talk about savory! Black beans and corn tortillas complemented them.

We all felt pretty good the next day and looked forward to the bullfight and barbecue. Parrots squawked, mockingbirds sang in the laurels and plane trees, sparrows and orioles jabbered, and the aromas of tortillas, beans, chorizo, and coffee pleasantly permeated the scene and accompanied scrambled eggs. Chatter filled the Zapatista camp.

Before long, Emiliano called for a rooster-snatching contest.

"I could take on a rooster," Harry said, "but I don't know about a bull."

"I do," I said. "You're not."

"Paco neither," Bruja announced.

I still tasted drunk turkey until nearly finished with breakfast. By then one of the Zapatistas had buried an irate red rooster to its neck in the middle of Yautepec's main street, and some of the men had saddled their horses.

"You start about thirty yards away and gallop full speed toward the rooster," Paco explained. "Stay just to one side of him. At the last minute you lean out of the saddle, grab the rooster by the neck, try to not fall, and yank him out of the ground."

We watched the first few riders. One fell to big applause, whistles, and cheers, but the successful ones grabbed the rooster flapping and squawking and trotted around showing it to everyone while holding it by the neck. Then another man reburied it.

"At least," I said, "this isn't bloody like a cockfight. But that little fellow sure is getting battered and tuckered out."

"Yes," Harry said, "hardly fit to kill and probably not much good with the hens."

Some riders wobbled like yesterday's turkeys and ran over the rooster, knocking it silly. That cost the rider points. When that happened they usually replaced the bird. We witnessed several substitutions. And more than one Zapatista, men and women, fell out of the saddle on that dusty sunny happy morn.

Harry did fine on his first attempt and didn't try again. I could have done it too, but Harry, knowing I'd show up some of those boys, didn't want me to try. Paco did well for his age, falling only once while grabbing the rooster two times out of three.

"That reminded me of the second Battle of Puebla," Paco said.

We sipped pulque while the rest of the Zapatistas and several local folks finished. Juan Silveti, instead of saving himself for the bullfight, tried right there with the others. I reckon if you're loco enough to fight bulls you can face a mostly buried live rooster.

"He rides well enough," Harry said, "but isn't much good at leaning over that far to grab the bird."

"They might have to cancel the bullfight if he keeps falling."

"He gets hurt bad, 'Miliano might have him taken out and shot."

Emiliano, by the way, lithe and lean and agile, showed up the other horsemen, no surprise. He scored three for three on the rooster grab, as graceful as a swooping eagle. Then he rejoined his subchiefs for more confab under the ahuehuete.

After a while we walked with Paco and Bruja to a little wooden bullring near the train station on the edge of the village, and at the corral we climbed wooden steps to get above the bulls to see them safely. Silveti showed up on our heels, so we introduced ourselves. I didn't know what to ask him that he might not have heard before, so I kept shut. Besides, he studied the bulls, as you could imagine. Paco talked with him some, however, and we all liked him. Silveti had a pigtail, same as Gaona and Belmonte, but combed his hair down over his forehead, a trait that became part of his trademark, along with his revolver and his cigar, his generosity and reckless courage.

The bulls were big and black. "They're scary," I said. "We're so close."

"Yes," Paco said. "That's the kind of bull Toluca turns out."

"But they don't seem as large as what we saw in Mexico City," Harry said.

Paco looped a hand through the air. "In the countryside, where doctors don't know much about horn wounds, we fight younger bulls. They're big enough but not so smart yet, so maybe they won't catch the *toreros*, who are also new and not so smart either."

"If they were real smart," Bruja said, "they wouldn't go out there."

"But they do," Paco said, "for they're a little loco too. Maybe we should find our seats. This won't be so formal, like what you saw in Mexico City. More fiesta."

As soon as they let the first bull into the arena, a man with a red cape lured him to the fence. Then another man jumped from the top of the fence right onto the bull. That man was Emiliano.

"What do you know," Harry said.

"No picadors, so we do that to weaken the bull," Paco said.

Emiliano gave it a sterling ride, leaped off, and someone else jumped on.

Harry stood.

I grabbed his arm and pulled him down.

He smiled and looked straight ahead, satanic, as though plotting.

When a bunch of guerrillas finished having the bull toss, bump, and trample them, and climbed back into the stands to continue getting drunk, Silveti took over. He had changed into a sequined jacket and tight pants, just like Gaona and Belmonte, and he strutted around the same and made a lot of cape passes everyone liked. He also stuck the sharp-pointed sticks into the bull's back, same as Gaona.

"Gaona does that much better," Paco said.

When he switched to a smaller piece of red cloth Silveti got tossed around a lot, inspiring a bunch of screaming. He also made plenty of passes that drew cheers and *olés*.

But the crowd that had favored him so much shouted insults and whistled when he couldn't stick his sword properly into the bull. I'd never heard such abuse.

"We'd better leave," Paco said. "This crowd might burn down the stands."

But the afternoon clearly showed us why they called him Juan Without Fear.

We headed back to camp, and Emiliano introduced Silveti to everyone, and we toasted the young fellow, not that anybody in that bunch needed an excuse to bend an elbow. To be friendly, I joined in.

When Harry started to stand first thing in the morning, his drinking leg gave way. He caught himself, sat back down on the blanket, and pulled on his boots.

"I noticed you had a big time yesterday," I said.

"My, oh my."

We enjoyed breakfast of scrambled eggs, black beans, pork chorizo, corn tortillas, and the blackest, stoutest coffee we'd ever tasted. Harry felt better right away.

"Sugar, I heard there's a rifle-shooting contest this morning."

"That so?"

"Paco says some of the Zapatista ladies been carrying on about how they can whip the britches off their menfolks."

"Wouldn't be surprised."

"Sugar, I think 'Miliano and the others have seen us around enough that their pride won't be ruined. Besides, I want to see the look on their faces."

I could hear Old Deuce dancing gleefully through Harry's words. "I'll get my Model 94 ready."

Some of the younger boys stood off and tossed tin plates into the air for us to shoot at, and I showed everyone how, even as we kept backing off to greater distances.

They put one of that day's turkeys behind a low barrier, and we took turns sniping at his head when he'd stick it up and look around. I killed one with my first shot, but no one else had any luck, and Emiliano called off the contest before I got to shoot again. After all, you couldn't get a turkey drunk if you knocked his head off first.

When we switched to cans for targets, the men joined in. I popped everyone's eyeballs out with the best rifle marksmanship that crowd had ever seen. Of course, most of them were farmers, but they had done plenty of shooting in battles and in practice, and they thought they were good. But only Emiliano with a Model 94 we'd imported for him, Eufemio firing a Winchester 73, and Paco using Harry's Model 94 came close to giving me any competition. Harry, known for pistol shooting, didn't participate.

"I will trade you carbines," Emiliano said, and he gave me a timid smile, his way of congratulating me without making too much of it. Eufemio, however, swore and spat and walked away, and before long got into a fistfight at a Yautepec pulquería called—this is my translation—God's Own Place.

"Margarita," Paco said, "I wished you'd been with us at Chapultepec Castle."

45

Emiliano occasionally held other meetings with his chiefs, but we never had another colorful congress like the one at Yautepec in 1915, for the way things soon developed, all the fighting had chased the party spirit out of the Zapatistas.

Early the next year, for instance, the federals pushed them out of Puebla, one of the few major cities they held, although Emiliano continued to control the countryside in that state, along with the rural areas of Morelos and Guerrero.

And a typhus epidemic struck Mexico City like the second blast from a double-barreled shotgun, being as so many folks already experienced extreme hunger, some of them forced to eat dogs and cats and rats, like during Huerta's takeover.

That year, 1916, we camped with Emiliano in the countryside at Tlaltizapán, so much healthier, and where plenty of crops and livestock kept folks going.

Fighting became sporadic but fierce. We stayed out of it, but I know Harry would have joined up if not for me.

"Etta," Harry said, "we can help 'Miliano by bringing supplies and running errands for him, delivering messages."

"We could acquire horses for him here and there too," I said.

"Yes, we have some experience in that profession."

Once we rode close enough to watch a battle from a hill and saw something we'd never imagined seeing in Mexico.

"Sugar, that's a flying machine up there."

About the time Harry pointed it out—it had two wings and wheels with a motor in front—something small fell out of it, hit the ground near some guerrillas, and blew up in a pop and a dust spout.

"A bomb," I said.

"Sure as shootin'."

A lot of Mexicans didn't believe airplanes existed, so you know a miraculous sight had occurred for plenty of folks.

Paco and Bruja joined us frequently, though they missed the airplane and didn't much believe us when we told them about it. Most of the time they stayed at the Hotel Delicias, even though Emiliano had abandoned Cuernavaca and federals returned.

"Federal money is going to still be worth something when the fighting ends," Paco said. "I don't think the rebel money will be."

"Like in our Civil War," Harry said. "But what if the rebels win?"

"They can't. Everyone is going over to Carranza."

"Not 'Miliano."

"Of course not. Never. But Carranza can't endure having my chief in a position of power. Carranza is an elite of the worst category. He will have to subdue my General Zapata or have him assassinated."

"I hope you're wrong," Harry told him.

"Me too. Either way, there will be a struggle for power. Obregón will have Carranza killed. And someone will have Obregón killed. Many terrible years lie ahead."

And the next unhappy thing we heard, a fact instead of an opinion, Pancho Villa couldn't keep his promise to send guns and ammunition to Emiliano.

"Sugar, I think we'd better pay another visit to 'Merica and Catalina."

"The port at Veracruz is open now."

"That'll be a heap closer for us."

Pancho Villa attacked Columbus, New Mexico, in this period of 1916. He wanted recognition from the United States and had become angry about supplies for Obregón traveling through our country to Agua Prieta, across from Arizona. Villa got our attention. Black Jack Pershing, nearby in El Paso at Fort Bliss, went after him. We heard plenty about the Pershing expedition while we traveled though Texas and New Mexico.

With America's help, Harry again shipped weapons and ammunition to Acapulco.

From New Orleans we wired Magaña to send someone to pick up Harry's purchases, and we took a freighter to Veracruz. When we docked, we boarded a train to Mexico City and the connection to Cuernavaca.

"General Pershing and his boys chased Villa all over northern Mexico," Paco told us. "He couldn't even find Villa's horse droppings. However, several of Pershing's airplanes are crumbling in the Mexican deserts being as the sun and heat warped and cracked their propellers. That grounded them."

And President Wilson began favoring Carranza, even banning arms sales to all other factions. Of course that didn't matter right then to Emiliano, and wouldn't, as long as Harry and America Connolly had their contacts.

In March of 1917, President Wilson officially recognized Carranza as Mexican president. We weren't at Emiliano's encampment when he got the news, a terrible setback for him. But we could imagine his disappointment and anger, knew Carranza would have to deal with both.

"First," Paco said, "Madero, who wouldn't act on land reform. Then the drunken fellow, Huerta, who had Madero assassinated. And now Carranza, who also doesn't care about land reform and is arrogant about his lack of interest in it."

The federals launched a big campaign, and things got mighty hot for us Zapatistas. They soon forced us out of

Tlaltizapán, so we set up headquarters at Jojutla. We got run out of Jojutla and went to Huautla.

And the way Carranza tried to defeat Emiliano is one of the shames on the country to this day. Under Gen. Pablo González, the federals went into village after village, rounding up the men. They sent them to work in the henequen fields of the Yucatán, virtual slavery, or to army training in Mexico City. They herded the women and children into specially created communities. And the federals burned their villages.

"It's terrible punishment," Paco said. "And it's not going to work. The people are loyal to my General Zapata."

So Emiliano continued to fight.

One time he dynamited the train near Cuernavaca and killed four hundred people, mostly soldiers, but women and children too, an awful tragedy, civil war. Recalling that makes me shiver. I'm glad I didn't see it. We felt relieved a few days later to learn that neither Paco nor Bruja nor Mrs. King had been on that train.

Along about cotton-planting time back home that year, one of Emiliano's generals defected to the federals. Two weeks later in a fight near Huautla, the Zapatistas whipped a large band of federals and captured most of the survivors, including their former general. Emiliano had him taken out and shot.

In April of 1917, I picked up a week-old newspaper and read about the United States entering the war in Europe.

"Says we have to help our friends over there on foreign soil," I told Harry.

"Admirable, helping friends. But it's such a long way off."

Emiliano's brother, Eufemio, drank more than ever, got nastier by the day. We quit inviting him to play cards and in general tried to avoid him. Around the middle of June, Eufemio beat up the father of one of his junior officers. The young officer sought out Eufemio, shot him dead, and defected to the federals.

1918 became much the same for the guerrillas, but Mexico City returned to normal after the awful typhus epidemic. Most of the fighting took place away from Mexico City, occurring especially in the north. So Harry and I spent more time in the capital, taking in the restaurants and concerts and horse races, plus renewing our acquaintance with the Sanborns at their pharmacy, where the ice cream tasted as delicious as ever.

"How do you like the remodeling?" Frank asked.

We looked around. It seemed like a different place.

"I see lots of stuff for sale," Harry said, "clothes and bottled things for women."

"Walter and I had been thinking about adding certain kinds of clothing and cosmetics from France. My boat had just docked at Le Havre when the fighting in France became so fierce in some areas. I grabbed a few items and caught the next boat back."

"Good you still offer ice cream," Harry said.

"Wait till you see our new place. We're negotiating with the owners of the House of Tiles to move there."

"That's where 'Miliano's boys hung out."

"Yes, but I hope they don't return. They scare the customers."

When the venomous hand of the Spanish flu struck in 1918, Harry and I lit out for Emiliano's camp once again, over at Tochimilco by now, and did what we could to warn his people about the flu and how to guard against it. But the epidemic got into the countryside too. It killed a terrible lot of folks, same as in the States and elsewhere.

Still, Carranza never eased up on Emiliano nor changed his position about the land.

And Emiliano's people never let him down. They worshiped him. I don't know how else to say it.

In early 1919 we had been lodging again in Mexico City at the Regis when Frank notified us that he and Walter had moved their business to the House of Tiles and asked us to the formal opening. "Invite the Monster of Morelos if you'd like."

We wired Paco. He and Bruja arrived in plenty of time.

Bruja, who had never seen the capital or tasted ice cream, sampled all flavors. "That might make you fat," Paco told her. "If it does I'm going to unload you."

But the beautiful young gypsy, and that's how we saw her, illuminated the store with her bewitching smile and ordered another dish of vanilla.

Paco and Bruja stayed only three days before returning to Cuernavaca.

"I have to get her away from this place before she's spoiled," Paco said.

And Carranza wouldn't move on the land problem.

And Emiliano wouldn't compromise.

Around St. Patrick's Day of 1919 the four of us visited Emiliano at Tochimilco.

He worried us, he seemed so sad. And at thirty-nine, Emiliano, five years younger than me, looked ten years older. We discussed him privately.

"What do you think, Sugar?"

"It's almost like he's dejected. I notice he'll get animated for a while, then sort of fade out of the conversation, like his mind's elsewhere."

"He still enjoys a drink and riding a good horse or being around a pretty woman."

But Emiliano seemed extremely preoccupied, had even lost some of his caution.

"No doubt unhappy about the condition of his people," Harry said.

"Yes. And resigned to their fate. And his, I suppose."

On April 11 we had just sat for breakfast in the Regis dining room when several newspaper vendors rushed in shouting the awful news. I bought an *El Imparcial*, glanced at it, and gasped. "Oh, no!" I whispered.

Harry hadn't understood the vendors. But he heard my tone, caught my expression. He scooted close and looked over my shoulder at the headline he couldn't read. But a photograph told it all: Emiliano's body, bloody, his shirt ragged, lay stretched out in the central plaza at Cuautla. Gawkers, mostly looking at the camera, surrounded it.

"Murdered," I said.

"The sons of bitches."

I paraphrased the article for him. "A federal officer named Guajardo takes what the newspaper calls 'the credit.' Says he feigned betraying Carranza, had even attacked some of Carranza's troops, trying to win Emiliano's confidence. It worked. Guajardo tricked Emiliano into meeting him at the Chinameca Hacienda, pretended to stage an honor guard of welcome, and gunned him down. Emiliano never had a chance."

"Damn!"

"Happened yesterday. So hard to believe."

The news stunned us, saddened, angered.

Emiliano had been our friend. But so much more important, he seemed to have the right idea for Mexico, that the land belonged to the people who worked it, that everyone should own some land, shouldn't have to work themselves into a grave for someone else.

"Somebody," I said, "has to try to fill Emiliano's boots."

"If there is anybody." Harry's expression became murderous.

Some of the other men and women having breakfast had jumped up and begun shouting happily and waving their newspapers.

"Must be Carrancistas," I said.

Harry, glaring, looked around the room, and I thought, *Oh-oh*. But he bit his lip and ordered a bottle of tequila, Herradura, I believe. I wept where I sat. And we toasted Emiliano. We didn't care who noticed that we refused to take part in their celebration.

A few days later we decided to go to Cuernavaca.

"See how Paco and Bruja are doing," Harry said.

"Federal influence shouldn't be so bad like in Mexico City."

"And they don't know us, Sugar. Besides, we'll be armed."

"Yes," Paco told us when we arrived at the Hotel Delicias, "this is still Zapata country. He's already been seen several times, high in the hills, alone on his white horse, *As de Oro*."

I hope Paco didn't think the look I gave him meant I thought him loco.

Harry said, "We've seen pictures of his body, his burial."

"Oh, yes. We know where he's buried. We just don't believe he's dead."

Gildardo Magaña took over the Zapatista movement. He and Emiliano's subchiefs decided that political means had become their only hope to save their gains and obtain their goals. Magaña continued to talk too much. But he was a politician of the first category.

With Emiliano murdered, however, we saw Mexico differently, felt different. One day under the magnificent red bougainvillea in Paco's hotel patio, Harry said it for me and him both. "I don't much like Mexico any longer."

"Paco and Bruja haven't changed."

"No, bless them. But with 'Miliano gone . . ." Harry looked away, looked back. "Most of the fighting's about over. Won't be so easy to acquire a payroll now and then."

"Think we should pull up stakes and head north?"

"Our time here seems over, Sugar."

"What about the Pinkertons?"

"I reckon they've closed the book on us. I'd like to find out."

"I wish we could find out without going there first."

Harry laughed. "We'll be cautious, Sugar. I imagine that polecat Charlie Siringo is too stove up with old age by now to come after us. Demaio too."

"I doubt they have any of our fingerprints."

"No. And we haven't posed for any pretty pictures since our wedding."

"Let's go," I said. "But we'll have to watch our step, especially at first."

"We're used to that. I could grow a beard."

"I could do my hair differently."

"Be good to live in the States again," Harry said. "I hope we can get jalapeños."

I agreed. Besides, all I ever did was hold the horses.

We recalled how pleasant San Diego had been that time we stayed at the Grant Hotel. We decided to try that quiet little border town first.

"I suppose we'll have to find a different way to make a living," I said.

"Yes. Our world there in the States is sure not what it used to be. Neither am I."

We told Paco and Bruja right away.

"If you are determined to go," Paco said, "it's a good decision. You should feel at home. San Diego is like Mexico in many ways. If we'd had a few more guns at Chapultepec and Buena Vista, the people of San Diego would talk Spanish to this day."

Carlota squawked. Bebito sang.

A few days later Paco and Bruja wished us well amid hugs and, from me and Bruja, tears. They put us on the train to Mexico City, from where we'd take another train to Veracruz, then a steamer north.

On the train we spent a lot of time staring out the window, enjoying the high-country scenery but reminiscing too, often about the same thing.

"I'll sure as shootin' miss ol' Paco and his gypsy witch," Harry said.

"That Bruja. She'll keep him going if she can continue to keep up with him."

46

At Veracruz, we boarded a Mexican steamer, a slow old bucket but she got us to Mobile safely. From there we had a grand reunion with my folks, headed for New Mexico to spend a few days with the Connollys, then to Utah, and San Francisco, along the way collecting our savings stashed long ago in one safe place and another, including a couple of banks. After a little sightseeing in San Francisco, and a fine seafood dinner at the Cliff House, we caught the train south.

Our new livelihood, not that we needed much money for a while thanks to previous activities, came with the Eighteenth Amendment, enforced through the Volstead Act: Harry and I had collided with national Prohibition. We first heard about it at Mobile, next from Pap, then all along the way. And everyone, looked like, studied how to circumvent it. We thought like plenty of others, not how to get a drink but how to make some money obtaining and distributing liquor. Such a business had several ramifications, and in San Diego my handsome enterprising husband soon fitted us in.

The car salesman, a paunchy little man with a mustache too big for him, probably to compensate for his baldness, gave me a headache with his jabbering.

"Name's Campbell," he said, "not soup, but cars. Ha-ha. Yes, sir, this is the best in the Studebaker line, the Big Six touring car, sixty horses, and she'll do a mile an hour for every horse.

Sits three in the front and three in back. Folding top. Keep it down or put it up if we ever have rain around here. Ha-ha. All the way from South Bend, Indiana. Starting this year, no more horse-drawn vehicles for Studebaker. Has a self-starter, a crank too, just in case." He laughed again, showed us how to start and stop it, use the choke, add gasoline and oil and water, turn on the headlights, shift gears, and turn.

Mr. Campbell drove off with a coworker and left us standing in the dirt street in front of our rental home alongside a dazzling new 1920 Studebaker, dark blue with white-wall tires, big seats front and back. We paid nearly two thousand dollars for it.

"You drive, Sugar." My husband, never afraid of bronc nor man nor wild beast, insisted on my handling the wheel, though he agreed to put on the spare tire if we had a flat and to crank if the self-starter failed. Harry watched the dust of the salesman's exit. "Talked so much he reminded me of Gildardo Magaña."

So I sat behind the wheel and we got the machine moving. I managed to steer it up and down the road, forward, then backwards, real slow, until I had the feel of it. I couldn't back up straight, frequently killed the engine, spun the tires, scared the neighbor's chickens, and nearly hit their fence. But at the end, laughing, excited, we felt proud. I left turning and high speeds for another day. I got good in a hurry.

When we sought a home to buy, I drove us through most of the city and into the backcountry. We found it on a little rise a few miles north of downtown, a one-story stuccoed house not five years old, with three bedrooms and an inside bathroom. Big wooden ceiling beams stuck through to the outside in the front, and red adobe tiles covered the roof. It had a small garage with double doors. Geraniums in flower boxes under the windows reminded us of Mexico. So did the rose bed. Cactus and sagebrush thrived on both sides. We purchased those lots as well.

"We might need the land someday, Sugar, if we decide to raise a horse or two."

"Or do some farming?"

"Anything but that."

From our front porch we had a wide view of the Pacific Ocean and could walk to it in ten minutes, though my husband, retired cowboy and former adventurer, usually wanted to go by car.

The Prohibition years in San Diego didn't resemble what I've read concerning Chicago, for instance, and other big cities. No one ever got arrested for smuggling liquor or bootlegging, and we never heard much about shots being fired. The Coast Guard chased a few rum-running speedboats, but never caught anyone. Lots of good liquor got pitched overboard to lighten an escaping smuggler boat, and the authorities captured goodly amounts of it.

We conducted most of our business at night in the back-country of San Diego County, driving through the hills into Mexico to pick up several cases of Scotch by way of Canada or champagne and wine that started out in France. We'd recross the international boundary near bucolic little Tecate, travel on bumpy dirt roads and cow trails into San Diego, and make deliveries to speakeasies or homes or restaurants whose owners had larcenous relationships with the local authorities. Occasionally we would rendezvous with a boat on the beach. Transactions like that.

Harry and I didn't give much thought to the illegality of our work, a universal practice condoned, overlooked, encouraged. We couldn't believe such a law so commonly broken and despised got passed by Congress and approved by so many states. Meanwhile, teetotalers remained teetotalers, and the tipplers kept on tippling.

Reminiscing about old friends one day put us in the mood to return to Mexico and have a big time with Paco and Bruja.

"He's about ninety," Harry said. "We ought to go soon."

We had been gone a year. A week later we headed south.

And we missed him. The Monster of Morelos had been done in by age and pneumonia. The brother of Paco's dead wife, running the Hotel Delicias for their eldest son, a lawyer in San Antonio, directed us to Paco's grave in the Cuernavaca cemetery. But he couldn't tell us what had become of Bruja, didn't know her as Inmaculada. After determining that she had left Cuernavaca, we went to Villa de Ayala, where Bruja and Paco had discovered one another. We asked around, using her correct name, but couldn't pick up her trail, although everyone knew Paco or had heard of him.

"Sugar, I don't know how else to find her."

"Me neither, damn it."

We returned to the north.

One reason San Diego didn't suffer the Prohibition violence of other cities had to be its proximity to Mexico. With Tijuana, Mexicali, and other settlements within an ace of the international boundary, folks could easily obtain liquor legally and cheap.

Tijuana, tiny and dusty and exciting, allowed all the freedoms that folks missed in the States.

For instance, a boxing promoter from San Francisco had opened a Thoroughbred racetrack right on the border in early 1916, seven years after the state legislature, in an outrageous folly under pressure from the do-gooders, banned pari-mutuel betting in California. And man must gamble. Tijuana had a first-class layout with the top runners, jockeys, and trainers from all over the States and Canada. We loved it, became regulars.

Right next to the track they built the Sunset Inn, dining, dancing, and gambling. Downtown Tijuana had important places too, including the San Francisco Café, real fancy, and La Ballena, which everyone called the Long Bar, with its full-size concave and convex mirrors that made you look ridiculously tall or short, fat or skinny.

Harry and I enjoyed the domestic part of our new life as well as the business end. I raised flowers in front of the house and on both sides. In the back, Harry tended our trees of peaches and plums, nectarines and persimmons, except when he went down the hill to Garnet Avenue and played cards with newly acquired cronies. I had to drive him down the hill and go pick him up too.

He worked in the yard without carrying his arsenal, but he kept one six-shooter and carbine handy in the trees.

We subscribed to *The San Diego Sun*. It included major news from Mexico, so we knew about Carranza's assassination the year after we left and that Pancho Villa got ambushed and killed in 1923, both acts probably on orders from Obregón, whom a religious fanatic murdered five years later at a banquet. It remained a violent land.

Also in that year, 1928, another news item excited us more. I ran with the newspaper into the kitchen, where Harry cleaned and oiled his Colt Bisley, even though he carried it only at night along with his inside gun when we picked up and delivered liquor, and in several years hadn't fired it or any other weapon except at jackrabbits and coyotes.

"Honey," I told him, so excited I nearly stuttered. "Good news. That varmint's cashed in."

Harry stopped oiling and looked at me. Of course he knew what I meant.

"Thank God." He stood and hugged me.

Charlie Siringo had died in Hollywood at the age of seventy-two. I read Harry the whole article. It mentioned Siringo's books, several of them published since the one about his Texas cowboy days. In the segment concerning his detective career with the Pinkertons, the article said he had "doggedly pursued Butch Cassidy and Harry Longbaugh, alias The Sundance Kid," throughout the United States and all the way to the Argentine.

Harry nodded. "'Doggedly.'"

The article called my husband and Butch anachronisms and misfits.

Then came the part that stunned us. It said Butch and Harry had been killed in 1911 by police during a shootout in Argentina, near Mercedes. An American salesman staying at a hotel in Mercedes identified them and told all this to the Pinkertons the next year. The Pinkertons didn't like taking the word of a drummer. But not much later Mary Seifert, the young fellow who had befriended us in Bolivia, told the Pinkertons he also had seen Harry's and Butch's bodies. The detective agency closed its files on us.

"Thank you, Mary Seifert," I told the sky in the direction of South America.

"So he misled them," Harry said, "for the protection work we did."

"Showed his gratitude. That had been dangerous country."

"I suspected he had us pegged. But what a favor!"

"Seventeen years ago," I said.

"Sugar, we'll have to go find Mary and thank him properly."

I knew Harry meant it, but I discouraged the idea. "We could try a telegram."

"If he's still there. Probably not."

"So the law hasn't been after you and Butch all this time."

"I can take the guns out of the fruit trees." Harry smiled. "Leroy is going to feel deflated now that he's not wanted."

I had only one mention in the article, where it called me a prostitute who had become Harry's mistress. How I hated that damn lie and whoever started it. Still, it's only one of the many fabrications related to me or Harry. I suppose I also felt disappointed that the article never gave me any credit for being part of our financial transactions. Still, I know what I did and how thrilled I felt in those marvelous times.

47

The biggest and best attraction in Tijuana opened down the road from the racetrack in mid-1928. Agua Caliente, they called it, for the old hot spring on its grounds, and it became famous worldwide almost overnight: hotel, two casinos, restaurant, swimming pool, greyhound track, beautiful white Mexican and Spanish mission architecture, arches and colorful tiles. The Deauville of the West, it called itself.

The Hollywood crowd and the wealthy from all over swarmed to Agua Caliente, along with ordinary folks who just wanted to enjoy a drink in public without fear of being poisoned by rotgut or arrested for violating the Prohibition law. Harry and I went frequently for the entertainment and meals, but he sat in on only one card game, didn't want to play there again. That made me happy. A fast crowd frequented both casinos, and Harry could spot cheaters. He'd have shot someone for sure.

"I'll stay with my local cronies," he said. "We're friends. Nobody cheats."

I even got Harry to dancing a little, especially to slow tunes in the hotel's Patio Andaluz. After a while he liked it and seldom stepped on me. If we went for dinner we dressed up, and Harry said we looked as elegant as any couple. He must have been right, since the press and public frequently mistook us for celebrities. And movie stars wandered all over the place. Our favorites were Johnny Weissmuller and Lupe Vélez, King of the Apes and the Queen of Spitfires. We saw a lot of Gilbert Roland, Mae West, Al Jolson, and Groucho Marx, to name a few. Once we spotted Jean Harlow and Paulette Goddard within five minutes of each other, a knockout blonde and a dynamite brunette.

"Sugar, they're a little younger than you, that's all."

"A lot younger, Honey. But thanks." My husband always knew what to say.

Even the doorman, Tony Castro, looked like a movie star, a slim young fellow with a slice of a mustache like Gilbert Roland's.

"Maybe working here you'll make some important contacts and land a movie job," Harry told him after we went to Agua Caliente enough that Tony remembered us.

When Tony laughed at that and I saw his grand smile, I agreed with Harry.

But Tony objected. "I'd have to leave San Diego."

Most of the workers, Mexican and American, lived in San Diego. By the way, he told us we tipped better than any of the big shots. We liked Tony so much we considered giving him our true identities.

"Reminds me of 'Merica," Harry said. "Taller is all."

A lot younger too. Harry often forgot he'd reached his late fifties, and America his late forties, although Harry's drinking leg occasionally reminded him.

Tony had a guest list, so that's how we learned of the imminent arrival of one of the most famous people in the United States.

"The help doesn't know whether to run and hide or line up for autographs," Tony told us. We sat in the lobby one day with a lot of other idlers when he walked in wearing a fancy blue suit with white silk shirt, blue tie, and white hat like the newspapers said, and surrounded by several tough-looking hombres: Al Capone, the notorious Chicago gangster.

"Little fellow," Harry whispered to me.

"And, they say, hyena mean."

We saw Capone just once more, the same evening he shot craps near the blackjack table where we watched W. C. Fields trying to beat the house.

I didn't want to see him any closer. Harry might have been on the far side of the law for a spell, but he had been just a cowboy gone wrong, defending himself, trying to get along. Capone was a deliberate hoodlum of the most heinous kind. I couldn't abide the skunk.

After enjoying the orchestra in the Patio Andaluz for an hour, and sipping a last Tom Collins, we headed for the front to ask for our latest new Studebaker to be brought up. So we had approached the main doors from inside when we saw Tony Castro and two other men talking near the driveway. Two nicely dressed couples awaited their turn.

The big doors, looking as though they could have come off a Colonial church, stood open, as usual, and we could see the other two men doing most of the talking while Tony mainly shook his head and tried to smile.

"Don't those two look like some of the gang that arrived with Capone?"

"They do, Sugar."

Their fedoras and dark suits couldn't hide the roughneck in them. We realized by their tone before understanding their words that they talked ugly. As we walked under the arch and started down the tile steps, we heard them clearly.

"But I'm saying I can't," Tony told them. "My job is door-man. I dispatch the valets to get cars for guests and call for them on the intercom, but I can't leave the door."

"We think you can, Mex," the taller one said. "He needs to go to San Diego."

"Mister Capone won't like this," his companion added.

"Look," Tony said, "one valet is off sick or drunk and the others are running like greyhounds trying to please everyone. And two other couples are ahead of your boss."

"We're gonna break your legs, you fancy Spic," the taller one said.

I'd heard enough. I usually kept shut, but this time I couldn't, Tony such a nice man. I stepped forward and told the gunsels what Tony had already explained to them and added a little. "Damn you. Don't talk to Tony like that. Leave him alone."

I must have caught Harry by surprise, but in a second he grabbed my arm.

One of the Capone boys told me in some of his rude big-city gangster lingo to shut up. You can imagine what trash like that would say.

Tony, bless him, stepped between us and told him to watch his tongue.

The fool pushed Tony nearly off his feet and began giving orders again and making threats. The other hoodlum smirked at me.

I slipped my right hand into my purse and found my derringer.

Harry stepped around me and Tony and knocked those two head over heels with one punch each, a left and a right. When they started to rise while reaching inside their coats, they discovered my husband standing over them with the muzzle of a revolver in their faces. Those two got up slowly and departed rapidly, frightened rats.

I turned to Tony. I saw the awe in his face for how fast Harry slugged those two and the way Harry got his inside gun out.

"We'll get our car, Tony." Harry holstered his Iver Johnson.

Tony thanked us over and over. "I've never seen anything like that."

"No," I said. "You wouldn't have." I took Harry's arm. "Let's go, Kid."

He gave me the funniest look.

I'd never called him that, and it just slipped out.

We let Tony wonder as I hustled us out of there.

"Must've lost some of my punch," Harry said. "Those two 'bout got up."

The next time we saw Tony I asked if he'd had any more trouble.

"Not a bit, thanks to the two of you. And they left town before long."

In late 1929 the Agua Caliente operators closed the track on the border and opened a beautiful new hippodrome across the street from the hotel and spa. We went on opening day, got to see Ruby Keeler, with Al Jolson wisecracking nearby, hang a horseshoe of flowers on the winner of the feature. We attended the races oftener than ever. I showed Harry how to understand the tout sheets, and he won modest amounts of money wagering. I won some myself but actually went for the excitement and to see the splendid horses running as well as being saddled and paraded.

We made friends with several trainers, Charlie Whittingham and Noble Threewit, for instance. They became highly successful on tracks all over the States. And we knew some jockeys, namely a couple who later became giants among those daring little men, Johnny Longden and Eddie Arcaro.

One of the grandest days there for us and everyone else who could squeeze in occurred in March 1932 when the big chestnut Australian champion, Phar Lap, easily won the Agua Caliente Handicap. Later we talked to Arcaro, who had watched from the rail, while Longden rode in the big event. He rode in Phar Lap's dust.

"What a race!" Harry commented.

"Folks," Arcaro said, "he's a terror, could have won by seven lengths."

Like racing fans the world over, we were shocked and saddened two weeks later to learn that Phar Lap, perhaps eating tainted feed, died in northern California.

The Great Depression worsened. Fortunately, we had our investments in paid-up property, not the stock market, so we didn't get hurt as much as lots of people.

One day in this same period as we watched a splendid sunset from our front porch, and commented about how the stock market crash hadn't much affected San Diego, we reminisced the way we often did about the old days.

"Sugar, what would you think of inviting 'Merica and his family to join us?"

"Give up their ranch?"

"They wouldn't want that. No, just work with us a while and build up a nice stake while Prohibition lasts. The kids would love the beach."

"Our own business, take off anytime. Pays well too. I'll write them tonight."

"Maybe ask 'Merica to get word to Leroy about our whereabouts."

Two months later while I watered our roses I spotted a man leaving a taxi in front of our home and walking toward the door. "Honey, you'll want to see this."

Harry came to the door and looked out. "Only one man swaggers like that."

Moments later the three of us sat on the porch sipping beer.

"Pard, you've put on weight," Harry told him.

"Pard," Butch replied, "you're as gray as I am."

Sure, everybody got heavier and grayer, but Butch's fat jaws and swagger made him recognizable anywhere. We sat on the porch and gave him a genuine homecoming enlivened by accounts of what each had been doing, and of course aided by some of our best imported whiskey. I took only polite sips.

"You know I felt sort of scared to go back to Utah and see the home folks," Butch told us. He watched the sea. "Not long ago I did it. I never got so many kisses and hugs, everybody so proud to see me. My pa. My sis. My brother." He paused, still didn't look at us.

I heard a sea gull call, saw one sailing nearby on the breeze.

"Ma was gone. I felt awful about that." After another pause, Butch faced us, tried to smile. "Rolled up with a friend in his brand new Ford. They was plenty surprised."

I felt sorry for Butch. He knew he should have visited his family long ago. I kept shut. Harry patted Butch's shoulder and refilled his best friend's glass.

The next night, we introduced Butch to the business. We walked outside and Harry swung the garage doors open. We assumed that with all his traveling and airs Butch would have learned to drive. I handed him the keys.

"You do it," he told me.

A week became enough for Robert Leroy Parker. He didn't like the work and couldn't sit still enough to enjoy the programs on our floor-model General Electric radio.

"Good time to visit the Grand Canyon," he said.

Always the fidgety traveler, Butch.

Harry said, "Don't stand too close to the edge."

We had about decided America couldn't get away when a few weeks later he stood on our doorstep. The poor little guy didn't have but four dollars in money.

"You and Miss Etta always help when I need it most, Kid."

"You'll earn it, 'Merica. And there's no danger of getting throwed and stomped."

We asked about Catalina and the children.

"We had a corn crop to get in and some horses to break and sell. The younguns have their own lives, but they come back to help. Anyway, that's why it took me so long to get here. Lupita and her husband and oldest boy are with Catalina while I'm gone."

America, quick to smile, nearing fifty, lean and strong, looked ready to ride, and still the nicest, politest, most loyal friend you could want.

"You can help with the driving," I told him. I saw his embarrassment.

"Oh, Miss Etta, Catalina does all that for us."

No matter. I knew the roads and shortcuts and all the lookouts. Besides, driving became an exciting change for me after my telephoning and bookkeeping during the day, arranging transactions and following accounts.

We gave America a nice advance, paid him well each week. He rode in the back seat every night, and how that boy helped! He made two of that Butch Cassidy when it came to work, not to mention his good attitude. As I've said, he virtually worshiped my husband. I will never again see the likes of America's admiration for Harry, not if I live to be as old as Isaac, son of Jacob.

America stayed for several weeks, happily counting his money every time we gave him a fistful. He'd never seen the ocean except through the bus window during the last stretch before reaching San Diego, and he marveled at it, loved walking the beach with us, picking up sand dollars and sea shells, skipping small flat rocks across the water. I took pictures with my Brownie. America made good company for restaurant meals in Tijuana and San Diego, pretended my cooking tasted as good as Catalina's, and, all of us in overstuffed chairs around the radio, relished sharing the soap operas in the afternoons. He liked *Just Plain Bill* the best. And he never missed Walter Winchell's broadcast.

"I wish we had electricity," America said.

When he prepared to rejoin Catalina, Harry gave him his remaining wages due and threw in a passel more.

Momma and Pappy died a year apart, 1932 and 1933. Thank the Good Lord they got to be old-timers, had all the family around them except us, but Harry and I had visited often and for a good spell each time. We were square with them.

When Prohibition ended in late 1933 we retired again.

By then we had our fourth Studebaker, though I continued to be the only driver.

This was a 1932 President, the luxury model, streamlined, white and tan, a six-passenger convertible sedan that, with the Depression, cost little more than we paid in 1920 for the Big Six.

Shortly before the Mexican government banned games of chance in the mid-1930s and forced an end to the fun at Agua Caliente except for the racetrack, a Spanish-dance couple began drawing big crowds to the Patio Andaluz. We had seen them perform at the Foreign Club in downtown Tijuana, but at Caliente they had a large, elaborate setting like they deserved, Eduardo Cansino and his daughter, Margarita Carmen.

"Hard to believe she's only fifteen," I told Harry one time during their show.

"She's a beauty, all right."

I squinted at him. "Has a little baby fat still, don't you think?"

Harry smiled and sipped his beer.

I predicted to Harry right then and there she'd become a big star someday. As Rita Hayworth, she did.

In 1937 we received a rare letter from New Mexico. I took it into the living room, where Harry sat listening to *Ma Perkins*.

"From Catalina," I said.

Harry motioned for me to sit on the arm of his chair. "Go ahead, Sugar."

"What if it's bad news? One of their kids got hurt?"

"Maybe it's good news. Maybe they're coming to visit." He lowered the volume.

It was bad: They had learned that Butch died in Oregon, where he owned a little hotel.

Harry gave a faint grunt. "I hope it's a false report." He turned off the radio.

"Me too, Honey. But America would have got it from someone he trusted."

Harry didn't speak for a moment, nodded. "How old was he?"

"Seventy-one, Catalina says."

Naturally, the news saddened Harry. "Never expected that. But I should have."

I went into the kitchen and returned with two jiggers and a bottle of Herradura, and we sat on the front porch and watched the ocean while toasting Butch and the old times.

"We made fun of him," Harry said. "But he was a good pard."

"I know, Honey. He surely was."

"One thing about being close friends with someone for such a long time, and even living for so many years apart in spells, you get used to having them in your mind and your heart, rather than at your side. Their death is permanent, a more sorrowful separation. But you can endure it. And in a way they're always with you."

I'd seldom heard Harry talk like that. We discussed Butch and good times all through supper and into the night. The next day I wrote Catalina to let us know where Butch got buried. Someday we could go tell him good-bye.

We didn't visit Tijuana so often in the late-1930s, but we'd go to eat at the San Francisco Café or the Foreign Club, some other nice spots, and we took in the races at Caliente. So we went in 1938 when Seabiscuit, sort of a national hero in those usually dismal years, won a special race there. We had a bigger day later that year when Seabiscuit beat Ligaroti in a match race at the new track up the coast in Del Mar.

World War II meant changes for everyone, directly in the fighting or not. I got a job for the duration teaching high school history, so many women being off in the military or working in the airplane factories. I enjoyed teaching again, kids in a class all the same age, so different from when I'd worked in those rural one-room schools of Alabama and Colorado, younguns ranging from tykes to big strong farm boys wanting to kiss you.

Harry was seventy-one when the United States joined the fighting in 1941, but he wanted to help. So he hired on as a guard at the big Consolidated Vultee Aircraft plant, which sent so many bombers and seaplanes out of San Diego.

"Are you familiar with firearms?" the interviewer asked.

"Well, sir, I do all right," Harry told him.

When Harry described the scene to me I laughed out loud.

48

During the last days of The Wild Bunch, plus our years in South America and Mexico, we enjoyed slam-bang heart-stirring times, doings no longer advisable.

And they became the period when so much false information originated about Harry and the others, including what little got published about me. With this writing, I tried to set things right. I added what happened later so that Harry's entire life, so wonderful and exciting, would be known.

Now I read that Butch's sister is considering a book where she'll say Butch finally visited her, their father, and a brother in Utah, same as Butch told us. I'm glad for them. Too bad his mother had passed on. The sister also says she has letters from several men who saw Butch in the States long after he and Harry were supposed to have been killed.

And there's a Hollywood movie in the works about Harry and Butch. A couple of young men are hired for it and are said to be handsome. I only hope they can act. But it's probably based on what has already been published, plus someone's imagination, which in many cases have been the same. It likely will even depict the alleged 1911 shootout, a cheap fabrication of the first category. Anyone who thinks Harry and Butch got killed, then or any other time, is as wrong as feathers on a hog.

I could set the movie folks straight, but I prefer to remain offstage, you might say. There'll be a time after I'm gone if one of you nieces or nephews wants to put the word out. Just keep in mind that my memory had weak spots but that I wrote this the best I could. I hope you'll remember that those were different times.

I am sorry to say that my husband, the handsomest man I ever saw, and the only man I ever loved, died in 1951. He had reached his eighty-second year but didn't look it. His heroic heart just quit on him in the middle of a beautiful Sunday morning while we talked over the olden days and watched the sea from our porch. I cried awhile. Then I took a sip of tequila for him, phoned Greenwood Mortuary, and wrote airmail to America Connolly and Catalina. Truth be told, I took several sips, Herradura, I believe.

A week later, with Harry in his coffin in the baggage car, the Connollys met me at the train station in Santa Fe. From there we rode in a big black sedan behind the hearse to an old Spanish cemetery in eastern New Mexico. It is surrounded by cactus and mesquite, an idyllic little spot where Catalina's people are buried.

I had my husband laid to rest as Harry Parker. That is how all the kinfolk knew him, and I didn't want to risk someone's stumbling onto his gravestone, the word getting out, then curiosity-seekers coming around and creating a spectacle.

"So long, Kid," America whispered when they lowered the casket.

Catalina and I hugged each other. We all cried.

Neil and the other boys are about to land on the moon now. I wish Harry could see it, so magnificent. And I'm about finished with this. When I'm done I'll put it in my trunk with my will and other important papers, including instructions for my burial alongside Harry, and how to find America and Catalina and the graveyard. You all know about my "Old West" trunk with our guns and souvenirs.

America and Catalina might be gone, though, by the time anyone tries to look them up, in case anyone is ever interested. With Catalina's letter about Butch's death I'll include where he's buried and the name he's resting under.

Maybe it's the schoolmarm in me, but I think people should know about us.

I'm bound to join Harry before long. After all, as I may have mentioned, if I live until November I'll be ninety-three years old. Naturally I've been mighty lonely at times in the nearly twenty years that Harry has been gone. Still, I've kept busy in the garden and around the house, and I've had my reading and good neighbors and plenty of correspondence to conduct. Most wonderful of all, I have a grand treasury of memories.

And I have no complaints. I had a really big time.

Made in the USA
Columbia, SC
26 March 2023

14340433R00220